E X E C U T E D

ALSO BY RR HAYWOOD

The Undead Series

The Undead Day One-Twenty

Blood at the Premiere: A Day One Undead Adventure

Blood on the Floor: An Undead Adventure

Demon Series

Recruited: A Mike Humber Novella

Huntington House: A Mike Humber Detective Novel

Book of Shorts Volume One

Extracted Series

Extracted

E X E C U T E D

EXTRACTED BOOK 2

R R   H A Y W O O D

47N RTH

Published by 47North, Seattle

www.apub.com

Amazon, the Amazon logo, and 47North are trademarks of Amazon.com, Inc., or its affiliates.

ISBN-13: 9781611099324
ISBN-10: 1611099323

Cover design by Mark Swan

Printed in the United States of America

'You do not pay me. You do not own me. You do not control me. The second you brought us back and explained why is the second you gave us the responsibility to deal with the problem. Can you understand that? You do not run this. This is not yours. This problem is bigger than you . . . the lack of care you have shown is staggering. I suggest, Roland, I really . . . really fucking suggest that from now you focus solely on providing the money and do nothing else that you can fuck up . . . Find someone with a military intelligence background . . . Find someone who knows what they are doing, because you don't.'

Prologue

2010

She walks into the diner. Two Slavic-faced men on the right at a table eating eggs over easy. She crosses the room to take a seat on a stool at the counter.

'Hey, Miri,' Joanie says as she pours the coffee into a white ceramic mug. 'Hot again.'

'Sure is.'

'Anything else?'

'No.'

Joanie moves off, replacing the coffee jug on the hotplate as she goes, as she always does. Miri tugs the smartphone from the back pocket of her jeans. She props it against the serviette dispenser and takes a sip of the strong, bitter coffee.

She filters the noises of the diner as she sips. The scrape of cutlery on plates. Low conversations. An old rock track on the radio, but it's low and muted.

The bubbled glass of the clean coffee jug gives her a view of the entrance to the diner. The reflection from a sliding glass partition between the counter and the kitchen shows her the toilet door. Her large-screen smartphone works as a mirror for the parking lot, and the highly polished stainless steel side of the chiller cabinet gives her the view of the two Slavic-faced men eating their eggs over easy.

California is a huge state. Bigger than Great Britain with a population of nearly forty million people, so two men in a diner mean nothing. Two men eating eggs over easy and drinking coffee while talking quietly are no different to the tourists, truckers and hikers all doing the same thing. America by definition is a land of varying cultures and genealogies.

Therein lies the problem. Therein is the tell. They are not tourists, truckers or hikers. They are dressed casually, and at a glance, they could pass for hikers, except for the lack of wear on their new boots and the fact they are dressed in denim when virtually all hikers now wear walking pants or shorts. It's also their pale faces and the overly casual manner of their eating. She has never seen them before, which means they are new to this place, yet they do not look around. Any normal person eating in a new diner or eatery would at least be curious. These guys are not. They are eating, sipping coffee and talking quietly, but to her they might as well be holding a signboard saying *We Are Bad Guys*.

She sighs inwardly with the sadness of a long life, then an instant later feels the thrill of being back in the game. The years fall away then come surging back with the bitterness of her retirement and being too old to be operational and left with a skill set no longer required. She reaches for her phone: one message will invoke a swift and brutal reaction.

She stops and lingers with her hand almost touching the phone, and in that second she realises how much she misses it. She hated her work at the end. Her moral compass had become increasingly warped. She started to question why they were doing things, and someone at her level should never question the ethics of the mission. If she sends the message, she will be back in the world of briefings, debriefings, meetings, clearance and intelligence gathering. She will be actively involved in choosing a relocation site, and they will expect her to work through her old missions to identify who it is that has decided to track her down to this diner. She would be a somebody again, but only for a very short time, and then she would be back to living in a no-place town doing nothing other than sleeping with one eye open by candlelight.

The future looks bleak. When she was active, she could never understand why retired agents committed suicide. Now she understands. It's the days and nights of memories of places, operations, kills, losses, missions and the never-ending motion of the machine they were a cog in. The nightmares come when you stop being active. The things you thought you dealt with and processed come back and make you scream out in the night. If she goes back, it will only make it harder to leave again.

Her hand lowers to the counter-top. Inches away from the phone. She stares at the reflection of the two men in the chiller cabinet and decides, in that moment, to do nothing.

Instead, she drinks her coffee and feels a sense of liberation. She can let go of her fear of the future because she knows she will be dead within two days.

She has been made. Tagged. Spotted. Seen. Located. The two men have not reacted outwardly, but right now one of them is keying a message into his phone, telling whoever they work for where she is. By tonight, they will have found out where she lives. By tomorrow night, they will have deployed resources and devised a method of attack, and at some point during the hours of darkness, they will come for her.

So be it. Better to die by the sword than lonely and forgotten in some shitty little town where she spends her days constantly looking over her shoulder.

Her time is over. She would never take her own life, but she can be passive in reaction to someone wishing to take it for her. There are no more missions. No more operations. She is too old to be a part of the machine, but too young to be left solely to her memories.

Miri finishes the coffee, drops down from the stool and walks out without a single glance at either of the two men, who in turn look everywhere else but at her.

When she gets back to her ranch-style house nestled in the open plains of the asshole shitty county, she finds a note pinned to the front door.

She reads it.

She does nothing.

She makes a light salad and does nothing.

She lies awake in bed and does nothing.

The next morning, she sweeps the wide porch and does nothing.

When the helicopter goes overhead, she does nothing.

She packs. She waits.

At dusk, she sits on her freshly swept porch with the Glock pistol wedged under her right thigh and waits.

If she were in charge of her assassination, she would devise a covert approach using stealth to gain the target property. Once entry had been made, she would advise that the subject first be incapacitated and then negated in a manner resembling a natural death. A gas leak. A hanging. Overdose by medication. If a search revealed the target was a gun owner, then that firearm could be used, by manipulation of the target's hand, to fire into the head. Or a simple robbery gone wrong is also very effective. Home invasion crimes at detached, isolated dwellings are not uncommon.

The motion sensors hidden in the scrub at the edge of her land ping softly from the receiver just inside the main door. She inclines her head and waits. The distance and the contours of the land will prevent them having line of sight yet, but no doubt they use night-vision aids and will eventually see her immobile in the chair.

The only reaction she shows is when the pings continue. Eight. She is impressed, flattered even. They obviously know who she is. They have sent eight operatives against her. She wonders who they are and narrows it down to three possible organisations, all Russian-connected. The Cold War may appear to have been a long time ago in the media, but the after-effects will forever be ongoing.

She sits and waits, with only the faintest increase in heart rate showing her expectation of immediate death. Five minutes, maybe ten at the most. She looks up at the sky. At the stars and the moon. The same stars and moon she has stared at from a hundred or more different cities on a hundred or more different missions. She thinks of the note on her door.

She could still call it in. One call would do it. She could hold them off long enough for the cavalry to arrive. She would be whisked away, and the threat negated and removed from existence by sunrise.

A scrape of a shoe. A tread of a foot. She rises, turns and strides into the hallway with the Glock held in a double-handed grip. A man is coming from the kitchen. Tall with swept-back dark hair. It is not possible for him to have gained entry without her knowledge. Every window is secured with motion sensors. Every door. Alarms would have sounded. Foot-pressure pads in the paths and grounds should have sent signals. A blue light spills from the kitchen behind him. He spots her a second later and flinches away with his hands coming up.

'Don't shoot . . . friendly . . . friendly!'

A British accent. She doesn't know him. She doesn't recognise him. He looks to be late forties, maybe early fifties. Younger than her generation, but only by a few years. She's met most of the British agents of her time.

'Miriam? Are you Miriam?'

'Who are you?' Miri asks, calm and controlled.

'I'm here to save you . . . You're about to die,' the man blurts. 'Right now, there are armed men coming to . . .'

'I know,' Miri says bluntly. 'Who are you?'

'Roland. My name is Roland.' He whimpers, staring at the gun in her hands. 'I don't know if you are Miriam . . . I mean . . . I couldn't find any pictures of you online or . . . but Ben said to find someone from military intelligence and . . . I mean, you weren't on the original list, but I should have realised we needed someone like you . . .'

Roland stops to draw breath and force a calmness into his voice that he doesn't feel at all. Safa and Harry are both dead. Ben is going to try and rescue them, but he will fail, and that leaves Roland back at square one, and there is no way he is going through it all again. Ben was right. They need professionals. He falters, still too scared to reveal who he is and what he knows, but also aware the risk has to be taken. This woman is going to die anyway. This house will be blown to pieces by an apparent gas explosion. He read the declassified reports detailing one of the attackers who defected to the US and informed the authorities what really happened. He exhales to gain composure and tries to look past the pistol in her hands. Being around Safa and Harry has at least hardened him somewhat.

'I need to extract you . . .' he starts to explain, but the words trail off when she lowers the gun, hefts the big black holdall on to her shoulder and stares at him with an air of expectation.

'I'm ready, Mr Cavendish,' she says in a flat, hard tone. 'We have work to do.'

One

The explosion is huge. The charges dropped in the warehouse detonate to scorch the air and send a shockwave that rips bricks from the walls and sends debris flying into the attackers. Bones are broken and lacerated. The petrol Miri poured before setting the charges explodes in flame that heats the air so quickly it fuses the material of the black covert clothing to the flesh inside them.

Many are killed outright. More lie writhing and screaming in agony from burns, breaks, lacerations and horrific injuries.

'Fall back.' Alpha's voice is calm. His manner controlled. This is why he is Alpha. This is why the five are who they are. They heard the pre-emptive click of the charges. It was this alone that made them drop and turn as the warehouse detonated. Only Echo sustains injury. A shard of a tibia from the first attacker embeds in his bicep. He spins from the impact, but grunts to swallow the pain and maintain focus.

The windows at the front of the building explode out. Glass flies far across the road. The fire roars, with flames licking through the new holes in the wall.

Alpha strides backwards with an arm up to protect his balaclava-covered face from the heat. The other four at his side in a line. Calmness in all of them. Not a flicker of panic shows. Bravo turns to see the bodies of Malcolm and Konrad being carried into the truck that seals the junction at the end of the road. Echo looks back at the buildings opposite the warehouse that they used as a base.

Alpha holds for another few seconds, assessing the carnage in front of them. If there is a way through, he will risk it, but the fire is growing bigger and more intense. The tang of petrol hits his nose. An accelerant was used. The ground was prepped in advance.

There is no choice. He pulls the phone from his pocket and thumbs the screen to dial the number.

'*Hello,*' the friendly female voice says when the call connects.

'*Mother, it's Alfie.*'

'*Alfie, darling. Are you okay? How's Berlin?*' Mother asks from her office, instantly knowing something has gone wrong. Calls from the field are only ever made when the mission is at a critical point. She doesn't reveal that thought process. Instead, she smiles into the phone to ensure her voice sounds as warm as it should be. She acts the part; she believes the part. She is Mother.

'*That show we were going to see?*' Alpha says, forcing himself, despite the carnage all around him, to hold a steady, friendly tone that matches hers. '*Been cancelled.*'

'*Oh, that is a shame,*' Mother says. '*Did it start?*'

'*Yes, it did, but I think a new actor did something they were not prepared for . . .*'

'*Oh dear.*' Mother tuts and sighs. '*So you never got to see the main act.*'

'*Afraid not. We, er . . . We did make two new friends though. They're with us now. Nice chaps, but very quiet . . .*'

'*Well, be thankful for small mercies,*' Mother says, closing her eyes to decipher the words. Two new friends will be Malcolm and Konrad. The mission was to wait for them to come out, then intercept before they could give warning or go back. Very quiet means they are dead.

8

'*Just a thought, Alfie. But do your new friends know of any other shows you can see?*'

Alpha processes her words in the blink of an eye. Dead bodies cannot talk. He frowns for a second as the penny drops. Dead bodies cannot talk, but they do yield information. '*Ah, I am so glad I called you now,*' he says, smiling under his balaclava to make his tone match the content of the conversation. '*That is a great idea. Yes, we'll ask them. There must be somewhere round here we can take them for a nice meal and a drink . . .*'

Mother taps the tablet on her desk, which brings a 3D, perfect-quality hologram operating system glowing in front of her. She swipes through the icons. Double-tapping and flicking to get the information she needs.

'*Shall I have a look for you, dear?*'

'*Great, thanks,*' Alpha says. '*Dad okay, is he?*'

'*Oh, your father is fine,*' Mother says, typing, reading, processing and speaking all at the same time as the air in front of her face fills with pages of information. '*Oh look – yes, there is somewhere. I can text you the details, if that's any good? Shall I contact them and book for you?*'

'*Mother, I don't know what I would do without you. Er . . . I was thinking about our other friends here. I mean, we did bring a lot to this show.*'

'*Oh, Alfie, darling. Now don't be silly. They can't go with you . . . They should have made sure the show went on, and you need to move fast to catch the next one with your two new friends.*'

A split second of a pause as Alpha looks at Bravo. '*Okay, Mother. I'll do that.*'

'*Speak soon, Alfie. Take care.*'

'*Yes, you too, Mother.*'

Alpha puts the phone away and glances round. A fire this size will draw the authorities. Emergency services will already be scrambling towards this location. He looks from his position to the warehouse and counts three operatives still alive. Another four are inert. Either dead or unconscious.

'Them?' Bravo asks Alpha, having tracked what Alpha was looking at. He already knows the answer. They all do.

'Staying here,' Alpha says. He lifts his submachine gun and fires at the first writhing figure. Bravo and Delta negate the others. Bullets fired into heads and centre of masses. Charlie fires into the inert bodies to ensure death is given. Injured people talk; dead people don't.

'*Exfil,*' Alpha transmits through his covert microphone as the last operative is shot.

The other agents with the truck at the far end by the junction stare at them, and even with faces covered, they telegraph shock at the executions they just witnessed, and to the last they take a step back as the five start running towards them.

'Fire in the hole.' Echo's arm hurts like hell, but he squeezes the detonation switch that sends the signal to the receiver in the charges set in the houses they used as observation points. A split second later, the front walls blow out so hard the bricks sail across the road to smash through the wall of the warehouse. The noises are immense. Windows breaking. Wood splintering. Gas mains flaming.

'*POLICE ARE HERE . . .*' An operative at the junction shouts the warning through the radio as the first sirens warble down the main street. A single police car forcing a path through the heavy traffic as the people going by try to snatch a view at the fire raging down the side street. Bystanders gather near the junction. People running from shops, stores and cafés in response to the explosions. The disguised workers who erected the screens that blocked the view draw weapons from tool bags.

'*Hold them off,*' Alpha transmits.

A second later, the windscreen of the police car is peppered with holes created by the rounds fired from the junction. Screams sound out. People that were running towards the explosions stop to yell, and either duck or start running away. More guns open up. Pouring fire into the police car with metallic dinks as the bullets strike the engine block. The two officers are killed outright. Control of the car is lost as it ploughs into the back of a taxi. The airbags inside the police car deploy as the already dead occupants slam forward. More sirens coming. More police cars with officers inside who heard the shots fired over the radio transmission from the first vehicle. The local police control room dispatches all units. Every officer on duty across the city bursts away from what they are doing and runs to vehicles that come to life with lights and sirens. Helicopters and drones are scrambled as the police control room staff move into emergency procedures.

Alpha reaches the truck with the four operatives at his side. An unmarked heavy goods vehicle used to block the junction and bring the operatives and the screens needed to seal the view. Now all that matters is getting the bodies away. Mother will not be pleased at the aborted mission. Alpha has to claw something back, and failing again is not an option.

He takes the front with Bravo. Charlie, Delta and Echo get into the rear with the corpses as the two uninjured agents work to apply a dressing to Echo's bleeding arm.

'*Keep them back, then bug out . . .*' Alpha transmits to the operatives in the street, knowing each is wearing lightweight clothing under their black covert kit and can strip down before running to blend into the chaos.

Two police cars pull up twenty metres away from the first one – now wedged in the back of the taxi. The officers draw pistols as automatic weapons open fire from the junction. A black-clad figure darts out to throw a flash-bang down the street. The officers return fire, plucking single shots with nine-millimetre rounds that lack the punch and range to be effective. The flash-bang explodes with a wall of sheer bright light and a huge detonation of noise. Alpha takes the chance to egress, pressing his foot down on the accelerator to move the truck out into the now-jammed road. Cars, bikes, trucks and delivery lorries everywhere. He rams them aside as he builds speed.

More police cars slew to a stop on both sides. The officers stunned by the flash-bang cover their ears and blink the retina burn away as they duck from the barrage of incoming fire.

Alpha builds speed as Bravo cocks his weapon and leans out of the passenger-side window to strafe down the street towards one of the police cars. People run screaming. Police officers fire handguns at the truck, heedless in the panic of the moment to the rounds pinging off the hard metal sides and slamming into the crowds of people trying to flee.

The operatives at the junction know they will be hemmed in, and start working to punch out and make a run for it, covering each other as they strip the black outer layers off to reveal normal street clothes. Smoke grenades and flash-bangs are made ready for release to create the distraction needed to bug out.

Bravo drops back inside the cab to change magazines, and uses the wing mirror to check the gap between them and the junction before glancing at Alpha. 'I think we're almost clear.'

The street blows.

The whole of the street from the warehouse already on fire to the junction detonates in one solid, rumbling explosion of bricks and tarmac. The whole of it. Every building.

Walls blow out. Concrete chunks, bricks and debris fly in all directions. The operatives left behind at the junction are reduced to molecular form. Dozens of innocent people in the street are killed. Buildings collapse. Huge holes form in the surface of the road. Flaming wood and parts of buildings rain down, causing chaos and panic. Pressure waves blast out down the street, knocking people off their feet. The immensity of the explosive force and the charge of energy makes the very ground seem to heave and shake. The truck rocks on its chassis. Car windows implode from bricks sailing through the air. The plate glass windows in the storefronts shatter into thousands of glittering pieces. Flaming chunks embed into wood. Smoke everywhere. Instant, overwhelming carnage.

The three agents in the back of the truck slam into the sides, falling over each other and the dead bodies of Malcolm and Konrad as the truck slews and bounces. Alpha grips the wheel. His face a mask of focus while he fights for control of the vehicle.

'What the fuck was that?' he shouts at Bravo as he steers left to avoid the huge chunk of masonry that just fell in front of the truck.

Bravo leans out to look back, seeing the fireball scorching up into the air and the huge plumes of filthy black smoke billowing up. He sees the debris behind them. Bodies lying everywhere. Cars on fire. It looks like a war zone.

'*Echo, old chap . . . did you do that?*' Bravo asks into his radio, his cultured tones so calm amidst the destruction surrounding them.

'*Negative . . . Not us. I repeat. Not us.*'

'*Check those bodies,*' Alpha says tightly as the truck trundles on down the carriageway, ramming other cars and vehicles aside.

'*At least no one is looking at us now,*' Bravo says.

In the back of the truck, Charlie and Delta work the bodies, going through pockets to pull wallets and phones. Society has moved on. People rarely use cash now. Everything is binary code, done by the devices they carry that link to their bank and are used to pay for goods and services. Governments still insist on physical identity cards. Even if they are embedded with chips that record biometric data.

'*Malcolm Phillips, born UK, and Konrad Johans, born Germany,*' Echo transmits, holding the two cards passed to him by the others. '*Er . . . Alpha, you there?*'

'*Go ahead,*' Alpha says from the front.

'*Malcolm Phillips was born on 4 April 2010 . . . Konrad was born on 20 June 2011 . . . Neither of these two are fifty years old . . . Both early forties, for sure.*'

'*Roger that. Stand by . . .*' Alpha says with a glance at Bravo, who inclines his head. Alpha dials the number and transfers the call to his earpiece.

'*Alfie, darling,*' Mother says in a tone that shows instant worry, '*are you okay? The news feeds are showing an awful incident going on in Berlin.*'

'*We've no idea what caused it,*' Alpha says, daring to push the boundary of coded speech in his desperation to tell Mother they didn't just make this happen. '*We're fine, Mother. We're away from any danger now. Listen, we've got our new friends with us. You'll need their details to book us somewhere.*'

'*Oh, that is good,*' Mother says, opening a blank document within the hologram display still hovering in front of her. '*Okay, I have a pen . . .*'

'*Malcolm Phillips, date of birth, fourth of April two zero one zero, and Konrad Johans, twentieth of June two zero one one. They look good for their ages though. I would put at around forty.*'

'*Oh, they do sound nice,*' Mother says, holding that pleasant tone while her fingers blur over the keyboard. '*I shall have a look for you . . . Is it okay if I call you back?*'

'*That's fine, Mother.*'

'*Speak soon, darling.*'

She works quickly, with a glance to the monitor fixed on the wall of her office that shows the news channel drone footage of Berlin. It looks terrible. A whole street blown apart like something from a war movie. Bodies everywhere. Dead, injured, mangled and writhing in agony as they scream out silently on the muted screen.

The dates of birth put Malcolm and Konrad at fifty-two and fifty-one years old respectively. Her team said they looked forty years old, not fifty. Ten years is a significant time gap in descriptions, and she knows her agents are exceptional at estimating ages from a glimpse alone. She accesses databases, search engines, Interpol and many more. Her hands swipe, lunge and drag to bring virtual screens forward, while others are pushed back or to the side.

An archived news report. She checks the date before reading on. *2052.* Malcolm Phillips and Konrad Johans died in a late-night car accident on a motorway in Hampshire, England.

> The two men, Malcolm Philips, aged 42, and Konrad Johans, aged 41, both worked for the estate of the late Roland Cavendish. Mr Cavendish was a former government minister and latterly entrepreneur who is believed to have committed suicide in 2046, although his body was never recovered. An early report from the accident investigations unit within Hampshire Police states they were involved in a high-speed, head-on collision. Police are appealing for witnesses . . .

She reads quickly. She processes the information and finds the memory of the news from that time coming to mind. Roland Cavendish walked into the sea. It was on the news because his death saved his family from bankruptcy, but his body was never found. Roland Cavendish worked for the British government and then moved into investments within the private sector. She pushes the virtual screen aside and brings up more search browsers to follow the breadcrumb trail.

Roland Cavendish yields far more results. She filters and discards tabloid or magazine articles. She scans his death reports, the investigation that went on after his apparent suicide and the eventual payout to his family. Family. She reads further, her eyes darting left to right to take it all in. A wife. A daughter. A son. Nothing to indicate the widow re-married. The daughter was seven when Roland died. The son was ten.

Maria Cavendish. Daughter of Roland and Susan Cavendish. Works for a hologram film production company. Mother delves into social media and punches through the weak firewalls and defences to scan the static images, holograms and vids of Maria Cavendish. Bookish in appearance. Straight dark hair. Curvy, bordering on fat. Average. That's the word. The girl looks entirely average, and she even has the average amount of social networking friends and acquaintances. The average number of replies to posts. The only thing about her that isn't average is the fact she obviously comes from a very wealthy family.

She follows the trail to Susan Cavendish. Wife of the late Roland. The beautiful widow. Mother pauses. Something in the back of her mind. The name Cavendish. She's heard it before, but not because of Roland. Something else.

She checks back to find the name of the son. Bertram Cavendish. Born in 2036. Three years older than his sister, Maria. Called Bertie by his family. Academically gifted. Yes, of course. Bertie Cavendish was one of the youngest persons in UK history to graduate with triple Master's degrees in advanced applied mathematics, theoretical physics and computer science. She delves further. Her sole attention and focus brought to bear on a young man with wild dark hair and the same features as his father. He looks amiable in the few images online. Quick to smile, and seemingly looking at something else in every picture. An archived news report from a few years ago when he obtained the three Master's at age fourteen.

> . . . so, like, I totally want to invent a time machine because my dad committed suicide and, like, then I can go back and totally ask him not to do the suicide . . .

◆　◆　◆

Alpha drives on past the fire engines, ambulances and police vehicles all heading in the other direction. Both of their masks off now so they look normal. Bravo holds a battered-looking tablet with a stylus to give the appearance of delivery workers chatting and organising their route. Bravo glances when Alpha reacts to his phone vibrating.

'*Alfie? It's Mother* . . .' She works hard to keep that tone soft and warm. '*I had a chat with your father, and we both think you should all come straight home. Berlin is too dangerous with all that mess going on . . . and we have a nice trip planned here for you . . .*'

'*Yep, okay.*'

'*We have booked your flights in one hour from Berlin to London . . . Do hurry, Alfie. We are so worried . . .*'

'*Okay, Mother.*'

Two

'Been called many things. Maureen. Monica. Maggie. Monique. M. Ma'am. Boss. SB, which stands for Stubborn Bitch. MB, which stands for Mad Bitch, and TB, which stands for That Bitch.'

She bites into the apple and chews while taking them in. Harry Madden. Commando from 1943. Safa Patel. Diplomatic Protection Officer. Ben is Ben Ryder. Saved the woman and kid when he was seventeen, then later stopped the terrorist attack. The last is the man she met when she first walked through the main room. Doctor John Watson. British by birth, but spent most of his medical career in the US.

'Now I'm Miri.'

She swallows the mouthful and leans back against the large table, while the others stare at her.

'Malcolm and Konrad are both dead.'

'How?' Safa demands.

'Shot and stabbed.' Miri takes another bite of the apple.

'By who?' Safa asks, her voice hardening. 'Ben, Harry, get ready. We're moving out . . . Where was it? Who did it? How many of them? Can you find the place again?'

Miri swallows and goes to take another bite, but stops with the apple an inch from her mouth. 'I don't know who. I do know where. I do know how many. I can find the place again.'

'What?' Safa asks, glaring harder. 'Who are you? Where's Roland? How did you get in here?'

'Safa,' Ben says.

'I asked you a question,' Safa says, louder now.

'You asked me a series of questions.'

'I said, who the fuck are you? How did you get in here? Where's Roland? How do you know Malcolm and Konrad are dead?'

'Safa, ease up,' Ben says, gently pulling her back. He looks at Miri. 'Who are you?' he asks politely.

'Miri.'

'Miri?' Ben takes in the woman. Swept-back blonde hair streaked with grey. American accent. Heavy lines on her face, a few of which hint at being scars. Cold eyes that look grey in this light. Tanned and weathered – someone who has spent years under the sun. Faded blue jeans. The sleeves of her checked shirt rolled mid-way up her forearms, the top three buttons undone. She looks anything from fifty to sixty years old, but she also looks sharp. 'I'm Ben. It's very nice to meet you.'

'Shake later,' Miri says as Ben walks towards her with a hand held out.

'Fair enough,' Ben says, dropping his hand. 'Forgive our surprise, but, er . . . can you explain what's happened, please?'

A nod at the show of manners. A glance at the positions of the others.

'I was extracted. Roland said you needed help.'

'Ah,' Ben says knowingly.

'We don't need help,' Safa says, moving out from behind Ben while gripping the back of a chair, ready to throw with a move noted but left unvoiced by Miri. Miri also notices the step Harry has taken out to the side. Casually and discreetly, but their positioning is tactically sound.

Ben, however, stays exactly where he is. 'I will ask you again,' Safa says. 'Exactly who are you?'

This part is not new to Miri. Walking into an established team is pretty much always the same. Safa clearly identifies herself as their leader. Miri has to gain that authority while showing she is not affecting the team dynamics but is taking overall control of the mission. She has to gain trust quickly, without asking or appearing to seek consent to do so. Every step is calculated. Every move is measured in advance. Miri remains calm. Showing control of the situation. Safa is growing angry. Miri is not. Control is already being asserted.

The only thing holding Safa and Harry back is Ben's reaction. Miri senses that to win them, she needs to win Ben first.

'Where do the pens come from?' A trick to defuse aggression and deflect tension. Casual, and asked easily. A master at work.

'What?' Safa asks, blinking at the weird question.

'Pens?' Harry asks.

'Pens,' Miri says.

'What are you on about?' Safa asks, the aggression rising clearly in her voice and manner.

'Roland gets them,' Ben says, holding his hands up in confusion. 'Or Malcolm or Konrad . . . I'm not sure . . .' He trails off at seeing Miri looking from her apple to the chairs and tables, then past them to the training equipment stacked at the far end.

'What the . . .' Safa says. 'You've got about three seconds to tell me who you are before this goes bad. Ben, move back now. Doc, you too . . .'

'Oh,' Ben says slowly, blinking as he connects the dots. He looks at Miri again, then round the room to the things she was looking at, to the food and drinks on the big table, to the swimming aid he made the two men bring back so he could prepare for the ocean rescue, to everything in the bunker and the bunker itself. 'Oh, I see . . .'

'Yes,' Miri says.

Ben drops his head an inch as he smiles that faint smile and rubs a thumb over his jaw. 'Holy shit . . . He got someone from military intelligence then?'

'Yes,' Miri says.

'Pens? What about the pens?' Safa asks, seeing Ben do *that move* he does when he's working things out. It catches her attention. The sight of him doing it. He hasn't done that for months. 'Ben? Who is she? Who are you? Where's Roland? We don't have time for this. Malcolm and Konrad are dead. Where are they?'

'Roland said you were smart,' Miri says to Ben.

Safa shifts a step, positioning herself ready to move in front of Ben. 'He is smart. What did you mean about the pens? Did Malcolm and Konrad die getting pens?'

'Er, no. No, she doesn't mean that,' Ben says quietly.

'If someone killed them for a pen, I'll . . .'

'It's not about the pens,' Ben says.

'She said pens.'

'Yes, but . . . No, she meant something else . . .'

'We don't even use pens . . .'

'Got a pencil,' Harry says, pulling one from his pocket.

'Okay, stop,' Ben says, looking at Harry and Safa. 'No pens. There were no pens. She means *who* gets the pens . . . Got it? Where do the pens *come* from?'

'From the fucking pen shop, obviously.'

'No, Safa . . .'

'Did you want my pencil, ma'am?'

'All of these things are the pens,' Ben says.

'What!?'

'The fruit, the equipment . . . all the stuff we use . . . They're the pens . . .'

'They're not pens.'

'No, Safa. I mean . . . so . . . Malc and Kon get everything we need, right?'

'Yeah, but they don't get . . .'

'Forget the bloody pens, Safa.'

'I would, but someone keeps on about them.'

'Christ! Right. Listen. Malc and Kon get everything we need. We don't know where from. We don't know how. We never go with them. Roland gives them the money and they get it. They are not surveillance-trained or . . . or know how to use countermeasures to prevent anyone finding them . . . Am I on the right track here?' Ben asks, glancing at Miri, who nods once. 'So I'm guessing someone tracked them to Berlin, right?' he asks Miri. This time she doesn't nod, but then she doesn't shake her head either. 'So someone found us . . . them . . . where they are . . .'

'Correct,' Miri says.

'How did you work that out from her saying about pens?' Safa asks. 'Who is she? Who are you?' She fires the questions out, irritated at not knowing what's going on.

'Safa, let Ben explain,' Doctor Watson says.

'I told Roland to get someone from military intelligence. Someone who knows how to do the things Roland is incompetent at. Roland has got her . . .' – he points at Miri – 'I mean you, sorry.'

'You know what ODNI is?' Miri asks.

Safa nods, once and curt, her dark eyes fixed on the older woman.

'What's that?' Harry asks.

'Office of Director of National Intelligence,' Doctor Watson says. 'I read a lot,' he adds when everyone looks at him.

'They oversee the whole intelligence community in the US,' Safa says. 'Which department are you from? CIA?'

Miri shakes her head. 'DIA,' she says. 'Defence Intelligence Agency,' she adds, so Harry can understand. 'Our remit was military intelligence. My background was military. Recruited during the Cold War.'

'I'm not buying it. She could be anyone,' Safa says. 'Why isn't Roland here to introduce you?'

'I was extracted two days ago and Roland is not here because I told him to stay home and await further instruction. I have something . . .' Miri says, leaning forward to reach round to her back. Safa stiffens. The grip on the chair tightening. Harry tenses, bunching power ready to launch at her. 'Stand easy. No threat. Piece of paper to show you.' She pulls a folded sheet from her back pocket and holds it out towards Ben. 'Read it.'

Tension in the room. Ben takes the folded piece of paper and moves back a step before opening it out to read the words written on one side. A smile twitches at the corner of his mouth, and again his head drops as his hand comes up to rub his jaw.

'What is it?' Safa asks, still holding Miri locked in her gaze. 'Read it out.'

'Okay,' Ben says, looking up to smile at Miri. He clears his throat and reads from the sheet.

'*Miri. Please do not be alarmed at finding this note on your door. My name is Ben Ryder . . .*' – he pauses at the surprised looks from Safa, Harry and the doctor – '*Tomorrow night, a man will come to you. He will arrive through a blue light in your kitchen. His name is Roland Cavendish. His son, Bertram, invented time travel in the year 2061. This seems absurd. The only way I can prove it to you is to tell you we know you went to the diner today and saw two men who you believed to be of Russian or Eastern European origin. You believe those men have tracked you because of your former life. You are correct. They will come tomorrow night and cause an explosion in your house, which will later be blamed on a gas leak. Your body is not recovered. Your body is not recovered because you go back with Roland Cavendish to a bunker in the Cretaceous period, where you will meet me, Safa Patel, Harry Madden and Doctor John Watson. Again, this sounds utterly absurd, but I know, from you telling me, that you have not reported your cover being blown for your own personal reasons . . .*'

'Shit,' Safa whispers.

'There's more,' Ben says. *Something causes the world to end by 2111. Bertram discovered it during his tests. Roland extracted us from our times because the bloody idiot used a computer program to match heroes. The man is incompetent. He is not capable of running this. We need your help. Please go with Roland . . .'* Ben trails off, blinking several times. He clears his throat and looks up at Safa, then across to Harry. 'Last bit to read out . . . It says, er . . . Well, it says, *In order to put Safa and Harry's minds at rest, tell them Safa's favourite film is* . . . er, well, it says *The Ben Ryder Movie*. And, er, her favourite food is now *the lemon-lime fruit thing in the bunker, but Harry prefers the awful thing that stinks of cheesy feet.* It also says Harry refuses to wear new boots, and the name of his first training sergeant when he joined the army was Gordon McTavish. *He was Scottish, and had a tattoo of a snake on his right arm. Safa's best friend before she joined the police was a girl called Tammy, but they lost contact when Safa joined up.'*

'Oh my god, it says that?' Safa asks.

'Yep,' Ben says. 'Few more too. Names of pets, schools. Stuff that someone wouldn't know . . . It's signed too. By us . . . All of us . . .' He holds the sheet up and walks over to show Safa and Harry the signatures. Doctor Watson rises from his seat to join them.

'Shit,' Safa says slowly. 'That your signature, Harry?'

'Aye.'

'Ben? That yours?'

'Yep. It's my handwriting too . . . I mean, I wrote this . . . all of it . . . but, um, I haven't written it yet.'

'Head fuck,' Safa mutters.

'That is definitely my signature,' Doctor Watson says. 'And, good lord, yes, my dog was called Meredith . . .'

'You called your dog Meredith?' Safa asks.

'If we re-extract Malcolm and Konrad, we confirm the existence of time travel to an enemy we do not know,' Miri says, instantly businesslike. 'The SA was attacked by either a PC or GA intent on securing the HB . . .'

'The what?' Ben cuts in, puzzled. Harry and Safa share his confused expression. 'I didn't get any of that.'

'Nope,' Safa says.

'Not a word,' Harry says.

'Staging area,' Miri says flatly. 'The SA was attacked by what was either a private company or a government agency intent on securing the home base . . .' She takes in the blank looks. 'The warehouse in Berlin was the staging area.'

'Ah, got it,' Ben says quickly, clicking his fingers. 'With you now. Yep. Staging area was Berlin . . . Er, what was the other stuff you said?'

'Private company . . .' Miri says.

'What, like a shop?'

'No,' Miri says.

'I'm not a soldier,' Ben says, holding his hands up. 'Insurance investigator.'

'I know. Ben Ryder. You saved a woman and child when you were seventeen, and were taken into the British equivalent of the Witness Protection Programme under the name of Ben Calshott. You were engaged to Stephanie Myers, who denounced you as a wife-beater after your death, which was caused by an explosion at Holborn train station in London following an attack by environmental activists. Safa Patel's parents are from Egypt and India. She joined the police following what you did when you were a kid, and then later moved into your equivalent of the Secret Service to protect the Prime Minister, having been influenced by your actions at Holborn. She died protecting him when the same environmental activists attacked Downing Street. Harry Madden, known as Mad Harry Madden. Commando deployed to a Norwegian fjord during the last world war. Information and knowledge. This is what I do.'

Ben listens intently, mesmerised by the way Miri speaks. Her tone somehow flat, but with that American drawl, and the words come out hard and fast. The last thing she said was so American too. The overt expressionism so unique to Americans. *This is what I do.* In those few words, he surmises Roland has told her who they are.

'I think she means a private military company,' Doctor Watson says with relish. 'Mercenaries. Guns for hire . . . rogues . . . The types of ne'er-do-wells likely to give their arms for the highest bidder in a world of shady deals in smoky back rooms,' he adds with a big grin as everyone else in the room looks at him for a few seconds.

'So,' Ben says slowly, looking back at Miri. 'The private military people attacked the warehouse in Berlin and killed Malc and Kon.' He realises he doesn't feel quite as bad as he should right now. Death isn't what it was. They have a time machine. They can go back and get them. That translates to *not being dead* in Ben's head.

'Crossfire, was it?' the doctor asks with a knowing nod. 'Got to watch the angles in the old firefight, you know.'

'So the home base is here, is it?' Ben asks. Along with not feeling as bad as he should about Malc and Kon *not being dead*, he also doesn't feel afraid or worried about the thought of armed people attacking a warehouse a hundred million years in the future. They are safe here. The one thing cemented in his mind is the complete impossibility of anyone ever finding them.

'We have immediate work to do,' Miri cuts in, placing the apple core on the table. She looks at the clothes Harry and Safa are wearing. 'Your physical state. Report.'

'Fit and ready to go, ma'am,' Harry booms, coming to attention.

'You're not bloody ready to go,' the doctor says. 'Harry and Safa have been out of it for two days. They need rest.'

'Belay the last from the good doctor,' Harry says officially, still standing to attention. 'Ready for duty.'

'Belay that belay,' Doctor Watson blusters. 'They need rest . . .'

'Had a good kip, ma'am. Ready to go,' Harry counters.

'What is it you require?' Ben enquires politely.

'Roland and his son. Extraction,' Miri replies.

'Oh, I can do that,' Ben says lightly. 'Doc's right. Safa and Harry need rest.'

'No way you're going alone,' Safa tells him.

'Why not? It's only Roland,' Ben says.

'Question,' the doctor says. 'Why do we need to extract Roland and his son? I mean, can't they just come here?'

'Bodies are evidence. Malcolm and Konrad will lead investigators to Roland. Roland's son is the inventor. Not good. Need extracting.'

'Right,' Ben says. 'Like I said, I can do that . . . Where are they?'

'No,' Safa says. 'We'll deploy as a team.'

'No,' the doctor says.

'No,' Miri says.

'Too many no's,' Ben mumbles, his forehead wrinkling. 'So where they are?' he asks Miri.

'Cavendish Manor. Hampshire. England.'

'Got it. So I just pop back and ask them to come and stay here, easy. Er, did you say manor? The cheeky twat lives in a manor house and he keeps us in a nasty bunker . . .'

'Roland and his son cannot stay here,' Miri cuts across him.

'I see,' Ben says, nodding at her. 'Sorry, not got a clue what you mean.'

'They require extraction, but they will not be staying here. Mr Ryder will come with me.'

'Mr Ryder will not go anywhere on his own,' Safa says.

'S'just Ben,' Ben says.

'I can do it, ma'am,' Harry says, taking a step forward. 'Ready to deploy. Feeling fine.'

Miri looks at him, at his drawn expression and the tremble in his legs that he can't disguise.

'Miri,' Ben says carefully, politely. 'Listen, the whole time thing is confusing, but we've got a time machine. We can go in ten years and it won't make a difference.'

'Negative. Need extraction now. Will happen. Has to happen.'

'Forgive me being rude,' Ben says, 'but you are wrong – it doesn't have to happen now. Safa and Harry have been out of it for a couple of days. Let them get better, and we'll all go in a few days. We've got a time machine . . .'

'Understand me,' Miri counters the second he stops talking. 'In the timeline I just left, the people who attacked the SA are examining the bodies of Malcolm and Konrad. They will link those bodies to Roland. They will connect that Bertram is the device inventor. They will immediately deploy to Cavendish Manor. If they gain Bertram, they gain a time machine. If they gain a time machine, the whole integrity of the timeline is ruptured.'

'That's over a hundred million years in the future. We can go to Roland's house whenever we want, and we can arrive at any time we choose. Those people are right now going to his house, but to us it doesn't matter. We've got the device.'

'Negative,' Miri says, her voice hardening. 'Once they gain a time machine, we lose.'

'Right, and what I am saying is that we'll always be able to go and get Bertram away from them because we have a time machine now.'

'Negative. Deploy now.'

'No. We can deploy when we want.'

'My agreement with Roland confirms I have authority. Roland and his son need extraction. That will happen now. If not, this will go to the US military. This is too big for you. Too big for Roland. We have to react to that timeline in real time. None of this is tested. None of this is known. We cannot take the chance on a system we do not know. Do not take what you think you know from science fiction and apply it now, Mr Ryder. Do not assume a thing because you think you know.'

'It's common sense,' Ben says, frustration showing.

'It is common sense formed from opinions of a subject you think you know, but we are dealing with an unknown entity. We will react accordingly to negate any and all risks, no matter how slight or negligible you perceive them to be. I understand your concerns and views, Mr Ryder, but they are just that: they are opinions. There is risk, and we *will* negate that risk. We will deploy now to absolutely ensure the safety of Bertram Cavendish. Failure to comply means the whole mission goes to the US military.'

Ben thinks to argue. To counter and persuade the woman she is wrong, but as much as he holds his beliefs strongly, so he can also see the validity of her argument, and the thought of a time machine going to any government, let alone the US government, is more a risk than anything else. He concedes and backs down, nodding to show supplication to her command. 'Safa, I'll be in and out. Like, super quick and super safe, and if it goes bent, then you and Harry can come rescue me . . . yeah? Good plan?'

'Shit plan. No. I didn't understand a word of what you both said. Is she being real? Does it need doing now?'

'Yeah, yeah, it does, but you and Harry have been in bed for . . .'

'Doc, give me and Harry a shot,' Safa says firmly.

'A what?' the doctor asks.

'A shot. Give us a boost.'

'A boost? No! You need rest, not . . .'

'We'll be manning up then. Harry, you fit?'

'Aye.'

'Safa,' Ben says carefully.

'Safa, my arse,' Safa says. There is no way she is letting Ben out on his own. He can handle a pistol and knows how to fight, but tactical awareness is an altogether different thing. 'Get ready, we'll deploy soon as we can. Doc, what *can* we take to help?'

'Safa, I just said . . .'

'I asked you a question,' Safa snaps, switching the glare to the poor doctor.

'Vit B make advances?' Miri asks, earning a frosty look from the doctor.

'They need rest,' he asserts.

'What's vit B?' Ben asks. 'Like, B vitamins?'

'Trials in my time,' Miri says. 'Natural energy boost. Does it work?'

'They do not replace the healing process a body requires,' the doctor says.

'Do it,' Safa orders. 'We'll get kitted.'

Three

To take five men out of a city in lockdown from what the public think is a terrorist incident, but what every intelligence agency, government and interested party believe to be the focal point of the hunt for the device, takes resources and power.

'We have a lead on the device inventor.'

That single phrase gives Mother more resources than she has ever had before. It gives her *all* the resources.

Every agent deployed throughout the world is suddenly at her disposal. Every researcher. Every asset. Every snitch, mole, hacker and back-office worker are made available and ordered, without excuse or failing, to focus on a large, detached manor house an hour south of London.

Commercial flights are out of the question. The five have literally just walked out of a gunfight and will be covered in trace chemicals that will register in the heightened airport security screening processes. That means a private jet has to be used, but filing a flight path with the aviation authorities creates an audit trail, and still does not circumvent customs and security services.

What it takes is a visit to the famous owner of a brand-name chain of fashion stores. An old-school visit with a brown envelope that contains original, high-definition time and date-stamped prints that show said married famous owner of the brand-name chain of fashion stores naked with a young man in a hotel room in Mumbai. That image, along with the passport of the young man showing his date of birth that puts him below the legal age of consent, means the famous man is only too willing for his private fast-jet to be used for a quick round trip to Berlin.

It takes off within fifteen minutes of the call from Alpha to Mother, and it takes fifty minutes for the jet to reach Berlin. During that time, the van containing the bodies of M and K is driven to a disused industrial estate, where a waiting operative sets it on fire and provides the five men with clean clothes.

They are taken to the airfield in time for the private jet to land and the famous owner to get out, shout at a poor, unwitting subordinate from the Berlin office of his fashion chain stores and get back in for the take-off. The owner does not say a word to the five men in his jet, but discreetly goes to the rear of the plane to stay out of sight.

That process gets the five out of Berlin, but it does not get them into London, and anything coming out of Berlin right now is subject to intense scrutiny.

So another jet is sent to Berlin from Paris. Another from Zurich. Another from Istanbul. Another from Barcelona, from Krakow, Moscow and five more from various cities within the continent. They file incorrect flight plans and cause chaos within the aviation authority's offices, and more at the private and commercial airfields they land at. Some wait a few minutes before taking straight back off. Some taxi about to draw attention. The pilot of the jet from Moscow gets out, pisses on the tarmac, then climbs back in and takes off. Attention is drawn and diverted, and every single one of those jets then aims for London.

Security services go into meltdown. The police are overwhelmed with reports of aircraft coming into the city with incorrect flight plans. The pilots on board those jets argue and bicker with each other for the right to land first. Air traffic controllers throw fits of panic, and, in the middle of it all, Mother's hands blur through the icons and programs hovering above her desk.

A mass brawl starts in the bar at Gatwick International Airport. A suspicious package left inside Terminal 7 at Heathrow. A truck fire outside the main doors to Stansted. A bomb hoax dialled into the police offices at Luton Airport. All of these things create enough of a distraction for the jet containing the five to land unobserved at Farnborough airfield in the north-eastern edge of Hampshire county in the south of England, as every airfield near London big enough to take commercial flights is put on standby to receive emergency landings.

The five, now dressed in smart business suits, walk through the small terminal. To say they adopt serious expressions and remark in the manner of business people delayed and frustrated at the chaos going on around them underplays the excellence of their craft. They *are* business people. The proficiency of their cover is superb in the display of behaviours that show they do not know each other, but realise they are all bound for the same executive meeting. They discuss the dismal pre-tax profits report produced by the fashion chain store, and nod and mutter in the way of people invested in such things who are frustrated at such delays and poor organisation.

The executive cars waiting at the airport take them on to the M3 motorway, first west towards Basingstoke, then south through increasingly narrow country lanes until they arrive at a wooden lodge five miles out from the small town of Alton, where Alpha strides in ahead of his team, already pulling ties from necks.

The large, open-plan lodge is packed with operatives, weapons stacked up, magazines being made ready, medic kits being sorted. Five sets of black combat gear identical to those worn by the five in Berlin wait by the table.

'I am Alpha. I have control,' Alpha says clearly, his voice carrying.

The energy in the room changes the instant they arrive. These are the five best agents known in their agency, probably the best in the country, possibly the best in the world. All five are together in one place at the same time. Every man and woman in that lodge making adjustments to kit, clothes and weapons glances over in the hope of gaining eye contact, to nod a greeting or make a show of the connection they may have once had on different operations, jobs and missions, but right now, those operatives are nothing more than cannon fodder.

'Secure line,' the operative at the table says, holding out a phone to Alpha.

'Stand by for briefing,' Alpha says, pressing the phone to his ear.

'*Go outside,*' Mother says. Alpha does as he is told, striding from the lodge as an army truck comes down the lane. He pauses to stare as the truck comes to a stop and a uniformed soldier jumps down from the front.

'Where do you want us?' the soldier calls over.

'Stand by,' Alpha replies to the soldier. '*Clear,*' he says into the phone.

'*We think the device inventor is R's son,*' Mother says. '*R is Roland Cavendish. His son is Bertie Cavendish.*'

'*I've heard that name,*' Alpha says, squeezing his eyes closed to try and sort through his mind.

'*Roland Cavendish walked into the sea in 2046. Body never recovered. Bertie was then in the press a few years later when he gained three Master's degrees at the age of fourteen . . . applied mathematics, theoretical physics and computer science.*'

'*Yes. Yes, I remember,*' Alpha says, thinking back to the national press coverage.

'*M and K worked for R. They died in a car accident in 2052.*'

'*Understood,*' Alpha says.

'*Good. Get briefed. We'll talk in a minute . . . For the purposes of everyone else, we are saying there is a new weapons system capable of mass destruction.*'

'*Got it . . . What happened in Berlin?*'

'*We will talk in a minute, Alpha. Get briefed.*'

'*Sorry, Mother. Why is there an army truck here . . .*' He turns to look, and blinks at the soldiers pouring from the back of it and the row of identical trucks behind it. '*Sorry, I meant why is the army here?*'

'*Ring of steel. Get briefed.*'

The line cuts off. Alpha pauses, sensing the size of the operation growing with every passing second. He walks back in as the lodge once again comes to instant silence. His eyes fix on the agent at the main table, which is now covered with maps, files and tablet screens glowing.

'Are you the briefer?' Alpha asks.

'I am,' the man says curtly.

'Brief will commence,' Alpha says, loud enough for everyone to hear. 'Go.' He nods at the man at the table.

'Target premises is Cavendish Manor.' The man tasked with briefing fires the words out as he taps a paper map before thumbing the screen of a tablet device that blooms out the hologram 3D image of a stately home. 'I've taken the trouble to map the entire area in order to establish the most accessible route in. This main road here,' he says, tapping the map while rotating the 3D hologram image of the house for no reason other than to try and impress the five, 'is the best route in . . .'

'That's a main road,' Charlie says. 'We cannot attack en masse from a main road . . .'

'There is a bridleway suitable for vehicles in the woodland to the rear of the target premises,' a voice calls out from one of the balaclava-wearing operatives gathered in the room.

'The bridleway does not show on the maps or satellite images,' the briefer snaps.

'Stop,' Alpha says, already irritated by the tone of the man and the lack of structure to the briefing. He turns to look at the operative who spoke out. 'You know this area?'

'Yes,' the voice says.

'How familiar?' Bravo asks.

'This is my patch.'

'Over here,' Alpha says, motioning the operative to come forward. 'You know what's going on?'

'Yes, Alpha,' the operative says politely. 'New weapons system capable of mass destruction. Snatch mission to secure Roland and Bertram Cavendish.'

'Mask up,' Alpha orders.

The woman rolls the black balaclava up to stare at the five. Brown hair tied back. Brown eyes set in a clear, healthy complexion. Slender and athletic. She takes the scrutiny without reaction.

'Rank?' Alpha asks.

'Two,' the woman says.

'Do you know this premises?' Bravo asks her.

'I know the location from horse riding in that area.'

'Horse riding?'

'Yes.'

'International circuit?' Alpha asks.

'Completed. Six offices,' the woman replies. 'Israel: combat, surveillance and counter-surveillance. Columbia: drug-trafficking infiltration. Siberia: counter-espionage. Nigeria: combat and advanced medics course. Beijing: surveillance . . .'

'I worked with her in Beijing,' Delta says.

'Final office?' Bravo asks, having counted five of the worst deployments on the planet, and wondering what the last one is and why anyone with so many deployments is still a Two.

'London,' the woman says. 'Twelve months' diplomatic surveillance and disruption.'

The five pause. London is the worst of all the offices. Twelve months on that rotation is exceptional.

'Name?' Alpha asks.

'Tango Two.'

'Why not Tango One?'

'I'm still Tango One,' an operative says dully from the crowd of black-clad figures.

The five look at Tango One, then back to Tango Two as Tango One thinks maybe he should have upped his game lately.

'Can you brief?' Alpha asks, clocking the filthy look sent to Tango Two from the briefer.

'I can,' Tango Two says, ignoring the filthy look.

'You are the briefer,' Alpha tells her, then points at the now former briefer. 'You are on report. Kit up. You're going in with the main group.'

'Knee injury,' the former briefer says with a look of panic at the prospect of deployment on a live mission, then instantly regretting what he just said on remembering he is talking to Alpha.

'Go away now,' Charlie tells him.

'Get familiar,' Alpha tells Tango Two as the former briefer makes a point of limping away out of sight.

Four

'You decent?' Safa asks, tapping on Ben's door.

'You're giving me a flashback saying that,' he calls out. 'And yes, I am . . .' He pauses as she pushes the door open, and stands with his hands out from his body. 'How do I look?' he asks with a grin.

'Your holster's on upside down,' she says, appraising him with one quick glance.

'Is it?' Ben asks, twisting to look at the holster. 'Oh shit, so it is . . . Bollocks.'

'And you wanted to go on your own, yeah?'

'Ready,' Harry says, walking from his room into the middle section of their suite.

'Boots,' Safa says.

'Aye.'

'Harry, we talked about this.' Safa rubs her forehead to rid the increasing fug clouding her mind.

'Aye.'

'You can't wear boots from 1943.'

'Aye.'

'Fuck's sake,' she says, looking from Harry's battered old boots to Ben fumbling with his holster.

'How you feeling?' Ben asks, glancing at Safa then Harry.

'Like shit,' Safa says.

'Then don't go. I can do it,' Ben says.

'Sure,' Safa says, dropping down to open the case containing the pistols brought in from the firing range outside. 'With your holster on upside down, yeah?' she asks, pulling a gun out. 'Harry.' She waves the gun at him as the big man looks up from his boots to the pistol.

'Nothing wrong with my boots,' he says as he takes the gun and slides the top back to check the chamber.

'Magazines,' Safa says, holding a few up to him.

'Good boots,' Harry says, taking the magazines.

'Old boots,' Safa says.

'Done it. Better?' Ben says, presenting himself like a child on the first day of school wearing his shiny new uniform. The other two glance, appraise, grunt and go back to loading and checking guns. 'Where's mine?' Ben asks, seeing Safa push one into the holster on her hip.

'Minute,' she says, pulling a third pistol from the container, which she starts checking.

'I can do it,' Ben says, holding his hand out.

'I know. Have you used these while we were out of it?'

'Yeah, did a few yesterday.'

'Did you clean them?'

'Yes!' he says, seeing her hesitation. 'What's up?'

'Nothing,' she says. 'Er, listen, Ben. Maybe me and Harry should go.'

'Eh?' He looks from Safa to Harry, who suddenly starts picking the crumbs from his clean shirt.

'It's different when people shoot back,' Safa says, as blunt as ever.

'What the fuck,' Ben says. 'You've trained me. I'll be fine.'

'I've trained you to fire a gun and fight unarmed, but that's not . . .'

'I'll be fine. It's Roland and his son. It's in and out.'

'Exactly. So maybe you don't need a weapon.'

'Safa, stop being a dick.'

'Ben, this is serious. A firefight is fucking horrible. One split-second delay and you get killed.'

'So, got a time machine. Come back and get me . . .'

'Stop fucking about,' she snaps, squeezing her eyes closed at the pain in the back of her head growing steadily worse.

'Safa,' Ben says, lowering his tone at seeing the blood drain from her face. 'Stay here with Harry.'

'No,' she snaps again, standing up to pass the pistol over.

He goes to take it, but she holds on, refusing to hand it over. 'Listen, you keep it holstered at all times. Do not draw it unless me or Harry tell you to. Okay?'

'Don't patronise me.'

'Ben! Listen to me. You either promise to keep it holstered or you don't go.'

'What?'

'I'm serious. I'm team leader. You'll stay here if I say so.'

'Are you taking the piss?'

'Orders are orders, Ben,' Harry mutters.

'Fine,' Ben says.

'Stays holstered,' Safa repeats, holding her eyes on his. 'Okay?'

'Fine,' he says again, smarting from her tone. He takes the pistol, his hands working fluidly and fast to slide the top, check the chamber, check the safety and listen to the moving parts. 'Am I allowed bullets?'

'Rounds,' Safa snaps.

'Safa, take it easy,' Ben says.

'This is a live job. Switch on.'

'Okay, okay, sorry . . .'

'Don't be sorry,' she mutters, passing him several loaded magazines. She watches him like a hawk as he loads and makes ready. They both do. Harry towering, massive and quiet, but as worried as Safa at taking Ben out of the bunker into an unknown situation.

'What?' Ben asks, clocking the look that passes between them as he holsters the weapon and secures the spare magazines.

'Nothing,' Safa says quietly. 'You okay now?' she asks, studying him closely.

'I'm fine. Honestly. I had ten days from when you . . . you know . . .'

'Died?' Harry asks.

'Yeah, died. I had ten days . . . The doc gave me different meds, and I feel fine now. Seriously,' he adds at the lack of assurance coming back from them.

'Okay,' Safa says after a pause. 'We'll get this done, then set up scenario training.'

'Awesome,' Ben says eagerly, then tuts at the hard glare. 'Fuck's sake . . . I'm fine. This is me now. That wasn't me before . . . I was sick . . . Now I'm not sick. I'm me again. I'm happy. I'm happy as fuck you two are back. Seriously I am. Stop looking at me like I'm a twat . . .' He trails off with a grin that grows wider as he spots the corners of her mouth twitching.

'Idiot,' she mutters, shaking her head, but at least smiling. 'Ready then? Harry, you fit?' She sets off, with the other two following her down the corridor to the main room. 'Ben, when we deploy, you need to stay quiet and listen to everything we say.'

'Yep.'

'No messing about once we're through.'

'Got it.'

'If I say to go back, then do it straight away.'

'Roger . . . Do I say roger? Is that the right word?'

'Just say okay.'

'Okay, roger.'

'If it goes bent, then stay behind Harry and me. Do not, and I repeat, do not run in front of us if we are aiming or firing.' She stops at the doors to the main room and looks back at Ben.

'Roger.'

'Stop saying roger. Harry and I will act as guards, so you go forward to make the two subjects move.'

'Roger that.'

'Twat. Don't ask them to do it. Tell them to do it. Force them. Make them move.'

'Roger wilco.'

'You're an idiot,' she tuts, pushing through the doors to see Miri drinking coffee and talking to Doctor Watson.

'Roger roger,' Ben mumbles.

'We're ready,' Safa says, watching the woman cast a look over them all.

'Comms?' Miri asks, seeing a lack of earpieces and radio sets on the three.

'Negative,' Safa says curtly.

'None?' Miri asks curtly.

'Affirmative,' Safa says curtly.

'No time now. Go without,' Miri says.

'Yes,' Safa says.

'Roger that,' Ben says as Safa groans inwardly.

The doctor rises from his chair with two mugs clasped in his hands. 'Something to help with the pain and fatigue.'

'Thought we were having shots,' Safa says as he walks over.

'So did I until Miri pointed out I cannot use the time machine to go and get them,' he says with a tight smile. 'Which means we have to make do with what we have instead.' He comes to a stop holding the mugs out to Harry and Safa.

'Don't I get one?' Ben asks.

'What is it?' Safa asks, peering into the mug, then up at Ben shuffling closer to join in with the visual examination.

'Nice,' Harry says, wiping his mouth after gulping it down in one go.

Safa shrugs and drinks it in one motion. She looks at Ben over the rim of the mug, almost laughing out loud at the earnest, interested expression on his face. Like the Ben that was here in the beginning. That Ben. The nice Ben.

'Was it nice?' Ben asks as soon as she lowers the mug.

'Was,' she says. 'What was in it?'

'Drugs,' Doctor Watson says with a lift of his eyebrows as he turns away back to his table.

'Do you feel anything?' Ben asks, looking from Safa to Harry.

'Only just drunk it,' Safa says.

Ben nods. 'Roger,' he says and waits for a few seconds. 'How about now?'

'Plan,' Miri says, drawing their attention.

'Ready,' Safa says, walking over to the table.

'No plan,' Miri says. 'Fluid. Snatch mission. Two adult males. Have any of you been to Cavendish Manor?'

'Negative,' Safa says.

'Negative,' Ben says, earning a look from Safa.

'No,' Harry says.

Miri continues without a flicker of reaction. 'Fluid. Go fast. Sweep through the target premises. Bertram is the priority. Get the son. Get Roland. Return through the Blue . . .'

'The what?' Ben asks.

'Blue,' Miri says.

'Time machine,' the doctor says from behind them.

'Time machine is Blue now, is it?' Safa asks, staring at Miri.

'Affirmative,' Miri says.

'Blue is cool,' Ben says, nodding happily.

'TM is better,' Safa says. 'We'll get *Roland*,' she says, casting a look at Miri, 'and his son, then back through the TM . . .'

'Blue,' Miri says.

'TM,' Safa says.

Silence.

'Device is Blue,' Miri says.

'Yeah, it's also a time machine,' Safa says.

Silence.

'Awkward,' Ben mumbles.

'Flip a coin?' Doctor Watson suggests amiably.

'You got a coin?' Ben asks him.

'Ah, no, afraid not,' he says.

'Harry, you got a coin, mate?'

'No.'

'Ah, shame. Miri? You got one?'

'Blue,' Miri says.

'TM,' Safa says.

'Righto,' Ben says. 'Er . . . vote?'

'Device is Blue.'

'We called it the TM *before* you arrived,' Safa says.

'Did we?' Ben asks, looking at Harry, who goes back to picking crumbs from his shirt.

'You were depressed,' Safa says, still looking at Miri.

'Depressed, not deaf,' Ben says.

'I have authority. Device is Blue. Fluid mission to . . .'

'Right,' Safa says brightly, turning to face Ben and Harry. 'Fluid mission. We go in, grab the two subject males and come straight back to the TM. Understood?'

'Aye,' Harry says, nodding eagerly.

'Roger,' Ben says. 'Grab the two blokes and come back through the Blue.'

'HAHA,' Harry laughs, grinning widely at Safa and Ben. 'It's funny because he keeps saying roger,' he explains, pointing at Ben.

'Urgh,' Safa says, shaking her head. 'I'm starting to buzz . . . What was in that drink?'

'I told you. Drugs,' Doctor Watson says.

'Feel awake now, I do,' says Harry. 'Oh aye, wide awake. You feel awake, Safa? I feel awake now. We should have a run when we get back . . . Safa? Ben? You up for a run later?'

'What did you give us?' Safa asks, looking from Harry to the doctor. 'It's like cocaine or something . . .'

'Um, not exactly cocaine . . .'

'What? You gave Mad Harry Madden cocaine before a live job . . .'

'It's not cocaine,' the doctor says, staring into the bottom of his mug.

'COCAINE,' Harry booms as Safa's body starts to tingle. Her vision grows sharper, clearer, her mind whizzing fast and wide awake. The pain in her skull gone and her limbs thrumming with energy.

'Holy shit,' Safa groans, shaking her head again.

'Really wasn't cocaine.'

'Fucking was,' Safa says, very loud and very fast. 'What the fuck are you thinking? Fuck it. We're going. We're off. We'll get moving. We're ready . . . Ben? You ready? Keep that weapon in the holster . . . I can't believe he gave us cocaine, the bloody idiot.'

'S'not cocaine.'

Miri gets the stopwatch on her wrist zeroed and ready, then finally lifts her eyebrows at the utter shambles going on in front of her. Unfortunately there is no choice but to press on. Roland and his son have to be secured. They are more important than any of these three idiots grinning at each other. Ben hasn't even had any drugs. Why is he so happy? The British are a strange folk, for sure.

Five

'Roland Cavendish. Last picture taken in the year 2046, so he will have aged,' Tango Two says, turning the 3D image so everyone in the room can see.

'Cosmetic surgery,' Bravo cuts in quickly. 'He may look the same as that. Exactly the same.'

'Understood,' Tango Two says, frowning as she reduces the image and brings the next one blooming up from the tablet on the desk. 'Bertram Cavendish. Son of Roland Cavendish. Twenty-five years old. Lives in the family home. Intel suggests Bertram is the inventor of the new weapons system. He is the primary target. Is that correct?' she asks, looking at Alpha, who nods. 'Also in the family home we have Maria Cavendish, known to family and friends as Ria – twenty-two years old, daughter of Roland – and Susan Cavendish, wife of Roland and mother to Bertram and Maria. Er, there are no orders regarding them?'

'Bertram and Roland are the priority,' Alpha says.

'Understood,' Tango Two says smartly before continuing. 'We have several army regiments currently deploying a ring of steel around the property. They are not tasked with entry but to secure the area only.' She blooms out the image of the manor house.

'How many agents and operatives have we got to deploy?' Alpha asks, reaching a hand into the hologram to turn the image.

'Thirty-two, not including your team,' Tango Two says immediately. 'Eighteen fully operational, eight coming to the end of their extended basic training packages and the remaining six are basic trained only.'

'Understood,' Alpha says. 'I'll take it from here, Tango Two. Good brief. We have a four-sided target premises. We stick with basic tactical colour coding,' he says, enlarging the image so everyone can see the hologram of the front of the manor house. 'The front is white side. The right side is green. The rear is black. The left side is red. Blue is the roof. Everyone clear?' A slight pause. A heartbeat and nothing more. 'Eight to white. Eight to black. Eight to green. Seven to red . . .'

'Forgive me,' Tango Two says, looking from Alpha to Bravo and then down to Echo while rapidly assimilating why Alpha has made a mistake, 'that is thirty-one. There is one unaccounted for.'

'Can you fastrope?'

'I can,' she says without a flicker of reaction.

'Training only or live deployment?'

'Both.'

'You'll deploy with us. When is the heli arriving?'

'Here now, half a mile away,' Tango Two says, allowing one single surprised blink in reaction to the information that she, only a Two, will deploy with the five via fastrope.

'Good skills,' Alpha says, offering her a nod. Snatch missions are unpredictable. They have to extract male subjects, and male subjects nearly always respond more positively to females.

'Ones will split to lead even teams,' Bravo says, addressing the operatives. 'Experienced Twos will assist their Ones. Is that clear? New operatives just out of basic will listen closely to their Ones and Twos. Is that also clear? The subjects are to be taken alive. All clear? Jolly good.'

The five take their kit to get changed in a back room, plunging the large, open-plan living quarters of the lodge into an awkward silence, with every Two wishing they were Tango and every One wishing she would piss off.

For her part, Tango Two feels the sudden pressure of being lifted to the top table but now not knowing if she should be issuing instructions, asking if everyone is ready or perhaps even going outside to avoid the thirty-one black-clad faces currently glaring at her.

She goes outside.

'I bet she's floating off the floor right now,' Charlie says, stripping his smart business suit off. 'She any good?' he asks Delta.

'Hmmm,' Delta says, tugging the corner of his mouth down. 'She's thirty and still a Two, but she's a woman, so . . .'

'Good enough,' Charlie says.

Bravo nods with understanding as he goes back to undressing. He thought he saw the flicker of a plan on Alpha's face when they all saw Tango Two.

'Have you checked in yet?' Bravo asks.

'Do it now,' Alpha says, opening the door. 'I need a secure line,' he calls out and waits a few seconds for the former briefer to run down with the phone. The man remembers halfway that he has a bad knee and adds the limp for the final few steps. 'You're a cunt,' Alpha says, taking the phone and closing the door in his face.

'*Who is?*' Mother asks as Alpha puts the phone to his ear and the other four wince.

'*The briefer,*' Alpha says honestly. '*Faking a knee injury to avoid deployment. He needs Siberia for a few months.*'

'*He'll get Siberia for a few months,*' Mother says curtly before switching to her nice motherly tone. '*So, Alfie darling. How are my boys holding up? Do put me on holo so I can see everyone.*'

Alpha mouths *sorry* as he pulls the phone away and presses a button that balloons Mother into the air above the handset in perfect, pin-sharp definition. Her pinched face glaring beneath the greying hair cut short and austere. Mother sweeps her gaze over the five half-dressed men and to the last they hold still. All respectful. All quiet and all waiting for her to speak.

'*Nice holiday, boys?*' Mother asks, her smile chilling the blood in their veins.

'Ma'am,' Bravo says, dipping his head.

'Yes, ma'am,' Charlie mumbles.

'Mother,' Delta mutters.

'*WHAT THE FUCK WAS THAT?*' Mother snaps before Echo can reply. '*Berlin is a mess. Have you seen it? You do not want to see it. It looks like fucking Beirut in the 1980s . . .*'

The five wait. Charlie with one leg in his trousers. Echo in his boxers with the bandage on his arm.

'*Jesus H Christ. How on earth did that go wrong?*'

'Unknown opposition prepped the warehouse,' Alpha says. 'Blew it as we approached.'

'*Professional?*'

'Definitely,' says Echo, the explosive expert amongst them. 'Charges and accelerants used in the room holding the device . . . but, er . . .' He pauses.

'*What?*' Mother demands.

'Looked like it was C4,' Echo says politely. 'Old way of doing it, ma'am.'

'*They've got a fucking time machine,*' Mother's states icily. '*They can use fucking dynamite taken from the dead fingers of Davy fucking Crockett at the fucking Alamo if they want. What about the rest of the street? You were only meant to destroy the observation points, not the whole fucking neighbourhood!*'

'Er, sorry, ma'am,' Echo says, 'but that wasn't us.'

'*What?*'

Alpha clears his throat, bringing Mother's glare back to him. 'That wasn't us. We blew the observation point only. The warehouse and the street was someone else.'

49

'*Fuck me,*' Mother mutters, looking away from Alpha to something in her room. '*They have a time machine. Every agent in that street is either dead or seriously injured . . . Shit and shit and FUCKING SHIT.*'

'Yes, ma'am,' Alpha says.

Mother leans forward, lowering her tone. '*I've got the fucking Prime Minister calling me every five fucking minutes. She has every other world leader calling her every five fucking minutes, all wanting to know if we have found it. Russia are pointing nukes at us. America are pointing half of theirs back at Russia, some at China and a few are now facing in our direction, gentlemen. We've got fucking NATO literally shitting themselves and every intelligence agency in the world and no doubt every fucking satellite now positioned over my fucking head! This is blown. We are blown. They know we went after it, which is bad enough, but we cannot confirm or deny, which makes them all think we HAVE A FUCKING TIME MACHINE!*'

The five stay silent. Not a muscle twitches.

Mother rubs her forehead and sighs heavy and long to force the harsh tone into something ever so slightly softer. '*Plan?*'

'Ground assault using thirty-one operatives attacking all sides of the target premises while we fastrope down on to a balcony on the white side,' Alpha says. 'Army on the perimeter for the ring of steel.'

'*I'm looking at the target premises now,*' the hologram image of Mother says while looking away to the side.

'Ma'am,' Alpha says, 'Tango Two is here. Said this is her patch. She briefed us.'

'*Oh, that is so nice for you,*' Mother says, still looking away to the side. '*I wish I could be happier, but I'm a bit busy picking up the pieces of a major European city currently in a state of emergency from a whole bloody street that just blew up during a gunfight for a fucking time machine . . .*'

'We're taking Tango Two in with us,' Alpha says.

Mother switches that hawk-eyed look back to the room. '*Good. Use her. Use anything you need to use,*' she says plainly, which is about as nice a tone as Mother gives when she is not impersonating an actual mother.

'*I have two attack helicopters ready in Portsmouth naval base. Flight time less than ten minutes. They will be overhead as the assault commences. Do you require further resources? I have Special Forces serials on standby and will start moving them towards. In short, gentlemen, I have every man and his dog capable of holding a shotgun ready to assist you.*'

The four look at Alpha in reaction to the fact that Mother wants to bring gunships to a fistfight. That is how serious this is now. That is how big it is.

'I think we have enough now,' Alpha says carefully, trying to figure out how two attack helicopters fit into a basic snatch mission.

'*Alive at all costs, but better dead than left,*' Mother says.

'Ma'am,' Alpha says in response, now knowing she wants the whole bloody house flattened if it means preventing anyone getting back through any device. 'Are you monitoring live time?' he asks.

'*Satellite is being positioned and I will be monitoring . . . And gentlemen? I will not be the only one monitoring this now. This has gone up the food chain. Do you understand? The PM is convening an emergency meeting for the Cabinet Office to eat cucumber sandwiches while they watch you. Good luck. I will be here for anything you need. Do not fail. Bring Tango Two up to speed on everything. She signed the waiver to be used as a honey trap. Use her if you need to. A female can still do things a male cannot.*'

The hologram cuts off instantly, leaving a heavy silence that hangs in the room as the five take stock and process everything she just said.

Five minutes later, the five march out into the main room. What they wear is identical to everyone else, and they select the same sidearms and submachine guns from the crates, yet they stand out. The aura oozes from them. The way they keep their masks rolled up like hats, the way they carry themselves and the complete confidence each conveys. The way each issues orders to everyone else with the supreme knowledge that they have authority. The operatives know they just spoke with Mother too. They had a personal conversation with Mother. That happened. Nobody ever talks to Mother unless they are being promoted or something has gone very seriously wrong.

'Ready?' Alpha asks, stepping outside to see Tango Two waiting by a black four-by-four with darkened windows.

'Ready,' Tango Two says, reaching up to start rolling her mask down.

'Leave it up,' Alpha says quietly as he walks over. 'Sets us apart,' he adds when Tango Two drops her hands to watch the operatives all piling out from the lodge. She suppresses any reaction to the micro-nuance that something so small works so well and he was right. Everyone else has their masks already down, as per procedure. Only the five refrain, and now her too.

They gather at their vehicle, pausing as everyone else loads up.

'Do you know the way to the heli from here?' Bravo asks.

'I do,' Tango Two says.

'Out,' Charlie says, opening the door. The driver complies instantly, rushing off towards the lodge. 'You drive,' Charlie says, looking at Tango Two.

She climbs in and works quickly to adjust the seat. Alpha takes the front passenger position, the other four go into the rear. Tango Two pulls away, following a different route to the other vehicles and sensing something else is going on.

'Mother wants you brought up to speed,' Alpha says after a few seconds' pause.

'Okay.' Tango Two stares ahead through the windscreen.

'What do you know?'

She glances at him, sensing this is an integrity test. 'Just what we've been told, sir.'

'Alpha, not sir.'

'Sorry. Just what we were told, Alpha.'

'No rumours?'

'Something to do with an advanced weapons system that everyone else wants,' she says honestly.

'Worked then,' Bravo says from the back.

'Worked?' Tango Two asks, her eyes darting to the rear-view mirror to see Bravo smiling at her.

'False rumours generated to hide the truth,' Alpha explains. 'Time machine. Confirmed to be in existence and in use. Actively in use, I might add. Berlin was a sort of staging area they were using. We did not know who. We launched the strike today, but that staging area was rigged to detonate . . . Watch the road, Tango Two.'

'Sorry, sir.'

'Roland Cavendish died in 2046, but is still alive now . . . at the same age he was when he died in 2046.'

'Fuck off,' she blurts. 'I am so sorry, Alpha.'

'It's fine. Watch the road,' he says again. 'Delta said the same thing.'

'I did,' Delta calls forward.

'We think Bertie Cavendish invented the time machine. We secured two of their operatives in Berlin. They died, but information they held has led us here. Understand?'

Tango Two nods quickly and swallows. 'Understood . . . Have you seen it?'

'We think so,' Alpha replies. 'Our surveillance suggests the device manifests as a bright blue light shaped like a door. Although we also believe it is mobile and the size can be altered.'

'Understood,' she says.

'His Majesty's government is very keen to ensure we secure this device before any Johnny Foreigner does,' Alpha says as they start bouncing down an unmade road towards the chopper waiting in the near distance. 'We had dozens of agents in Berlin. Mother said they're either dead or seriously injured. Bad for them. Good for you. Positions are suddenly becoming vacant. Juliet One was killed last month. Mother said you'll be getting her position. That puts you in the top ten. India

One was also in Berlin. If he's dead, then you make ninth agent . . . Do you understand what I'm saying, Tango Two? Mother needs results. At any cost. This is a snatch mission, but we are prepared to do *anything* to secure either that device or the inventor . . .'

Tango Two nods, a gritty reality sinking in. She signed the waiver because all the other female trainees signed it. It was expected. The expectation is that agents will do *anything* to serve their country.

'Are we clear, Tango Two?'

'We are, Alpha. Very clear.'

Six

'BLUE,' Harry shouts, seeing the device come instantly to life as Miri activates the tablet in the portal room. 'VERY BLUE.'

'STOP SHOUTING,' Safa shouts.

'HAHA,' Harry laughs.

'Fuck me,' Ben mutters, shaking his head as he stares at them both, then looks round to a somewhat defensive Doctor Watson.

'Wasn't cocaine,' the doctor says again.

Miri looks up at them from the tablet held in her hands. Finding Cavendish Manor was easy. It was logged in the software system as *Roland's House* for a start. That fact, along with nearly everything else, appals her. The lack of security is staggering. The lack of care taken for something so powerful. In her mind, it's like asking high school kids to look after a nuclear arsenal.

She places the tablet down and draws her pistol from the holster, which makes Safa instantly counter-draw with a speed that even Miri finds impressive. A second of eyes locking. Of Safa's pupils now huge from whatever drugs she has been given, but staring intently.

'Er, everything alright?' Ben asks carefully.

'Weapons check,' Miri says, making a point of turning away from them to eject the magazine from her pistol.

'What for?' Safa asks, the words coming too fast and too loud.

Miri checks the weapon and reloads with a show of confident hands that have done the same many times before.

'I said, what for?'

'Coming with you,' Miri says.

'Are you asking me or telling me?'

'Argue later.' Miri holsters her gun and picks up the tablet. She thumbs the name *Roland's House* and glances up as the device once again bathes the room in shimmering blue. 'Blue is live. I'll go first,' Miri says as Safa rushes past.

'I'm on point,' Safa says. 'Harry behind me. Ben next, Miri on rear . . . Shit a brick, I am buzzing my tits off . . .' She goes forward through the wall of iridescent light with Harry hot on her heels. Both with pistols drawn and held double-handed, pointing down. Ben blinks once and follows them, still wincing as he touches the light, as though he can't quite believe he'll pass through it.

Miri goes last, hiding her irritation. She starts the stopwatch with a glance at the time on the tablet and passes through, leaving the good doctor staring at the blue light with the crushing knowledge that right now, he is the only human being on earth.

◆ ◆ ◆

'Where the fuck is the handle?' Safa whisper-snaps as Harry bunches up behind her from Ben bunching up behind him from Miri coming through.

It may be a large wardrobe for clothes, but four people now make the space feel very cramped and confined. Especially with Safa pawing at what she thinks is the door while cursing at why it won't open.

Ben blinks round at the tight space now bathed in blue from the portal shimmering behind them. Safa moves back, tutting at Harry in her way, while still moving too fast and too wired from the drugs in her system.

'Move over,' Safa whisper-snaps again, trying to glare at Harry, who tries moving away, which physically shifts Ben into Miri, who pops into the Cretaceous period, nods at the good doctor and returns to the chaos in the closet.

'. . . said I can't bloody find it,' Safa says, her voice growing louder as her pistol clunks against the inside of the closet door.

'And I said they don't put bloody handles on the inside,' Ben whispers back, trying to peer round Harry to Safa. 'There won't be one.'

'Then how do we get out, Mr Smartarse?' Safa asks.

'Push the bloody door,' Ben groans, then yelps as Harry stands on his foot.

'I am pushing the door . . .'

'Sliding door,' Miri says quietly from the back.

'Miri said sliding door,' Ben relays the message.

'Hang on, I think it's a sliding door,' Safa says.

The sound of rollers as light bathes the room to reveal four armed people peering out into a very large, luxurious bedroom. Safa's pistol lifts to aim as she sweeps. In her peripheral vision, she sees Harry doing the same, then two more joining in.

'Put your gun away, Ben.'

'Why?'

'Because I bloody said so. Put it away.'

'Fine,' he says, pushing it back into the holster.

'Is the safety on?' Safa asks.

'Didn't take it off,' he mumbles.

'Moving out,' Safa says, striding into the bedroom to point her pistol at the bed, at the set of drawers and the mirrors, while Harry points his at the door, at the corners and everything else. 'Room clear,' Safa says, nodding too fast as she realises her heart rate is too high. She draws a deep, steadying breath and blinks a few times.

'Nice room.'

'DOWN,' Safa shouts as she, Harry and Miri spin round to aim at the poor doctor falling back with his hands up.

'It's me,' he whimpers.

'What the fuck?' Safa asks. 'What are you doing?'

'Thought you might need a medic,' he says, trying to stand upright and regain his dignity.

'Who said you could come? This is a live job, for fuck's sake,' Safa says.

'You try being the only person on a planet, and see if you like it,' Doctor Watson retorts, blustering and red-faced as Miri rubs the bridge of her nose.

'Jesus,' Safa growls, knowing how bad they look in front of Miri. She tries to focus and switch on, but finds herself blinking rapidly again and twitching her head and shoulders. 'This is a shower of shit . . .'

'Safa and Harry abort,' Miri says. 'Return to HB. Me and Ben will proceed.'

'HB?' Ben asks with a puzzled frown. 'What was that again? Hungry bunker?'

'Home base,' Safa says tightly. 'We're fine. Doc, go back . . .'

'I shall wait here and guard the portal,' he replies quickly.

'Fine. Just don't bloody move anywhere,' Safa says.

'You can rely on me,' Doctor Watson says bravely.

'Said the drug dealer,' Ben mutters as Safa goes back to the bedroom door being glared at by Harry.

'I'll go first,' Safa says, getting in front of Harry. 'I'll look right, you look left,' she tells the big man. 'Ready?'

'Aye, when you've been in a war with tanks,' Harry says loudly.

'What?' Safa asks. 'Never mind. Right . . . ready?'

'You said left,' Harry says.

'I meant right! As in okay . . . We're going . . . now . . .' She opens the door to sweep out with her pistol up and aimed to the right as

Harry surges past to aim left. Ben nods in admiration at how cool that just looked. Like something from a movie. He still doesn't feel scared. This is only Roland's house. The baddies were all in Berlin about an hour and a half ago; there is no way they'll get to here in that time. Wherever here is.

'Where are we?' he asks Miri.

'Roland's house,' she replies, giving him a blank look.

'No, I mean what country?'

'I told you. England. Hampshire.'

'Ah, right, yes, you did say that,' he says amiably as Safa groans that her side is clear.

'What?' Ben asks at the sound of dismay. He walks out of the bedroom to look down a wide corridor. First or second floor, judging by the view from the windows. Doors on both sides. Everything quiet.

'It's bloody huge,' Safa says.

'Yeah,' Ben says. 'Nice house.'

'I mean, it will take ages to clear.'

'Clear?' Ben looks around, then over at the big windows and the view of the gorgeous grounds outside. A summer's day. All pretty and picturesque. Like something from a postcard. Willow trees and manicured lawns. He leans over a little to catch sight of what looks like a pond or a water feature further down in the grounds. 'It's daytime,' he adds.

'And?' she asks.

'Well, it's a big house, but it's still a house. Bedrooms at the top and the living rooms on the ground floor . . . which is where most people tend to be in the daytime, and if the son is an inventor, then he'll probably have an outbuilding or a garage, I would have thought.'

'Oh,' Safa says, staring with drug-induced fascination at the way his lips move and the sparkle back in his eyes. She takes in the scar on his face and how different he looks now after the decline he suffered over the last few months.

'Safa?'

'Huh?' Safa asks, blinking at Ben. 'Yep, downstairs then. Harry, where are the stairs?'

'Er, right there,' Ben says, pointing to the top of the stairs a few metres away.

'Yep, good . . . er . . . Harry? Seen any other stairs?'

'Aye, when you've been in a war with stairs.'

'Shush,' Safa whisper-shouts, blinking at Ben's scar.

'Need to move,' Miri says bluntly.

'We are,' Safa says, giving her a withering teenager's look and even adding a tut before heading towards the stairs.

'Maybe we should just call out?' Ben suggests as they start descending, and feeling left out by everyone else holding a pistol while he is strolling down with his hands in his pockets. 'Harry's got a loud voice.'

'Aye,' Harry says.

'No,' Miri says from the rear. 'Go faster. Stay quiet.'

'*Go faster, stay quiet,*' Safa mimics in a voice that she thinks is under her breath but instead comes out really quite clearly and leaves a very awkward silence hanging in the air.

They reach a landing and establish the portal was on the top floor of a three-storey house. Again, the main wide corridor leads in both directions, with rooms going off. Light and airy, with paintings and pictures hanging from walls. Bespoke tables stand nestled here and there with vases of perfectly arranged flowers on the top. Safa focusses on trying to widen her eyes and stretch her jaw while craning her head over side to side. She blinks constantly; her whole body feels full of energy. Harry is the same, and has to physically stop himself from whistling a jaunty tune.

The descent continues as they move down the last feature staircase, which widens at the base directly opposite the double-sized entrance doors. Miri holds position at the back, watching the others intently, studying everything they do.

Ben stays in the middle, casting an appraising eye over the fixtures and fittings. The signs of affluence are everywhere. Roland is minted. His house is just incredible, and Ben knows the price of property in Hampshire even back in his time was astronomical. As they reach the bottom, so the first sound of voices is heard from the ground floor somewhere at the rear of the house.

Safa pauses at the bottom, holding still with her head cocked. Harry taps her shoulder, indicating a hallway running off at the back of the huge, atrium-like lobby.

'Faster,' Miri mutters from behind them.

Safa speeds up, striding into the inner hallway. Harry close behind. Both with pistols gripped and held down. Ben rushes after them.

Safa stops with a hand held up in a closed fist. She waves it once, then turns it into a flat palm and points towards an open set of doors ahead on the right. Voices within. Male and female. The clink of cutlery on a plate. A chair scraping on a wooden floor. Safa peers back to nod at Harry and Ben, and catches the wave from Miri urging her on.

Hundreds of hours of drill and training kick in as Safa surges through the door into the room. The pistol lifts automatically as her eyes take in the three people at the table.

'POLICE OFFICERS,' she shouts, 'STAY STILL, STAY STILL . . . DO NOT MOVE . . .'

Roland and the two women freeze with forks raised to mouths, eyes wide with fright.

Harry strides past her to the French windows at the back of the dining room giving a view of the perfectly striped lawn beyond.

'What the . . .' Roland mutters, food falling from his fork. Ben takes in the room. The gorgeous hardwood dining table. The fine china plates. The gleaming silverware. The expensive ornaments and artwork dotted about the room. The sheer luxury in which Roland lives while they were cooped up in a sterile bunker and ate fruit and eggs listening to him moan about the cost of everything and how hard it was to get money.

Two women at the table sitting either side of Roland. Both dark-haired. One older. One younger. Ben takes in the older woman's dyed hair and smooth skin that speaks of cosmetic alteration. The year here is 2061. Roland died in 2046. Ben looks again to the younger woman wearing glasses. Black hair and blue eyes, pale skin. She must be Roland's daughter. The older one must be his wife.

'BEN!' Safa snaps at what her drug-addled mind takes to be him gawping. 'Get them moving . . .'

Safa's voice brings sense back to Roland, who drops his fork. It lands with a clatter on the fine china plate as he rises from his hardwood, antique dining chair.

'What the hell is going on?' he demands. 'Miri? What the . . . Safa, put that damned gun down . . . Why are you here?'

Susan rises quickly to move closer to her daughter. Protective, while clearly very frightened. 'Roland? What's going on? Why are they here? You said they wouldn't come here . . .'

'Hi,' Ben says quickly, seeing the worry on Susan's face. 'Sorry for the intrusion. I'm Ben. You must be . . .'

'What the fuck?' Safa growls. 'Stop chatting . . . Move!'

'Extraction now,' Miri says from the doorway.

'Extraction?' Roland asks, looking from Miri to Ben. 'What?'

'Attack on the warehouse . . .' Miri says.

'Roland, please ask them to put their guns away . . .' Susan says, her voice quavering.

'I can explain,' Roland says, glancing at his wife. 'Miri, what . . . Why are you here? I gave no authority for you to . . .'

'NOW,' Safa shouts. 'Up . . . Get moving . . .'

'You must be Safa?' the younger woman says, staring in awe.

'You must be deaf. MOVE NOW,' Safa retorts. 'Ben, get them fucking moving . . .'

'BOSCH INCOMING . . .' Harry's eyes take in the tree line bordering the perfectly striped lawn that disgorges heavily armed, black-clad figures. His huge voice booms, making Roland yelp.

A wall of noise thunders towards them. Harry steps back, suddenly unsure at a sound he thinks he knows. Like propellers on an aircraft, but different. Everyone else instantly connects the sound to helicopter rotor blades creating air displacement as a chopper goes overhead to drop down over the perfect lawn. It holds for a second. The pilot inside easily visible. The chopper lifts a bare second later. Ropes thrown out from the sides unfold as they drop, with black-clad figures already positioned on the landing skids ready to rappel.

More rotor blades thunder in. Heavier, deeper, more solid and serious. Safa goes with Miri to look out of the windows. Both of them catch sight of the gunships coming in low and the figures now sprinting across the lawn. Black-clad. Balaclavas. Submachine guns. Professionals. Further back, they spot the motion of more forms and catch sight of camouflage-wearing soldiers close to the tree line.

'Son,' Miri says, noting the time on her wristwatch. 'Where?'

Roland balks, unable to comprehend the noises outside and the questions being thrown at him.

'Bertie's in the cellar,' Ria says, rising from the table to look out on to the grounds.

'Sir! Sir!' A man runs into the room from a door on the side leading to the kitchen. A smart black suit, white shirt and white gloves.

'Is that a fucking butler?' Ben asks. 'Have you got a butler?'

'Men coming, sir,' the man blurts. 'From the front, sir. They have guns, sir.'

'An actual butler,' Ben mutters. 'You cheeky sod . . .'

'I SAY, MIRI?' Doctor Watson shouts down the stairs. 'GOT SOME CHAPS RUNNING ACROSS THE GRASS. ALL DRESSED IN BLACK AND CARRYING GUNS . . .'

Seven

The five and Tango Two check weapons as the heli flies low over the lawn. Alpha readies himself on one side. Bravo on the other. Charlie, Delta, Echo and Tango Two wait between them.

A tap on the arm. Delta motions for Tango Two to lean in. She bends forward so his mouth is next to her ear.

'Mother's watching us,' he shouts over the noise of the rotors above them, his hand lingering on her arm. She looks at him as he points skyward, and nods. The abstract notion settles for a bare second that something in low orbit in space is now watching them in perfect clarity and detail, and that signal is being fed to Mother right now.

She swallows and draws a deep breath. She took the shittiest deployments on offer. She did the worst, the very worst. The nasty, dirty and bitter jobs that no one else would touch. She killed, tricked, lied and fought her way through all of them in service to her country and for a career she was dedicated to. The pressure made her worried she was already getting too old and that she should have been a One years ago. It felt like nothing she was doing was making any difference, but now she is being watched by Mother, who also knows her name. This is it. This is the time to impress.

She thinks about the information Alpha just gave her. A time machine is in existence and in use. That makes this mission the most important there ever has been and possibly ever will be. She glances round to the five, feeling the thrill inside at being in such exalted company and catching Delta as he winks before turning towards the door. These men are almost godlike in the way the others view them. They have commanded armies and run operations of a scale that would make most generals balk. There is nothing bigger than this right now, and she is at the front as it happens.

'*Target premises ahead.*' The voice of the pilot comes calmly through their earpieces.

'*Roger that,*' Alpha replies. He waits for the heli to get closer and spots the units moving through the woodland bordering the house. A tap on his shoulder. Charlie waving for him to look up and ahead at the two attack helicopter gunships coming in from the opposite direction. Alpha nods.

The heli turns and drops with such speed the six feel their stomachs flip, heave and turn over as it manoeuvres to face back towards the house. An instant view gained of the open French doors and signs of movement within.

'*Armed people inside that room,*' the pilot relays before moving the heli forward towards the designated balcony.

'*MOVE FAST NOW,*' Alpha orders into his radio. '*Secure the targets . . . Pilot, get us in position.*'

'*In five,*' the pilot says calmly, adjusting the stick in his hands to ease the thrust as he gains the space over the balcony. '*Deploy ropes.*'

'*Rope out,*' Alpha says.

'*Rope out,*' Bravo says.

Both of them release their coils that fall to hang down from the sides of the craft.

'*In three . . . two . . . one . . . Deploy deploy deploy . . .*'

Alpha grips, pulls out and drops at speed with the thick gloves gripping the rope to control his descent. Bravo matches his rate on the other side, and as soon as the gap is created, Charlie and Delta come sliding down. As Alpha and Bravo land, Echo and Tango Two rappel down. The whole thing takes but seconds. The pilot watches closely and yanks the stick the second the last pair land to give lift as the heli roars and sails up and away.

Echo rushes in, a small shaped charge is taken from a pocket and stuck to the lock on the double doors. 'Clear,' he says.

'Clear,' Alpha says as the others duck and turn away.

The explosion is only small but enough to destroy the lock and enable Bravo's right foot to kick the doors in. Weapons up. Lasers activated that hold steady as they pour through Roland's bedroom towards the door as the first shots are fired.

Miri hears the heli drop and knows the fast ropes are being deployed. She sees the attackers coming across the lawn and knows the same numbers will be coming at the sides and front of the house. She glances up at the military gunships looming larger by the second, and from all these things she gains the measure of their opponent that must be the British government deploying with all its might. An image of a world map flashes in her mind that narrows down to the small county of Hampshire, which contains the British naval base of Portsmouth and the squadrons of Royal Marines and Special Forces units. Instant concern that this opponent is too big to take on. Only the US and Russia can surpass the Brits when they set their minds to something – and right now, that something is a man in the cellar of this house, and that man cannot, under any circumstances, be given over to any government. In the same whirling stream of conscious thought, she considers that her own side consists of a drugged-up Commando from the Second World War, an equally drugged-up police officer and an insurance investigator. Bad odds. Damn bad odds.

'Your son,' she says quickly. 'Priority . . . Take us to him now.'

'Who are they?' Roland asks, backing away from the windows.

'Now!' Miri says, aiming her pistol at Ria's head.

The dull explosion reverberates through the house as Echo blows the doors on the middle floor. Glass smashing from somewhere else. Voices shouting. Helicopters thudding. The pressure grows.

'No, please!' Susan screams, rushing in front of Ria with tears streaming down her cheeks.

'I'll show you,' Ria says.

'Now . . . go . . . go . . .' Miri says, her voice clear but hard.

They pile into the hallway and down towards the atrium lobby, hearing boots thudding on the floors above them and doors being kicked open. Ria leads them on from the lobby into a huge drawing room resplendent in ivory-coloured sofas and armchairs. Thick rugs on the floor and a huge crystal chandelier hanging from the centre of the ceiling. Safa and Harry run with the group, both with pistols still out. Miri winces from the pains in her hips and back.

'Call him . . .' Ben says. 'Tell him to get to us.'

'No phone,' Ria says. 'Bertie won't use one.'

'He'll hear the heli and come out,' Safa says, rushing to gain the front position.

'Cellar is soundproofed,' Ria replies.

'Hold,' Safa says as they reach the next door.

'No time. Go,' Miri says.

'This way.' Ria runs on through a games room, past a billiards table as Ben tuts and casts a withering look at Roland. She reaches a discreet door at the back and heaves it in, pushing the handle down as she goes. The difference is immediate and stark. Old peeling paint on the corridor walls. Worn floorboards underfoot. The old servants' access routes and walkways. She runs fast, staying ahead of Safa and the rest, who crash through the door and down the corridor. Explosions are heard. Flash-bangs and stun grenades being thrown into rooms before the attackers charge in.

That tells Safa and Miri the house is breached. Harry just ploughs on, still feeling the thrum of the drugs running through his body.

'Down there,' Ria pants, coming to a wooden door that she goes to open.

'WAIT.' Safa pushes forward to gain the door. 'Move back.' She shoves Ria away, creating room to open the door and surge in. 'BERTIE?' Safa yells, rushing down an old set of wooden stairs. Music sails up at them. Beethoven's Fifth Symphony in a wall of noise pumped from speakers that render her words unheard.

She barrels down, with Ben behind her. Miri grabs Roland and Susan, forcing them to wait, then checks behind to see Harry staring back the way they came.

Safa turns sharply at the bottom of the stairs into a wonderland of light, of machines, of stripped-down electrical devices. Of posters of heavy metal bands, pop groups, Japanese anime illustrations and reproduction prints of Monet and Constable. Colours everywhere. Vibrant primary shades daubed on the walls. A drawing of the time machine etched on a huge piece of paper pinned to the wall. Schematics, blueprints, diagrams, hand-drawn sketches and piles of books stacked everywhere. Tools litter the sides. Old hand tools with worn wooden handles next to tiny, surgical-style scalpels and grips.

She spots the man sitting at a desk swaying side to side as he drums his fingers over the wooden surface in front of him in mimicry of the music. She shouts out, but the music blares too loud. She runs forward, veering round an old shop store mannequin fitted with robotic arms and legs and camera lenses for eyes.

Bertie plays the music, and for a few wonderful seconds his mind is full only of the chords. A hand on his shoulder that grips hard and twists him round. He turns smiling up into the face of a person he recognises as Safa Patel screaming something at him. Bertie lifts a hand in greeting, then smiles wider when he spots Ben Ryder behind her.

'Hi, Bertie,' he shouts, his words as unheard as Safa's.

She says something and wrenches him off his feet as Ben moves in to grab his arm and start dragging him towards the stairs. The same height as his dad but leaner. The same dark hair, but whereas Roland's is neat, Bertie's is unkempt, shaggy and sticking up in clumps.

With Beethoven filling his ears, Bertie is dragged across his workshop to the wooden stairs. He looks up as he goes, seeing his sister at the top beckoning him to run faster. Another woman too. Older, with greying hair. Ben runs behind him, pushing him to go faster. Safa coming up last. Bertie reaches the top and finds a huge hairy gnarled hand gripping his wrist as he flies off his feet to look up into the bearded face of Mad Harry Madden.

'Hi, Harry,' Bertie says, grinning widely while being awe-struck at the sight of him. 'You're, like, totally huge . . .'

'Go now,' Miri shouts.

'Roland,' Safa says, grabbing his arm to spin him round, 'is there another way up to the top floor?'

'What?' Roland gibbers in confusion and fear.

'Servants' stairs,' Ria blurts.

'She's so pretty,' Bertie says, staring at Safa. 'You were right, Dad . . .'

'Please, will someone tell me what's going on?' Susan asks, clutching to pull Ria and Bertie closer.

'PEOPLE IN THE HOUSE . . . LIE DOWN WITH YOUR ARMS OUT . . . PEOPLE IN THE HOUSE . . . LIE DOWN WITH YOUR ARMS OUT . . .'

The voice is enormous. Amplified through a loudspeaker fitted to the helicopter. It hovers metres from the front of the house. The pilot's words boom clear and deep.

'We should do as they say,' Roland says quickly.

'Go,' Miri says to Ria. 'Back stairs . . .'

'We have to get into the drawing room,' Ria says, gripping Bertie's hand.

'Which one is that?' Ben asks.

'We came through it,' Ria says.

'The ivory room?'

Ria nods quickly. 'There's a door next to the fireplace . . . Goes to the middle floor, then out on the landing and up the next flight . . .'

Alpha holds his arm up. Fist clenched. *Hold*. His submachine gun gripped in his right hand as he listens to the radio traffic.

'*White side breached . . . We're in through the main doors in the lobby.*'

'*Black side breached . . . We came in through the dining room. We saw them running out the room.*'

'*Green breached. Negative contact. We came through a games room and drawing room . . . We can see the other agents in the lobby.*'

'*Red side breached . . . We can hear you in the lobby . . .*'

'*This is Alpha. Commence room clearance to search ground floor. Alpha to pilot. See anything?*'

'*Pilot to Alpha. Negative.*'

Tango Two conjures an image of the house in her mind and the four groups of attackers all sweeping through to meet in the lobby. She leans over the railing to look down at the operatives kneeling next to the now open front door. The red lasers glowing bright and straight from the weapons held ready as the operatives get ready for a game of hide-and-seek.

'Keep your mask up,' Bravo whispers at Tango Two. 'If we find them, you will communicate. We are here to help them. We are here to assist. We do not want to hurt them. Understood?'

'Got it,' Tango Two says with the bitter thought that she is only here because she is female.

They have to go fast. There is no option. Speed and daring is all they have now.

'PEOPLE IN THE HOUSE . . . LIE DOWN . . .'

The amplified voice continues as Ria leads them back through the servants' corridor to the door into the billiards room. She stops when she reaches it. Already breathing hard from the running and the fear.

Safa goes to the front again. Not speaking this time, but gripping Ria's arms to pull her away. She listens closely, leaning in towards the closed door. Her pupils huge. Her whole body still buzzing. Silence on the other side. Maybe they haven't got this far yet. Doesn't matter anyway. In her head, she plots the route ahead. Out of this door, across the billiards room, into the drawing room and through the next door to the flight of stairs. Not a big distance to go. They can make that at least.

She turns to look at the others. Harry at the back and everyone else between them. She locks eyes on Miri, who nods the order to go.

Safa draws a deep breath, grabs the handle and bursts into an empty room. Pistol up and aimed. She strides clear of the door as the others come out behind her. Scrape of shoes. Whimpers of fright from Roland and his wife. Ria telling Bertie to shush.

Safa aims for the exit door that leads into the drawing room, approaching it from an angle. A quick glance back. Everyone is out of the corridor. She pushes on to charge through the door and spots the eight kneeling figures looking into the atrium lobby. More attackers beyond them. Glowing red laser sights in the air.

Miri spots them next and notices their identical appearance to the people in Berlin. Ben's eyes widen. His hand falling towards the pistol on his hip. Harry comes last, taller than the others and seeing over them to the soldiers in the room ahead. Roland screams out. Susan gasps. Ria flinches from the noise. The trailing operative turns quickly to check his route behind. He's only a Three. Fresh out of basic training and his heart is already going like the clappers; now it thunders and booms as he spots Safa in the lead lifting her pistol to aim.

71

'CONTACT . . .' the young Three screams. Operatives start spinning round, aiming their guns.

Safa pauses as a voice inside remembers the police rules of engagement. She sees a threat, but not an immediate risk to life. Miri senses Safa's lack of killer instinct and thinks this mission will end right here. She checks her watch, muttering the minutes to herself.

Red lasers flash through the air. Men and women screaming the word *contact* out to repeat and relay. The heli outside and the amplified voice thundering 'PEOPLE IN THE HOUSE . . . LIE DOWN . . .'

Wide stance. Double-grip on the pistol. Face a mask of focus and aim. Safa overcomes the internal reasoning and fires once. She twitches the aim. Fires. Twitches the aim and fires a third. All three rounds gain kills. All three find their mark as three corpses fall dead on the floor with brains blown out.

Miri blinks, stunned, not expecting the perfect placement of shot from Safa, who aims at the door and fires steady rounds to send the rest of the attackers scattering.

'HARRY, WITH ME . . . BEN, GET THEM THROUGH . . .'

Harry is already surging forward, using his bulk to push through into the drawing room. Shots come back, designed to suppress. The house fills with gunfire and the ping of rounds ricocheting off walls.

Safa holds for Harry to join her, then goes forward. The pair side by side firing single shots one after the other through the doorway. All concerns about drugs, fast heart rates, trembling limbs now forgotten. They stride to the door, firing again and again. Ben glances at them as he drags Bertie across the room towards the door being wrenched open by Ria.

'Magazine,' Safa says calmly. The one in her pistol drops away as the fresh one comes up in her spare hand to be rammed in. She looks back to see Ben staring at her. 'Go,' she says, just as calmly.

'Magazine,' Harry says, remembering the lesson from Safa that people now say magazine when they run out of bullets. What's wrong with *I'm out* is beyond him, but he does it anyway.

'FLASH-BANG,' Safa yells, seeing the object fly through the door. She drops and turns, squeezing her eyes shut. Harry copies her a fraction of a second later. The grenade detonates as Ben turns away. A blinding explosion of light and a huge booming noise that makes his bones shake. Miri is through the door, grimacing as she grips Bertie and drags him up the stairs.

'IN IN IN . . . ALPHA WANTS THEM ALIVE . . . GET IN NOW . . .' a voice from the hallway bellows, urging the agents to go forward.

'Ben, go!' Safa screams, her head swimming from the sensation of the flash-bang.

Ben hesitates at the door. He closed his eyes before the flash-bang detonated, but the retina burn still got through his eyelids. Colours and stars flash in his vision. His hearing muffled. His head spinning. He looks up to see Miri dragging Bertie, then back to see attackers steaming into the room towards Harry and Safa, both still rising from the floor.

His hand draws the pistol before his mind can assess what he is doing. That same hand lifts, flicks the safety off and fires the pistol at the doorway as he strides across the room.

Time slows like it has done before. Everything in perfect clarity. No panic now. No concerns. He tried to fight back at Holborn, but he didn't know how to fire a gun then. He didn't know to compensate for the recoil or the sensations and noise. Now he knows.

He empties the magazine into them. Twitching the aim to send rounds through the centre of mass. Bodies drop, screaming. Submachine guns return fire. Ben dives to the side as Safa and Harry both do the same. All of them taking to the floor to roll and snatch what shots they can in the close-quarters firefight.

The attackers fall back, scrambling from the room as the pistol shots slam into the frame and door. More bodies lie dead. Blood smeared and splashed across the ivory sofas, and armchairs now puckered with bullet holes. The thick rugs ruined. The floor scuffed and dented. A surreal second of awareness as the thought of insurance flits through Ben's mind and the idea of someone from his old firm coming to assess the damage. *So exactly how did the massive gunfight happen again?*

'Back . . . back . . .' Safa scrabbles up and runs, lurching to grip Ben's arm, heaving him up as Harry rises to fire a few more rounds through the doorway.

Safa pushes Ben towards the door, then drops to kneel and cover Harry falling back. The three of them get through and start up the wooden stairs. Ears ringing. Chests heaving. They change magazines as they go, with Safa once again leading them to the top to see Miri looking at the watch on her wrist.

'We need to go,' Miri says. Her tone flat. Her eyes hard. 'Door ahead.' Miri points up a short distance to a plain wooden door. 'Girl says we go out, turn hard right and through the next door for the last flight of stairs. You take point.'

'Move,' Safa says, forcing the others back against the walls to let her squeeze past.

'We should just surrender now,' Roland begs. 'Ben, tell them . . . see sense . . .'

'They'll kill Bertie,' Ria says, staring at her father, with disgust and shock etched on her face.

'They might not . . .' Roland says weakly. 'Why don't one of you run back and get Malcolm or Konrad to change the coordinates to here?' he suggests with a flash of brilliance only a true coward could summon at such a time.

'Dead,' Miri says bluntly.

'What?' Susan gasps. 'You brought Malc and Kon back?'

'You did what?' Ria asks, the disgust growing by the second.

'I needed their help,' Roland sputters.

'You said you did it on your own,' Ria says. 'You said it was just you doing everything . . . We could have seen them.'

'I'll go and talk to them,' Susan says, trying to draw composure, despite the abject fear gripping her insides. She holds Ria and Bertie close. Nodding to herself. 'I'll go down, okay? I'll . . . Let me talk to them . . .'

'Mum, no,' Ria says, the tears falling fast down her cheeks. 'They want to take Bertie.'

'Is that true?' Susan asks, looking round to everyone apart from her husband, who cowers back in his own state of panic.

'It is,' Ben says. 'They'll probably kill him if they can't take him.'

'I see,' Susan says softly. 'Then I can buy you time to get him away,' she adds, summoning pride and dignity back into her voice. 'I will go down and . . .'

Miri considers the option, but knows exactly what will happen. They'll grab the mother and inflict instant torture to draw Bertie out. What son could ever stand by and listen to his mother screaming in pain? Sacrificing one to save many is a valid option, but right now it will not work. This is the level of the game. The other side have gunships. Enough said.

'No, we go now . . . We run for the top floor . . . Nobody stops . . . Understood? Bertie must get through . . .' Miri says.

◆ ◆ ◆

'*Agent down . . .*'

'*Fall back, fall back . . .*'

'*DO NOT FALL BACK . . . Bravo, get down and lead them through . . .*' Alpha orders, seeing the chaos in the lobby.

'Be happy to oblige,' Bravo mutters. 'Anyone with a flash-bang can throw it in that room now,' he says, pointing at the door of the drawing room as he runs down the stairs.

Bodies lie dead and injured. Blood everywhere. Bullet casings shining on the floor. The pressure grows. The need to secure the target, while very aware of the satellite feed overhead and Mother listening into their comms. How can over thirty operatives fail to secure a handful?

'They're scared to return fire.' Charlie voices his own thoughts.

Alpha doesn't reply. The quandary is clear. Shooting back means a dead target, but then he also heard a woman shouting the name Harry. That must be Safa. If Safa and Harry are in this house with Roland and the inventor, then it means the device is active. The portal is open right now. He cannot let them get through it.

'*THIS IS ALPHA . . . SHOOT TO KILL . . . MAXIMUM AGGRESSION . . . MOTHER, IF YOU CAN HEAR ME, DEPLOY THE SOLDIERS TO THE GROUND FLOOR . . .*'

'*About bloody time,*' Mother's icy voice quips. '*Soldiers to you, Alpha.*'

Flash-bangs sail through the door. Tens of them flying together on orders from Bravo. The figures drop, turn and cover their heads as the grenades detonate in a deafening cacophony of explosions that seemingly boom together in one sustained, thunderous clap. The house shakes from the pressure waves sent out. The windows in the drawing room blow out. The air charges, becoming thick and hot with the stench of chemicals and black smoke billowing out into the lobby.

'IN IN IN,' Bravo roars, his strong, cultured, private-school tones so loud and deep. He goes first, his submachine gun raised and ready as his laser sight cuts through the smoke. Flames lick at the sofas and armchairs. The once glorious chandelier now smashed to bits on the floor. The walls blackened and the door Ria led them through hanging open. Bravo fires at it. Emptying his magazine as he marches forward. More guns join in as the Ones and Twos left in the lobby rush after him. The rounds slam into the wall and door. The wooden frame shreds apart, with splinters flying off. Voices from outside. Boots running that crunch over the gravel laid to the front of the house as the soldiers charge at the front door and burst through to a scene of carnage.

Bravo drops to a knee, ignoring the smouldering bodies scattered about the floor. A change of magazine and he rises to go forward, but stays low to hook his arm through the door, firing the submachine gun one-handed. The second he fires, the pistol rounds slam into the wall behind his hand. He drops lower, squeezing the trigger before scooting back to change again. As he scrabbles away, he glances up along the wall, tracking the rise of the stairs to where he thinks they level out.

'*STAIRWELL TOWARDS YOU . . .*' Bravo roars into the radio, aiming to fire into the top of the wall. The rest follow suit. Submachine guns spraying fire to shred the wall and ceiling apart, with bricks, plaster and wood flying everywhere. 'FIRE INTO THAT WALL,' Bravo orders the first soldiers running in. They drop to their knees with assault rifles braced into shoulders to strafe along where the wall meets the ceiling.

Harry runs with his arm covering his face. Noise everywhere. Rounds slamming just inches away. The submachine-gun rounds ricochet and lose all momentum from hitting hard bricks. The bigger rounds in the assault rifle get through. Embedding in the walls and gouging splinters through the floorboards. Debris grazes his shoulder and arms. Splinters cut across his face. He drops low, pinned in place from the barrage of fire.

Miri checks her stopwatch. 'Five minutes, six seconds, five minutes, six seconds,' she mutters to remember. Lodging the numbers in her head.

'*WE'VE GOT THEM PINNED,*' Bravo shouts into his radio. The ruined carpet now thick with shell casings.

Miri blinks and looks down past the heads to Harry lying flat. Her breath held. Waiting. Listening.

'GO NOW, GO NOW,' Harry roars. The big man knows they are pinned. He rolls on his back to change the magazine in his pistol. He'll charge down and out. He'll give them something to aim at. The boy has to get away.

'HOLD' Miri shouts, raising a hand and seeing the look of intent on Harry's face.

Bravo grins. He's got them held in place. They can't come down. They'll either die there or give up. He turns towards the door with his hand lifting to the radio mic to transmit the situation and suggest they look for the exit point from that corridor. As he does so, he hears the instantly recognisable thud of a heavy machine gun. The years of experience make him drop instantly. Sudden sustained firing coming into the room. Rounds whizzing over him, slamming into walls, furniture and people. The kill rate is staggering. Blood flies everywhere. Soldiers and operatives screaming out. Bravo snakes towards the hallway, screaming into his radio that someone outside is firing in.

In the corridor, Miri holds her hand out, indicating for everyone to hold. All eyes on her. The sound of the heavy machine gun comes clear over everything else. Her hand drops. 'Now,' she says, looking at Safa.

Echo staggers from the door ramming into his back. The five agents turn as one to see a face they all know. A face made famous from a time she stood on duty outside Downing Street when bored photographers became captivated by her beauty and snapped away to plaster her image in every newspaper and website, and those same pictures that were released again when that same woman died saving the Prime Minister. They all recognise Safa Patel, but they all know Safa Patel has been dead for over forty years. That split-second surprise that gives Safa the edge to press the attack with a mask of pure aggression as she rushes into their midst with her hand moving round to aim and fire the pistol.

A blur of motion as Delta's hand shoots out to grip the barrel of the gun in Safa's hands, preventing it rising. Safa counters, twisting as she slams her hip into Delta, ridding his grip.

Alpha comes next. His submachine gun let go so he can dart in from the side to grab her wrists. Safa pulls back enough to slip his grip. He comes with her, his hands cycling to gain purchase. She turns quickly, plucking the trigger as Alpha gets one hand under the pistol to throw the aim high and blow chunks out of the ceiling.

A fist thrown by Echo comes from Safa's side. She lets go of the pistol and rotates to block and slam the blade of her right hand into his throat. He saw it coming and moved away an inch to deflect the power, but still reels back, gagging from the impact.

Another hand coming from the other side as Charlie joins the fray. Safa blocks, ducks, grips his arm and tries for the break at the elbow joint. Charlie counters the move and rotates his body to jerk his arm free. A foot comes at Safa's knee joint. She lifts her leg to absorb the blow on her boot while slamming a fist into a black-clad face. Tango Two comes in from behind, still stunned that the woman fighting them is Safa Patel. Safa detects the motion and bends forward to back-kick as she throws a punch into the groin of Delta coming at her. Tango Two veers at the last second and tries to grab Safa's ankle. Safa spin kicks over to rotate her body to face Tango Two and goes forward with hard punches raining out that batter Tango Two away.

'*UP HERE . . .*' Delta roars from the floor, his hands clutching his genitals from the hard punch given by Safa. Operatives and soldiers in the lobby, too afraid to run into the drawing room, snap heads up to the balcony above them and start running for the stairs.

Safa ducks, spins and blocks the fists and feet coming at her, and for a couple of seconds she holds them at bay. Neither winning nor losing. Neither gaining nor giving ground. One against five. The speed she generates is stunning. The acute, intrinsic grasp of situational close-quarters combat is almost beautiful.

Harry steams out and into the fight. The blink of an eye. He takes in the situation and knows he cannot fire for fear of hitting Safa. He slides the pistol into the holster and kidney punches Charlie, who sags from the power of the blow.

Alpha turns, ducks, weaves and comes in fast to tangle Harry's feet with a vicious leg sweep. Harry takes the impact on his shins without a flicker of reaction and goes fast to meet the body of Alpha. Huge hands grip the leader of the attackers and sends him smashing into the railing of the landing. Harry powers forward, intent on kicking the man over. Delta comes in with a nasty blow to Harry's right ear that snaps his head over, buying time for Alpha to recover.

Ben runs into the fray, slams Delta down to the ground and tries to stamp on his head. Delta rolls. Tango Two punches the back of Ben's head and again feels that surprise at seeing the face of Ben Ryder as he staggers away.

Alpha pushes off from the bannister to surge into Harry, aiming low with a rugby tackle that drives Harry back into Roland and Susan trying to squeeze past them, with Miri and Ria dragging Bertie towards the next door.

Harry and Alpha go down in a heap, with Alpha on top slamming hard fists into Harry's head. Alpha can fight. He is Alpha. He is the best at this. He will not lose. He punches hammer fists into Harry's eyes, nose and mouth.

Delta sees Safa facing off with Tango Two, and rushes her from behind. Lifting her off her feet and down the landing as Tango Two darts out of the way. Operatives charge up the main stairs. Ben tries to block a punch from Echo, but gets battered back from the blows coming too hard and too fast. He spent six months being thrown about by Harry and Safa, but his mind was gone. He'd do well against normal people, but these are not normal people. They are highly trained and highly experienced at this very thing. Ben runs backwards from the barrage of blows slamming into his skull. He should get angry, scared even, but his mind runs clear without a trace of panic as he stops going back and purposefully runs forward into the fists to take Echo down.

Harry takes the punches. The fists slamming again and again. Alpha risks a look round. Echo is on Ben. Safa has been taken down by Delta, with Tango Two close by. More agents are running up the stairs. Bravo is coming with more up the hidden stairwell. He spots the targets trying to get through a door, and knows this day is won. Charlie is running at them, and there is no way they'll get through him. One glance tells him none of the people with the targets have fighting ability.

A second for him to look round. A second for the sense of victory to lodge in his mind. A second for Harry to change and become the thing that gave birth to the legend of Mad Harry Madden. A switch in his head that prompts a whole new state of mind. As Alpha looks down, he sees someone else staring up at him. Their eyes lock. Alpha sends the punch down. A hard one delivered with every ounce of strength that is summoned by the sudden knot of fear in his gut caused by the utterly crazed eyes staring back at him.

That punch is caught in a huge hand that grips and twists. Instant pain in Alpha's arm as it rotates the wrong way. A hand on Alpha's throat. Mad Harry Madden rises up, lifting the lead agent with the strength of one arm alone. Alpha's feet leave the floor. His right hand still gripped in Harry's fist. His left hand scrabbling uselessly at the fingers round his neck that squeeze to cut the air and blood off. Bravo comes through the door. Seeing the mass brawl underway. Harry looks at Bravo. Bravo looks at Harry. Alpha looks at Harry, then at Bravo. Harry throws Alpha at Bravo.

Susan sees the threat with that protective maternal instinct driving her every move. She sees the black-clad figure coming hard at them and runs to stop him. Charlie slams into her, driving her back into Roland, then sets to work battering the group senseless. Bertie tries to fight in defence of his parents, but is back-handed away. Susan and Ria keep lunging at Charlie, desperate to protect Bertie. Roland cowers, screaming in horror.

Miri snatches a glance at her watch: *six minutes two*. She lurches to grab Bertie, heaving him up and into the wall as she covers him with her own body. Ria is thrown at them by Charlie. She crumples into a heap as the agent stalks forward to finish them off. Charlie goes in for the kill on Miri. His hands lifting as his mind forms the intent to snap her neck and then deal with the others. Miri looks up at him, and the last thing Charlie sees before the high-velocity round goes through his skull is the absolute lack of compassion in her eyes.

Delta flinches at the round whizzing past his head and sees Charlie shot dead. Another round comes in, millimetres away and smashing a huge chunk of wall away behind him. He blinks, goes to duck and finds Safa's hard boot ramming into his groin for the stupidity of losing focus.

As Delta drops, Harry roars past to slam into the first few coming from the stairs. Huge hits are given by his big fists bunched and ready. Men sail over the balcony, to land with sickening crunches of bones breaking. Harry attacks anyone foolish enough to come near him. Booting operatives and soldiers back into those coming up the stairs, who cannot fire for fear of striking the agents behind Harry.

One agent ducks, feints and rolls to come up behind Harry with a knife pulled from a belt. He surges in, the blade lifted and ready to sink in. The shot comes from outside, taking him off his feet and into the wall. The huge boom clear above the heli blades thundering overhead. Another shot comes. Another operative is taken off his feet. Harry rages. Battering everyone around him as soldiers and operatives are snatched away by the gunshots booming outside.

'WHO IS THAT?' Safa bellows, rolling away before jumping to her feet to run and join Harry.

'*TANGO TWO, WHERE ARE YOU?*' Mother's voice clear on the radio, demanding her location.

'*Landing, middle floor.*' Alpha snatches a reply amidst the carnage.

Tango Two blinks in the confusion at hearing her name. No time to think why. No time to think of anything. She looks back to see Bravo and Alpha trying to rise, and Ben rolling away from Echo before surging up to his feet and kicking the agent in the ribs so hard it sends Echo scooting across the floor. She sees Miri grabbing Bertie back to his feet and wrenching the door open. She sees Harry and now Safa dominating the group still trying to breach the stairs. She sees Ben launch himself into Alpha and Bravo as they try and rise. His skill way below that of everyone else, but viciously violent nonetheless.

Wild and chaotic. Frantic and frenzied. Bertie is the important one. She runs for the door, reaching it at the same time as Susan, who once again tries to gain time for Bertie to get away. Tango Two slams her bodily into the wall, reaches down, grabs an ankle and pulls up as she runs on.

'BEN . . . DOOR . . . GO GO GO . . .' Safa yells.

Ben bursts away from Alpha and Bravo. A hand shoots out, grabbing his boot. He goes down hard, but scrabbles to keep going as Alpha and Bravo lunge after him. Harry spins, seeing Ben held, and starts running towards him.

'BERTIE, NOT ME . . .' Ben screams out.

'*WHERE IS TANGO TWO?*' Mother demands again. None of them can reply. None can free the seconds to press the radio button and speak.

Harry falters, turning for the door as Delta takes him from the side through the doorway of the second flight of stairs. Safa screams out and runs to go after them. Roland pushes in, clambering over Harry and Delta fighting on the floor, his mind lost to panic and thinking only of escape. Ria grabs at Delta and heaves back with enough force to allow Harry to rise and surge up the stairs. Delta goes after him, heedless of the screaming woman grabbing him from behind.

Ben pulls his leg free and runs for it, gaining the doorway a second before everyone else. Instant compression as they all surge in and up. Echo screams at operatives to follow him as he runs for the main stairwell.

Eight

Miri gains the top of the stairs with Bertie. The pains in her hips and back are immense. Her vision swims. She cannot take this kind of movement now. Her body is too battered and broken from the things she has done. She grits her teeth and ploughs on, with the sole focus of getting him through the portal to safety. She fires her gun as she runs, sending rounds back, heedless of who they hit. Tango Two drops flat as the bullets go whizzing overhead. Harry and Delta still scrapping in the confined space. Safa and Ria behind them. Ben behind them. Everyone else coming up the stairs.

Miri's gun clicks empty. Tango Two rises to sprint hard. Powering down the corridor as she watches Miri run while changing magazine. Everything frantic. Everything a blur of instinct and countermove to the things everyone else does.

Delta heaves Roland aside. That slight motion buys time for Harry to grab at Delta's hair and launch him backwards and down to the floor. Harry drops hard and sends a fist into Delta's face, knocking him clean out.

Miri bursts on to the top landing. Her right hand holding the gun up. Her left hand gripping Bertie who runs on, shocked to the core and rendered mute.

'HERE,' Doctor Watson shouts. She rushes towards him as Echo throws the flash-bang up the stairs and sprints up with his eyes squeezed closed and his hands clamped over his ears.

The detonation is sickeningly loud. Bertie takes it open-eyed, and screams out at the pain. Miri staggers into the wall. Her legs suddenly weak and rubbery. Her head swimming.

Hands grip her arm. She tries to throw them off, but hears the tones of the doctor shouting at her to run. She keeps her grip on Bertie. Dragging him towards the room as the doctor looks back to the stairs now alive with soldiers and black-clad operatives.

'STOP,' Tango Two shouts. Doctor Watson goes faster, his own heart thundering as he heaves Miri and Bertie through the door. Only one room to cross to reach the glowing portal at the back.

Bertie's legs give out. The pain in his eyes and ears is too much. Miri sinks down with him, unable to take his weight. Doctor Watson tugs at them to get up.

Harry dashes out from the door into the small group of operatives running past. That impact sends several sprawling, buying a second's worth of distraction for Safa, Ria and Ben to come through after him. Safa and Ben go straight into the fight. Fists lashing out, grabbing arms to break and using legs to trip. Roland crashes through. Seeing his daughter jumping on the back of an operative, he runs on past towards the door to the room holding the portal.

They fight as they run. All of them. A pressing, seething clash of form against form. Harry plucks Ria from the back of the man she is trying to blind with her thumbs before booting the almost blind operative away.

Tango Two runs into the room, seeing an old man trying to help the target male. Doctor Watson snaps his head up, his face full of fear. He screams out and charges. His hands lashing out wild and unaimed as he thinks to beat the woman back. Tango Two side-steps neatly, letting him sail past as Miri blindly raises her gun in the direction of the noise. Tango Two darts to the side and rushes for the hand holding the pistol. Miri fires, the gun slamming up from the recoil as Tango Two snatches it from her hand.

Tango Two spots the blue light shining from the open door of the walk-in wardrobe. Mesmerising colours that ripple and dance across the surface. There it is. That's the time machine. The doctor bounces off the wall with a gargled yelp and staggers back. He turns and screams out again as he commences his second charge at the woman. Tango Two again steps out of his way and sends a foot into his arse, propelling him into the closet and straight through the portal. She sees it happen. She sees the man go through.

A mass of people reaches the door in a confusing, chaotic, wild, brawling, seething bunch of grunts and hisses, of bones snapping and blood spraying. Roland pushes through them. Screaming in fear and terror for his own life as he runs and dives through the portal. Tango Two tracks him going across the room then to Safa Patel, Ben Ryder and the other big guy with the beard fighting like demons to keep everyone else back.

'*WHERE IS TANGO TWO?*' Mother demands again, her voice rising to a screech.

'*TOP FLOOR . . . I HAVE THE TARGET MALE,*' Tango Two transmits in a frantic shout in the utter chaos of the moment.

Miri's head catches up to the fact the gun is not in her hand anymore. She rises and grabs Bertie, trying to drag him towards the blue light. Heedless of the female agent still holding him. Heedless of anything and everything. Consumed only with the need to get Bertie away.

'GET TO BERTIE . . .' Safa bellows.

'BERTIE, GO . . .' Ben screams out, his own face streaming with blood.

'GO, BERTIE . . .' Ria shouts.

'GET OUT, LAD,' Harry roars.

'Get through . . . Get through . . .' Miri mutters the words over and again as Tango Two spins to see the older woman tugging on his arm, desperate to get him away.

Ben breaks free of the mass, diving towards Tango Two, who darts back with Bertie firmly in her grip. She has a pistol. She could shoot him, but he's Ben Ryder. She could shoot the other woman, but it's Safa Patel. Indecision renders her hopeless as someone slams Ben down from behind.

Safa thrusts her head back into the face of the male grabbing her. She breaks his nose, then kicks into his shins and pulls free. She aims for Bertie and not Tango Two. A black-masked figure dives out, grabbing Safa's trailing leg and bringing her down. Again Tango Two stares almost slack-jawed at the woman she knows is Safa Patel twisting to fight back at the man holding her.

'BERTIE, RUN . . . RUN, BERTIE,' Ria screams out.

'*WHERE IS TANGO TWO?*' Mother's screeching voice repeats the question. Tango Two winces, confused and jarred. She sees Echo lurching into the room, his hand already on his radio ready to transmit.

'*WITH ME, TOP FLOOR . . .*'

'*GUNSHIPS . . . TOP FLOOR . . . FIRE NOW, FIRE NOW . . .*' Mother screams.

The engine pitch of the gunships changes again as they drop and start to turn. Tango Two feels the pull coming from Miri heaving on Bertie's arm.

'*KILL TANGO TWO . . . KILL HER NOW!*' Mother rages into the radio, into earpieces and through loudspeakers to be heard clearly by everyone in the room. '*KILL TANGO TWO . . . GUNSHIPS . . . TOP FLOOR, FIRE NOW, FIRE NOW . . .*'

The chain guns on the gunships come to life. The noise is overwhelming and blots out all others sounds. Huge rounds slam into the top floor of the house, smashing through bricks that sail down in chunks. The gunships turn slowly, strafing from the ends of the house towards the middle. Nothing in this room will be alive within a few seconds.

A shot snaps Tango Two's head over. Echo firing at her with his face so beaten one of his eyes is sealed closed. She lifts and fires with an instinct that makes her react before she can give it conscious thought. The round hits Echo's throat, spinning him back and away. She fires again, the second shot killing him outright. That instinct takes over. Indecision leaves. Hesitancy evaporates.

'*KILL TANGO TWO . . . KILL HER NOW . . .*'

Someone lurches at her. She fires at the figure, killing him instantly. She twitches and fires again. Shooting another one down. She aims and fires into the back of the one fighting with Safa. He screams out, releasing his grip. Tango Two fires again. She goes backwards towards the blue light, one hand holding Bertie, the other aiming to fire at anyone coming at her.

Tango Two snatches a glance at the older woman still tugging on Bertie's arm, and turns to heave and send them both staggering through the blue light.

Safa vaults up to lock eyes on Tango Two firing past her, and tracks the shot to one of the soldiers. Everything on instinct. Safa saw the woman push Miri and Bertram through the portal. No time to think. She grabs Ria and heaves the girl towards Tango Two, who pushes her on towards the blue light.

The chain guns get closer, destroying everything in their trajectory of fire. A missile launched from one of the gunships strikes and explodes at the end of the house that shakes and vibrates from the huge detonation. Dust and plaster rain down from the ceiling. A second fires in. A third.

Tango Two braces, aims and fires the last of the rounds. She kills her own team as Harry grabs Safa and Ben and runs towards the blue light.

The chain guns hit the ends of the room. The rounds powering through the bricks with ease. Daylight floods in from the walls blown away. They won't make it. Tango Two can see it. There is no way anyone else will get through that portal.

A bright blur swooshes up from the ground outside and slams into the side of the gunship on the right side. Flames scorch up as the impact sends it slewing through the air into the other one. Propellers strike propellers. Metal pings off and spins across the expanse into the house. The chain guns still firing. The gunships' engines whir louder as the pilots fight to control the craft now coming across the grounds towards the house.

Seconds bought, but it's enough. Tango Two's eyes go wide. Someone runs into her, driving her off her feet and back towards the wardrobe. Noise everywhere. Fire, flames, smoke, explosions. The two gunships hit the house with a deep crash of twisting metal and solid ringing thuds. Tango Two goes through the blue light as the gunships crash through the wall into the room. She goes screaming from the noise and the sheer overwhelming awe of seeing such a thing.

She lands hard on her back. Still screaming. Still shouting. Still believing she is in the house. The pistol drops from her hand and it takes seconds for her to realise the only sounds in this bare concrete room are coming from her and the others crying and gasping.

Flames billow through the blue light only a few feet away. She tries to scrabble back and away from the wall of heat that stinks of aviation fuel. Ben, Harry and Safa all tangled on top and underneath her.

Miri crawls as fast as her pain-ridden body will let her. Round the back of the portal to the tablet device left on the side that she grabs and thumbs at, half-blind and half-delirious. The blue light cuts off and with it the flames and heat instantly end.

In the bunker room, they lie gasping, heaving for air, sweat burning eyes. Cuts, bruises and welts show everywhere as Miri mutters the time on her watch to herself, then sinks down on to her back while thinking maybe she got it wrong about Safa, Harry and Ben.

Nine

'No threat . . . No threat . . .'

'Don't fucking move . . .'

It's not over. Not yet. Not by a long way. Miri lies on her back, gasping for air, listening to the voices around her.

'Ben, hold her hands . . . Harry, get up . . .'

'I'm not resisting . . .'

There is work to do. Work that has to be done now, but Miri doesn't want to move. Her body hurts like hell. Old injuries that remind her how battered her body is. She summons the fortitude to finish what has been started. The situation has to be made safe.

Focus slowly returns. Her hand goes to her hip to check her pistol, and it takes a second or two for her mind to catch up that it's back in the house on the floor of the bedroom. Did she drop it? No, the female agent took it. Her head snaps over to see the female agent face down on the floor with Ben on top, holding her hands behind her back.

'Hold her tight,' Safa orders, her voice hoarse, blood dripping from her bruised face. 'Harry . . .'

'Yep,' Harry groans, rolling from his back to his front then up to all fours. Blood drips from his nose on to the concrete floor, his right eye swollen, a deep cut on his upper arm bleeds freely down his elbow.

'Why were they trying to kill you?' Ben asks, his voice rough and low.

'I don't know!' Tango Two says quickly.

'Not now,' Safa says.

'Mum?' Ria looks up. Huddled at the edge of the concrete room having crawled to grab and hold her brother. Roland lies nearby, curled up in a ball, whimpering in fear. 'Where's Mum? Where is she? MUM?'

'Harry, you fit?' Safa asks.

'Aye,' the big man says, coming to his feet wiping a swollen hand across his bloodied nose.

Ria spots her dad, the older woman, the doctor and the others. She sees one of the attackers on the floor being held down, but not her mother. 'MUM? WHERE'S MUM?'

'I'm not resisting,' Tango Two says.

'Shut up,' Safa says, her voice weaker than normal, the back of her skull pounding. Her legs feel heavy, and she keeps blinking to stay focussed.

'DAD?'

Roland stirs and lifts his head. His face ashen and drawn. His eyes red from crying. He swallows and stares blankly for a second before his brain starts processing exactly where he is.

'DAD? WHERE'S MUM?'

'What?' Roland says weakly, looking round. 'She, er . . . Susan was . . .'

'Take this,' Safa says, nodding at Harry to take the pistol. 'You move and you die,' she tells the agent.

'I am not resisting,' Tango Two says in the same rough voice as Safa. Her own head spins, pain in her skull, flashes of light in her vision, but she stays still despite the pain of Ben's grip on her wrists.

'Mum . . . She . . . She . . .' Ria gasps the words out, her voice breaking with emotion as Safa glances at her then goes back to the woman pinned down.

'Where's Susan? What's going on?' Roland asks, his voice growing firmer as the risk of immediate peril starts to abate.

'CAN'T HEAR ANYTHING . . . I CAN'T HEAR ANYTHING . . .' Bertram screams out with sudden panic. His shouting voice adding to the bedlam in the room.

'It was the flash-bang,' Safa says, blinking as she looks over at him, then realising he can't hear her. 'You . . .' she shouts at Ria. 'Comfort him . . . The effects pass . . .' She shakes her head again and looks down at the woman being held on the floor. 'Weapons?'

'Knife on my belt,' Tango Two says.

'Firearms?'

'Pistol only . . . I dropped it when . . .'

'Keep her hands held . . .' Safa cuts in, working down one side of the agent's body to check for concealed weapons.

'What we doing with her?' Ben asks, his voice strangely muffled in his own ears. He stretches his jaw and blinks to try and rid the flashes of light in his vision. 'Why were they trying to kill you?'

'Ben, not now. Do this first . . .' Safa says. 'Move your head back a bit, you're dripping blood on my hands.'

'Sorry,' Ben mumbles, leaning away to rub his cheek on his shoulder.

'Go back,' Ria says. 'We have to go back . . . Get Mum . . . Mum's there . . . She didn't get through . . .'

Roland takes it all in quickly, with a sense of instant shame that he ran off and left his family behind. He crawls to Bertie, extending a hand to his son's shoulder.

'GET OFF HIM,' Ria screams, pulling her brother away. 'You left us . . . You bloody left us . . .'

'Ria, I . . . I . . . I was trying to draw them away,' Roland says, forcing belief and sincerity into his voice.

'WHERE'S MUM?' Ria screeches the words out. Panicked and terrified.

'Stop shouting now.' The glare from Safa robs the air from Ria's lungs. The sheer intensity coming from her. The bruises and cuts on her face shining with sweat and blood. 'Open the portal,' Safa says, still breathing hard as she looks round at Miri. 'We'll throw the bitch back out,' she adds, pointing down at Tango Two.

Miri clambers to her feet, swaying on the spot as she tries to look round. 'She stays,' she whispers hoarsely before staggering towards the door.

'Where you going?' Ben calls out.

Miri doesn't reply, but puts her hands out on to the walls to steady her balance as she walks down to the last set of rooms in the corridor. She goes through the middle room, past the blue chairs and into one of the bedrooms to pull the black bag out from under the bed. She pauses, blinking and breathing, before setting off back towards the portal room.

'Get up,' she tells the doctor as she walks back in. He nods dumbly, with shock etched on his face. 'Get sedatives ready . . . Do it now . . .'

'I demand an explanation,' Roland says, mutating the anger at his own cowardice into something resembling an attempt at authority. 'What the hell were you thinking? Where is my wife? You put my children in danger and . . .'

'I CAN'T HEAR ANYTHING . . . MY EYES . . . RIA, MY EYES . . .' Bertram screams out again and again, clutching at his sister. His vision strobing with flashes of light. Pain in his eyes, ears and skull. His hearing muffled.

'YOU LEFT US,' Ria shouts at her father. 'WHERE'S MUM? GET MY MUM . . .'

'Jesus,' Safa mutters, wincing at the noise coming from the Cavendish family. Her own head hurts. Every muscle in her body hurts. Her head is swimming. Her vision is strobing, but this noise is too much. 'SHUT UP . . . ALL OF YOU . . .'

Tango Two stays passive and still as Safa methodically works down her body searching for weapons. She feels the same as they do.

Confused. Hurt. Shocked and stunned. Too many things have just happened in too short a space of time. Training kicks in as she works to gain what information she can. She isolates voices. Attaching each to a name and already gaining a sense of the dynamics.

'Clear,' Safa says, staggering back from the female agent. 'Harry, keep that pistol aimed at her. Miri? What now?'

Miri stops next to the inert machine. 'Need coordinates for the basement.' She unzips the bag, reaches in and pulls out a lump of C4 explosive fitted with a detonation timer.

'Blowing it?' Safa asks, unaware of the sway in her body.

Miri nods.

'Good. He had plans all over the place down there.'

'Mum didn't get through,' Ria says with tears spilling down her cheeks. 'She didn't get through. Go back . . . Please go back and get her . . .'

'We can't,' Ben says, softening his voice as he speaks to Ria. 'Listen to me, Ria! Listen to me. You have to stop shouting. Comfort your brother . . .'

'I demand an explanation. This is my bunker. This is my . . .'

'Roland,' Ben says, the soft tone evaporating instantly as he growls the words out. 'One more word from you and I will batter you senseless . . .'

Roland's mouth opens ready for the retort. Ready to reclaim his authority, but the hard glares coming from Safa, Ben and Harry stop him before any sounds are formed.

'Got it,' Miri says, scrolling through the list of previous destinations on the tablet and shaking her head at how they have all been saved. *Cellar*. It cements in her mind the need to see this through. She sets the timer on the C4 to ten seconds, before pressing the saved destination on the tablet and confirming it to open. The blue light comes on. Beautiful and mesmerising. Tango Two turns her head to stare properly without the worry of bullets flying everywhere. The room is quieter now. The screaming has stopped. She twists to see that the girl is comforting the target. Smoothing his head while holding him close. She spots Roland Cavendish floundering, as though unsure of what to do or say.

'Push her through,' Safa says, clocking the agent looking about the room.

'She stays,' Miri says.

'She's the fucking enemy,' Safa snaps.

'Look through, confirm it,' Miri says, glancing at Safa.

'I'll drag that bitch through and confirm it,' Safa says, moving towards Tango Two.

'Stand down, Miss Patel,' Miri says, halting Safa in her tracks as Tango Two holds very still. 'Confirm the location.' Miri points at the blue light. 'I do not know what it looks like . . .'

Safa glares at Tango Two as she walks to the blue light and quickly leans through, holds position for a second, then comes back. 'Yep, that's it.'

'Hold here,' Miri says. She takes the tablet and C4 with her through the portal into the basement. An instant transition of time and place. She was expecting to hear the noises, then remembers the basement is soundproofed. A glance round. A need to understand the place where the inventor works. A desire to investigate and seek knowledge, while knowing she has but seconds. She spots the desk. Something catches her eye. Sheets of paper strewn over the tabletop. It's 2061 here. They use tablets for everything, not paper. She moves over to grab the sheets, and hears noises coming through the door Safa and Ben left open at the top of the stairs when they took Bertram out. No time to wait. She has to go now. She sets the timer, places the C4 down on the desk and rushes back through the portal, thumbing the screen and shutting it down the second she gets through.

'What's that?' Ben asks, looking at the sheets of paper clutched in Miri's hands.

'On his desk. All I had time to grab.' She goes to move off, but stops. She has to know. Nothing can be left to chance. There could be another time machine in the basement. She has to be sure the C4 detonated. She looks at the two poles holding the music speaker-like objects and waits another few seconds, which fill with the sound of Ria, Bertie and Roland all sobbing.

'Need to know,' she mutters and moves the poles to face away from everyone. Once set, she stands back and presses the saved destination. The blue light comes on. Heat and flames roar through and up to lick the ceiling. Tango Two stares, entranced, as Safa lifts an arm to cover her face. Miri switches it off. Satisfied the explosion has worked. Only then does she glance at the sheets of paper and spot the hand-drawn schematics of another device identical in design to the first, but with a red glowing field instead of blue. She holds it up towards Ben. 'That's why we went now . . .'

'Fuck,' Ben says.

'SOUND WON'T GO THROUGH,' Bertram roars, his vision returning enough for him to snatch a glance at his papers held by Miri.

None of them ask him what he means, they work to stay focussed and alert in the room now made hot and charged by the flames that came through the portal.

One job done, but there is more to do. So much more. Miri slowly lifts her head to look at the next task and takes in Roland, Bertie and Ria. She looks down to the female agent. She planned for Bertie and Roland, but not the other two. Never mind. Missions are always fluid.

'I have authority?' she says, staring at one person.

'What?' Safa says as she realises the last question was directed at her.

'I have authority?' Miri asks again.

Safa takes her in through fresh eyes. At what the older woman just did. At what she went through and the relentless vicious determination to get Bertram out the house. 'Fuck yes,' Safa snorts. 'You have authority . . .'

'Miri?' Ben asks in alarm at seeing the woman sway unsteadily. 'Maybe you should sit down.'

'No time. Sit later. Doctor? Sedatives, now.'

'I'm coming, I'm coming,' Doctor Watson mumbles, rushing into the room with a large bag.

'Roland, son, girl and the prisoner,' Miri snaps, trying to clear her mind to think ahead.

'What?' the doctor asks weakly.

'What?' Roland asks just as weakly at hearing his name.

'Sedate them.'

The doctor mumbles a reply and drops to a knee with a grimace as he unfastens the latches on the bag to let it fall open. With shaking hands, he gets a syringe out and works to fit a new needle protected by a bright-orange plastic cap that he bites off and spits aside. He pushes the needle through the rubber seal on a vial, turns it upside down and pulls back to fill the syringe with the clear liquid.

'What is that?' Ben asks.

'What are you doing?' Roland asks at the same time, alarmed at the sight.

'Sedative,' the doctor says. 'It will help calm you down.'

'I want Roland and prisoner out. Not calm,' Miri says.

'What?' Roland says. 'What the hell?'

'You did it to us, remember?' Safa says.

'Hang on,' Ben says. 'Miri, what's going on?'

'I do not know their medical history. Administering a sedative beyond the prescribed dose could be harmful.' The doctor joins the babble of voices rising again.

'Do it now,' Miri says, ignoring his question.

'And I say again . . .'

'Now, Doctor,' Miri says with an edge to her voice. 'Or *I* will.'

'I want it noted that I am against giving medications beyond the prescribed limit.'

'Why are you knocking him out?' Ben asks, holding a hand out to stop the doctor.

Miri's whole face changes, morphing into pure anger as she strides towards the shocked doctor and snatches the syringe from his hand. 'We do not have time for this. How did they find the staging area? Who led them there? How did that information get out? Why did that person help us? Is Roland passing information right now? Muscle or vein?' she barks, dropping next to Roland.

'Get your hands off me,' Roland cries out at Miri reaching for his arm.

'Muscle!' the doctor blurts, seeing the needle going towards Roland's arm.

'Harry, roll him over,' Miri orders.

'GET OFF ME,' Roland yells.

'Now, Sergeant Madden,' Miri orders. Harry responds to the tone. Dropping to grab Roland, flailing and screaming. He rolls him easily. Pinning him face down.

Miri doesn't hesitate. She drives the point of the needle into Roland's backside and pushes the plunger down halfway. Roland cries out, trying to buck and get free.

'How much did you give him?' Doctor Watson asks in shock at the half-empty syringe.

'Hold her,' Miri says, moving towards Tango Two.

'Miri, let the doctor do it,' Ben says quickly as Tango Two twists her head to follow the action. She looks back to Roland. Already his voice is losing volume. Whatever they gave him is working fast. She knows she is next.

'I'm not a threat,' she says quickly. 'I don't know that man. I don't know any of you.'

'Stay still, please,' Doctor Watson says, moving towards the woman.

'No, please . . . please,' Tango Two says. 'I'm no threat . . . I want to . . .'

'It's just a sedative,' Doctor Watson says, trying to sound soothing and professional but coming across clipped and terse.

'Do it now, Doctor,' Miri orders.

'No, please,' Tango Two says, gritting her teeth as the needle pushes through her trousers into her backside. She feels the jab and the hotness of the liquid going in, and knows it's too late to say or do anything. She breathes calmly, easing her heart rate. Miri watches her, seeing that lack of panic and the control exerted.

Tango Two goes quietly, closing her eyes to relax and let the drugs take her down. The voices around her grow softer, fainter, further away. It's warm here. Safe. She feels nice. Sleepy. Her eyes close, heavy and drugged, as she sinks down into darkness.

Ten

An austere, sterile room. Concrete walls. Concrete floor and ceiling. A single metal-framed bed. A metal shutter on the wall indicates the placement of a window.

Tango Two stirs, rising through the layers of sleep to open heavy eyes that snap shut from the glaring light overhead. She winces, lifting a hand to shield her eyes that slowly open to peer out. She feels dizzy and slow-witted, as if hung over.

She sits up too quickly and a wave of nausea sends her sinking back down with a groan. She breathes it through, forcing her mind to work. *Cavendish Manor. The gunships. Mother ordered me to be killed. I shot Echo. I shot other agents. The portal. I went through it. They injected me. I was sedated.*

Injuries?

She tenses muscles and checks for sensation and feeling. Arms okay. Legs okay. Head okay. Sore and fatigued, but everything seems to be working.

Senses?

She clicks her fingers to hear the sound while sniffing at the trace of antiseptic hanging in the air.

She opens her eyes again, just a crack at first and then slowly wider while her pupils adjust to the light.

She can see, hear, smell and move.

Sitting up, slower this time, she looks round the concrete room. Like a cell, but not a cell. She has sheets. *Sheets can be used as a weapon or for self-harm or to aid escape.* She leans over to see if the bed is bolted to the floor. It isn't. Cells normally have the beds bolted down so they can't be used to barricade the door.

Why did Mother order them to kill me?

She hears a drip and freezes to listen. Another one. She looks down to see blood on the sheet covering her body and only then gains the sensation of hot liquid in her nose. Her hands come away smeared in blood. Nosebleed. She starts feeling her head again, grunting, tutting and wincing at the feel of her swollen eyes, cheeks and the sore points all over her skull. That was some scrap in the house. Flashes of memory come back. Safa Patel fighting five of them on her own. The big bearded guy called Harry lifting Alpha off his feet.

She pinches the fleshy bit underneath the gristle on the bridge of her nose and looks round again. A metal shutter on the window and a solid metal door are the only other features.

With her hand raised to her face, she spots her bare arm and only then looks down at herself and the plain black vest top she is wearing. She pushes the sheet away to find her legs covered in soft cotton, grey tracksuit bottoms. A pull cord on the waist of the jogging bottoms. *That can be used as a weapon. A ligature for suicide or to use to strangle someone from behind.* Someone changed her. She sniffs again and lifts the top to look at the cuts and bruises on her body that smell of antiseptic. She was cleaned too. They've given medical aid, changed her into clean clothes that have a pull cord and placed her in a room with a bed that isn't bolted down.

The dizziness comes again when she tries to stand. She braces, closing her eyes and seeing if it will pass or get worse. It eases off. At the door, she listens, expecting to hear something. Nothing. She pushes the handle down and blinks in surprise when it opens. The next room is bigger. Three ugly blue chairs at the end underneath the exposed window set under a rolled-up metal shutter. Daylight outside. A quick glance at the blue sky before she turns to scan everything else.

Two more doors stand open opposite her. She walks out gingerly, peering through both to see metal-frame beds, clean and unused. Two more doors. One looks like it leads out. She checks the other one and finds the bathroom. It looks brand new. Stainless steel fittings and with three plastic cups, three toothbrushes and three towels placed neatly on the side.

Thirsty. Hydrate.

She fills a cup from the tap on the sink and takes a testing sip before guzzling it down in one go. The water is cool and refreshing and a tiny step towards being revitalised.

Why did Mother want to kill me? What did I do?

Toilet. Toilet paper. Shower. Towel. She picks up one of the toothbrushes. It's solid plastic and not one of the flimsy things they use in detention centres. *This could be a weapon too.* She grips the end with the bristles and holds it up ready to stab out. Pressure on her bladder. She puts the toothbrush down, moves over to the toilet and discovers she is not wearing her own knickers. That's disgusting. These are plain black and similar to hers but not hers. Something about not wearing her own underwear repulses her. She sits down and urinates while looking round. *No noises. Nothing. It's so quiet.*

She flushes and moves to the sink to rinse her hands, freezing at the sight of herself in the mirror fixed to the wall. Her whole face is battered, bruised and swollen. She reaches back to pull out the hairband and runs her fingers through her shoulder-length brown hair to untangle the knots. She fixes her hair back into a ponytail, grimacing at the sight of herself, but knowing it looks worse than it is. She is walking unaided, which is incredible after a fight like that.

Face rinsed. Hands washed. Teeth brushed. Feeling clean and ready gives a psychological boost and in turn helps set the mental preparation for what is to come. She stops, looks down at her chest and grabs her boobs, realising she isn't wearing a bra.

She goes into the middle room with the three chairs and prods one with her bare foot. Not bolted down either, and it feels light. She could throw it as a distraction. She looks round, assessing, evaluating. No visible lenses, but then they've become so small now they could be anywhere. She closes her eyes and draws a slow breath to try and gain any sense of being watched. They said in training never to ignore those senses. If it feels that way, then assume it is that way. She doesn't get that voyeur feeling now, but then also considers the fact that she just woke up from being drugged.

Perimeter.

She goes to the window to further the assessment and evaluation. To know what the ground outside is. Where the nearest structures are. How high up is she? Where are the hiding points? *See. Smell. Hear. Plan, think and always be prepared.*

Why did Mother do that? Why? What happened? I was with the target male. I secured him. Why?

Ten minutes later, she still stands at the window. Staring. Just staring. Her heart, which had almost jumped out of her chest, now settles back down to a normal rhythm.

Dinosaurs.

She finally thinks to look around. She is on the ground floor of a concrete structure on the side of a hill that sweeps down to a huge valley currently filled with what appear to be dinosaurs.

Another ten minutes pass and she again tries to look around, unaware that her nose has started bleeding again.

Assess. Evaluate. Summarise.

Alpha said there was a time machine. He said Bertram Cavendish is thought to be the inventor. The snatch mission failed. They were opposed.

The opposition was Safa Patel, Ben Ryder, a big man with a beard who was strangely familiar. Harry? They called him Harry.

Mother ordered everyone to kill me. She ordered the gunships to fire on us. Why?

Safa Patel.

Ben Ryder.

Dinosaurs.

Is the old woman in charge? The dynamics in the room they came into after Cavendish Manor suggested that Roland thought he was in charge. They were all arguing with each other. Yes! She remembers now. She remembers the old woman saying to Safa if she had authority. Like a question, but not a question. *Is the team here undergoing change?* A change in leadership always creates a power vacuum, which is a thing to exploit.

Okay. The time machine is real. She went through it and now she is in the distant past. *Cretaceous? Jurassic?* She knows history, but not enough to determine her precise location. Either way, those periods spanned tens of millions of years and were hundreds of millions of years before humans emerged as a species.

Footsteps. She turns from the window to face the main door. She listens for what comes next to determine the number and types of locks, but hears only the scraping of metal on metal. A bolt? The door swings inwards. She waits, passive and calm. Safa Patel walks in and stops on seeing Tango Two.

'Seen the dinosaurs?' she asks bluntly.

Tango Two stares at her. Seeing the same bruises, swellings and cuts on the other woman; but even with that slight disfigurement, she is clearly and recognisably Safa Patel.

'You deaf, fuckstick?'

'What?' Tango Two blurts.

'Dinosaurs? Seen them?'

'Er, yes. Yes, I have . . .'

104

'We're in dinosaur times,' Safa says. 'Cretaceous.'

'Oh.'

Safa shrugs. 'I sounded smart then. I don't know what Cretaceous is.'

'Oh,' Tango Two says.

'You look like shit. Good. Serves you right for being the bad guys. Miri said I can't ask you why you helped us. So fuck off and don't tell me anything.'

'Okay.'

'Doc said nothing's broken.'

'I . . .'

'You got my knickers on. Clean though. It's gross wearing someone else's pants.'

'I see.'

'Your boobs are bigger than mine, so no bra.'

'Right.'

'I changed you. You're the bad guys, but I didn't let any men see you naked.'

'Thank you.'

'Miri said Ben and Harry aren't allowed to talk to you.'

'What?'

'She said you might honey-trap them. She meant shagging. Don't try and honey-trap me either, or I'll punch you in the face.'

'What?'

'Don't try and run off, otherwise the dinosaurs will eat you.'

'Right.'

'Or I'll shoot you and leave you for the dinosaurs to eat.'

'Um.'

'And the nosebleeds are something to do with the oxygen or something . . . Doc's given you meds. You'll be fine, so stop whining. Man up.'

'I . . .'

'Miri said I'm not allowed to carry my sidearm when I come and see you . . . in case you take it off me. I said there was zero chance of anyone ever taking my gun from me unless it was from my cold, dead hands, but she said no. So I don't have a sidearm. But you try anything and I will kill you with my bare hands. Got it?'

'I . . .'

'Stop gabbling. I hate gabblers. Got it?'

'Yes.'

'There is nowhere to run. The portal is shut off and the thing that makes it work is encrypted.'

'Okay,' Tango Two says, blinking as she tries to keep up, while staring mesmerised at Safa.

'Your nose is bleeding,' Safa says. 'Miri will debrief you later. You want some food?'

'Food?'

'Yeah. Food. To eat. Are you English?'

'Yes, I'm English.'

'Stop gabbling then. Doc said it helps to eat.'

'Yes, food would be nice. Thank you.'

'I'll come back with food.'

Tango Two stares as Safa about-turns and marches out, slamming the door closed, with that single scrape of metal coming after.

◆ ◆ ◆

'Miri?' Safa stops at the door of what used to be Roland's office and looks in to see the older woman sitting behind the rough-hewn desk reading a newspaper. The rest of the room is bare and sterile. Anything left by Roland is now gone. Out with the old and in with the new. Safa snorts at the thought as Miri folds the newspaper neatly in half.

'Come in. Report.'

'She's awake,' Safa says, walking to the desk. She thinks to sit down, but gets the sudden feeling of being back at work in front of the divisional commander and almost comes to attention when she stops.

'Sit down,' Miri says in that blunt, hard voice. Her own face still bears the marks of the fight. Bruises and swelling, but Miri remains devoid of expression. Simply waiting for Safa to continue.

'Thanks.' Safa sits down. 'Seemed fine. I told her what you said.'

'All of it?'

'Yep. Well, I said it in my words, but yeah.'

'In your words?'

'In my words,' Safa says, locking eyes. 'In the way I speak . . . With my words . . .'

'I know what . . .'

'Then why ask?'

Miri concedes the point with a twitch of eyebrows. 'Did she say anything?'

'Nope. She said yes and no, and said she understood. She's seen the dinosaurs. Ben's idea of leaving the shutter up worked. She was polite. Didn't ask anything.'

'Good,' Miri says, picking the newspaper back up. 'Be yourself with her. It is the right strategy at this time. Take her drinks. Take her food. Put her at ease and comfort. Chat with her.'

'I'm not the chatty type, and isn't that a bit weird for a prisoner? And why did her side try and kill her? And why did she help us? And where's Roland? And . . .'

'I am working on it.' Miri unfolds the paper and starts leafing through the pages, as though to find the section she was previously reading.

'The answer in that newspaper then, is it?'

'That is all for now. Thank you.'

'So what's happening now?'

'I said that is all, Miss Patel,' Miri says, lifting her eyes back to Safa.

107

'Where's Roland?'
'Somewhere else.'
'Why?'
'Sterility to prevent risk of cross-contamination of knowledge.'
'I don't know what that means.'
'Ask Mr Ryder.'
'Patronising. Is that the same as Bertie and Ria?'
'Yes.'
'Right,' Safa says, rising from the chair. 'Thanks for the chat.'
'Welcome.'
'Door always open, is it?'
Miri reads the newspaper. Safa tuts and walks off.

Eleven

Footsteps. She turns from the window to face the main door. The footsteps stop. The door swings inwards. She waits, passive and calm, as Safa Patel walks in carrying a tray. Tango Two looks to the door left open and then to the tray and the bowls of fruit, eggs and a steaming mug of coffee. She spots the cutlery too. A stainless steel knife, fork and spoon.

Hot coffee in the face. Throw the mug. Grab the fork. Stab for the eyes. Go for the door.

Safa puts the tray on the seat of the chair and steps away to look down at the same things then back up at Tango Two. A second's worth of silence. Safa's eyes hard, but the challenge is clear.

'I'd win,' Safa says. 'Even with hot coffee in the face.'

A flash of memory at seeing Safa holding them off on the landing single-handed.

'Thank you,' Tango Two says, remaining by the window.

'Anytime you fancy attacking me, just have a go and see what happens.'

'Thank you,' Tango Two says, still remaining by the window.

Silence. Neither move. Neither speak.

'Eat then.'

'Now?'

'Yes, now. I can't leave you with a knife and a fork. You might shove them up your arse.'

'Right,' Tango Two says carefully, walking gingerly towards the chairs.

'Pack in the acting. You aren't that hurt.'

'Thank you,' Tango Two says, offering a submissive look at Safa. She sits down on the middle chair.

'That fruit is nice,' Safa says. 'We haven't got much left now though, because you killed Malc and Kon, so we can't get any more . . .'

'Wasn't me,' Tango Two cuts in quietly, politely. 'I believe that was in Berlin? I didn't come into the operation until Hampshire.'

'Still your lot,' Safa says.

'Of course,' Tango Two says, reaching for the bowl. She looks at the chopped-up chunks, instantly recognising them from the smell and appearance, then wondering why Safa mentioned the fruit. When did Safa die? It was 2020. The attack on Downing Street. This fruit was developed years after her death. She looks up and smiles politely, stealing another studied glance at Safa.

'Stop gawping at me,' Safa says, then narrows her eyes. 'Are you honey-trapping me?'

'No,' Tango Two says quickly, still averting her gaze.

'Try the lemon-lime thing, that's my favourite. Ben likes it too. Harry likes the cheesy-feet marrow thing, but that is gross.'

'Melemime,' Tango Two says, stabbing a chunk of the lemon-lime fruit to hold up.

'What?' Safa asks.

'Hybrid cross-pollinated from a melon, a lemon and a lime. Melemime.'

Safa steps forward to look closer. 'Ben will love that. What's that plum thing called?'

'This one?' Tango Two asks, using the fork to push a chunk of fruit in the bowl. 'That is actually a combination of vegetables and fruit. Potato, sweet potato, plums obviously, nectarine and kiwi.'

'What's it called?'

'Plumtato.'

'Are you taking the piss?'

'Not at all. That is the name. In English anyway. They call it something else in Germany, where it was developed. Are you Safa Patel?'

'Yeah. So did they make loads of different ones? The fruits, I mean. And are they nutritionally good? I figured they were, but . . .'

'Er, yes. Yes, several were developed, and yes, very nutritionally good. They were designed to get children back to eating fruit after the obesity epidemic. The cheesy marrow thing you mentioned is a very acquired taste. Marrow, yams, fermented beans and . . .'

'What's it called?'

'Marrowyam.'

'Marrowyam? I'll tell Harry,' Safa says, stepping back as Tango Two chews thoughtfully on the chunk of melemime.

Questions whirl and spin through Tango Two's head. She needs to know what happened, but is experienced enough to go patiently and slowly. Build a bond. Stay passive and non-threatening. She clears her throat, as though worried. 'May I ask, was that Ben Ryder?' She speaks as lightly as she dares, even focussing on choosing another chunk of fruit to make the opening test question seem innocuous.

'Yeah, Miri said you'd do this.'

'Pardon?' Tango Two says, blinking in confusion.

'Cultivate. We got trained in it in the force. Because we guarded politicians, we had people trying to get close to us. Cultivate us. Like, make friends and find things out.'

'Right,' Tango Two says, still polite as before. She blinks again and forks another chunk of fruit. 'I apologise. I was just surprised. I mean . . . Safa Patel and Ben Ryder . . .'

'And Harry Madden,' Safa says with a slight grin at seeing the woman freeze as she lifts her fork.

Harry Madden. Mad Harry Madden. The Second World War in the mid-twentieth century. She looks up at Safa and allows the surprise to show. 'Mad Harry Madden?'

'Yep,' Safa says. 'Reason I'm telling you that is so you know who you have to get through, if by some divine miracle you get through me. Ben Ryder and Harry Madden.'

'I see,' Tango Two says, lifting the fork to her mouth.

Safa sits down on one of the other chairs. Making small talk is not her area of expertise, so instead she just watches Tango Two eat.

Tango Two takes the positioning in, but shows no reaction. She was expecting instant interrogation. Sleep deprivation, and for food and water to be rationed. That another strategy is being used is jarring and confusing. There should be two guards. One to come forward. One to stay back. She senses something like awkwardness hanging in the air. Like Safa wants to say something, but doesn't know what to say.

'You train a lot then?' Safa asks. Looking at her athletic build and the muscle definition in her shoulders and arms. Not bulky, but toned.

'Pardon?'

'Exercise.'

'Oh. Er, yes. Yes, I do.'

'Me too. Go nuts if I can't train.'

'Same,' Tango Two says, slowing down in her eating to give time for the conversation to grow. 'You exercise here?'

'Running outside, circuits . . . Got some combat training equipment in the main room. Basic stuff, but you can train anywhere really.'

'Motivation is a state of mind.'

'Bloody right,' Safa says in agreement.

'Is it safe to go outside?'

'Yep. It's nice. View is amazing.'

'I saw.' Tango Two offers a smile and nods at the window.

Safa tuts. 'We didn't have a clue when we got here. I mean, where we were. Ben said to leave the shutter up so you'd be able to look outside.'

'I see. Seems a good idea.' Tango Two has no clue if it is a good idea or not, but knows to be agreeable. She chews slowly, thoughtfully. 'Certainly a jarring place to wake up in.'

'Say that again. You finished?'

'Oh, yes. Thank you. That was very nice.'

◆ ◆ ◆

'Hey,' Ben says as Safa walks back into the main room carrying the empty food tray. 'Alright?'

'Fine,' Safa says. 'She seems alright actually. Beardy? How's the face?'

'Sore,' Harry says, sitting at the table with Ben.

'Back in a mo.' Safa dumps the tray and walks through the next set of doors down to Miri's office. She stops to see the woman reading from either another or the same newspaper, which she folds and places down on the stack on her desk. A bigger pile rests on the floor nearby. Notepads and pens on the tabletop with an old smartphone, the earphone wires stretched across the desk.

'Report.'

'Same as before. Chatted a bit. Didn't really say anything. Talked about exercise.'

'Good. She may go silent to try and draw you out. That is fine if that happens. Be yourself, as I said before.'

'Weird,' Safa mumbles. 'I told her who Harry is. So she knows who she has to get through if she thinks of escaping.'

Miri doesn't reply.

'That was it,' Safa says.

'Thank you.' Miri lifts the newspaper up.

Safa sighs. 'We're almost out of food.'

'We need money to get supplies.'

'Whatever. Get money then.'

'I am working on it,' Miri says, reading the newspaper.

'Fuck me, you're not Roland, are you,' she mutters as she leaves.

'Correct. I am not Roland.'

Twelve

'Wake up.'

'Huh?' Tango Two's eyes come open as she sits up to stare round in the split-second panic of waking too fast from a deep sleep. She breathes hard. Not recognising where she is until the pennies start dropping one after the other. The first question in her mind is the same as the last thought before she slept. *Why did Mother order them to kill me?*

'Are you hiding behind the door with the toothbrush?' Safa's voice calls through.

'What? No . . . I'm . . . I'm in bed.' Tango Two says, her voice rough from sleep.

'Hope you are,' Safa says, overly stating each word as the door handle starts going down. 'I mean waiting to attack me, not that I hope you're in bed. Bollocks . . . I am coming in . . . in case you wanted to attack me . . .' The door opens. Safa looks in. Tango Two stares out. Safa shrugs. 'Get up, breakfast.'

'Yep. I mean, yes. Yes, of course,' Tango Two says, blinking and forcing her brain to kick in. She slides off the bed, expecting the same wave of dizziness that kept coming yesterday. It comes, but weaker. Mild even.

'It goes quickly,' Safa says, seeing her holding the bed. 'Use the ablutions, as Harry calls them. I'll wait here.'

'Of course,' Tango Two says politely, walking from the room as Safa steps back from the door. She notices Safa is dressed differently, in jeans and a plain black T-shirt, with her boots on. She spots two mugs on the tray and glances again at Safa before going into the bathroom.

'No rush,' Safa calls out, picking up one of the mugs.

'Thank you,' Tango Two calls out. She goes for the toilet first. Sitting to relieve her bladder and hardly believing how well she slept last night. She expected to be tossing and turning. She expected nightmares, but she slept soundly, and that was after spending most of yesterday dozing. *What happened? Why did Mother tell them to kill me?*

How long has she been here? She tries to focus, feeling surprised at the lack of grasp she has on time. Two days? Three? This is the third day. Yes. Yes, it is. She shakes her head to try and clear the fug in her mind.

Miri visited yesterday. She walked in, looked round and nodded to Safa, who walked out. Then Miri sat down on one of the blue chairs and opened a paper notepad. She said she was called Miri and that they were going to debrief. She asked what happened that led to Tango Two being here, and listened as the agent recounted the events. Tango Two was truthful, but basic. She gave facts, but no opinion. She studied Miri, as Miri studied her. Sitting positions. Posture. Eye contact. Tone of voice. The way Miri held the pen, and every nuance available.

Once Tango Two finished her account, Miri did not ask any questions, but said thank you and left.

Later, while Tango Two was dozing on the bed, the doctor came to check her injuries. Safa was present the whole time. He gave her some pills to take and said they were just anti-inflammatories and pain relief. She was given food again too and drinks throughout the day, and every time she felt the jolt of knowing the woman bringing them was Safa Patel.

She rinses her hands and checks her reflection. The swelling is already going down. The bruises are still livid and she's still sore everywhere, but healing quickly. She washes her face, dries off and walks out to see Safa by the window, clutching one of the mugs between her hands.

'Have a shower, if you want.'

'I can later,' Tango Two says politely.

'Sleep alright?' Safa asks after a time, watching the other woman start eating. Tango Two didn't think she would be hungry, but her appetite is strong and she tucks in. Just fruit, eggs and coffee, but it's so nice.

'Very well, thank you,' she replies.

'Does that here,' Safa says after another brief silence. 'I sleep like a log. Harry does. Ben didn't for a while, but he was messed-up on bad meds and . . . some other issues. He sleeps alright now.'

Tango Two eats, knowing when to stay quiet and hoping Safa will feel the need to keep talking. All information is good information.

'Nice day,' Safa remarks, looking out the window. 'Doc said you can go outside later for some air. Said your injuries are fine. I said I can give you some more, but he didn't find it funny. Ben laughed. Harry smiled a bit, but then Harry doesn't laugh out loud that much. Sounds like a donkey when he does though.'

Tango Two eats and listens. Nodding and making noises when appropriate.

Safa suddenly stops and grins with perfect white teeth showing through her darker skin tone. 'Miri said that happens too.'

'What's that?' Tango Two asks, wishing she had teeth like that.

'Said cultivating can happen without you saying anything. We got trained like that in the police for interviews when we question the bad guys. Something about the use of silence to make the suspect need to speak. I was shit at it. My questioning technique was *Did you do it? Did you do it?* I'd ask that twice, then get bored and give up.'

Tango Two laughs. She was ready to force a fake laugh, and is surprised when the real thing comes out instead.

'Yeah, so, stop cultivating me with your silence.'

'Okay,' Tango Two says.

'At least you don't make noises when you eat,' Safa says after a few seconds of being unable to stay quiet. 'Harry does. He's a squelcher. Hate squelchers. Ben's not too bad.'

'The doctor looks like a squelcher,' Tango Two says, risking an observational comment.

'Fuck yes,' Safa says with a snort of humour. 'Mr Squelchy Face, like *yamyamyam*, with all liquidy noises. I'd actually shoot him at mealtimes and use the time machine to go back and get him if I could.'

'Gross.' Tango Two smiles while noting the things said. *Mealtimes. They eat together. The time machine is normal to them. How long have they had it? How long has Safa been here? Where are Bertie and Roland?*

'Is that girl okay?'

'Which one? Ria?' Safa asks.

'I don't know her name,' Tango Two lies. 'She was crying when we came through . . . Her mother?'

'Yeah, her mum got stuck in the house,' Safa says, quite emotionlessly too, which is also noted. 'I think she's okay. Her and Bertie aren't here now. Miri took them somewhere after you were sedated.'

'Oh,' Tango Two says, amazed at the information flow.

'And that twat's gone too.'

'Er, who, sorry?' Tango Two asks.

'Roland.'

'Oh, right, not a nice man then?'

'He's an idiot,' Safa scoffs. 'Did you see him run past his own kids and wife trying to get out? Complete coward, and totally out of his depth with all this.'

Tango Two pauses for a split second at the information coming from Safa. She considers a counter-bluff. That Safa is giving what she has been told to give. It doesn't feel like that. It feels normal. Like chatting. 'Roland is Bertram's and Ria's dad? Is that right?'

'Bertie. He doesn't like being called Bertram. Anyway, stop cultivating me.'

'Sorry, I was just . . .'

'Yeah, he is their dad. I'm glad he's gone, personally. Ben is too. Miri is cool. That's the last of the fruit anyway. Miri and the doc are going out for supplies later. You allergic to anything?'

'Er, no. No, I don't think I am.'

'Not peanuts? I can get some peanut soup if you are.'

Tango Two smiles, sensing the joke within the threat. 'Er, no . . . but, er . . .'

'What?' Safa asks as the agent trails off.

'I am allergic to strawberries. Fresh strawberries.'

'Are you?' Safa asks, amazed that anyone could be allergic to strawberries.

'Oh, yes,' Tango Two says seriously. 'Really very allergic. Especially when they are served with fresh cream . . . and chocolate. I'm very allergic to chocolate.'

'Dick,' Safa tuts, shaking her head, but smiling all the same.

'Strawberries,' she chuckles to herself as she walks down the corridor back to the main room. She hasn't had either for a long time. Safa isn't bothered about food, and only really views it for the nutritional content, but right now she really wants some strawberries and chocolate. She considers the prospect that she has been cultivated, and dismisses it almost instantly. She couldn't give a shit if she is cultivated. She'd beat the shit out of the woman without blinking.

She pushes in to see everyone standing round one of the tables and Miri holding the notepad that now seems to be glued to her hand.

'We should get strawberries,' Safa says, lifting an eyebrow at Ben and Harry who both turn to look at her.

'Strawberries?' Ben asks.

'Yeah, and chocolate. Prisoner just said about strawberries and chocolate, and now I really want them.'

'Not cultivated then?' Ben asks.

'You didn't even know what cultivated meant until Miri explained it to you,' Safa says, walking over to dump the tray on the big table. 'We're running out of stuff, Miri.'

Miri pauses from writing on the pad to look up.

'Just saying,' Safa says, joining them at the table loaded with belt kits, holsters, pistols, magazines and new radios with earpieces. 'We should just get Malc and Kon back. They were good at getting the pens.'

'We cannot get them back,' Miri says, placing the notepad down. She lifts one of the belts up and loops it round her hips, ready to fasten.

'Why not?' Safa asks, taking her own belt that she starts feeding through the loops on her trousers.

'I have told you why not,' Miri says.

'No, you went *waffle waffle, blah blah* while Ben looked all serious and creamed his pants.'

'Safa,' Ben laughs, his belt secured on his waist. He takes a pistol and starts checking it through, ignoring the looks from Safa and Harry. 'How is our prisoner anyway?'

'Malc and Kon, Miri,' Safa says, ignoring Ben.

'No.'

'We'll get them back. I'll do it. Outside the warehouse, right? I'll be back in, like, five minutes . . . How do you use that thing?'

'No.'

'The encrypted thing,' Safa says.

'No.'

'The tablet thing,' Safa says, looking at Miri with a smile. She takes a pistol and starts the same checks that she taught Ben.

Miri speaks slowly. 'M and K do not have a suitable point at which they can be extracted. Taking them from any point will take them away from you before I arrived, and taking them from outside the warehouse doesn't happen because it would have happened and it did not happen.'

Safa nods, narrows her eyes and makes a sound, as though in agreement. 'That a no then?'

'It's a no.'

'We can't just leave them dead,' Safa says, pushing a magazine into her pistol. 'I bet they're bored shitless.'

'What?' Doctor Watson asks, looking over the table after watching them all getting ready.

'Me and Harry were bored shitless when we were dead,' Safa continues. 'Weren't we, Harry?'

'Aye.'

'You're in a good mood,' Ben remarks.

'Yep. I am. So we'll get them back,' Safa says confidently. 'You and Ben work it out, and me and Harry'll go get 'em. Anyway, why were they trying to kill her? You figured it out yet? And where are we going?'

'Multiple questions elicit multiple answers,' Miri says. 'A police officer should know that.'

'A police officer should know that,' Ben says, smiling at Safa.

'I've told you, I was a shit copper.'

Miri sighs, checks her pistol, fits the magazine, pushes the weapon into the holster and looks at Safa with a glint in her cold grey eyes. 'Do you know what smurfs are, Miss Patel?'

'Smurfs? The little blue things?'

Thirteen

'ARE YOU A SMURF?' Safa demands, twisting the grip on his wrist harder. He yelps and cries out. Pleading in his eyes. 'I SAID, ARE YOU A SMURF?'

Organised crime works on many levels. Prostitution. Drugs. Gambling. Craps games in basements. But all of those things generate cash. Some is put through business to be laundered. Some is spent. The vast bulk is paid into domestic accounts, then moved to offshore accounts in countries that don't ask questions.

'What?' the man says, stammering in fright.

America is an advanced country. Even in 1998, the banking system will trigger if consistent large cash deposits are made.

'Don't what me. Are you a fucking smurf?'

'My arm, man . . . Come on, dude . . . What the . . .'

The smurfs are used to deposit cash. They meet in busy places like mall car parks. The head smurf hands the money out and the smurfs go banking.

'I asked twice. Bored now. I'll break your arm off and shove it up your arse . . .'

The man stares up in horror, unable to comprehend why this beautiful woman with a bruised face and an English accent is beating him up.

A good smurf can deposit one hundred K in one working day. We find a smurf and follow him back to smurf HQ. We will stay discreet. We will remain covert. We will not show out or do anything to draw attention.

'*Safa!*' Miri's voice in her ear.

'Hang on,' Safa tells the man, adding another twist that makes him gasp in pain, '*I think I got one,*' she says, pushing the button on the wire threaded under her shirt.

'*What did you not understand about the word discreet?*' Miri asks, her voice for once showing some emotion – pissed-off emotion, but emotion nonetheless.

'What the fuck?' A deep voice speaks out. Safa snatches her head up to see a big man walking slowly into the alley. 'What'choo doin'?' he asks.

'Piss off,' Safa says, squeezing harder on the wrist in her grip as the man yelps again.

The big man walks slow. His eyes taking in the scene in front of him. A woman holding Lucas by the wrist. He cocks his head, showing mild concern.

'You're a big boy,' Safa says, taking his size in.

'You a cop?' the big man asks, his voice deep and rumbling. His shoulders wide. His arms thick and bulging with muscle. A thick gold necklace round his neck. Gold rings on his fingers. Gold teeth glinting in the dirty rays of the Los Angeles sun filtering through the skyscrapers and made foul by the millions of cars, trucks and people.

'Er,' Safa hesitates, 'sort of . . . Used to be . . . Best say no, not now.'

'Not a cop?' The big man is still walking towards her.

'Maurice?' Lucas yelps as a look of relief washes over his face. 'Get this crazy bitch off me . . .'

'Morris?' Safa asks, chuckling to herself. 'Nice name.'

'My granddaddy name, and it's *Maureece*,' Maurice says with a hard glare.

'Oh,' Safa says, offering a shrug. 'I don't care. Fuck off.'

'You British?' Maurice asks. His instincts tell him she looks like a cop.

'Are we bezzer mates now?' Safa asks. 'Fancy coming to mine for a pizza? Fuck off. ARE YOU A SMURF?' she asks Lucas again, going back to the arm-twisting.

'*SAFA!*'

'Fuck's sake . . .' Safa mutters. '*Yep, go ahead, Miri.*'

'*Where are you?*'

'*Some filthy, stinking, dirty-arse alley with my new best friend, Morris. He's coming round for pizza later.*'

'*What?*' Miri asks.

'What?' Maurice asks.

'Bloody Yanks are deaf,' Safa mutters. 'Right, one more time, then I start breaking things,' she tells Lucas. 'Are you a smurf? Actually, I think you are, so just tell me where the smurf house is and stop pissing about.'

He moves fast for a big man. Safa is beautiful and a woman, but Maurice will mess her up the same as anyone else. Rules are rules, and no one touches his crew.

Safa smiles. Her dark eyes twinkling as she offers a prayer of thanks to the gods of back-alley fights. She pauses, holding Lucas's arm to let Maurice close the distance, and in so doing she gauges speed, motion and how he conveys himself into a fight. By the time Maurice has taken five steps, she knows he is used to dominating by his size alone.

He swings. She ducks, and comes up showing him a middle finger, having dropped the wrist she was holding. Maurice swings out. She weaves, back-stepping and still holding the middle finger up at him. Goading his temper to explode. Maurice's eyes glare with rage. His pride dented. He lunges fast and angry. Safa goes to move back to draw him on, then closes in with her right knee into his groin. That right leg comes down to the floor to reposition, then flies up to strike into the side of his knee. The flat of her left hand hits Maurice's right ear, bursting his ear drum. The flat of her right hand hits his left ear, doing the same again. She stamps down, breaking several toes, and simply steps away as he topples from the points of agony blooming in his body.

Ben runs past the alley, stops and runs back to look down at Safa standing over two bodies. 'What the fuck?'

'Hey,' Safa says, smiling at him. 'Got two. You get any?'

'What?' Ben asks, coming to a stop as Harry does the same and first runs past, stops then runs back into the alley.

'Smurfs. You get any?' Safa asks.

'We're not fishing, Safa,' Ben says, looking at Lucas then at Maurice.

'Big lad,' Harry says, stopping to look down at Maurice.

'Miss Patel,' Miri says, striding down the alley.

'Oh, I'm in the shit.'

'Discreet. Covert,' Miri says, looking with distaste at the groaning Maurice and the too-terrified-to-run-away Lucas.

'Yep,' Safa says. 'Thought we were catching them. Misunderstood. Apologies.'

Miri goes to reply, but spots the earnest look on Safa's face and the wry smiles of Ben and Harry. She should chastise. She should berate and give punishment. Orders are to be followed. Anything less is a loss of discipline. Then again, this is the game and they are in it, and this game has no rules. To play at this level means needing people like Safa. People who can do this. Damn. She wishes she had had Safa when she was active.

'Good work,' Miri says instead, noting the surprise in Safa's face.

'Eh?' Safa asks.

'Please follow my orders in future, but good work,' Miri says curtly.

'Fucking freaks, man,' Lucas wails, looking up in horror.

'Harry, get him up,' Miri says.

'Roger that, ma'am,' Harry says, stepping towards Lucas.

'I am sorry, Miri,' Safa says, feeling strangely repentant. There's something about Miri that makes her want to earn her respect and thanks.

'He's up,' Harry says, holding Lucas by the scruff of the neck, the poor man now on tiptoe as he stares at the group around him, seeing the bruises, cuts and swollen eyes from the fight in the house two days ago.

'I will ask you once,' Miri says, fixing him with her cold grey eyes. 'Where?'

'Where what?' Lucas asks meekly. 'Ma'am,' he adds with a weak smile.

'All yours,' Miri tells Safa, turning away.

'NO!' Lucas bleats. 'No, no, no . . . I can't say anything – they'll kill me.'

Miri slowly turns to look upon the young man. 'So will we,' she says with absolute conviction.

Ben starts going through the big man's pockets, pulling out wads of banknotes.

'I can't,' Lucas says, his voice trembling with fear.

Ben stands up, holding the thick wedge of cash. 'Can't what?' he asks mildly, nicely. Harry lowers Lucas, sensing the new approach. He even reaches out to adjust Lucas's clothes, pulling them gently back to order with a friendly smile. 'Mate, what's your name?' Ben asks.

'Lucas.'

'Okay, listen, Lucas. We're not going to hurt you, okay? You need the money, right? We get that. There's got to be a few thousand here.' Ben offers the cash over, holding it in front of Lucas. 'Yours,' he says. 'Go somewhere else.' Lucas looks at the money, then up to Harry, who smiles again and nods at him, reassuring and pleasant in manner. 'We're going to take their money,' Ben says, looking at Lucas. 'All of it. We need it more than they do. Where is it, mate?'

Lucas blinks a few times, his hands reaching for the money held by Ben. Lucas handles tens of thousands of dollars every day. He banks it for them, but Maurice always knows exactly where he is. This is different. Maurice is down. He can go. He can get out of LA. Go east. He licks his lips, his eyes furtive and cunning.

'Tell you what,' Ben says, smiling kindly. 'Show us where it is, and we'll cut you in. How about that?' That does it. Ben spots the flash of greed in the street hustler's eyes. 'How much they got?'

'Millions,' Lucas whispers.

'Have you seen it?'

Lucas nods, staring at Ben.

'Is it in a house?'

Lucas nods, still staring at Ben.

'Where in the house?'

'Bedroom at the back. Just stacked up. Like, massive, man. Like, so much of it . . . They got men though, loads . . . Guns 'n' shit.'

'We got guns,' Ben says, 'and shit. What's the address?'

'Cut me in, yeah, man?'

'Cut you in,' Ben says.

'I don't gotta go in though . . .'

'Nope, we'll do that.'

Fourteen

'Tell me what happened that led you to being here,' Miri says, the note-pad on her lap. She looks at Tango Two, absorbing, analysing, examining, assessing and knowing fully well the same is being done in return.

Tango Two recounts what she said before. She stays basic. Offering fact but not opinion. She speaks calmly, politely. Holding eye contact where it should be held, and looking away when it is right to do so. When she finishes, the room falls into silence. She does not fill it with sound or speech.

'What is your codename?' Miri asks.

'Tango Two,' Tango Two says.

'Thank you,' Miri says, closing the notepad and standing up. Something is different. Tango Two can sense it.

'Safa will be back soon,' Miri says, closing the door as she goes out. Tango Two stares at the door closing and hears the scrape of metal that she has now seen is a thick pin going into a clasp. That's it. No bolts, no padlocks, no keys. Remarkably simple, yet also remarkably effective.

She prowls the room. Thinking furiously. *Why isn't Miri asking me more questions? Does Miri know why Mother ordered them to kill me? Why isn't the questioning more intense?* Tango Two cannot see the angle. *It doesn't feel right.* Safa brought food yesterday afternoon and could barely hide the grin on her face. Energy was pouring off her too. She was playful and joking. *A guard should not be playful and joking.* It takes months or even years for that level of relationship to grow.

She avoids going near the window because the view is so spectacular it makes her stand for hours and forget everything else. She is also sleeping soundly at night. She thought she must have been drugged to be sleeping so deeply, but she wakes naturally, feeling alert and refreshed.

The whole of it plays on her mind. Questions going round and round. Frustration showing.

'You decent?'

Tango Two immediately changes to that passive-submissive appearance of feet together and her hands held in front. 'I am, yes,' she says. She expected Safa to come later, but Miri has only been gone half an hour.

'Hi,' Safa says, pushing the door open to grin at Tango Two.

'Hi,' Tango Two says. She spots the huge smile and frowns, still wondering what's happened that feels different.

'Want some air? Miri said you can go outside, and the doc seems happy with your injuries.'

'I'd love some, thank you,' Tango Two says, offering that polite smile, while feeling a thrum of excitement inside. Her senses sharpen. Her eyes hardening as she follows Safa out the door to see her set of rooms are at the end of a long corridor lined with metal doors, all the same as hers. It feels empty and somehow new. She can't say why, but she listens to what her senses are telling her.

'Do you know what smurfs are?' Safa asks, turning to walk backwards with that grin showing again.

'Smurfs?' Tango Two asks. 'The little blue people?' She catches glimpses into rooms identical to hers. One middle room with three blue chairs and doors leading to bedrooms.

'That's our rooms,' Safa says, slowing to point in a door. Tango Two hesitates, feeling jarred and weird. She stops behind Safa and peers inside. She could grab Safa's neck in a chokehold, but the memory of her fighting the five agents in Cavendish Manor once again swims through her mind. Safa is too tough. Too fast. *Stay passive.* She looks inside the rooms to show interest. The difference is striking. The same dimensions, but with rugs, bookshelves, lamps, paintings on the walls and soft furnishings, giving a lived-in feel.

'Same as mine,' Tango Two says.

'Yep, all the same,' Safa says, motioning up and down the corridor. 'Have a look at these,' she adds and walks on down to the next door. Tango Two follows, and again stops to peer in.

'Oh, wow,' she says softly. She knows the response was expected, so duly gives it, but she also means it. The rooms are amazing. Armchairs have replaced the blue chairs. The furnishings have been given thought, instead of the ad-hoc nature of the ones Safa just showed her.

'Go in,' Safa says, nodding at her.

'Thank you,' Tango Two says, still hesitant, as though fearing a trap. She blinks at seeing the first bedroom, which looks so cosy and warm. So snug. She tries to stiffen her resolve and remember why she is here. 'Very nice,' she says. 'You share a set of rooms?' she asks, suddenly thinking of all the empty ones she just saw.

'Yep, woke up in there, so just kinda stayed really,' Safa says. 'Ben did these though, with Malc and Kon's help. I think they did it actually, but it was Ben's idea. Either that, or the famous Ben Ryder is good at soft furnishings.'

'Quite,' Tango Two says, smiling at Safa. 'How long have you been here?'

'Stop cultivating me!'

'Sorry.'

'Six months . . . ish . . . Maybe a bit more, dunno. Anyway, stop spying. Did I tell you Miri wanted to call the time machine the Blue, but I said the TM was better? What do you think?'

'Er, right, well, er, both have strong points, and I can see the equal benefits of . . .'

'You'll get splinters in your arse if you're not careful.'

Tango Two smiles back, still confused, but counting the rooms and working out the length of the corridor, noting the surface of the floor and how it echoes from the sound of Safa's boots, but not from her bare feet. She follows Safa down to the next set of doors, feeling that weird conflicting sense of threat while the voice inside tells her there is no threat.

A big room. A long table at one end. Cups, plates, cutlery and things to use as weapons. Her eyes sweep round, taking in the rough-hewn tables and chairs. This is where they eat. A training area on one side. Almost like a dojo, with soft mats on the floor. Boxing gloves, head guards, rubberised bats and sticks against the wall. Safa said they train for combat in the main room. Tango Two spots Ben Ryder and Harry Madden standing with the doctor at a table stacked high with money. US dollars. Lots of US dollars, used banknotes too, judging by the tang of grease hanging in the air. Safa just said smurfs. Smurfs are used to deposit illicit funds. They took a smurf out yesterday and backtracked to the main stash.

Why do that? Why steal money? Is this a criminal operation? Terrorists? Fanatics? Government organisation? No government agency would use some-thing as important as a time machine to disrupt a shitty money-laundering operation. It could be a terrorist organisation. Terrorists need money, but then criminals are easier to exploit than fanatics. The profiles of Safa, Ben and Harry don't fit anything illegal or immoral. All three stand for decency, honesty and courage. But then greed and power can change anyone.

With luck, this will be a bog-standard organised crime syndicate. She'll put the charm on Ben or Harry first chance she gets. If that fails, she'll go for the doctor. The thought repulses her. Ben and Harry are both physically attractive. The doctor isn't, but then men are men, and Alpha said she must do whatever it takes. Tango Two has no idea why Mother ordered her to be killed, but if she can bust this operation, maybe she can erase whatever hostility against her has formed.

'Look at you, still being a spy,' Safa laughs. Tango Two immediately drops her eyes.

'Good morning,' Ben says, turning from the table at hearing Safa. 'How you feeling?'

'Er, fine, thank you,' Tango Two says. She keeps her voice low and timid, and offers a glance up to Ben then across to Harry, playing on the stereotypes of big strong men needing to protect a vulnerable woman.

'Hello, miss,' Harry says, offering her a friendly nod.

'Hello,' she replies. She blinks several times. Emphasising her nerves, while knowing that fluttering, feminine eyelashes sends a subconscious signal to heterosexual men. She widens her eyes at the last second. Like a doe. Meek and bashful. Tiny variances of her body language that start planting seeds.

'We stole loads of money from bad guys,' Ben says, pointing at the huge pile of money.

She nods, then lifts her head to peer over and to show the slenderness of her neck. She adopts an air of being impressed. Men like to be heroes. They seek validation of their exploits and derring-do. 'Wow, that's a lot of money.'

'Want a coffee?'

Tango Two feels a fresh jolt of surprise at realising Safa is at the main table and not immediately next to her. She has been left with space around her. She checks hips, seeing no pistols worn. 'Er, yes. Yes, please,' she says, flicking her gaze constantly to the three men at the table holding the money.

'Poor Maurice,' Ben says with a laugh. 'Safa had this guy in an alleyway, Lucas . . . Little guy . . . She was asking him politely where the smurf house was when Maurice tried to intervene.'

'I wasn't polite.'

'Huge,' Ben says to Tango Two. 'Maurice, I mean. Almost as big as Harry.'

'Aye, big lad,' Harry says.

'Oh,' Tango Two says in a tone suitable to show genuine interest while conveying a sense of worry at the topic of the conversation. *This is good. They are relaxed and laughing. Not a hint of aggression or sullenness. Not a foul look from any of them.*

'So you okay then?' Ben asks, softening his voice. 'You look bruised. You sore?'

'Oh, yes, I am a little,' she replies, touching the bruises on her face while offering a brave smile. 'I'm fine though, really.' Hurt, but brave. Vulnerable, but trying not to show her fear. *Protect me. Help me. I am feminine. You are masculine.*

'You got me a cracker in the back of my head,' Ben says, rubbing it with a wince. 'Still bloody sore.'

'I am so very sorry,' she says earnestly. 'I was following the orders given . . . Truly, I did not know who you were . . .'

'Ah, it's fine,' Ben says, sensing her discomfort. 'Safa got you a few times, by the looks of it.'

'Yes. Yes, she did,' Tango Two says. She clocks the glances between Ben and Safa, and immediately detects the chemistry between them. She responds instantly by switching her gaze to Harry. 'Were you hurt, sir?'

'Ach, it's Harry, miss,' Harry says. His voice is so deep. So masculine. *I am feminine. Protect me.*

'Harry, thank you,' she says softly. 'You look bruised.'

'Had worse, miss.'

He speaks simply and honestly, without a shred of boasting.

'I'd say between ten and fifteen million dollars,' Doctor Watson says after a thorough medical examination of the pile of money, which consisted of counting one wad then multiplying it by lots.

'No way?' Safa says from the table. 'Fuck me, Roland would have a fit.'

'Miri's not Roland, that's for sure,' Ben says, looking back at the money.

'Say that again,' Safa says.

'Miri's not Roland, that's for sure,' Ben says, grinning at Safa tutting and calling him a twat.

Miri is not Roland. Roland was in charge. Miri is now in charge. Tango Two wishes Roland was still in charge. It's far easier to manipulate a man than a woman. There has been a recent change in leadership. *Good. Easier to exploit.*

'Right,' Safa says, walking over with two mugs, 'that's yours . . . but actually they're both black with no sugar, so it doesn't matter, but fuck it, have that one anyway.'

'Thank you.'

'Don't throw it in anyone's face,' Safa says.

'Okay.'

'And stop trying to honey-trap Ben and Harry.'

'Pardon?' Tango Two balks at the suggestion, staring wide-eyed in innocent response, then immediately worries she overplayed it.

'We'll go outside,' Safa says, offering a grimace at the money. 'That stinks. Do you want breakfast now or you okay for a minute?'

'Money always does smell,' Doctor Watson says. 'Handled by so many people.'

'I, er, I can wait . . . sure,' Tango Two says quietly.

'You coming out?' Safa asks Ben and Harry.

'Aye, I'll have a smoke,' Harry says.

'Yeah, I'll come out,' Ben adds.

Safa takes the lead. She is Safa. She always takes the lead. She goes through the doors into a second corridor, holding it open again for Tango Two, who in turn holds it open for Ben Ryder behind her. The surrealness of it hits again. She is holding a door open for Ben Ryder.

134

'Thanks,' he says, smiling nicely. She smiles back. Coy and shy. A quick flutter of lashes as she looks down and away.

They walk through with Safa giving a running commentary. 'That's Malc and Kon's rooms, which we're leaving as they are UNTIL WE GO AND GET THEM . . .'

'No,' Miri's voice comes from somewhere.

'You're in a good mood again, Safa,' Ben says, grinning as Safa flicks him a middle finger.

Flirting. That was flirting.

'And that's the portal room. Oh, I forgot to call you a shithead for killing Malc and Kon.'

'I am so sorry for their loss, but it wasn't me,' Tango Two says, struggling to understand the jibe. It should be malicious and full of spite, but despite the foul language Safa uses, nothing she says is spiteful or malicious, just very direct. Safa has influence here. The way she speaks and moves. A sense of leadership about her. *Be friends with her. Get her onside.*

'Anyway, so that's the portal room where you first came in . . . And that's Roland's office, or at least it was. It's now Miri's office,' she says.

Tango Two stops behind Safa to look through the door at Miri behind a roughly made wooden desk. Sheets of paper stacked up. Notepads one on top of each other and a sizable stack of newspapers on the floor. She spots an ancient-looking electrical device on the desk. Like an old smartphone. It still has wires wrapped round it. No one uses wires anymore.

Miri stares back, seeing the passive, easy way the agent looks round while scrutinising every detail. 'Are you telling the prisoner our secrets, Miss Patel?'

'Only the shit ones, Miri,' Safa says, walking on. 'So, this is important. This thing is a . . . a thing that makes it . . . so it . . . Ben, what is it?'

'Filtration system,' Ben says as Safa stops below the machine fitted to the sides and above a door at the end of the corridor. 'That door leads outside,' Ben explains. 'We might have bacteria or things on us that could harm the world out there; likewise, we could take something from outside to another time era and cause harm . . .'

'Cross-contamination,' Tango Two says.

'Exactly,' Ben says. 'We pause underneath that and it apparently neutralises anything harmful.'

'Understood,' Tango Two says. 'Tech labs use them all the time.'

'Yeah, Malc and Kon fitted them.' Ben pauses, offering a down-turned smile. 'And we haven't killed everyone yet . . . As far as we know anyway.'

'You'll love this,' Safa says, pushing the door open. She pauses and walks through to the outside world. Tango Two follows. Staring up at the metal fittings that look like old air-conditioning units, then stepping through.

'Round here,' Safa calls out.

Tango Two complies dutifully. Walking on springy stems that are like grass, but much thicker. The air too. She could eat it. It's so gloriously pure. She walks round the edge of the bunker. Wooden chairs left outside. Weatherproof gun containers. No locks on them. A range set up for firing. A table at the side. She goes closer to Safa, knowing that is what she is expected to do, and looks down the side of the hill. All other thoughts cease. All worries fade. The view she saw from her window is a mere snapshot of this vista. The valley is so big. So wide. So long. So full of life.

It's like the air is taken from her lungs and the blood drains from her brain. Like her legs are suddenly not hers. She staggers in shock. A big hand on her elbow. A deep voice asking if she is okay. She blinks up at Harry, not faking the heavy blinking this time. She nods and looks back down the valley.

'Takes a while to adjust,' Ben says from close by.

'Understatement,' Safa mutters.

The magnitude of it dwarfs her. The sheer incomprehension of being so far back in time that it renders her entire existence meaningless. She is a speck of dust and nothing more.

The creatures are so big. Even at this distance, and without proper scale, she gets the measure of them. Long necks. Broad backs. Huge legs. Tails that go on forever.

So many different types too. Big ones. Small ones. Single ones that look enormous in comparison to the others. Herds that cluster together. Shimmering lakes of water. Thickets and copses of trees. Wide-open spaces.

Tango Two didn't realise Ben was next to her. She can see the scar on his cheek. She looks to her other side at Safa. The shape of her eyes. The darker skin tone and pure black hair. She looks past her to Harry. *When did he move away?* The man is enormous. His chest is bloody massive. His bushy black beard and unruly dark hair. He lights a cigarette and blows the smoke out with the manner of a contented man, but she saw him fight. She saw him lift Alpha off his feet with one hand. Visions of him holding the operatives off at the top of the stairs fill her mind. The strength of the man. The vicious way he fought. Now he looks completely at ease, so calm and genial. He senses her watching, and turns to smile.

'Did you want a cigarette, miss?'

'No. No, thank you,' she murmurs.

Too many thoughts. Too many sensations. She faces forward and looks down to a world lost and now found again.

'I don't know why they tried to kill me,' she says suddenly, without any idea she was going to say it. She feels instantly stupid and berates herself harshly inside. A loss of control brought on by the shock of being here.

Ben frowns and goes to speak, but drops his head to scratch his jaw, and doesn't notice Safa staring intently at him.

Miri stands by the window in her office. A wire running from the single earphone in her left ear to the smartphone in her hand. Her cold grey eyes tracking the four outside.

'Ah, bollocks,' Safa says with a sudden groan. 'We didn't give Lucas his cut.'

Fifteen

Tango Two sleeps deeply. She lay in bed for a while thinking about the day. They spent a while outside staring in silence until a screech made her jump back. The others pointed up at two black objects plummeting towards them. At the last second, they both opened their wings and sailed over the ledge to swoop down the valley side. They were like pterodactyls from the holomovies, with big, curved beaks and enormous wingspans. She couldn't help but laugh in wonder at the sight, and ventured closer to the edge to watch them once again tuck their wings in to drop like missiles, then soar up on thermals, seemingly dancing round each other.

She then listened as the other three told her about the time they ventured up into the forest and described the creatures they saw. The plants and bugs. A spider nest, then a small dinosaur that ate the spiders. She even pulled a sympathetic face at Harry shuddering in memory. Big men don't like bugs sometimes.

When they went back inside to get food, Miri was gone and the portal was shining blue and glorious. Ben asked the doctor where Miri was. He mumbled he didn't know and went back to reading a newspaper. Safa then said they were eating outside because of the stench of the money.

They later explained how they got the doctor from the ocean and how Harry and Safa *died*, but didn't die because Ben went back for them. They were *dead* for ten days, but they were never dead because Ben went back to the exact time they were in the ocean.

Throughout the day, she didn't probe or ask questions other than to clarify points of the discussion. She also laughed a lot. The humour between them was very strong. The quasi-bantering, flirting abuse between Safa and Ben. The dry quips from Harry. Tango Two kept forgetting to flirt, and listened with rapt attention. When she did remember, it often felt too forced, too clumsy and too weird. Like the mere attempt was instantly deflected by the energy between them.

From the whole of it, she understood that Ben suffered a reaction to the medication given when they first arrived. It made him decline into severe mental depression almost to the point of suicide. Something happened that started a fight between Harry and Ben. The fight ended badly, and Harry and Safa rescued the doctor to help Ben. This was only recently too. *Is that something to exploit? To pit Ben against Harry. Maybe when the time is right, she can tell Harry she is scared of Ben, that he frightens her, the way he looks at her . . .*

The rest of the day was spent the same. She ate lunch and dinner with them and wasn't locked in her room until evening, when Miri came back.

One thing became very clear. Ben is very intelligent, and it was obvious he was struggling not to ask questions and find out more about her. When he did start, he either got a comment from Safa or stopped himself. That told her Miri has control and has given explicit instructions.

They didn't even ask her name. She felt a bit strange at that. Like she wanted them to ask. She almost told them, but held back.

All of those thoughts came and went in the five minutes it took to get into bed and fall asleep. Now she snores in a sleep deeper than she has had for a long time.

Safa sleeps. Harry sleeps. Ben was reading for a few minutes, but now sleeps with the book dropped on his chest. Doctor Watson snores loudly. Like a walrus having a fight with a whale.

Miri does not sleep. There is work to do, and she doesn't sleep so good these days. These days? She snorts to herself in the shadows of the alley in Berlin. She hasn't slept soundly for years. Many years.

She thinks about the Blue and how the British government tracked it. The fact the staging area was attacked means someone found it. How?

It was while debriefing Roland that she found out about the mass brawl in the bunker that resulted in several hired men being killed and several more being seriously injured. It took all day, but eventually she was able to witness Malcolm and Konrad loading the injured men into a van.

Reading the newspapers taught her the world descended into more private wars, and private wars need mercenaries. Mercs get injured the same as soldiers, so a smaller industry flourished, with private hospitals that give treatment for cash. Berlin has two private hospitals, and she now stands in the shadows of an alley across the road from the one closest to the staging area.

This kind of work used to be time-consuming and gritty. Weeks or months would sometimes be given to backtracking to find trails of evidence. Having a time machine certainly makes it easier. The concept of time. The ability to see what is ahead and plan accordingly, and for someone like Miri that is a powerful thing.

The sound of engines brings her attention fully back to the clinic over the road. Two private ambulances stop outside the brightly lit private hospital. Five men dressed in the green jumpsuits of paramedics disembark and chat noisily as they stretch, as though from a long journey. One of them takes a tablet and starts checking the vehicles over, looking in the back, overtly doing a standard equipment check.

She lifts the single-lens, military-grade sight-magnification device to watch as the man holding the tablet saunters into the clinic towards the pretty woman behind the reception desk. They talk for a while. They start flirting. Subtle and carefully done.

The other four paramedics go into the clinic. The one with the tablet stays with the woman at the desk. A short while later a different exit door opens and six men in hospital gowns are helped to the two ambulances. They are hurt, and move as if they are drugged or medicated.

Miri switches the view to the man at the desk and the way he is leaning towards the woman, who in turn is making eyes back at him. Miri waits. Holding the view. One of the other paramedics goes in and says something. The man at the desk turns, and after a few seconds walks out with some lingering smiles at the receptionist.

The two ambulances drive off. Miri watches the receptionist use a smartphone. Sending a message? Something in her manner suggests she is trying to hide what she is doing. The way she glances up and round, but keeps the phone low before swiping it off and going about her duties.

Miri lowers the lens and thinks. The man Harry lifted up on the middle floor of the house was the man at the desk. She recognised a couple of the others too.

Several factors come to mind. The first brings a surge of irritation that Roland led the British government to them. He might as well have opened the door and invited them in. How the British government got wind of the device in the first place is now a moot point. They know it exists, and if they know, then you can be damn sure the US, Russia and China also know. The Brits had no right to try and deal with it on their own. They should have sought help. The incident in Berlin would have focussed attention. The attack on Roland's house would have done it too, and the two incidents were only a couple of hours apart in real time.

If the world's superpowers even suspect the Brits have a time travel device, it could trigger a nuclear war. Heck, this very thing could be what causes the world to be destroyed by 2111.

Her mind processes the new information and applies it to everything else she already knows to gain the path ahead. There is always a path ahead. There is always a way through it. That's her job. To find it then fix the problem.

She pauses before returning to the Blue. Enjoying the buzz inside. She's back in the game and at the very front. This is her pitted against the whole world. Her mind against everyone else's. There are no rules now either. No politicians saying what can and can't be done. No budget restrictions. No policy demands. No protocols. This is the game, but with every rule stripped away, and it feels glorious. She even has a team. She thought they were inept, but how they handled the attack in Cavendish Manor was sublime. With training, her team could be exceptional pawns to deploy and use. They have a high moral code, and that can be manipulated.

One thing is damn sure. She has to remain in total control, and that means Roland can never be let near the Blue or the team ever again.

Sixteen

Night follows day follows night. It always has. It always will. The hours of darkness finally recede to a new dawn of a new day, and Safa Patel comes wide awake with the blink of an eye and the realisation she hasn't exercised for six days now.

'Get up, beardy, we'll train before breakfast.' She bangs on Harry's door, pausing to listen to the gruff affirmations coming from inside.

'Mr Ryder? This is your fuck-early wake-up call . . .'

'Piss off.'

'Get up. We'll train before food.'

'Said piss off.'

She cracks the door open to see him pulling the covers over his head and snuggling further down the bed.

'Safa.' His muffled voice comes through the blanket. 'Safa? I know you're standing there . . . Piss off . . . Seriously . . . Fuck's sake,' he mumbles, pushing the cover from his head to see her grinning. Weak daylight behind her from the window in the middle room. Dressed in knickers and a vest top. Her hair tousled. Her teeth white. He blinks, squints then groans to hide the bad thought that popped into his head. 'Okay, I'll get up in a minute.'

'Do you like Miri?'

'What!?'

'Miri. Do you like her?'

'Safa, I literally just opened my eyes . . . Yes. Yes, she seems fine.'

'I like her. Do you trust her?'

'Oh, my god, Safa . . . Yes. Yes, I trust her.'

'What about Tango Two?'

'Huh?'

'She seems alright, doesn't she?'

'What were you expecting?' Ben asks with only one eye half-open.

'Should I ask her if she wants to train?'

'What the actual fuck?' Ben blinks as the bad thought pops into his head again, and wishes she wouldn't lift her top to scratch her back like that. 'If I say yes, will you go away?' He drops his forehead on to the pillow, making a point of not looking. 'She is a prisoner though, Safa,' he adds.

'Yeah, but the bad guys tried to kill her . . . Okay, forget it, just an idea.'

'Ask Miri.'

◆ ◆ ◆

'Miri? You awake? It's Safa . . . Miri? Miri?' Safa stops knocking and calling out to lean closer to the door and listen.

'Help you?' Miri says, standing in the doorway to her office, fully dressed and already holding a notepad and pen.

Safa spins round, stunned that someone wakes up earlier than her. 'Can the prisoner train with us?'

'Yes.'

'Because . . . What?'

'Yes.'

'She can?'

'Yes.'

'What, just like that?'

'Yes.'

'Why did they try and kill her?'

'Working on it.'

'Er.' Safa pauses, expecting to have to argue. 'She seems alright, doesn't she?' she adds in a rare show of deep thought.

'She is a prisoner,' Miri says bluntly.

'Yeah, but, you know, seems okay for a prisoner,' Safa says. 'You training with us?'

'No.'

'Why not? We'll go light. We're all still a bit sore from . . .'

'No. Anything else, Safa?'

'Er . . . nope, don't think so. We're running out of food.'

'I will re-supply today. Anything else, Safa?'

'Malc and Kon . . . When are we . . .'

'Goodbye, Safa,' Miri says, walking back into her office. 'The pistols are now secured in the last set of rooms by the exit door. I have fitted a clasp with a combination padlock. The number is 01899.'

'That's my collar number,' Safa says. 'In the police . . .'

'I know. Enjoy your training.'

'But . . .'

'Train, Miss Patel. Train hard. I need your team fit and ready for deployment.'

'Roger,' Safa says, sensing she is being told to piss off.

◆ ◆ ◆

Tango Two comes awake suddenly, the same rapid surge from deep slumber to wide awake in a few seconds. She sits bolt upright in bed as the knocking comes again.

'Coming in,' Safa says, pushing the door open to look at Tango Two. 'Fancy training?'

'What?' Tango Two whispers, then coughs to clear her throat. 'Sorry, what did you say?'

'Training. We're doing phys. You fancy it? Nothing heavy. We're still sore.'

'Right,' Tango Two says, staring with the look of someone who has come awake too quickly. 'I don't have a bra.'

Safa nods. 'Bouncy boobs, yeah, that's not funny. We threw yours away. Had blood on it. Er, I've got a spare one, it might stretch a bit . . . Any good?'

'Er . . . yes. Yes, thank you.'

'Sports bra, so it'll be stretchy anyway.'

'Right.'

'I'll go get it.'

'Okay,' Tango Two says as Safa marches off, pulling the outer door closed behind her. This is very good. The bond is already starting to show. She suspects counter-cultivation is underway, but that's fine. Spending time with them is exactly what she needs to do. Another thought pops into her head as she rushes into the bathroom. Safa was a police officer, Ben investigated insurance and Harry was in the Second World War. How can they be trained to a high level of counter-cultivations and manipulation?

It doesn't matter. It means she gets time with Ben and Harry, and she needs to maximise that opportunity. Should she shower? Does she smell? She sniffs at her armpits, and has a shower.

'OUT HERE,' Safa calls through the door. 'ON THE CHAIR.'

'Thank you,' Tango Two calls back. She washes, dries off, then winces as she puts the still wet knickers on. She washed them in the sink last night and they're still damp. As she puts the grey tracksuit bottoms on, she realises the wet knickers will make the material of the trousers wet, and damp shows on grey cotton too easily. She frets for a second. Not wishing to be seen with wet knickers under her bottoms. Should she take the knickers off? But then she would be naked under the bottoms. She could ask for another pair and suspects being given only one set of underwear is part of the strategy. To ask for something leaves her open for leverage. She will have to suffer and try to look as good as she can with what she has.

She scowls at the bitterness that thought leaves in her mind. Mother tried to kill her. These people are being decent and nice. Is she worried about her appearance solely for the prospect of honey-trapping Ben or Harry?

Shit. No shoes. The bra is bloody tight too. She squeezes into it, giving what thanks she can for it being Lycra and stretchy. Oh, actually, it makes her boobs look huge. That's a good thing, plus she can honestly say it's not her fault as the bra is too small.

With a hundred thoughts in her head, and for the first time since joining the British Secret Service, Tango Two feels like a twat. Her boobs are squashed, her arse and groin are wet and she doesn't have any shoes. She frets and berates herself as she waits for Safa to come back, then realises, with her mouth dropping open, that the main door isn't closed.

She peers out into the corridor. Bending forward from the waist to look down. 'Hello?'

'COME DOWN,' Safa shouts.

Tango Two blinks. Ponders for a few seconds, then waddles down the corridor with one hand plucking at her wet knickers through the jogging bottoms and the other tugging at the bra under the vest top. She has to look as good as she can with what she has. *Switch on and work now.* 'Er . . . hi?' she says meekly.

'Morning,' Ben says, standing in the middle room with one foot on a chair as he bends over tying his laces. He looks half-asleep with his voice still deep from slumber.

'Morning,' Harry says, walking from his room and glancing at her wet jogging bottoms and chest bulging through the vest top in a polite *avert-the-eyes-quickly* way that makes Tango Two actually blush and want the ground to open up.

'I am so sorry, but I don't have any . . .' Tango Two says as Safa strides out from her room holding a pair of trainers.

'Will they fit? Miri's going for supplies today, so we'll get you some gear.'

◆ ◆ ◆

'Ben,' Safa snaps.

'What?' Ben asks, looking up at her.

'Stretch properly, you'll pull a muscle.'

'I am.'

'You're not.'

Ben stretches properly, grimacing at the pain in his hamstrings.

'Better,' Safa says, almost bent double as she forces her chest into her knees.

Tango Two stretches. Bent over the same as the others to ease the muscles in the backs of their legs. It's so beautiful out here. The sun just rising to bathe the world in glorious orange hues. Noises screech from somewhere above the hillside. A thunderous racket of wood snapping, then it goes silent.

'That happens,' Safa says, seeing her looking round while bent double.

The gun containers are gone. They must have been locked away somewhere.

'Shoes fit okay?' Ben grunts the question out, red-faced from bending over.

'Bit tight, but fine, thank you,' Tango Two says. The tips of her toes are pushing against the end of the shoes, and if she runs any distance she'll create blisters on her heels from not wearing socks. A wet arse.

Squashed boobs and feet, and she's looking across at Ben Ryder and Harry Madden while Safa Patel is telling them to stand up slowly.

They stretch each muscle group. Going slowly and carefully, easing into each stretch. Tango Two knows she isn't the only one still a bit sore from the fight they had. The big fight. The one where she was fighting against these three. That one.

'. . . off if you want,' Safa says.

'Pardon?' Tango Two asks, realising Safa was talking to her, and instantly chastising herself for the lack of focus.

'Shoes, take them off if they're too tight. You'll get blisters and fuck your toes up.'

'Er . . .'

'We're only staying out here,' Safa says, nodding at the side of the bunker.

'I, er . . . I'll keep that in mind, thank you.'

'You are very polite,' Harry says to her, pulling his right arm across his body with his left hand digging into the back of his right elbow.

'I, er . . . Thank you.'

'She is polite,' Ben says by way of conversation. 'Safa's not polite,' he adds by way of observation.

'No,' Harry says.

'Fuck you,' Safa says mildly.

Tango Two grins. She didn't want to grin, but she does. She coughs to hide the giggle that suddenly threatened to come out.

'You okay?' Ben asks at the strange sound she just made.

'Fine,' she smiles at Ben, then remembers Harry is the one she should be flirting with and switches to smile at him instead.

'You okay, miss?' he asks at seeing the strange smile.

'Fine.' She stops smiling.

'We'll run for a bit, then stretch again,' Safa says.

Tango Two follows the others to the imaginary start line, which is marked by the corner of the bunker.

'Just gently,' Safa says, jogging on at a very gentle pace.

She stays with them. Jogging lightly up and down. Her toes hurt. She wants to take the shoes off. She views the ground for debris that could harm her feet, but sees nothing. What about insects? Does the Cretaceous period have insects? What about poisonous plants? She reaches the start line, about-turns with the others and runs back up. Nope. The shoes really have to come off.

'Limping,' Safa says, jogging next to her. 'Take 'em off.'

They all stop as she bends, pulls out the laces and places the trainers neatly to the side.

'Ready?' Safa asks.

'Yes, thank you.'

She stays with them. Jogging lightly up and down and feeling the spongy foliage under her bare feet with the instant relief from not having her toes cramped.

The pace builds up steadily. Nothing frantic. Nothing too fast. Just easy. Safa dictates the pace, and from that, Tango Two begins to understand Safa is actually very good at this. She knows they all got hurt, so adapts to allow for it.

It feels nice to be moving, and that air is so pure. She glances down the valley side then at the sky and runs up and down. She starts breathing more heavily, and hears Ben and Harry do the same. As the pace increases, so Tango Two starts to sweat lightly, and again notices the same with the two men. Safa isn't even breathing hard, she looks as fresh as when they walked out. Tango Two has a high level of fitness, but Safa must be in another league.

'I'm going to push a bit more, but stop if you want,' Safa calls across. She reaches the start line, about-turns and applies some power to her legs. The others follow suit. Keeping pace. At the next turn, she goes a bit faster. Not sprinting, but fast enough to get their arms pumping. To the last, they each feel the pleasure of the motion. Lungs expanding. Legs thrumming. Heads clearing.

'I'm done,' Harry says as he slows at the start line. His head still tender from the battering Alpha gave him.

'Yep,' Ben says at the next turn, easing to jog past the imaginary line.

'Stop if you want. Not competing,' Safa says.

'Thanks,' Tango Two says. She feels like she should stop so it doesn't appear she is trying to compete, but it's nice to be running.

Safa applies more speed to the end of the bunker and belts it back down. Tango Two stays at her side. Arms pumping. Legs buzzing. Lungs opening.

'Out,' Tango Two gasps, running past the start line.

Now Safa goes for it. There is no risk to anyone now. She sprints hard up and down. Turning fast with a fluidity that is a joy to watch.

'Water,' Ben says, nodding at the cups next to the flask on the table. 'Help yourself.'

'Thanks.' Tango Two pours a cup while watching Safa. The woman is incredible. Her level of fitness is far greater than she initially thought.

Ben sips his water and muses over the thoughts he had of Safa this morning when she came into his room.

In truth, those thoughts were simply her climbing into his bed so he could sleep next to her. That's all it was. That sleepy fug of wanting someone to hold. Now he feels like a creep for thinking it, and looks away. She came into his room when he was sick. He remembers it vaguely. No, he remembers it perfectly; the vagueness comes from his state of mind at that time, like it wasn't him. Safa is beautiful, but she is more than that. She is perhaps the single most incredible person he has ever met. Just to know her is an honour, and for that reason he banishes any thoughts of anything else. The memory of the ocean pops into his mind. Did they kiss? He thought so at the time, but now, looking back and remembering the waves and the noise, the fear, the adrenalin and pure frenzy of it all, he isn't so sure. Ah. Be a decent human being. Don't be a dick.

'Fucking fuck, that was so fucking good,' Safa exclaims to the world as she finally stops. Ben chuckles and turns back to see her bent over with her hands on her knees. She stands straight, breathing deep to regulate her diaphragm. A look from her to Tango Two. A simple glance that Tango Two immediately understands. She pours a cup of water as Safa walks over. 'Thanks, shithead,' Safa says, still breathing hard, but only sweating lightly.

People in service used to do this all the time. Give abuse by way of endearment. The British Secret Service doesn't promote the use of banter. Instead, it promotes individual excellence and an allegiance to the service itself. Is being called a shithead a term of endearment, or is Safa actually being abusive?

'Few circuits?' Safa asks everyone.

'Yep,' Ben says.

'Aye,' Harry says.

'Thank you,' Tango Two says.

◆ ◆ ◆

Miri moves back from the window. The wire stretches from her left ear to the smartphone in her hand. At the desk, she puts the device down, and sits with her palms flat against the rough-hewn wood.

Time passes. Time will always pass, but time is not fixed. Every action has a reaction. Every behaviour elicits a behaviour in response. Understanding behaviours is what she does. Stripping away all the frills to scrutinise the bare bones of the individual. To see them react when passive and when threatened. To see the perception of them through their own eyes and through the eyes of others. To know all those things and apply them to everything else.

She stays motionless. Focussed. Entirely and utterly focussed, and loving every minute of it.

After a time, she hears them filing in through the back door and grabs the top newspaper from the pile beside her desk. She opens it somewhere near the middle and adopts a perfect persona of being absorbed.

'. . . yes, but I am still sore,' Ben says, humour in his voice.

'So how does it feel knowing both women did more press-ups than you?' Safa asks. Miri listens to the tones and inflections. She hears Tango Two laugh and a comment from Harry.

'Ma'am,' Harry says, passing by her door with the prisoner behind him. Tango Two looks flushed and rosy. Smiling broadly from the endorphins released by exercise and the humour of the others.

'Mr Ryder, Miss Patel. A word. Sergeant Madden, take Tango Two into the main room.'

'Roger,' Harry says. Miri clocks the uncertainty that flits across Tango Two's face at hearing she will be alone with Harry. The chemistry between Ben and Safa is strong. Tango Two will see that. The doctor is too old and not such an intrinsic part. Miri knows Harry is the viable option.

'What's up?' Safa asks, breathing hard from the exercise and looking ridiculously healthy.

'You okay?' Ben asks, wiping the sweat from his forehead with the back of his arm.

'Good training?'

'Er, yeah, fine,' Ben says. 'Why?'

'The prisoner? Any issues?'

'Seems okay,' Safa says. 'Did more press-ups than Ben anyway.'

'I said I was still sore.'

'Sore loser,' Safa coughs into her hand.

Miri folds the newspaper she was reading. 'I will be going for supplies. What does the prisoner need?'

'Everything,' Safa replies.

'What's happening with her?' Ben asks. 'She's been here six days now.'

'I'm working on it.'

'I appreciate that, Miri. I'd like to know your plans.'

'And I will tell you when the time is right.'

'Or, you know, maybe you could include us a bit more now. We're debriefing with you every day. I guess you're going to Roland, Bertie and Ria too. Tango Two is briefing with you. How long does that process take?'

'As long as it takes.'

Ben draws breath. Safa stays quiet. She knows how frustrated Ben is at not knowing. They talk about it a lot.

'We're not idiots.'

'No, you are intelligent people. You, Mr Ryder, are an exception ally intelligent man, and I will include you when I can, but there is a process. Give me time to do my work.'

'Fine,' Ben says. It's the same answer she always gives. 'So it's okay for the prisoner to spend time with us?'

'For now, but you will understand, all of you will understand, that it is my decision what we do with the prisoner. The world is at risk. We will not lose sight of that.'

'What's that mean?' Safa demands.

'Means she's not sure,' Ben says.

'You going to kill her?' Safa asks, the alarm showing clear and obvious. 'She seems really nice.'

Miri stares at them, letting the silence speak volumes. 'Provide me with a list of the things you need. I will be going shortly. Thank you, Miss Patel and Mr Ryder.'

Seventeen

'Trainers.'

'Thank you.'

'Normal clothes for chilling out and stuff.'

'Thank you.'

'Proper tracksuit bottoms for training.'

'Thank you.'

'Stop cultivating me.'

'Sorry.'

'Bras . . . So I forgot to ask what size you were. I'm 34B. Miri and me guessed you'd be 34C?'

'I am.'

'Alright, big boobs, don't go on about them.'

'I really wasn't.'

'Sports bras and a couple of normal ones . . . No lacy shit, so don't try and honey-trap Ben or Harry.'

'Right, of course not,' Tango Two says, staring at the bed now piled with clothes.

'It all looks okay,' Safa says, standing next to her. 'I was worried she might get crappy stuff. They went to a Walmart in Milwaukee. How messed-up is that? She got them with the doctor. Oh, that bag has loads

Executed

of toiletry bits, shampoo and things. I said to get conditioner. If she got cheap stuff, just say, and you can use mine. Malc and Kon got decent kit for us before you killed them. She put tampons in there too.'

'Thank you.'

'Do women still have periods in the future?'

'Yes.'

Safa tuts. 'Bit shit. Do you get moody?'

'Me? Er, well, we take medication, so we can . . . you know . . .'

'What?' Safa asks.

'Not have a period if we're on an active mission.'

'Oh. They have that in my time, but doesn't it mess your body up? I never took it, but then I don't get that moody. Not like crying and things, like some women do. Bit of tummy pain. Do you get that?'

'Yes, unfortunately,' Tango Two says with a grimace.

'Ha! Look at us, having girly period chats. Who is cultivating who?'

'Indeed.' Tango Two smiles back at her.

'Is she debriefing you?'

'Miri?'

'She's debriefing us, but she takes ages. But you're . . .'

'She's debriefing you?' Tango Two asks, cutting in without realising it.

'Yeah, we only met the same day we got Bertie and Roland out.'

'What?' Tango Two says, clearly shocked.

'Stop spying, shithead.'

'I'm not! You just told me.'

'I'm joking. Yeah, so she takes ages with us, but you're done really quickly.'

'She doesn't ask me anything,' Tango Two says, dropping her voice a little.

'What, nothing?' Safa asks.

157

'Well, I mean, she asks me what happened that led to being here. That's it. Oh, and she asked my codename. Why haven't you asked my name? My real name, I mean.'

'Miri said not to. So . . . is this not normal then?'

'Pardon?'

'What we're doing with you. Is it not normal?'

Tango Two hesitates and suppresses the urge to be honest and say, no, it's not bloody normal; it's not anywhere near normal. 'I guess so,' she says instead.

'Has she asked why your side tried killing you?'

'No. Nothing. Why? Do you know something?' Tango Two asks, then instantly berates herself again for forgetting to keep her guard up.

'Me? I don't know anything,' Safa admits. 'I keep asking Miri, but she just says she is working on it.'

Honesty. Raw honesty. There is no doubt in Tango Two's mind that Safa is being brutally open. She sighs and shakes her head. 'I don't know, Safa. Really, I've got no clue.'

'Did you do something then? Or maybe something you didn't do? Like shoot Bertie? Maybe they told you to shoot Bertie, and you didn't. Was that it?'

'No. We just had to secure him. I mean, they did say we could kill if it prevented escape, but I had him. I had him right there with me.'

Stop it. Stop opening up. Be reticent and passive. Be ignorant.

'Got to be a reason.'

'I . . . Safa, has Miri asked you to ask me all this?'

Safa looks at her in earnest, a slight twitch at the corners of her mouth. 'I'd tell her to fuck off if she did. I don't play games like that. Never have and never will.'

Tango Two searches for a sign of deceit, but again feels only pure honesty. She can't help but like Safa too. There is something about her. Her humour. Her direct way of speaking.

'I don't lie. I hate lying. If I knew why they tried to kill you, I'd tell you, and if Miri told me not to tell you, I'd just tell you to fuck off. So you're an agent?'

'In the British Secret Service.'

'What's that?'

'It's, er, well, it was formed after you actually.'

'Me?' Safa asks, pushing some of the clothes aside to sit on the bed.

'After the attack on Downing Street . . .'

'My attack?'

'Yes, it was, er . . . So you don't know any of this?'

'Not a clue.'

'Right. Did you know it was the same group that attacked Ben at Holborn station?'

'Fuck, no way. Was it really?'

'You really don't know this?'

'No! Hang on, come for a coffee and tell Ben at the same time.'

'Er,' Tango Two says, looking down at the clothes she has been wearing for several days.

'Oh, yeah, get changed,' Safa says, standing up. 'You don't have to come for coffee.'

'No, I would like to.'

'Okay, shithead. I'll wait out here.'

Think. Stay clear. They are pumping you for information. These are the entry topics to get you talking. Be smart. Be earnest. Stay passive. I am not a threat.

'That feels better,' she says, walking out to the middle room.

'Yeah?' Safa asks, taking in the new clothes. 'Fit alright?'

'Perfect, thank you,' Tango Two says, smiling at her. She feels different now too. Less jarred and more human from the boost of being comfortable in the clothes she wears.

She follows Safa down to the main room, blinking at the big table stacked high with food. Bowls of fresh fruit and vegetables. Tins,

159

packets, bottles, jars. Trays of eggs. Loaves of bread. Jars of coffee. Boxes of teabags and tubs of powdered chocolate to make hot drinks with. Books too. Stacked on one of the other tables. Loads of paperbacks in all manner of colours. Ben and Harry walk in from the other set of doors, both carrying more supplies that are set down by the food table.

'You look better,' Ben calls over. 'Everything fit okay?'

'Fine, thank you,' Tango Two says, strolling to the table piled with books.

'Reader?' Harry asks, walking over.

'Love reading,' she replies. 'Do you?'

'Oh, aye,' he says in that rumbling, deep voice. 'It's all so different now.'

'Oh, of course. So . . . what did you read, er . . . well, before?'

'Anything really. Was hard to get books in the war. Read the same things all the time. Lot of westerns and romance.'

'Romance?' she asks, smiling up at him.

'Ach,' he says easily, 'what's this one?'

'Oh, er . . . maybe not a good choice.'

'*Fifty Shades of* . . .'

'What about this one?' Tango Two says quickly. 'Harry Potter.'

'Harry Potter? Western, is it?'

'Er, no, more, er . . . well, fantasy. Wizards . . . It's about a boy who goes to wizard school. I mean, it was written decades before I was born, but it's a classic.'

'What's a classic?' Ben asks, walking over.

'Harry Potter,' Tango Two says.

'Oh, you'll love it,' Ben tells Harry. He smiles at Tango Two, then regards Harry with a mock-studious look. 'Hagrid?'

'He does, yes,' she says as Harry looks slightly bemused.

'Coffee,' Safa says.

'Thank you,' Tango Two says, taking the mug. 'Do you read?'

'God, no, bores the shit out of me,' Safa says. 'Ben, Tango says the same people that attacked you at Holborn did my one at Downing Street.'

Tango. Safa shortened her codename. Tango Two notes it silently. 'Environmental activists,' she says. 'That's why my service was formed.'

'Your service?' Ben asks.

'British Secret Service. After Holborn, they armed all the British police, and then a few years after Holborn, they attacked Downing Street. The government realised just how organised the terrorists were becoming . . . I mean, that attack nearly killed the Prime Minister . . . Safa, did you know you were credited for saving his life?'

'Was I?' Safa mutters. 'Shame. Fucking prick.'

'Pardon?'

'Nothing. So what happened?'

'They formed our service. British Secret Service. Modelled in some ways on the CIA, but they amalgamated all the previous intelligence services. MI5. MI6. Special Branch. Counter Terrorism.'

'And you're an agent with them?' Ben asks.

'I am, yes.'

Miri walks in, silent and seemingly absorbed in her own thoughts. Tango Two notices the other three glance over at her, then carry on as normal. Who runs this whole thing? She still doesn't know the reason for it. The purpose. Who is in charge of Miri?

'Clothes fit?'

Tango Two blinks up at Miri. She zoned out again. Lost focus. *Switch on and do your job.*

'Yes. Yes, they do. Thank you, that was very kind.'

'Not kind,' Miri says. 'Necessary.'

It is not necessary. It is the opposite of necessary. Necessary would be denying food, water, sleep and clothing in exchange for a flow of information.

'What's happening now then?' Safa asks brightly.

Miri stays quiet for a second and sips at a can of Pepsi. Her eyes look more blue than grey in this light. 'Tango Two will come with me,' she says. 'Safa, you will get your team ready for deployment . . .'

'On it. Armed?' Safa says, rising from her chair with a sudden switch to business mode.

'Affirmative,' Miri replies. 'Tango Two, with me, please.'

'She's just got new clothes, so don't shoot her.'

'Make ready, Miss Patel.'

'I'm so cultivated,' Safa mutters, then shrugs because she doesn't care one bit if she is cultivated or not. 'Right, come on, beardy . . . Ben, you fit?'

◆ ◆ ◆

'Sit down.'

Tango Two pulls the chair a fraction of an inch. Miri clocks the slight movement: an effort to control her environment. Tango Two sits with her knees together and her hands holding her coffee mug. Neither defensive nor open. Passive. Not a threat. Miri notices the position: too defensive. She is using the mug as a shield. Miri sits down behind the desk as Tango Two looks round, taking in the stacks of newspapers and magazines. Boxes pushed against the wall.

'Who do you work for?' Miri asks.

'The British Secret Service.'

'How long have you been an agent?'

'Eleven years and three months.'

'How old are you?'

'Thirty.'

'What is your position within your organisation?'

'I am a Two.'

'Explain.'

'Agents are based on a hierarchal structure. Lead agents who are fully trained and experienced gain the position of One if they are sanctioned by Mother. I am a Two. I am working towards being a One. Trainee agents are a Three.'

'How many agents does your organisation have?'

'I don't know.'

'Explain.'

'We are discouraged from asking questions of each other in a social capacity. We are discouraged from seeking information about the organisation other than to serve our professional needs.'

'How many agents does your organisation have?'

'Seventy-eight work within the One, Two and Three structure. Those agents are forward operators. They lead teams, conduct operations and investigations. We have many operatives who assist those agents.'

'Do not ever lie to me again. How many operatives?'

Tango Two cannot stop her reaction of guilt at lying, her cheeks burning in shame at the harsh tone Miri used. *Who is this woman?*

'Over five hundred,' Tango Two says.

'Funding. Explain.'

'We are funded by central government. We have primary responsibility for non-police domestic security, terrorism, counter-terrorism and overseas interests.'

'Your experience. Explain.'

'Combat. Surveillance and counter-surveillance, and counter-espionage. Diplomatic surveillance and disruption.'

'Do you know why we are here?'

'No.'

'Why did they attack you?'

'I really don't know.'

'Did you do anything to provoke them?'

'No.'

'Do you know Bertram Cavendish or any members of his family?'

'No.'

'Tell me what you know.'

'You have a time machine. Bertram Cavendish invented it. You had a staging area in Berlin. That is what I knew prior to Cavendish Manor. I now know you have Safa Patel, Ben Ryder and Harry Madden, along with Doctor John Watson, who I have not previously heard of, and you, of course. I do not know anything else of any significance.'

'You do.'

'Only what I have gleaned. You followed a smurf to get money. I do not know why you need the money or the reasons you took it. Neither Ben, Harry nor Safa have revealed anything of significance, but may I say thank you for the clothes and the care you have shown. What are you planning to do with me? Do you know why they attacked me?'

'Tell me what happened that led to you being here.'

'The same as I have previously told,' Tango Two says carefully, politely, passively. To show any degree of irritation will create an opening for an interrogator to take advantage of. She repeats the same account. Factual. No opinions offered. Only what she saw.

'Thank you. Return to your rooms, please. Tell Safa to secure you.'

'Sorry?'

'That is all, Tango Two. Return to your rooms. Tell Safa to secure you.'

'Okay, hang on,' Tango Two says, blinking as she shuffles forward on the chair. 'You want me to walk back through this . . . this place on my own to find Safa and ask her to lock me in my rooms?'

'Yes.'

'I could run outside.'

'The dinosaurs will be glad to see you.'

'Listen, I am a trained . . .'

'Now, Tango Two.'

'Yes, ma'am,' Tango Two replies instantly at the tone and absolute authority of the older woman.

She does it too. She walks from the office down the corridor, into the main room and over to the big table, where she stands to finish her coffee. She glances at the knives, forks and other things she could use as weapons and considers taking something to conceal. She could slide a fork or a knife off the table when she puts her cup down, but dismisses the notion the second it forms. She might be under observation. They might count all the equipment, and anyway, what would she use it for? To do what? Go where? Force is not the way forward. Compliance and passivity are the best options. Something else too. Something nagging in the back of her mind.

She walks back up the corridor and stops at the open door to see Harry standing in the middle room reading Harry Potter and Safa pulling her hair back to tie off with what looks like an old scrap of grey material.

'Hi, er . . . Miri said to . . .'

'You going back in your rooms?'

'Yes. Yes, I am. Miri said to ask you to lock me in.'

Safa laughs. 'How fucked-up is this?'

Eighteen

Miri looks up from the tablet as they file into the portal room.

'Briefing. Ready? Fort Bragg. America. Largest military base in the world at the time we are attending, which is zero two hundred hours mid-winter in the year 2009. Place of entry is the main storage depot for personal-issue weapons. We are increasing our armoury because . . .'

'We need to go back and support us at Cavendish Manor,' Ben cuts in.

Miri notices the lack of reaction from the other two. No, not a lack of reaction, more a sense of expectation. She knows Ben worked it out very quickly and explained it to the other two.

'Very good, Mr Ryder. That is correct.'

'So it definitely was *us* firing outside the house?'

'It was and it will be,' Miri says.

'So it's *us* giving *us* support? The *us* inside the house? In effect then, we've already done it because it already happened, which means we've already got the guns and so we *will* go and get these guns and train . . . but why Fort Bragg?' His head drops; the frown crosses his features. His hand rubs at his jaw as he looks up at Miri. 'Ah, yep, yep, yep, you were US military intelligence, so I am guessing at some point you were posted there, so you know this location. That makes sense because the armoury inside the base doesn't need to be secure because it's *inside* the base. Okay. I've got that. Why not a factory? I guess that's because the US military is so bloody big they won't know or simply won't care if a few guns go missing. Right. Yep, got it. Happy now.' He stops talking and slowly becomes aware of everyone staring at him. 'What?' he asks.

'Nothing,' Safa says, looking away quickly.

'Bit bloody risky though,' Ben says. 'Going into an American army base, I mean. Are you sure we go there? Maybe we go somewhere else . . . Like the Kremlin, or somewhere less dangerous than the biggest . . .'

'Be fine,' Harry says, slapping him on the back. 'Yanks never lock their stuff up. We nicked it all the time.'

'Really?' Ben asks, recovering himself as the room fills with the glow of the portal shimmering to life.

'Had a tank away from them in Italy.'

'A tank?'

'Aye. Then a frigate in Portsmouth.'

'A what?' Ben asks as Miri tilts her head at Harry.

'Frigate,' Harry says. 'Ship.'

'You stole a ship?' Ben asks.

'And a tank,' Harry says.

'Heard about that ship,' Miri says.

'What did you do with it?' Ben asks.

'We rammed a German battleship with it.'

'What about the tank?'

'We kept that.'

'Oh,' Ben says.

'Good tank.'

'Right.'

'We should get a tank, ma'am,' Harry suggests.

'We're not getting a tank,' Ben says.

'Who the fuck are you?' A deep American voice booms out. They snap from staring at Harry to the man leaning through the portal glaring round the room. 'This a Spec-Ops thing?' the man asks. Buzz-cut hair. A hard face and strong jaw. Army fatigues on his upper body.

'Soldier,' Ben says, stepping quickly in front of Safa, who was about to launch at the portal. 'What are you doing?'

'Staring at you,' the soldier fires back. 'Seeing as this is in my goddam armoury . . .'

'Staring at you . . . *sir*,' Ben says, sounding each word out with perfect delivery and complete authority. He takes a step forwards and stops with his hands on his hips to glare at the soldier. 'Waiting?' he adds quietly.

'What?'

'You said we had this area clear,' Ben says, glancing at Miri. 'This area should be clear. That was the agreement. How can we test holographic equipment if we have bloody soldiers poking their heads in every five minutes? And rude soldiers at that. Rude soldiers who don't know HOW TO SAY SIR!'

'Stand down, soldier,' Miri barks, her accent suddenly noticeably firmer, harder and distinctly American. 'Sir, I can assure you this area should have been cleared.'

'Well, it's not bloody clear, is it?' Ben says, withering in delivery. He moves towards the portal with an air of utter confidence. 'Well, go on, piss off.'

'What?'

'THE OFFICER GAVE YOU A COMMAND,' Harry roars, striding at the soldier.

'Sir, yes, sir!' The soldier snaps a salute and draws back.

'Follow through,' Miri whispers.

Ben and Harry march through the portal with that instant transition not just from one room to another, but to a completely different place in terms of oxygen, the smell of the air and the feel of the world around them. Instantly colder, and the air taken into lungs a hundred million years ago mists as it is exhaled. Ben glares round a vast room, pointedly ignoring the two soldiers as Harry walks straight at them.

'OFFICER ON THE DECK. TEN . . . SHUN!'

Instant compliance. Both come ramrod straight to snap salutes. Harry glowers, simmering with aggression that terrifies the two young men. 'Shower of shit,' he growls. 'Pair of miserable little squaddies. DO NOT EYEBALL ME, SOLDIER . . .'

Miri and Safa come through. Safa holds back with Ben, while Miri moves to stand next to Harry.

'What the hell are you doing here?' she demands. 'Who ordered you here? Was it Captain Dayton? I told him this area is to be clear.'

'Ma'am,' one of the soldiers says, with another salute. 'Captain Dayton is away this weekend, ma'am. Leave, ma'am. Said to count the rifles, ma'am.'

'Punishment detail?' Harry barks.

'Sir, yes, sir.'

'What did you do?' Miri asks.

A look between them. Worry and angst filling their features.

Harry leans round them to make a point of noticing the playing cards on the floor behind and the stubbed-out cigarette butts. Open cans of soda. Empty food packets and army-green blankets rolled up and used as seats. He tuts once. Disdainful and disgusted.

The blood drains from the soldiers' faces. One even squeezes his eyes closed at being caught out, because their futures are suddenly filled with days of court martials, trials and sentences of hard labour for a long time to come.

'I asked a question,' Miri snaps.

'Stole a jeep, ma'am,' one blurts.

'Crashed it,' the other says.

'Into the General's staff car.'

'Killed his cat, ma'am.'

Ben snorts a laugh, then coughs to cover it and turns away.

'You are both in deep trouble,' Miri says.

Ben pauses, watching them closely, choosing his moment. He moves closer and sighs heavily. 'This test should be covert,' he says to Miri. 'These two have seen it.'

'And they will pay for it,' Miri says.

'Doesn't stop the test from being blown, does it? They'll tell everyone. They'll go back and say what they saw. What then? This has been months in the planning. The British Army does not want this spoken about. Generating holographic illusions is meant to be secret.'

'Ach, I'm sure we can have an agreement,' Harry growls, moving closer to the two men. 'I'm sure an understanding can be reached here.' He stops a hair's width away from one. Glaring as though waiting for a response, before moving to do the same with the other one. 'Do you want to be court-martialled for dereliction of duty, son?'

'No, sir,' the soldier blurts meekly.

'My commanding officers do not have my level of patience and tolerance. My commanding officers do not want this spoken about . . .'

'Sir.'

'Sir.'

'I AM A SERGEANT, NOT A SIR.'

'Sergeant!'

'Sergeant!'

'You will not discuss this. You will not mention this. If you discuss this or mention this, I will find you. Are we clear?'

'Yes, sergeant!'

'Yes, sergeant!'

'Ma'am,' Harry says, stepping away and speaking calmly, as though nothing has happened. 'Just lads having a game of cards on their ref break, ma'am. No harm done, ma'am. Seem like good lads, ma'am.'

Miri holds position, as though deliberating, before shooting a glance at Ben, who nods once and waves a dismissive hand.

'Leave us,' Miri tells them both. 'Our test will be done in thirty minutes, at which point you can return. I will be speaking to Captain Dayton to ensure these rifles are counted correctly. Are we clear?'

'Ma'am.'

'Ma'am.'

'Dismissed.'

The two about-turn into each other. Both swear. Both about-turn to face the opposite direction and set off before one realises and turns to run and catch the other. It takes seconds for them to cross the vast room, but finally they walk out the far door.

'What the fuck!' Ben releases the breath he was holding. 'Jesus Christ . . . Did that just happen?'

'That was incredible,' Safa says, grinning at Ben and Harry. 'Ben! You reacted so quickly.'

'Aye, was very good, Ben.'

'You were brilliant,' Ben says, staring in awe at Harry. 'Miri? That okay?'

'Fine,' Miri says. 'They won't say a word.'

'How can you be so sure?' Safa asks.

'I saw them when I was here. Month from now. I remember they both panicked and snapped salutes when I walked past. Had no idea why at the time.'

◆ ◆ ◆

Drab olive-green shelving units line the walls. Each one a segment bolted to the next, and each containing assault rifles that stand lined in perfect symmetry. More units given over for the storage of sidearms, sniper rifles, light machine guns, heavy machine guns and ground troop missile-firing systems.

'Come on, Ryder,' Safa says, shoulder-bumping him. 'That was seriously cool though.'

'Thanks.'

She holds her dark eyes on him for a second before walking over to join Harry inspecting the closest batch of M4 assault rifles. She pulls one out to turn over in her hands. 'These are only semi, Miri.'

'Over here,' Miri says, pulling what looks to Ben to be an identical weapon from a different section.

'What's the difference?' he asks.

'These,' Safa says, waving a hand at the closest, 'are the rifles issued to the soldiers. Semi-automatic and burst fire only. 'Those though,' she says, leading them both over to Miri, 'are the ones the US Special Forces use, and are fully automatic. Harry, have a look. These are good weapons.'

'Light,' he rumbles, hefting the weapon. He turns it over, checks the balance, then taps a fingernail against different parts and sections.

'Twenty of these,' Miri says, pulling another two from the rack.

'Twenty?' Ben asks.

'Spares. Breakages. Planning.'

'Right, okay,' he says. 'So how do we go back, and what do we do? At the house, I mean?'

'Later.'

'Why later? Why not now?'

'Later. Twenty of these,' she counts them out. 'Get familiar with them. You need to be fully conversant. Train for stoppages, blockages, malfunctions. Start using radios, and understanding basic commands and hand signals. Safa, I want them at your standard as soon as possible.'

'What are we doing with Tango Two?' Ben asks as they walk back to the portal.

'You are very intelligent,' Miri says after a pause.

'And what?' Ben asks when she doesn't continue. She still doesn't continue, but goes with them into the portal room to stack the rifles against the wall. She still doesn't continue then, but moves back into the armoury.

'Barrett fifty-calibre, semi-automatic sniper rifle,' she says, stopping at a section holding several enormous guns. She hefts one out, grimacing at the weight and the pain in her lower back, hips, joints, ankles and everywhere else.

'Ma'am,' Harry says, taking the weapon from her. His eyes show pleasant surprise at the size of the weapon, which looks normal when held by him. 'Fifty calibre?' he enquires politely.

'Fifty calibre,' Miri says.

'Is that big?' Ben asks.

'It's big' Safa says.

'Oh. Why do we need big?' Ben asks.

'Dinosaurs,' Miri says.

'Oh.'

'And firepower.'

'Oh.'

'Browning heavy machine gun,' Miri says, stopping at another section as the others gather round to stare at the huge gun.

'What calibre is that?' Ben asks.

'Also fifty,' Miri says.

'Oh. Why do we need another fifty?'

They look at him.

'What?' he asks.

'Sniper rifle,' Miri says, pointing back to the Barrett fifty-calibre sniper rifles. 'Machine gun,' she adds, pointing at the machine gun.

'Oh,' Ben says, then shrugs.

'Single aimed shots,' Miri says, pointing back. 'Suppressing fire,' she adds, pointing at the machine gun.

'Oh,' Ben says. 'The dinosaurs firing back then, are they?'

'No.'

'It was a joke.'

'I know, Mr Ryder. I am laughing on the inside.'

'Ha!' Safa snorts.

'M72 light anti-tank weapon,' Miri says, stopping at the next section.

'That's a rocket launcher.' Ben looks from the long metal tube to Miri. 'A bazooka.'

'Not a bazooka.'

'Looks like a bazooka.'

'Single fire. Point and shoot. Remarkably simple to use,' Miri says. 'Twenty of these.'

'Twenty? How big are these dinosaurs?'

'Very funny, Mr Ryder.'

'Ha!' Safa snorts again.

'M67 fragmentation grenade. Fatal radius five metres. Severe injury to fifteen metres.'

'In case the bazookas don't work?'

'In case the bazookas don't work, Mr Ryder. Two cases.'

The kit is carried through, and each passage shows the instant change from mid-winter to a higher oxygen density and greater heat and humidity. They scurry back and forth. Carrying crates of ammunition, grenades, rocket launchers and the heavy, frame-mounted machine guns.

'Done?' Ben asks, placing the last box on the floor of the portal room. 'Sure we don't need a jet plane?'

'A what?' Safa asks.

'Jet plane,' Ben says.

'What the fuck is a jet plane?'

'What? It's a jet plane.'

'Oh, you mean like a plane?' Safa asks.

'Yes, a plane. A jet plane.'

'Like a bang-tank?' Safa asks.

'What!? That's not the same thing.'

'Or a pew-pew laser gun?'

The easy banter continues as the new kit is taken from the portal room to be locked inside one of the bedrooms in the last set of rooms.

Harry sees Miri wince as she stands up from lowering the rifles.

'We can finish this, ma'am,' he says quietly to her in the corridor as they walk back to the portal room.

'Thanks.'

'Good lord,' the doctor calls out, standing with his hands on his hips surveying the weapons. 'Are we going to war?'

'With dinosaurs,' Ben says. 'Those are for aimed shots and that one is for suppressing fire.'

'Twat,' Safa says. 'What they called again?'

'Um . . . one is Barrett and one is Brown.'

'Browning. Which one is which?'

'Dunno. Apparently we're getting a jet plane anyway,' he tells the doctor.

'Are we?'

'Dick,' Safa chuckles.

'And a bang tank,' Ben adds drily.

'We should get a tank, ma'am,' Harry says, lifting two heavy crates of ammunition with ease. 'Very handy is a tank.'

'Are we really getting a tank?' the doctor asks.

'Doctor, word please,' Miri says.

'Of course,' the doctor says, winking at Safa as he goes past towards the door. 'Carry on, troops,' he adds brightly.

'Tango Two. Injuries. Healing?' Miri asks, sitting in her chair behind her desk.

'Ah, well,' the doctor says, assuming a serious, deep-thinking look. 'In short, yes, she is fine,' he adds simply. 'What's happening with her?'

'Her physical state?'

'As I just said, she appears to be fine. Why? What are your plans for her?'

'Ria and Bertie?'

175

'Both fine,' Doctor Watson says, sitting down heavily to get comfortable. 'What's the plan then, eh? Got something cooking, have you?' he asks with a wink and a nod. 'And anyway, Miri. I told you to rest, not to carry heavy boxes and machine guns.'

'Tango Two mental state. Any concerns?'

'No. Surprisingly. She is healing and appears physically healthy. She is eating. She is drinking fluids. She undertook physical training with the others. I have no concerns for her. She is bright-eyed and bushy-tailed, as they say. Right, so, as her medical practitioner, I would like to know what your cunning plans are, eh? Cunning, I bet. Cunning and secret. Oh yes. Why did her own side try and kill her?'

'Ria's mental state.'

'Ria is consumed with grief,' he says in an instant change to a serious tone. 'I will monitor that as she transitions from her normal life, taking into account her support networks have been taken away. Bertie is . . .'

'Thank you, Doctor Watson. That will be all.'

'Plans, Miri?'

'Thank you, Doctor Watson. I have work to do.'

'Right, well, I shall go and count some pills.'

'You do that.'

'One thing I would say is that confining Tango Two to her rooms without stimulation will of course have a negative effect and potentially invoke a decline in mental health similar to that which Ben suffered. She is fine now. She has been here only a few days, and she is young and robust, but any length of time will not be healthy.'

Miri listens intently. Her eyes narrow with the slightest of motions that shows her attentiveness. 'Thank you, Doctor.'

'Are you going to execute her, Miri?' he asks quietly, all trace of joviality gone.

'Thank you, Doctor. You have been very helpful.'

'Helpful is my middle name.' The joke falls flat. Silence, sudden and awkward. 'It's not. It's Hamish actually, but . . . Ah, right, you are looking down at your desk, which indicates the conversation is now at an end.'

Miri thinks with her hands flat on the warm, wooden surface. The others pass the doorway, glancing in to see her almost frozen. Back and forth they go. Carrying weapons. Carrying boxes. Talking. Joking.

She takes one of the notepads from the desk before walking out into the corridor to stare at the bare walls, then down towards the main room for long seconds of deep thought. 'Safa?'

'Yep,' Safa says, walking backwards carrying a heavy crate of ammunition with Ben.

'I will be busy for the next few days and not always here. You are in charge in my absence. I want you fit and ready.'

'We are fit,' Safa says.

'None of you are in peak condition. Increase your training to be ready.'

'I beg your fucking pardon?'

'Do not keep the prisoner confined to her rooms. She can come out if the weapons are secure. Train with her. She may have skill sets and practical knowledge that you are lacking.'

'Lacking? What the . . . We are fit. We're bloody fit as anything . . .' Safa protests.

Miri holds the silence for a second. 'Good. Then work harder.'

'Where are you going?' Ben asks before Safa can explode in righteous fury at being called unfit and lacking.

'Train,' Miri says, striding into the portal room. 'Get better. Work harder . . .'

She smiles to herself at the bluster coming from Safa as she programs the tablet to bring the Blue back to life.

The game is underway.

Nineteen

Pressure can be described as continual physical force.

Mental pressure is the perception of continual force, although the force is not always apparent.

It's not apparent now. It's subtle and very suggestive, but by degrees it is increased, and with it the atmosphere within the bunker grows with each passing day.

Miri uses language like an artist with constant studied, deft touches.

The prisoner can be given more freedom. The prisoner can move about freely if the weapons are secure. The prisoner can eat with you. The prisoner should train with you.

Miri suggests one thing while meaning another to create a penetrating, yet unseen jarring sensation, while all the time working to shape a new reality. A groomer. A player. It's what she is. It's what she does.

The days roll on. *You need time to heal and I am working.* That's the answer she gives when Ben asks what she is doing and why everything is taking so long. She suspects Ben knows a great deal more than the others, but she also knows that he is intelligent enough to keep those thoughts to himself – and she would know if he didn't, because of Safa.

Safa is pure honesty. There is absolutely no deceit with that woman. If Safa thinks it, Safa will say it, and if Ben relayed his suspicions, then

Safa would voice them. Safa has not voiced them, so therefore Ben has not spoken of them.

Work harder. Get fitter. Be better. Do more. Why are you relaxing? Why are you drinking coffee again? Work.

A team gels and excels when there is a defined hierarchy. Miri knows that. She pushes them to knit and bond with each other. She has to be careful though. Too much, and it looks tyrannical. Too little, and she runs the risk of over-familiarity. *Good work today. Relax tonight. It's a nice evening – you should eat outside with the prisoner.*

To plan at this level means to see and know everything, and that takes time, but she has a time machine, and what would have taken her months to achieve in the past can now be done in weeks.

I want to see the surrounding area. The prisoner can come with us. Harry will arm with a Barrett rifle. Ben and Safa will arm with pistols. The prisoner will be given a pistol, but not a magazine. A spare magazine will be carried by Safa and given to the prisoner in the event of an incident serious enough to warrant the use of live rounds. Do you all understand?

That was exactly two weeks after Cavendish Manor. Fourteen days since Tango Two was taken captive. Miri gave them the brief and watched as they kitted up and made ready.

The weather was changing. The humidity was growing stronger every day, the precursor of what Harry and Miri recognised as a rainy season. They set out after breakfast. Doctor Watson tagged along too, dressed in a sleeveless fishing jacket, baggy khaki shorts, long socks pulled up to his knees, rugged walking boots, a floppy hat and a pair of huge binoculars hanging from a strap round his neck.

They were all sweating by the time they walked up the steep bank to the plateau above the bunker. Insects buzzed and lifted in swarms as they moved slowly through the long grass. The huge Barrett fifty-calibre rifle was strapped to Harry's back. All of them save the doctor armed with a pistol in a holster.

Miri spent a long time in that clearing. Walking back and forth. The doctor moved here and there, studying insects, flowers and plants, and staring through his binoculars. The other four stayed together, chatting easily with hands resting on butts of weapons.

'Bet I can draw faster than you,' Safa said after growing bored at Miri and the doctor pissing about.

'Bet you can't,' Tango Two said, smiling back at her.

'I so bloody can.' Safa pulled her pistol from the holster to eject the magazine and the round in the chamber. 'Safe, unloaded.' She showed the weapon to Tango Two before sliding it back in.

'Seriously?' Ben laughed, taking the magazine from Safa.

'Ben, count down from three,' Safa said as Tango Two pulled her own pistol out to check.

'Safe, unloaded,' Tango Two said.

'I know it is,' Safa said.

'I know you know, but I'm just confirming,' Tango Two said.

'Whatever. Ready?'

'Ready.'

Miri was absorbed in her own work of measuring distance by footfall, but she heard Ben counting back from three and saw the blur of hands as Safa and Tango Two drew to aim.

'Mine!' Safa exclaimed.

'Best of three,' Tango Two said.

Safa won. Then it was winner stayed on, and she drew against Ben too. He unloaded his pistol magazine and handed it to Tango Two, who held it in her hand while laughing at being beaten by Safa. Miri counted her steps, but clocked the prisoner was now holding a magazine of live rounds, while a pistol rested in a holster on her hip.

Safa won again. Ben took his magazine back, then Safa and Harry played. Safa won again and extolled the virtues of good sportsmanship by calling the others *slow twats*. Tango Two won against Ben, but drew level with Harry. Ben won against Harry, but Harry complained that his big hands made it harder to draw as fast as Ben's *dainty hands*. Miri counted steps. The doctor stared at insects.

The application of force to create pressure. Create an environment for a bond to grow. Water the seeds and study the results.

'Firing practice?' Miri asked as they finally walked back to the bunker after spending half a day traipsing about the clearing and tree line. It was the right time to stay with them and join in. Friendly, but not close. Polite, but not familiar.

'What about Tango?' If Safa thinks it, Safa will say it.

'She can join us. Firing-range protocols will apply at all times and she will only be given live rounds at the firing line.'

'Don't shoot us, shithead.'

'I won't.'

An afternoon of obliterating paper targets pinned to a sandbag firing wall. An afternoon of drinking coffee and holding competitions. The doctor asked to be shown how to shoot. They each took turns to guide and show him. Tango Two included. Firing-range protocols were adhered to at all times, but as the afternoon wore on, so the acute awareness of *the prisoner* having access to live rounds abated.

'We've got a time machine, so if you do shoot us, we'll come back and shoot you,' Safa said when they began.

'And that makes no sense at all,' Ben said.

'It does.'

'It doesn't'

'It so does. If Tango shoots us, we can just come back and shoot her with the time machine.'

'We'll be dead. How do we come back from being dead?'

'Fuck you, egghead.'

And so it went on. Ben explained timelines. Miri listened. The doctor joined in. Harry chuckled as Safa got confused. Tango tried to explain, but got herself confused in the process until the topic reverted to the *so if we go back and shoot us as kids* line of thought.

'Ensure the prisoner is locked securely. You've had a relaxing day. Work hard tomorrow.'

Those were her parting words as Miri left them that evening. Give a little and grow the bond, then take some away to imbue the insidious, jarring feeling.

The days rolled on.

Tell me what happened that led you to being here.

Tell me what happened up until I arrived.

Why did Mother order you to be killed?

Why did Mother order me to be killed?

What food does the prisoner like? Do you all like Chinese food? Make sure the prisoner is locked in securely. The prisoner can take a lamp from the other rooms into her quarters.

The application of pressure. Tango Two is a prisoner. A captive. Do not trust her, but give her freedom. Do not like her, but spend time with her. Do not let your guard down, but give her a loaded gun.

'How long have you been here?' Miri asked as she walked *the prisoner* back to her rooms after a communal feast of Chinese food eaten while they all listened to the rain lashing the windows.

Tango Two had to think of the answer. The days had all merged in her mind. *Time is different here.* There are no clocks on the walls. No watches. Their body clocks work with sunrise and sunset.

'I think three weeks?'

It had been twenty-three days. A highly trained captive should know exactly how much time had passed.

'Goodnight,' Miri said, pulling the door closed.

'Night, Miri,' Tango Two said.

She turned from the door towards the bathroom as the familiar clunk of the bolt came, but it was different. A different sound. Like it wasn't rammed home properly. At that moment, she felt comfortably full and relaxed from the meal and felt no need to investigate. Tango Two used the bathroom, her bathroom, and made her way into the bedroom, her bedroom. She turned on the lamp, her lamp. She pulled back the soft throws on the bed, her bed, and she thought about the door and the bolt and why Mother tried to kill her. She thought about the Chinese food she ate and the jokes with the others. They even had a bottle of beer each. She smiled to herself at the memory of Harry scowling in distaste and saying *this fizzy stuff is not ale.*

She got into bed and turned off her lamp. She lay in the darkness, listening to the rain on her window, and thought about the door and the bolt . . .

She stayed barefoot, as she knew the floor of the corridor made no noise when walking without shoes. She paused near to the other rooms. No lights on inside. She pushed the door open to the main room, heavy with the pleasant scent of Chinese food, beer and the smells of the others. Smells now so familiar and homely, but this is not her home. A sense of duty kicked in. A sudden internal reminder that she is not part of whatever this is.

A loose rivet was all it was. One single rivet that allowed the bracket of the bolt to slip down. It was solid when she first got here, but she figured it must have worked loose over the last three weeks.

She moved across the main room to the doors on the other side and silently pushed through to see Miri's office empty and the corridor bathed in blue with light spillage from the portal room. Her heart rate increased. Her senses ramped. She listened carefully, but heard nothing other than the rain lashing the bunker outside.

Fortune favours the brave. Your allegiance is to your country, to your service. Agents are selfless and will give everything and do anything for their country.

She stopped at the doorway to the portal room and stared in at the shimmering blue light, seemingly alive with the motion of colours pulsing across the surface. The tablet was on the side. The screen was glowing.

Berlin 2061.

Home.

Right there. She moved towards it. Trepidation and excitement mixing in equal measure. She could go home. She swallowed and hesitated. She is an agent. She has duty and allegiance. This is not her time or home. These are not her people.

As the uncertainty of those seconds stretched, so she heard the strike of a match and darted back into the corridor to see the rear door slightly open. The smell of a woodbine floated down. Her eyes flicked to the portal, then back to the door. She is an agent. She has duty and allegiance.

She stepped silently through into the night air and the pouring rain to see Harry standing under a huge umbrella propped against one shoulder. His free hand holding the cigarette that curled smoke up to roll round the underside of the material. She stayed in the lee of the building, protected from the drenching rainfall. Harry smoked. Facing away. Huge, yet passive.

Thoughts whirled through her mind. She is an agent. Alpha told her to do what it takes. Mother tried to kill her. The portal is open. Harry is alone.

She took a further step out to let the rain drench her hair and run down her face to drip from her nose and chin, and she waited. She waited for the rain to soak her top to make it cling to her body. She waited for the chill of the water to cause the physical reaction to her nipples under the flimsy, sodden material. She arched her back slightly and lifted her chin to show the slenderness of her neck while widening her eyes like a doe. They were taught this. They were given lessons on how to look and appear vulnerable and alluring. Alpha said to do what it takes. She is an agent. She has duty and allegiance.

'Hey,' she said softly, quietly.

'Miss,' Harry said without turning to look.

She opened her mouth slightly, tucked her bottom lip between her teeth and waited for him to look at her.

'The bolt broke on my door,' she said when he didn't turn.

Harry tutted as though mildly irritated. He took a drag on his cigarette and plumed the smoke to curl up into the sky. 'Didn't go through it then.'

She moved into his peripheral vision. 'No . . .' She trailed off and waited while her hair became slick against her scalp and the top clung to her frame. Still he didn't look. Still he didn't react. 'Should I?'

A pause. A second in time passing as he lifted the cigarette to his lips. 'Not for me to say now, is it?'

She blinked and felt the confusion tugging at the back of her mind again. The confusion that comes each time she thinks she knows what to do. 'Do you miss home, Harry?'

He finally turned to look at her with a glance down and a sadness showing in his eyes. 'Got a job to do.'

'What job?' she asked. She moved closer, arching her back a bit more, showing the vulnerability, biting her bottom lip, but seeing only calmness and decency coming back. A sudden feeling of guilt surged through her. A feeling of being dirty and cheap. Crimson bloomed in her cheeks.

'You're getting wet, miss.'

She tried to brave it out for another few seconds. Her nipples were hard and straining through the top. Her neck was slender and shapely. Her eyes large, but tears pricked and fell down her cheeks with the rivers of rain. She folded her arms quickly and lowered her head to stoop with shame. 'I'm so sorry . . .'

'Ach,' he moved next to her, sheltering her with the umbrella as a huge arm went over her shoulders, drawing her in as the sobs threatened to break from her chest.

'They'll kill me.' She drew a quavering breath. Not acting now. No pretence either. Just raw confusion and emotions pouring out. 'If I go back . . . they'll kill me . . .'

'But you're here. Not there.'

'I can't stay here, Harry. I'm an agent. I don't know what to do . . .'

'What's your name?'

She snorted a humourless laugh at someone finally asking who she is. 'Emily. Emily Rose.'

He nodded slowly. 'Nice name.'

'I've never done that before,' she said suddenly, searching his eyes. 'Thank you.'

'No bother.' He smiled down as she closed her eyes and felt the weight of his arm resting on her shoulders. His calmness spread through her. His aura soothing her frantic mind.

'I bet Safa thinks my name is fake.'

'Aye, probably.'

Twenty

Miri walks from the portal room to her office and places the brown paper bag on the table, then slides the smartphone from her back pocket, connects the wire and pushes the earpiece into her ear.

It's been twenty-five days since Cavendish Manor. Twenty-five days for Ben to become increasingly frustrated at not knowing what Miri is doing. Twenty-five days for everyone to heal from their injuries.

Miri switches the phone off, winds the cable round the middle, picks up the tablet and the large brown paper bag and heads down the corridor to the back door and out into the inky blackness of a Cretaceous night.

'Ah, Miri,' Doctor Watson says, sitting up in his chair. 'All well?'

'Doctor.'

She moves to the wooden table used to strip the weapons and places the bag and tablet down. 'Eaten?' she asks no one in particular.

'We had a lovely meal,' Doctor Watson says, 'and heard an incredible story of a stolen frigate ramming a German battleship.'

Miri roots in the bag. The atmosphere is friendly and relaxed. She looks round to see Harry at the end closest to the corner. Ben next to him. Emily, then Safa and the doctor at the other end. Good positioning. She takes in the stretched-out legs from Harry and Ben that tell her they are both relaxed in the company they keep. Same with the doctor, who did sit up straighter, but now eases back down. Safa and Emily are more upright, but that is due to their natural manner rather than any show of being guarded or pensive. All of them barefooted, relaxed and conversing with warmth and humour.

The thrill is there. The thrill at taking the next step in the game.

'Strawberries,' Miri says, pulling the first punnet out. 'Got a few,' she adds, placing more down. 'And chocolate.' Big bars of milk chocolate come out of the bag.

'Seriously?' Safa asks, rising from the chair to walk over.

'You said you wanted strawberries and chocolate,' Miri says, as though confused, but using that second to take in the ever-so-slight blanch on Tango Two's face that confirms more than the agent will ever know or realise.

'No, it's great,' Safa says. 'Fuck me, we've got strawberries and chocolate,' she adds with a grin at Emily. 'Bet you're glad you didn't escape now, eh? Ah shit, you said you were allergic . . . Never mind, more for me.'

'Allergic?' Ben asks, looking at Emily.

'Um?' Emily says, holding a mock-questioning look.

'Oh,' Ben chuckles, 'I thought you actually were then. Thanks for this, Miri.'

'Enjoy,' Miri says, turning to walk back. 'Oh, I have a problem.' She holds the tablet up. 'I loaded this with some data and footage, but I can't make it work now. The tech is from your era,' Miri says, looking at Emily.

'Would you like me to try?' Emily says as Safa starts handing out the punnets. Harry takes his with a smile as Ben holds his thoughtful gaze on Miri for a second.

'Thanks,' Miri says, handing the tablet to Emily. 'Can switch it on, but the operating system is unfamiliar.'

'How did you load the data then?' Ben asks, immediately regretting asking such a stupid question when Miri is clearly playing a hand.

'Asked a kid in a café,' Miri says in that flat American drawl.

Emily swipes the screen to see familiar icons glowing within the square, then looks up at Miri. 'It's working – what was it you wanted?'

'Loaded images. Can't find them.'

'In the images folder, which is through here . . .'

'Can you make them 3D?' Miri asks.

'Er, sure.'

'Put it on the table,' Miri says, as though to watch and learn.

'This icon here accesses the images folder and . . .' Emily trails off with her fingers hovering over the screen when she sees one of the images in question.

'That one,' Miri says, pointing to another icon. 'How do I play that footage and make it 3D?'

'Er, right, of course, like this: tap the image and two smaller icons appear. This one is conventional, and this is for 3D.'

'The kid said it will come out,' Miri says. 'How do I do that?'

'Like I said: 3D.'

'Show me, Tango Two. Make it play now.'

Emily double-taps the screen, then selects the 3D option. An image immediately blooms out from the device to fill the air above. A static shot, just a grey blur that is instantly recognised by Ben, Safa and Harry, who all shift position to watch intently. 'So to play it, you just swipe left, then to pause you swipe right. Really simple.'

Emily swipes the holographic image. Sound immediately comes. A slight hiss, then the sound of rotor blades. She moves back to her seat, conscious of the earnest looks of the others now staring at the footage.

Ben frowns at Miri. Questions in his eyes. She doesn't show any reaction, but moves back, as though to watch the footage herself.

The footage blurs with the distinctive motion of a camera lens trying to focus. The noise of the rotor blades increases in pitch as the camera is given lift and rises smoothly into the air a few feet.

The footage of the world in 2111. The footage Ben, Harry and Safa saw in Roland's office. The end of the world.

Emily watches the grey rubble, confused and not understanding what it is she is seeing. As the drone moves, she spots the charred remains of a child's doll, and frowns deeper.

The other three have seen the footage before, but not like this. Not in 3D in perfect, pin-sharp, high-definition quality bloomed out in the air.

More rubble. A ruined building. Debris strewn everywhere. Window frames of buildings, bathtubs and household content, charred, broken, filthy, old and lying everywhere. More buildings come into view. A whole street that shows the same thing. Roads buckled and broken. Tree stumps dead and withered. A lack of life. A feeling of an empty, sterile place.

Emily watches as more streets come into view. She spots cars and vehicles, then railway lines. Bigger buildings. A city. They all show reaction at the first capsule from the London Eye. Then more of them littering the ground. The drone goes over the Thames. Putrid brown water filled with jagged shards and shapes hidden by the flowing tide. Westminster Bridge broken and slumped in the river. The Houses of Parliament destroyed. The clock face from Big Ben lying amongst the squalor.

Miri swipes right. The footage cuts off. Silence behind her.

'What did I just watch?' Emily breaks that silence.

'The end of the world, my dear,' Doctor Watson replies heavily.

'Good, at least I know how to make that work,' Miri says, as though to herself. 'Now, I have another image. I click it? Is that correct? Tango Two?'

'Her name is Emily,' Safa says.

190

'Huh? What? I mean, yes, just, er . . .'

'Got it.' Another image blooms out from the tablet. The atmosphere now thick and charged. Miri carries on, as though ignorant to the change. 'How do I make it bigger?'

'You, er, you need to swipe the edges to rotate it and, er, to enlarge it, you take both sides and pull out . . .'

'That's Roland's house,' Safa says. 'Cavendish Manor.'

Again, Miri stands back in assessment of the image in front of her. The same 3D, pin-sharp, high-definition quality now showing Cavendish Manor. Seconds pass. Plant seeds. Water them. Let nature do the rest.

Silence broken only by Harry and the doctor eating strawberries. Ben watches Miri closely and takes a strawberry from his punnet. Everything Miri does is for a reason.

'Can I touch the image without moving it?' Miri asks.

'Er, you, er . . .' Emily clears her throat and blinks rapidly several times before rising to walk over to the tablet. 'Press this and it locks the image in place.'

'Thank you,' Miri says. She stands back, staring at the image and eating a strawberry. 'We'll start planning the secondary attack tomorrow,' Miri says, as though reaching a decision. She takes the tablet from the table and a punnet of strawberries, and starts heading back towards the bunker with the glowing hologram hovering in front of her. 'Good night.'

'Night, Sun Tzu,' Ben says quietly. Miri pauses, a twitch at the corner of her mouth.

'Night,' Safa calls out.

'Ma'am,' Harry says as she passes him.

Emily takes her first strawberry and bites into the soft flesh. It tastes divine. Perfect even. Juicy and full of flavour. Her mind runs frantic and fast with a pressure applied and exerted by a master at work.

'Warm,' Ben says conversationally.

'Is,' Harry says in reply, stretching his legs out.

'Balmy,' Doctor Watson says.

'Balmy,' Ben says, holding a strawberry up in acknowledgement. 'Good word.'

'Was,' Harry says in reply.

'Want some chocolate?' Safa heads over to the table to pick a few bars up to carry back, throwing one to Ben and Harry as she passes.

The heavy machine gun. The sniper shots. *Barrett. The joke that Ben didn't know the difference between a Barrett and a Browning.* The gunships being fired on from the ground. *Ben called them bazookas.* The bunker. The isolation from the world. Smurfs. *Maurice.* Money. Supplies. The empty rooms. *Malcolm and Konrad got everything for us.* Realisation finally sinks in. This is all they have. It's just them. *Three heroes from history. The end of the world.* Emily leans forward as everything slots into place one after the other. Her heart hammering. Her head spinning.

Ben watches the connections form on her face. The more he knows her, the more he struggles to understand how an agent, such as she appears to be, is so slow at working everything out.

'So nice,' Safa says, munching contentedly.

Emily shuffles on the seat and looks up to a night sky filled with millions of stars shining down. She doesn't know where she is in the world, and wonders if they are the same stars in the same places from her time. Why did Mother tell them to kill her? Alpha ordered the gunships to open fire, and she didn't want to die in the room of a house for a thing she did not understand.

Ben rolls his eyes and bites his bottom lip with frustration. She's had over three weeks to work it out.

'Emily Rose is clearly a shit spy name anyway . . .'

She turns to smile as Safa grins back with her white teeth showing stark against the darkness of her features.

'Emily Rose?' Safa laughs. 'That's so made up.'

'No! It's my real name,' Emily says with an instant grin.

'It's a lovely name,' Doctor Watson says.

'Is,' Harry says.

'You worked it all out yet?' Ben asks.

'I don't know,' she admits honestly.

'It's just us,' Ben says. 'To stop what Miri showed you.'

Emily doesn't reply, but stares, silent and thoughtful.

'Anyway,' Safa announces. 'What's your real proper name?'

'That is my real proper name!' Emily laughs again.

'Whatever. Eat your strawberries, or I'll steal them.'

Miri sits at her desk, staring at the hologram image, with the smartphone on the desk and the wire stretching up to her ear. Ben is good. He's smart. Miri likes that.

She ponders as the doctor wanders in, says goodnight and retires to wage war on the whale. The others stay outside. Chatting. Laughing. Genial voices. The seeds she planted have formed roots. The roots are strengthening, but are they strong enough yet? It took ages to loosen the rivet enough for it to appear to be a natural breakage.

'Night, ma'am,' Harry says, passing by when they start filing back in.

'Night, Miri,' Ben says, lifting a hand as he passes.

'Still up?' Safa asks.

'Safa, word please. Tango Two, you also,' Miri says.

'What's up?' Safa asks, walking into the office with Emily behind her. 'And her name is Emily . . .'

Are the roots strong enough yet? Miri pauses, listening for the door in the corridor to close, which signals Ben and Harry have both moved on. 'I have a mission.'

'Okay,' Safa says slowly with a glance at Emily.

'There is a woman,' Miri says, watching them both closely. 'She is very attractive. Flirtatious. I need information from her. Do you think Ben will be suitable to extract what . . .'

'Over my fucking dead body,' Safa blurts. 'Ben's not going anywhere near some rancid, diseased whore.'

Emily stares at her in surprise at the vehemence in her voice. Miri stays expressionless, but calculating every reaction.

'Fuck off,' Safa tells them both. 'Not a chance he's doing anything like that. He's a decent man. Who is she? I'll get the information.'

'My concern is that the information will be within a device she has . . .'

'No worries,' Safa says. 'I'll get it from her. Where is she? What do you need Emily for?'

'If you let me speak, Miss Patel . . .'

'Okay,' Safa says, either ignoring or ignorant of the rebuke.

'I do not know if it is appropriate to take the phone from her, or if it should be examined in situ. The technology is from Tango Two's era . . .'

'You want Emily to go on a mission?'

'Me?' Emily asks.

'Not with Ben though. I'll do it,' Safa says. 'You up for it?' she asks Emily.

'Are you serious?' Emily asks, turning from Safa to Miri.

'Do you now know why we are here?' Miri asks her.

'The footage,' Emily says. 'Ben just said . . .'

'What year is she in?' Safa asks. 'This attractive woman that isn't going anywhere near Ben, I mean.'

'2061.'

'That's . . .' Emily says.

'Your time,' Miri says, finishing her sentence when Emily trails off.

'Let me get this right,' Emily says. 'You are suggesting taking me outside of this place to my own time? I am an agent. It was my side trying to stop you . . . You do not know me well enough to . . .'

'Your side,' Safa scoffs. 'What, the same people that tried to kill you, yeah? And you walked right past the portal the other night and went outside with Harry instead . . .'

'Do you know why they were trying to kill me?' Emily asks, looking from Safa to Miri. 'I keep going over and over it, but . . . I didn't do anything wrong. I had Bertie. I had him . . .'

'Dunno,' Safa says.

'Safa and I will be with you, and after seeing what she did to Maurice, I have no doubt she will be able to deal with you.'

'The world ends?' Emily asks. 'How? What happens?'

'We don't know yet,' Safa says. 'Bertie filmed that footage, then he went back and got his dad.'

'Roland?' Emily asks. 'You said before that Roland tried killing himself.'

'So where's this whore then?'

'Tango Two?' Miri asks.

'Emily,' Safa says.

'Tango Two,' Miri says, ignoring Safa.

'Emily,' Safa says, ignoring being ignored.

'Do I have your word you will not try and escape or alert your people?' Miri asks.

'Say yes,' Safa says.

Emily blinks and goes to speak to voice the hundred or more questions whizzing through her head that suddenly drop away to leave an empty void. 'Sure, why not,' she says, amazed at herself for saying it. 'I give you my word.'

Twenty-One

'What?'

'Yeah, and I said there is no way you are going near her, so Emily is going with me.'

'What?' Ben asks again. He looks at Harry in the middle room, then back to Safa in her room and blanches at seeing her pulling her top off. 'Shit, sorry, Safa,' he turns away quickly.

'What for? I've got my bra on. You're blushing, Ben.'

'I'm not. It's hot.' He clears his throat. 'You sure it's a good idea?'

'What?' Safa asks, trying to choose between a black vest and a black T-shirt.

'Taking Tango . . . I mean Emily with you. Out of here, I mean.'

'She gave her word,' Safa calls back.

'That's very noble, but she's a trained agent, Safa.'

'Miri said she can do it. Miri asked her actually. The whore has a phone. Miri doesn't know if we can take it away, so Emily might need to examine it in situ.'

'Er, why is she a whore again?' Ben asks. 'You decent yet?'

'Yep,' Safa says, holding the vest and T-shirt up.

'Safa!' Ben says, turning away again at seeing her laughing while still in her bra.

'Twat,' she chuckles. 'She's a whore because Miri said she's attractive and flirtatious and wanted you to go and speak to her, so like I said . . . I told Miri there is no way anyone like that is going near you.'

'Right,' Ben says, looking at Harry clearly enjoying himself. 'Er . . .'

'Cos I'll be jealous.'

'Jealous?'

'Yeah.' Safa decides on the black T-shirt and tugs it down over her head. 'You're my Ben Ryder, not some other woman's Ben Ryder.'

'Safa?' Emily calls out, leaning through the door.

'Ready?' Safa asks.

'I am,' Emily says, looking down at herself, then across to Safa. 'We're matching.'

'So?'

'Draws the eye if we look the same. I thought we had to be covert. Miri said . . .'

'Oh,' Safa says, looking from herself to Emily, both wearing black T-shirts. 'Fair one. I'll change my top . . .'

'Something different to me.'

'This?' Safa calls out.

'That's a black vest top.'

'Yeah.'

'No,' Emily says. 'Something not black.'

'Something not black,' Safa repeats, looking round the room at her black clothes. 'Ben, you've got white T-shirts. Can I use one?'

'Er, yeah, sure, hang on,' Ben says, heading into his room.

'Never been very good with clothes and things,' Safa tells Emily.

'It'll be baggy,' Ben says, walking back with one.

'S'fine, it'll hide the pistol,' Safa says, tugging her top off as Ben swears and turns round again.

'You can stop laughing, beardy,' he mutters, slumping down into the chair next to a chuckling Harry.

'Sharing clothes, eh?' Harry says. 'My Ben.'

'Piss off.'

'I told Ben he's not allowed near attractive, diseased whores,' Safa says quietly in her room to Emily while pulling the white T-shirt on. 'He blushing now?'

'Oh, yes,' Emily says, leaning out the door to spot Ben's rosy cheeks.

'That better?' Safa asks, presenting herself to Emily.

'Fine,' Emily says. Even in just a baggy white T-shirt and jeans, Safa looks stunning. 'Leave your hair down,' she adds quickly as Safa goes to tie it back. 'Looks more natural.'

'Yeah?' Safa asks.

'Looks fine,' Emily says. 'Your hair is lovely.'

'Needs cutting. Haven't touched it in, like, six months.'

'I can trim a bit for you later.'

'Yeah? Cheers. Think I've got split ends. Is that a split end?'

'Show me . . . Yep, it's fine though. We'll just take a bit off. So where are you putting the pistol?'

'On my belt at the back.'

'Turn round,' Emily says, looking down at the hem of the T-shirt in relation to the waistline of the jeans. 'Should be okay.'

'We're off,' Safa says, coming out of her room.

'Safa, you sure about this?' Ben asks, lifting his head from his hands.

'Be fine. Miri's coming with us too.'

'Is Emily going to be armed?' Ben asks.

'No, I won't be,' Emily says before Safa can answer. 'I gave my word.'

'Maybe me and Harry should come. Like, just be near or something.'

'We'll be fine,' Safa says. 'Come on then, spy lady with the fake name Emily.'

'Emily?' Ben says as the two women move towards the door. She looks back at him to see his expression has hardened. His gaze on her and her alone. The man who took on five gang members when he was seventeen. The man who attacked the terrorists at Holborn and took the battering from Echo on the landing. She looks to Harry to see the same thing and a hint of the man that lifted Alpha off his feet and brought a German base to its knees.

'I promise,' she says softly, the words catching in her throat at the subtle, yet staggering sense of threat suddenly conveyed.

'Christ,' Safa says, looking from Ben to Harry. 'Silly twats. You'd make me cry if I knew how.'

'Ach,' Harry says, genial and smiling. 'My Ben.'

'Fuck's sake,' Ben groans.

'My Ben,' Safa laughs, heading out the door.

Twenty-Two

'So is there anything going on between you?' Emily asks while they wait in the portal room. Hardly believing she is even asking, or even interested to ask. She is about to go back through the time machine to her own time, after being asked to do so by the woman holding her captive. She should be planning to run or secure the device. She should be doing many things, but right now she is actually really quite interested if Safa and Ben are a couple, and even thinking ahead to later and cutting Safa's hair.

'Who? Me and Ben?' Safa asks. 'Nope. I think we kissed, but . . .'

'You *think* you kissed?'

'In the ocean. When Ben came back . . . We were sharing an oxygen bottle, and I was breathing for us . . . so I think we kissed . . .'

'Oh,' Emily says, as though that was the most natural story she has ever heard.

'And, er, this one night . . .' Safa stops herself. 'Tell you another time.'

'Ready?' Miri walks into the room and hands Safa a pistol and spare magazines.

'Ta,' Safa says. She loads a magazine, checks the safety, then holsters the weapon before presenting her back to Emily. 'See it?'

'Only just,' Emily says.

Miri holsters her own pistol, hidden by the tails of her checked shirt. 'Get shirts. Easier to conceal a weapon. We're going in blind. I know the subject's home address, but not who she lives with. Subject's name is Clara Jacobsen. We arrive two minutes away in an alleyway during the hours of darkness, but there will be ambient street lighting. We go out the alley. Turn right. Walk down to the junction. Turn left. Walk down to the junction. Turn left. Seventh building. Entrance on the ground floor, white side front. Terraced property. Area looks semi-affluent. That means access to whatever devices are used to summon emergency services. Most urban cities in the western world have a police response time of under four minutes. Is that still the case, Tango Two?'

'Less,' Emily says. 'Drones are dispatched with pre-set coordinates. They move fast on a flight plane reserved for their sole use. If anyone calls the police, we can expect eyes on us within two minutes or less.'

'Subject has a phone. She works in a private hospital. Injured persons from the bunker were taken there. Your agents took those males from the clinic. After they left, the female subject used what appears to be a phone to send a message. I want to know who she is communicating with, and what is in that phone.'

'Got it,' Safa says.

'Understood,' Emily says, feeling strangely in work mode, except for the fact she doesn't work for these people. She works for the British Secret Service.

The blue light comes on. Mesmerising and shimmering. Emily has seen it before, but still she stares, captivated. 'It's beautiful,' she says quietly.

'Safa, on point. I'll take rear. Tango Two middle.'

'Emily,' Safa says. 'She gave us her name, so . . .'

'Take point, Miss Patel.'

Safa takes point, pulling a told-off face at Emily before walking through the light. Emily blinks at the sight of a person disappearing in increments, then bursts out laughing when Safa's hand comes back through with the middle finger sticking up.

'Go through,' Miri says.

'Sorry.' Emily winces at laughing, at looking unprofessional, then worries why she is even concerned at looking unprofessional. A rise in her heart rate as she steps through into an alleyway. Time travel. Instant and without sensation. She spots Safa grinning. This would never happen in the British Secret Service. A joke would never be played, not in training, and certainly never in a live mission. No flippancy. No banter. Just work.

'Ready?' Miri says, coming out behind her. 'Move normally. We're three women walking.'

The three women walk from the alley into a standard residential, inner-city Berlin street. High buildings. Ornate windows. A transition to dirty, polluted air and the smells of traffic, people, cooking, living. The sounds of a city. Harsh lights overhead.

Emily feels the jolt of moving from somewhere so pure to a hundred million years in the future. Her head wants to spin, but her mind is set for work. She could run right now and chance it. She could ram an elbow into Safa's head and just sprint. If she screamed rape or fire, she'd draw attention. She stands a chance at least. Why isn't she doing it? This is her time. Her world. *Do something.*

'You okay?' Safa asks, her eyes narrowing slightly.

'It's just weird,' Emily says earnestly.

'I told Greta to tell him to go. She should not be treated like that. Honestly, but she never listens. Just never listens to anyone. Such a stubborn woman.' Miri comes to life. Her voice animated with pitch, lilt and tone. Her face active to convey the words in fluent German as Safa glances over to a couple walking past on the other side of the road.

'Christ, Miri,' Safa whispers once the people are gone. 'Was that German?'

Emily concedes the expertise shown. The accent was very good, and the delivery and tone were perfect. She spots a man walking towards them. His eyes flicking left to right in that zoned-out way of walking when someone is familiar with the world around them.

'Of course, Greta was the one who had the affair though,' Emily says in fluent German. 'I mean, she was treated badly, but she was the cheater, so maybe he should be leaving her, or they could just, you know, work it out and move on . . .'

'Very good,' Miri says once the man has gone past.

'Look at you two,' Safa says, nudging Emily with her elbow. 'Wish I could do that.'

'What other languages can you speak?' Miri asks Emily.

'French, Spanish, some Arabic dialects, although not well. My Mandarin is good. Cantonese is okay.'

'Russian?' Miri asks, in Russian.

'*Da*,' Emily says. 'I forgot Russian,' she adds, in Russian.

'Beautiful language,' Miri says, in Russian.

'Not as beautiful as English,' Emily says, in English.

'Clever bastards,' Safa mutters, wondering if Ben can speak any languages.

'Did you have to learn them?' Miri asks.

'A second language is essential,' Emily explains. 'But I'm lucky. I can take new languages easily . . . Been doing it since I was a child, and of course the intracranial information dumps help enormously.'

'What the hell is that?' Safa asks.

'Only works for children. Like a skull cap they wear at night that sends information into the brain. My family had an early version. I could speak French by the time I was five, but neither of my parents could speak it.'

'Does it work with everything?' Miri asks.

'No. Languages are the main thing. Everything else needs context. Maths, sciences . . . core subjects – they all need contextual understanding relative to the world and experiences. Like I said, children work well, but as the body develops, so the thing within the brain ceases to receive the intracranial flow.'

'Fuck,' Safa mumbles.

'Seventh building on this street,' Miri says as they turn the corner. Five men ahead walking towards them. Three white. One black. One Arabic.

'Agents,' Emily whispers, adding a broad grin to Safa, as though in response to something said. She reaches out while chuckling and laughs as she tugs Safa's T-shirt down at the back, covering the pistol.

'Brits?' Miri asks, leaning forward to laugh at the joke Safa said that made Emily pull her top down.

'No,' Emily says, still grinning. 'Yours. Yanks.'

'Know you?' Miri chuckles, pointing at Safa's top.

'No,' Emily says, pushing her arm round Safa's shoulders, as though to soften the joke they just made. 'I am sorry!' Emily says in German, loud and laughing as she hugs Safa and laughs. 'It was funny though.'

'Very funny,' Miri grins, speaking out in fluent German as she looks across at her two friends.

'Don't speak,' Emily whispers to Safa. 'Haha! Your face when I said it. You were, like . . . *Did she just say that?*

Safa does nothing. She doesn't have to. Emily and Miri take over, both laughing and gabbling in German. She glances ahead to the five men. All hard-looking, but trying to appear normal. To the last, they glance at Safa and smile, but that's nothing new to Safa. Normally, she would scowl or even tell them to piss off.

'*Guten abend*,' Miri says politely as they pass.

'*Guten abend*,' Emily calls out, still chuckling from the joke with Safa.

'*Gootten aband*,' one of them says in what he thinks is a fluent German accent, but sounds like an American trying to speak German.

'That was an awful accent,' Emily says quietly.

'Go slower,' Miri says, risking a glance round.

'How did you know they were Yanks?' Safa asks.

'Just one of those things. Way they dress and look.'

'Low end,' Miri states. 'Berlin must be full of them.'

'We were told it was a new weapon of mass destruction,' Emily says. 'Everyone knew something was going on.'

Why is she saying that? Why is she doing this? They were American agents. She could have shouted for help. They would have responded. Done something. This is not her mission. This is not her job. She has to snap out of this.

'That's it,' Miri says, nodding ahead to the seventh building. Lights on inside behind window coverings.

'Take the door,' Miri says to Emily. 'Your German is better than mine.'

Emily falters for a second, trapped between being drawn into this game and desperately trying to remind herself she is not one of them.

'Problem?' Miri asks.

'No,' Emily says. It does make sense. Miri's accent is good, but it carries a trace of American. Emily's German is perfect, even capturing the imperfections of speech that native Berliners use. She starts forward, staring up at the door.

'Safa is right behind you,' Miri says with a warning edge to her voice.

'You asked me,' Emily says, pausing halfway up the set of steps to the front door. 'I have given you my word . . . and we just walked past five American agents.'

Emily knocks, and that in itself shows training. The knock is polite and friendly. Three taps. Not too hard. Not spaced apart. The science of showing no threat. She adopts a friendly countenance in case she is being watched through a peephole or camera. Footsteps inside.

'Movement,' she whispers, turning her head towards Safa. Neither of them notice Miri drawing her pistol to hold low at her side as she watches the front door.

The hairs on the back of Safa's neck prickle. She heard the heavy footsteps too: a solid body wearing big boots on wooden floorboards. Her senses come alive. Her eyes hardening. A very faint metallic click. Safa can't speak languages. She isn't good with clothes and hair, but she can bloody tell when a man with a gun is about to open a door.

'Move back!'

Her hand whips out to wrench Emily away as the door cracks open. Safa hits it hard, ramming it into the face of the man, sending him staggering back as she slips through, weaves to the side and snatches the pistol from his grip while slamming the heel of her right hand into his nose already broken from the impact of the door. She turns as she moves, snatching a view of four men in the front room pointing guns at each other over the head of a woman kneeling in the middle of the floor. Two Asian males. Two Slavic. The woman's face a mask of mascara, blood and tears. Her clothing torn, livid welts on her face, neck and exposed breasts.

Emily powers into the hallway behind Safa with an instinct urging her to attack. She spots the man going down and sees his pistol in Safa's hand.

No time to think. No time for thoughts. Everything on instinct and gut reaction. Safa pulls the gun from the holster in the small of her back as she spins, and throws the pistol taken from the man to Emily.

Emily snatches it from the air as she steps through and drops to a knee, aiming at Safa.

A split second as Safa's eyes go wide on realising what she just did. A mistake made. An awful, terrible mistake in the heat of the moment, brought on by growing too comfortable with a woman who is a prisoner, not a friend. Her own pistol has too far to travel to aim at Emily.

There are armed men behind her. Everything taken in within the blink of an eye.

Miri saw the pistol being thrown. She saw it as she surged up the steps. She catches a glimpse of Emily aiming at Safa, and four armed men moving quickly. The thrill inside. *The thrill of the game. Are the roots strong enough?*

Emily aims and fires. She doesn't hesitate. She is a trained agent. The bullet leaves the pistol, spinning through the air at a velocity too fast to see. Safa tries to move, but the round whizzes millimetres past her ear to strike the closest one of the four men bringing his aim at Safa.

'DOWN,' Emily shouts.

Safa drops to her back, aims up and fires into another with a double-tap to his centre of mass that sends him flying back off his feet. The men return fire with wild shots.

Miri fires once from the doorway into the man Safa hit on the way in as he tugs a secondary pistol from a holster on his belt. She kills him outright. Emily fires twice more into the third man in the room. Safa rolls to aim and shoot into the last.

'Two down,' Emily reports.

'Two down,' Safa calls out.

'One down,' Miri shouts.

Silence. Ears ringing.

'Clear the house,' Miri orders. 'Less than two minutes.'

'Cover me.' Safa surges up to her feet and strides forward into the room. Emily at her back, covering the points of danger.

'Shit,' Safa hisses. 'The woman's dead.' Safa drops to check and be sure, but she can see the position of the entry wounds in her back means the rounds would have gone through her heart, spine and lungs, killing her instantly.

'All dead,' Emily says, checking the other bodies in the room.

Safa moves across the room to the doorway at the end that leads into the kitchen. Emily stays close, but leaves enough reaction space while factoring for crossfire, angles, escape routes and points of potential attack.

'Clear,' Safa says, sweeping through the kitchen with her pistol held double-handed as she tracks round.

'Upstairs,' Miri says.

'Go,' Safa says to Emily.

Emily takes the lead, sweeping back through the front room to the hallway and over a bloodied corpse to mount the stairs. Everything on instinct. Everything on gut reaction. No time for thought. No time for thinking. She aims as she rises. Safa close behind her, but leaving space for reaction while instinctually factoring for crossfire, angles, escape routes and points of potential attack.

'Three rooms. One ahead. Two to the right.'

'Covering,' Safa says, aiming towards the two doorways on the right at the top of the stairs. Emily goes forward to the one ahead.

'Bathroom, clear.'

'Proceeding,' Safa says, moving to the first door on the right. She kicks it open and surges in. 'Bedroom, clear.'

'Proceeding,' Emily says, moving on to the last door as Safa comes out and covers the hallway. 'Bedroom, clear.'

'House clear,' Safa calls down.

They move swiftly down the stairs to Miri in the front room standing over the dead body of Clara Jacobsen. 'Silly girl,' she says quietly, almost sadly.

'You get her phone?' Safa asks.

Miri holds it out, or what remains of it anyway. 'Destroyed.'

Safa takes in the device, smashed and broken from a stray shot. 'Not our day then,' she mutters.

'These are Chinese and Russian agents,' Emily says, holding passports taken from the pockets of the dead men. 'Looks like they were arguing over the woman.'

Miri looks at her, then round at the bodies. 'Clearly,' she states.

'Chinese, Russians . . . the Yanks we walked past,' Safa says. 'How many people are after us?'

'Everyone, by the looks of it,' Emily says.

'Exfil,' Miri says, glancing at her watch. 'One minute twenty.'

'We might be able to retrieve data from that phone,' Emily says. 'Keep it.'

They run from the house into the street, using a burst of speed to create distance. Safa and Miri re-holster. Emily tucks hers into the front of her waistband and pulls her T-shirt out to cover the bulge. 'See it?' she asks.

'Looks like a big willy,' Safa says.

Safa starts smiling. She tries to stop, but can't help it. She coughs to clear her throat. Emily stares ahead, the corners of her mouth twitching. She looks to Safa, who suddenly snorts a laugh and covers her mouth while looking away. Emily grins, then tries to stop grinning.

'Big willy?' Emily asks as Safa snorts again.

They get into the alley, one older woman wincing from the pain of running and two younger ones trying not to giggle.

Miri knows their reactions are caused by endorphins and adrenalin kicking in. To anyone else, it would look cold, callous even. A lack of care for human life. It isn't that at all. This is normal to the people in her world. People just died, but Safa and Emily are highly trained professionals doing what they have been trained to do, and what's more, they did it very well.

Very damn well.

As the first drones whir overhead, fitted with tiny flashing blue and red lights, so they reach the alley and run down to stop at the blue, shimmering light. As they slow down, Emily pulls the pistol out, pops the magazine, slides back to empty the chamber and holds it all out to Miri.

'Thank you for your assistance,' Miri says, taking the gun.

'Anytime,' Emily says as Safa walks through the blue light then sticks her hand back out with her middle finger sticking up again. Emily snorts a laugh, then covers her mouth in embarrassment. 'Sorry. She is funny though,' she says.

'Safa is unique,' Miri says quietly, studying the agent. Emily looks back at her, at the cold grey eyes that are impossible to read.

Miri nods at the blue light. 'After you, Tango Two. Perhaps you could make me a coffee.'

Twenty-Three

Ben drums his fingers on the table. Harry turns a page. Ben stares at the door and continues drumming his fingers on the table.

'Miri doesn't do anything without a reason.'

Harry looks over the top of his book, then goes back to reading.

Ben drums his fingers. Harry turns a page.

'She's doing something.'

'Ach. Probably.'

Ben drums his fingers and stares at the door. Harry exhales noisily through his nose and smiles wryly to himself at Ben's increasing frustration. Voices sudden and loud. Safa laughing as she walks through the corridor and pushes into the main room with Emily close behind her. Ben immediately spots the butt of the pistol poking out of the holster in the small of Safa's back and the complete lack of attention Emily is paying to it. An energy between them. The glow of a post-adrenalin rush.

'Everything okay?' he asks needlessly as Harry lowers his book.

'Fuck, yes,' Safa says. 'Apart from the five bad guys we killed,' she adds, trying to sound and look sad for a second. 'But, oh my god, Emily was so cool . . .'

'Yeah?' Ben asks, watching the two women grinning from ear to ear. 'What happened?'

'Miri said she wants a coffee,' Emily says. 'Anyone else?'

'Love one,' Ben says.

'Tea, please, Emily,' Harry says.

'Big willy,' Emily laughs, walking over with Safa to the main table.

Ben thinks while watching them, the way they laugh and joke with each other. It's nice to see. Safa is changing. Becoming more open and friendly. Emily is drawing Safa out of herself, and for her part, Safa has Emily laughing most of the time with the blunt way she speaks.

It was Safa who pulled him through his decline. The pressure on her must have been immense. To sustain belief in him day after day for six months was incredible. Now she is slowly relaxing and becoming more human. Safa even admitted quietly, when they were alone, that she'd never really had friends before. *Not proper mates. You know what I mean?*

Emily is still a prisoner though, and that situation is still to be resolved. Ben knows everything Miri does is for a reason. This mission tonight was done for a reason, and while everyone has been worried about cultivation, maybe the cultivation has been happening on another level.

'What about the girl and the phone?' he calls out.

'Killed,' Emily says, grimacing as she turns to reply. 'Two Chinese and three Russian agents were arguing over her as we arrived . . .'

'Oh, right,' Ben says, leaning forward on his chair and listening intently.

'Two Russian agents,' Safa says.

'No, three. The one you took out at the door was Russian too.'

'She was already dead then?' Ben asks.

'Sadly not,' Emily says. 'Killed when they opened fire. We took them out quickly, but . . . well, not quickly enough. The phone Miri wanted was shot too, but she might be able to retrieve data from the chip.'

'Thanks,' he says, as Emily carries his coffee over.

'Seriously, Ben. I've never seen anyone move as fast as Safa . . .'

'Sure,' Ben says, thinking hard. '*Sorry . . . tell me again what happened . . .*'

'*Safa . . .*' Emily's voice, groaning with humour.

Miri cocks her head slightly. The wire stretching from her ear to the smartphone on the desk in front of her.

'*What?*' Safa's voice. Humour.

'*You're presenting your pistol to me again.*' Emily's voice, humour.

'*So?*' Safa's voice.

'*Seriously, Safa.*' Emily's voice. '*You are, like, the worst guard ever.*'

'*Hang on.*' Ben's voice. Concerned. Inquisitive. '*Where was this? Where did it happen?*'

Miri listens as Emily and Safa recount the mission. The way they both speak in turn and fill in gaps the other left out. The tone of their voices, and both speaking a little faster than normal from the excitement of the mission.

'*You went to her house? This being the woman who worked in the clinic Malc and Kon took the guards to . . .*'

'*Yeah, her house.*' Safa's voice. '*What's that look for? You going all egghead again?*'

'*You went to her house?*'

'*Fuck me, Ben. Yes, we went to her house.*'

'*And the other . . . agent people were already there?*'

'*Yes!*'

'*And that seems normal to you, does it?*' An edge to Ben's voice. Miri stiffens, ready to rise from the chair. She's pushed Ben as far as he can go.

'*Er . . . well, she kinda lives there?*' Safa's voice, still with humour.

'*Why? What's wrong with that?*' Emily asks.

'*Ben? Where're you going?*'

It's time.

Miri pulls the earpiece from her ear, slides the phone off and stands up to head into the main room to see Ben already on his feet walking towards her.

'We need to talk,' he says, his eyes brooding, his whole manner set with a decision formed.

'Later.'

'No.'

'Mr Ryder . . .'

'Now.'

Miri glares at him. He glares back. She about-turns to stride into her office with Ben right behind her.

'Close the door,' Miri says, stopping to stand with her arms folded across her chest.

'What the fuck was that?'

'What?'

'You know damn well what, Miri. You took them to that woman's house with five agents inside.'

'Poor luck, Mr Ryder.'

'Poor luck, my arse. We've got a time machine. We could go anytime. You would have cased it out. You would have known they were inside.'

'I am honoured by your opinion of my capabilities, but . . .'

'Don't patronise me. That girl died . . . That might not mean anything to you, but it . . .'

'That *girl* sold the lives of six men under her care for money. Greed and stupidity killed her by playing multiple agencies, each of which warned her exactly not to do that very thing. Yes, I knew they were there. Yes, I had already completed my investigation, but this *is* my work, Mr Ryder. These are *my* methods and this *is* what I do.' The passion in her voice makes him blanch. 'Do not question me. Do not question my methods. You are smart and your frustrations are duly noted, but therein lies the discipline you need to work at this level and the stomach to cope with it.'

'*Quis custodiet ipsos custodes?*'

She widens her eyes and bursts out laughing with a sound so unexpected it robs the heat from his temper. She looks away, then bursts out laughing again when she turns back to him. 'Seriously, Ben? *Who polices the police?*'

He shrugs. 'Sorry, bit trite.'

'That was beneath you.' Her whole manner suddenly animated and alive with humour. 'It will be concluded tonight.'

Ben chuckles softly at himself and the situation. He can't help it. The sudden warmth of the woman invites him to break the tension. That he is being played is obvious. 'What about Emily?'

The smile fades away, taking the warmth from her face with it. The eyes grow cold and hard again with an instant transformation that sends a chill down his spine. He gets the sense he is being shown what she can do. A glimpse of the master. 'I need to speak to her . . .'

He tuts and shakes his head, refusing the urge to be cowed in her presence. 'You're not giving anything away, are you?'

Miri reads him closely. His reactions to her sudden humour, then the ease in which she took that warmth away. That he can overcome nerves and retain his focus is testament to his natural abilities. She draws a breath. Slow and long. Her lips purse with a thoughtful gaze that flits over her features. 'Has to be that way. For what it's worth, you've probably worked it out correctly.'

'Wow. Now that was patronising,' he counters, and earns a twitch at the corner of her mouth. 'Has she worked it out? Emily, I mean. Has she said anything to you? She's asked us loads of times.'

'She hasn't worked it out.'

'But she's an agent.'

'Tango Two has a range of exceptional skills, but is lacking in advanced cognitive function.'

Ben can't help but smile at the reply. 'So she's a bit thick then.'

'She is a highly trained agent . . . Just not a very good one.'

'Roland? Bertie and Ria?'

'Let me get through tonight, Ben. We can talk more tomorrow. Send Emily in, please.'

Twenty-Four

'Debrief,' Miri says, sitting down behind her desk.

Emily sits down. She feels hot. The mission, and now laughing with Safa, has made her cheeks flushed. She waits. Staring over the desk at the older woman. Nerves kick in. The overwhelming sense that Miri is always ten steps ahead in every conversation they have, which is how she imagines it would be meeting Mother face-to-face.

'Why did they try to kill you?' Miri goes straight in with the question and watches the agent closely. Examining every nuance of reaction. The direction of the eyes, the posture, the breaths taken, if the woman swallows, if she tilts or inclines her head. The tone of voice; if it is made stronger or weaker with effort. This is the game, and the thrill of being back is strong.

'I don't know,' Emily says quickly.

Miri waits. Questioning a trained agent is entirely different to debriefing a normal person. Emily is trained to not only withstand questioning, but to read the interviewer as much in return to gain leverage and understanding. The whole thing is a mind game. A pitting of mental agility.

Or so Miri thought when she first started debriefing Emily.

In the end, it comes down to the simplicity of the fact that although both are trained, Miri has decades of experience and Emily really has not worked it out yet.

Emily knows this process is coming to a close. The pressure builds. Her heart rate rises slightly as she looks across at Miri, with a sense of foreboding and dread growing inside.

'Our debriefs are concluded.' A cold voice, a hard voice. The dread grows. Emily swallows and blinks several times. 'You will meet me in the portal room in five minutes,' Miri says, rising from the chair.

The power of Miri hits her. A surge of worry inside. The mystery of the woman, the aura of utter authority. She searches the older woman for any sign of emotion, but sees only cold grey eyes staring back, and an absolute belief grows in Emily that Miri would kill her without hesitation.

'Where am I going?' Emily asks. 'Do I need to say goodbye to the others? Safa has been a friend to me. I owe her a goodbye if I am . . .'

'Five minutes, portal room.'

'Miri, if you are going to execute me then you can do it here.'

'Do not tell me what to do. Five minutes, portal room,' Miri says, walking from the office to her own set of rooms. Emily pushes her hands through her hair, that feeling of dread growing. She knows what's going to happen. She is an agent. She is not one of them. She is the enemy within. Tonight was a test that she's failed somehow. She did something wrong. Maybe Miri thought she was aiming at Safa. She turns to explain, but realises Miri has gone, leaving her entirely alone. She thinks of the footage of the end of the world and the hologram image of Cavendish Manor they saw outside. Why did Mother order her to be killed? Miri knows something. Does Miri work for Mother? Thoughts flash through her whirling mind as her stomach flips and plunges.

She turns for the door. Not seeing and not looking at the pistol left on Miri's desk. In the corridor, she pauses to stare into the portal room at the shimmering blue light of the time machine left open, and thinks only of not being here. Of not training with the others outside and eating eggs and fruit. Of not joking with Safa and talking about missions and the things they've done. Emily never had a friend before. Not a real one. Her role was so serious she couldn't bond with anyone outside of her organisation. This is it. She did something wrong tonight. She failed somehow, but she knows she is still a trained agent who was taken captive, and the end was always going to come.

She pushes into the main room, ashen-faced and with all trace of the post-mission buzz now gone from her manner.

'Miri told me to meet her in the portal room in five minutes.'

'Why, what's going on?' Safa asks, her own grin fading at seeing Emily's state.

'She said . . . She said the debriefs are concluded.'

'Like, finished?' Safa asks.

'She left me in her office,' Emily says, blinking several times before moving across the room towards the others. Harry looks up from his book. 'And the portal is open. I just walked past it . . .'

'Fuck knows,' Safa says. 'She say where you're going?'

'No, just to meet her in the portal room. I said if she is going to execute me to do it now . . .'

Harry rises from his chair. 'There'll be none of that now,' he rumbles.

'I said . . .' Emily says, feeling a rush of emotion. 'I said . . . I said I wanted to say goodbye if I was going . . .'

'She wouldn't,' Safa says firmly, shaking her head, but then glancing at Ben with worry in her eyes. 'We just did a mission together . . . You had a weapon and . . .'

'I mean, if she is going to do that, then . . .' Emily's voice breaks as she fights the urge to cry. 'I'm the enemy and . . . But . . . I'd rather die here than . . . And Mother told them to kill me. If I go back, they'll kill me . . . I . . . I like it here . . .'

'Ach,' Harry says, deeper and stronger as he moves towards her, seeing the tears spilling down her cheeks.

'*I'm an agent.*' Emily's voice, trying to inject some firmness in her tone, but just sounding more scared. Miri walks back to her office, listening intently and spotting the pistol is where she left it. She rolls her eyes and tuts softly. '*I know the risks . . . But listen, thank you for being my friends . . .*'

'*Hey, no, stop that.*' Ben's voice. '*She won't do that . . .*'

'*Like fuck she will.*' Safa's voice, the aggression rising. '*I'll ask her . . . Where is she?*'

'*Safa, no.*' Emily's voice, speaking quickly.

'*She's not doing anything to you.*' Safa's voice.

'*She might have to.*' Emily's voice, full of emotion, quavering. Miri listens, knowing exactly what Emily is feeling because she orchestrated it. Emily thinks of herself as a highly trained agent, but has simply been exposed to a level of manipulation she has never experienced before. '*Listen, I'm an agent . . . If Miri has to do it, then . . .*'

'*No,*' Safa snaps.

'*I can't just stay here forever, Safa,*' Emily says. '*And if I go back, then Mother will kill me . . .*'

'*Can't just execute someone because . . .*'

'*You would have done it,*' Emily says.

'*I didn't know you!*' Safa's voice. '*I'm telling you right now I won't let her . . .*'

'*If Miri says it's the right thing, then it's the right thing,*' Emily fires back. '*She must know why Mother ordered me to be killed. Tonight must have been a test or . . . I don't know! I just . . .*'

'*Oh my god, what the fuck?*' Safa says, her voice rising with disbelief.

'*No.*' Ben's voice, calm and assured. '*It's not that. Stop panicking. It's fine.*'

'*You know something.*' Safa's voice. '*Ben, what? What's happening?*'

'*It's fine. Just go with Miri. You'll be fine.*'

Miri smiles again. *Who polices the police?* She likes Ben.

'*WHAT?*' Safa shouts. Miri chuckles.

'*I said it's fine. Emily, you must have worked it out by now.*'

'*Worked what out?*' Safa shouts again. '*What? Ben, for fuck's sake . . .*'

'*Oh my god! Seriously? She's outside with us when we attack the house. That's why her side were told to kill her. They saw her. They saw her outside. It's bloody obvious. She comes with us when we help the us in the house.*'

Silence. Miri laughs softly at the vision in her head of the others' faces.

Time to move. She pulls the earpiece out and strides from her rooms up the corridor to the heavy metal door and pauses to listen to the voices inside.

'Oh my god,' Ben calls out. 'I just said she won't kill you.'

'I would,' Emily says honestly. 'You might be wrong, and in this situation I would execute . . . And if she sends me back, then I'm dead anyway because Mother will . . .'

'What?' Ben asks in disbelief.

Miri tuts softly. This is why the woman is still a Two.

'Tango Two,' she calls out, opening the door.

'Coming now,' Emily says quickly.

'Are you going to kill her?' Safa asks, glaring.

'Oh my days,' Ben groans.

Miri stays as Miri is. Expressionless. Revealing nothing. Reading everything. Seeing all. 'Has the agent cultivated you?' Miri asks as bland and flat as ever, and all the more striking for it.

'No, I haven't,' Emily insists.

'That,' Miri says quietly to Safa, 'is what cultivating is.'

'MIRI,' Safa shouts, her face flushed with anger.

'Yes, I cultivated them,' Emily says coldly. She smiles humourlessly and sighs. 'Fuck it. Well done, Miri. We going then?'

'Dear god,' Ben groans again, slumping down in a chair. 'I give up.'

'My advice,' Emily says to Miri, 'from one agent to another . . . get professionals. These three amateurs aren't capable or competent.'

'Emily,' Safa says, 'stop it . . .'

'With me,' Miri says simply, pushing through the doors.

'You three need to toughen up,' Emily says, turning back at the doors to look at them. 'I would have killed you all within a week . . .'

'It's been over a week,' Ben mutters. 'It's been over three weeks . . .'

◆ ◆ ◆

'I would rather you killed me here, Miri. I don't want to . . .'

'Shut up.'

Emily blanches at the harsh rebuke, the sting showing in her cheeks. She tries to rally to keep going, but that same energy from Miri gets to her. Blagging or bluffing Miri just isn't right. She follows the older woman into the portal room with her heart jack-hammering and her mouth growing dry.

'I just want to say . . .' Emily swallows to try and speak normally with composure and dignity as Miri arches an eyebrow, shakes her head and lifts the tablet. 'I want to say thank you for the decency of . . . and the . . . I mean, the kindness you have bestowed and . . .'

'Can you move silently?'

'Pardon?'

Miri looks up at her as the blue light blinks out. 'I said, can you move silently?'

'Yes, but . . .'

'You will not make a sound. You will not speak. You will watch and we will talk after. Am I clear?'

'What?'

'Am I clear?'

'Yes, but . . . Listen, Mother will kill me if I go back, so . . . I mean, it's nice here and . . .'

Miri jabs at the tablet. The blue light comes back on. Bathing the room once again.

'Move silently. Follow me,' Miri says, placing the tablet down before going through the portal.

Emily blinks again, feeling as if she's always several steps behind when speaking to Miri. She looks at the tablet, then at the light, and with her mind spinning, she walks through and sees Miri standing in the darkness with her finger pressed to her mouth, indicating silence. The stench of rotten, damp air hits instantly with an immediate impression of being underground. An absence of light. She looks round to bare concrete walls that drip and ooze gunk. The only light is from the portal bathing the corridor in an eerie glow.

Miri twitches her head for Emily to follow. The older woman moves off down the corridor, placing her feet carefully to avoid stepping on any of the debris left strewn about. Emily moves in the same way, lifting to place her feet with each step thought in advance to avoid scuffing or noise.

The corridor is long and the light from the portal fades the further they go, plunging them into deep shadow. Miri uses a small pocket torch to light the ground. Shining so they can both see where to tread. They reach a corner and move round to an old metal staircase. Miri goes carefully. Emily the same. Descending the cold metal stairs. Emily catches sight of Russian letters and symbols. An old Soviet installation. She wonders if the execution will be done here, but then realises she is not now expecting to be killed. She would have been shot the second she stepped through, and Miri is exposing her weapon side to Emily as they move.

At the bottom of the stairs, Miri again pauses to press her fingers to her mouth. Emily nods. Miri reaches out with a warm, dry hand and gently takes Emily's wrist. The torch goes off, and as the darkness hits, so Emily detects the essence of light coming from round the corner. A voice too. A male voice calling out angrily. Miri guides her on, moving from the stairwell into a wider space. Up ahead, Emily sees the bright, glowing lights coming from one of the cells and someone sitting outside on a chair. A man inside the cell talking.

They go slowly, drawing closer. Emily strains to see. To understand. Her eyes trying to take everything in at once. The realisation comes sudden and unexpected.

'Okay?' The voice comes out, as though the person on the chair is shouting towards them. Miri scrapes her shoe on the rough floor, creating noise.

Emily watches. Taking it in. Trying desperately to keep up with Miri's mental agility and understand not only what she is seeing, but what it means and why she is being shown it.

A squeeze on her wrist. The torch comes back on as Miri leads her back to the stairwell and up the metal steps to the corridor bathed in blue. Emily follows. Stunned and silent. They go through the portal into the bunker as Emily sighs heavily.

'Why did you show me that?'

'Not here. Wait,' Miri says. She picks up the tablet, turns off the blue light, keys in another destination, then activates it again. The light comes back. Miri nods at Emily to follow her and once more steps through.

The frustration and confusion return, but Emily dutifully goes through and immediately squints from the harsh daylight blinding her. A hand comes up to shield her eyes as she makes out Miri wearing sunglasses and lighting a cigarette in a huge, open field of thick grass. A blue sky overhead dotted with clouds. Powerlines in the distance. The rumble of heavy traffic somewhere far off. An old shed behind them, the portal shining in place of the open doorway.

'Where are we?' Emily asks, looking round, then back to Miri. 'You smoke?'

Miri looks at her and lifts an eyebrow. 'Obviously.'

'I mean . . . Okay,' Emily says, trying to order her thoughts. 'What's going on, Miri?'

'Do you need more confirmation on what you just saw?'

'What? No . . . I saw it . . .'

'It hasn't happened yet.'

'What?'

'Time machine, Tango Two,' Miri says, blowing smoke into the air. 'Damn, I shouldn't smoke,' she adds in the first really human thing Emily has heard her say. 'Bad for you,' she says, looking at the cigarette in her hands. 'They banned yet?'

'Er, yes. Yes, they are,' Emily says weakly, her mind spinning.

'Good. Black market strong?'

'Yes,' Emily says again. 'Why am I here? Am I being released?'

'Ben was right. Hell, I think he knew before me, or damned well suspected. He's got a grasp on this. Your side tried to kill you because they saw you outside Cavendish Manor with us. Mother used a satellite to monitor the event. The time now is two days after that. You can leave. You can say you were held captive for two days and escaped, or be honest and say I let you go. I don't care which.'

Emily moves closer, mesmerised by the words spilling from Miri.

'If you are still concerned that your side saw you outside with us, you can disappear and start a new life, but if you walk away, then you're on your own. I can't protect you.'

'But . . .' Emily blinks and rubs her head. 'Miri . . .'

'If you go back to your side, you tell them what you saw just now. Tell them what you know. It will change the timeline, but I do not care. Time is not fixed, and I will bend it to my will. I will bend it to fix this. If you leave now, there is a very slight chance Mother will not kill you. At the very least, you will be tortured, but you know that. Damn, I love smoking. You ever smoke?'

'No,' Emily whispers, unable to take her eyes off Miri.

'You want to go, then go,' Miri says, nodding in the direction of the traffic noises. 'But you tell your side that Maggie Sanderson says hi.'

Emily staggers back, her mouth open. Her stomach flips, heaves and twists. Everything fits. Everything makes sense. 'You?' she whispers.

'Finally,' Miri mutters. 'Yes. Me,' she adds with the bitterness of the years all showing on her lined and weary face.

'Your son . . .'

The look comes; Miri's head snaps up. Fury of a kind Emily has never seen before.

'You have a time machine,' Emily says, the words a gasp.

'I am a professional,' Miri spits.

'You have Harry Madden, Miri. You have Safa Patel and Ben Ryder . . . You have me . . .'

'You know shit, little girl. You know nothing of what an agent is. You play at it. What we did, we did first. Where we went, we went first. Go beg in a public square in Yemen for two months with camel shit smeared on your face so no man looks at you for a chance at a shot that some politician never green-lights. You do not speak of my son. You do not ever speak of my son . . . Mission first. Professional. Take an oath and stand by it.'

'Miri, I . . .' Emily falters, too many things in her mind at one time. Miri is Margaret Sanderson. Maggie Sanderson. The original Mother. The first. Undercover. Covert. Kill missions. Cold War. Africa. The Middle East. Harry Madden. Safa Patel. Ben Ryder. Maggie Sanderson. Every trick learnt, every practice, every policy, procedure and training package refers back to Maggie Sanderson because she did it first. She died in 2010 at her home in California. A multiple hit from forces working together that had spent years tracking her down. It only came out a few years ago, but her body was never recovered.

'It was on the landing.' Miri forces the anger from her voice, which resumes the dull, hard, emotionless state she has perfected over a lifetime of service. She winces as she drops to a crouch to stub her cigarette out and puts the butt in a small plastic bag taken from her pocket. Her body hurts. Everything hurts. 'You're the Brits. The good guys, right?' she stands slowly, looking up to see Emily still hanging off every word said and the look of almost comic shock etched on her face. 'Someone has a time machine. The Brits have to secure it because they're the good guys, right? You were fine with that. You go to the house and commence the attack. You were fine with that.' She turns to face Emily with utter, vicious power dripping from every word spoken. 'You find opposition and you are fine with that, but at some point during that fight, you stopped being the good guys.' Miri points at her. Holding her entranced. 'You had so many. We had so few. You had gunships. We had pistols.' She runs her fingers over the top of the bag, securing the ziplock. 'When that flash-bang was thrown, you saw an old man and an old woman trying to get a young man away from dozens of armed attackers. You realised it was wrong. Do you remember you stopped attacking us before the order to kill you was given? Maybe you had it in mind to go through the portal and try and work from within. Maybe negotiate. Maybe spy. Maybe cultivate. Maybe hell knows what. Damn bullets flying everywhere. Who can think in that chaos? I never could, and sure as dammit nobody else can. Maybe Ben. Ben is rare. I do my thinking after. That's what I always did. I think. I plan and I execute to make sure that shitstorm can't happen again.'

She pauses, before looking back at Emily. 'At some point in every agent's career, they start an ethical debate within their own mind. Black and white becomes grey. The agent thinks it is the world that changes. It never is. The individual evolves. Seen it. Had it. You are younger than average, but that's all it is. Damn.' She takes another cigarette and lights it. She coughs from the smoke, her face flushing from the exertion.

'You should stop,' Emily says quietly.

'Tell me what to do young lady,' Miri says, glancing at Emily, withering, contemptuous, full of furious energy.

Emily closes her eyes as the frantic thoughts whirling in her mind start to settle and find order. 'You bugged us,' she says after a time.

'I bugged every damned room in the bunker. Are you surprised?'

'No,' Emily mumbles. 'Safa is a good person,' she adds, speaking louder.

Miri rolls her eyes, frustration showing at the agent for her emotional needs. Agents can't afford emotion. She goes to snap, to voice the anger, but swallows it down. *Be softer. Be easier. Emily is not you.* 'So are you, Tango Two, which is why you do not have a bullet through your skull. I heard every conversation. You had a half-assed attempt at cultivating, but Safa won you over. Gotta love that girl. Wish I had her years back. Half the shit wouldn't have gone down if we had Safa.'

'I didn't cultivate,' Emily says, needing to say it, needing to be believed. 'I mean . . . I was going to. I was. I thought about Ben first, but the chemistry between him and Safa put me off. Then I got to like Safa and didn't want to do anything with Ben, so then I thought about Harry. But it felt wrong . . . Then I thought about the doctor, but he's so old and he squelches when he eats and . . . and I . . . I just . . .' She trails off, quiet and thoughtful as Miri bites the frustration down.

'I left the door open for you. I left the portal on for you. The only thing I didn't factor was Harry being outside. Tell me, what made you stay?'

'I like them,' Emily says quietly. 'I actually really like them. They're so different to anyone else . . . I didn't have friends before . . .'

'Safa held off five of you on her own. She went into that house tonight before you, and I even blinked. You ever see anyone else do that?'

'No,' Emily admits honestly.

'Me neither. I need Safa. Ben too. He's smart. He doesn't panic. I need that.'

'Ben's exceptional.'

'I need Harry. The man is fearless. You see him throw those men?'

'Tell me what you want, Miri. Tell me what to do.'

Miri smokes and looks over at Emily, then round at the beautiful English countryside, so different to what she is used to in California. *Tell me what to do? Hell. She's never heard an agent say such a thing.* 'You want to go?'

Emily thinks. She looks round at the field and the hedgerow and up to the blue sky that should all feel like home, but it doesn't compare to the sterile bunker and the Cretaceous sky they have on the hill that looks down into the valley. She should be homesick for this, for here, but she sat outside on a balmy evening and ate strawberries and chocolate. She told Safa she would cut her hair. She smiles at the thought and being called fuckstick, spy, shithead and twat every five minutes. She's laughed more in the last twenty-five days than the last ten years. She has introduced Harry Madden to Harry Potter, stood with him under an umbrella in the rain and played a game to see who could draw faster. She did that.

She can go back to her side now and claim the victory, but with a very real risk of being killed, and suddenly it's so obvious. She is on an operation run by Maggie Sanderson in a team of Safa Patel, Ben Ryder and Harry Madden.

Miri rolls her eyes at the painstaking indecision in the agent. This is a no-brainer. Why is she even thinking about it? She puts the cigarette out and places it in the bag with the first. 'You can take these with you. Mother will DNA test them and confirm you're being truthful. It's all I can do to help buy you back into your club.'

'Thanks,' Emily says.

'Jesus wept. Pick a side, Tango Two, but I will win . . . And if I don't, then everyone dies.'

Twenty-Five

Water pools on the floor. Dripping from bodies and hair. Soaked. Breathing hard. Faces flushed. Clothes drenched and tight against bodies. Harry pushes a hand through his beard to remove the excess moisture. Safa flicks her head to the side, spraying droplets from the strands worked loose from her ponytail. Ben shifts to free up his right hand to rub it down his leg in a vain effort to dry it.

'Ready?' Safa asks.

They stare at the Blue. Grim with determination.

'Okay,' Safa says, 'on three . . . One . . . two . . . three!'

She goes first. Running through the blue light with her assault rifle up and aimed, sweeping round in a circle. She holds position, assessing the ground on all sides before sticking a hand back through the light with a thumbs-up.

Emily goes through. Her own assault rifle braced into her shoulder as she aims round.

'Clear,' Emily snaps. 'Move out.'

'Moving out.' Safa paces further across the uneven ground and drops to a knee. The rain pelting into her face. A wall of water pouring from the sky. It's hot too. The humidity is staggering. She shakes her head to rid the droplets of water going into her eyes. 'Clear.'

Emily's hand goes through the light. A thumbs-up to Harry, who comes running through. His right hand holding the heavy machine gun to his waist. His left hand holding the big metal box of belt-fed ammunition connected to the weapon. He moves out and drops to a knee with the butt of the heavy machine gun pressed into his stomach. 'H clear,' Emily reports.

'B out,' Safa says tightly.

Emily's hand goes through to give the signal. Ben comes running into the rain and heat and humidity.

'I'm out,' he says.

'On me.' Safa starts moving ahead at a brisk pace while aiming and checking the front and sides. Emily runs past Ben and Harry to gain the front with Safa. The two side by side going forward to press the attack. Faces fixed. Eyes set and glaring. Water pouring down cheeks to drip from jaws. Hair slick to heads.

'LEFT SIDE, LEFT SIDE,' Emily shouts, opening fire into the figure looming from the tree line. The air erupts with gunfire. The figure drops back. The pace increases. The pressure on.

'HOUSE AHEAD,' Safa shouts, seeing the stately home through the driving rain.

'RIGHT SIDE,' Ben shouts.

Emily spins to seek the figure and fires a strafing burst to suppress anything coming. She twists back to the left and fires again. Safa presses on. Watching ahead. A figure moves. She fires a controlled burst.

'CONTACT AHEAD,' she yells.

'LEFT SIDE,' Emily shouts.

The air fills with gunfire from ahead, from the left, from the right. They run fast. Sprinting towards the house.

'GRENADE,' Safa roars, seeing the object flying through the air. They drop into the mud. All four landing on their backs to keep weapons clear of the gunge beneath them. A huge boom, a flash of light as the flash-bang detonates. 'UP! UP!' Safa screams out, vaulting on to her feet to strafe round from the right side to ahead. Emily a split second behind her, on her knees, then up on to her feet, strafing left side to ahead. Magazines come out. Magazines go in.

They move on. Flash-bangs blow. Disorientating. Loud. They press towards the house.

'HERE,' Safa yells. She drops to a knee and aims ahead to the windows of the house. Sweeping her view across the ground-floor windows, past the front door to the windows of the drawing room as Harry places the Browning down on the bipod. The metal box of ammunition goes down. His right hand finds the trigger. His left stabilises the belt feed. 'FIRING,' his huge voice booms. The gun comes to life. A solid, heavy, sustained thud of a large-calibre weapon. He aims at the window of the drawing room as Safa and Emily turn in circles to give Harry cover as he fires. Figures are seen and fired at. Gunshots sound back. Flash-bangs explode. The noise is immense. Ben lifts his weapon and aims through the sight. Breathing as deeply and as steadily as he can. The fucking thing weighs a ton. He spots a figure through the sight and fires. The recoil whams into his shoulder. He braces, snarls and recovers the aim to fire again into the tree line.

'MOVE ON,' Safa shouts. Harry rises, pulling the gun up with his right hand still on the trigger and his left clutching the box. Safa leads. Emily covers her. The path is picked. The firefight continues. Water plumes from the explosions going off all around them.

'BEN,' Safa shouts.

Ben moves up as Harry fires a heavy machine gun from the waist. His whole body juddering from the recoiling impact against his frame. Ben lifts and aims at the house. He does as he's told and finds the front door as the marker, moving up and to the right to see through the second-floor windows. He aims, fires and works to steady his body, then fires again. The huge boom of the fifty-calibre sniper rifle so distinctive. He moves position. His right foot hits mud and slides. He goes down ory.

hard. Shouting from the pain of hitting the ground while trying to keep his rifle up and out of the surface water.

Harry covers. Safa and Emily drop to either side and pull Ben up. He aims for the door, but his breathing is wrong now. He can't aim properly. The sights are wavering. He fires anyway.

'SLOW DOWN,' Safa shouts.

He winces, breathes and shoots again.

'MOVE OUT . . .' Safa gives the order. They move on, running now. To the last, they flinch at the sound of the chopper blades filling the air, whumping so deep and full of bass. They aim for the corner of the house. Sprinting while guns fire and water plumes from detonations. Smoke billowing from somewhere on the right. Then more on the left. They run down past the side of the house towards the back. Safa in the lead. Ben and Harry in the middle. Emily at their backs.

'FASTER,' Safa shouts. They slip and slide, cursing foully. They run and shake heads to rid water from eyes.

'HERE,' Safa shouts again. Harry moves to present his back to Ben. Ben slings his rifle to the rear and works to pull the missile launcher from Harry's back. Safa and Emily fire at the tree lines, into the air, at anything that may pose a threat. Magazines are changed fast. Everything frantic and rushed.

'Got it,' Ben grunts, pulling the missile launcher free from Harry's back by unclipping the straps holding it in place. He steps back, flicks the sight up, readies the weapon and aims as the air fills with explosions, chopper blades and gunfire, and his view is obscured by water in his eyes and thick smoke billowing everywhere. 'READY,' he shouts.

'FIRE,' Safa shouts back.

'BANG . . . WHOOSH . . . BANG AGAIN . . . OH NO, THE CHOPPER'S BEEN HIT . . . CRUNCHBANGWALLOP . . . MAYDAY, MAYDAY . . . ARGH!'

'FALL BACK,' Safa shouts, trying not to laugh.

'RETREAT,' Ben shouts.

'FALL BACK, NOT RETREAT,' Harry bellows.

'RUN AWAY,' Ben shouts as Emily bursts out laughing. 'LEG IT . . .'

'Ben,' Safa gasps, 'stop it . . .'

'RUN AWAAYYYYYY.'

'GRENADE! DOWN! DOWN!' Emily shouts the warning. They drop again on to backs as the boom sounds out and sends a plume of water sailing into the air.

'UP, UP.' Safa springs to her feet, firing in the direction the grenade came from. She glances back to see Harry and Emily rising, but Ben lying on his back in the water. 'BEN, GET UP . . .'

'I'm hit,' he cries out. 'Go on without me . . .'

'Fuck's sake . . . GET UP,' Safa shouts.

'Tell Wuffles I love him,' Ben says.

'GET . . .'

'I can't . . . The chopper landed on me . . . Go on . . . Run for your lives!'

'BEN. . .' Safa says, marching back as Emily turns away laughing. Harry lowers the heavy machine gun and turns his face to the rain while chuckling.

'Poor Wuffles,' Ben says.

'GET THE FUCK UP,' Safa shouts.

Ben looks at her, his eyes finding hers as the corners of his mouth twitch. She tries to stay angry, but bursts out laughing and kicks surface water at him. 'Who the hell is Wuffles?' she asks, giving in and lowering the rifle from her shoulder.

'Our dog,' Ben says, as though the answer is obvious.

'Such a twat,' she says with a smile touching the corners of her mouth.

The noises cease instantly. The whump of the chopper blades, which were still going despite the missile strike, now ends as the gunshots stop, and the air falls silent save for the pattering of rain striking the ground and trees.

'Best time yet,' Miri calls ahead, walking through the house dressed in an army-green poncho with a bag over one shoulder and a tablet held in her hands. 'Despite Ben slipping,' she adds, emerging from the side wall of the house, which shimmers as she passes through.

'Not fast enough,' Safa says, looking at the hologram of the house.

'My aim was off after slipping,' Ben says, heaving himself up to his feet using the butt of the huge sniper rifle to brace on the ground.

'Things happen in live missions,' Miri says.

'ARE WE FINISHING?' Doctor Watson shouts from somewhere in the rain.

'Harry, tell him we're taking five,' Miri says, coming to a stop as she thumbs the tablet and presses the wrong button, which makes the air fill with the sound of the chopper and gunfire for a second. 'Wet hands,' she murmurs. The sounds stop again. She looks back at the house and presses another button as Roland's stately home blinks from view. 'It's all just binary,' she says to herself.

'TAKING FIVE,' Harry bellows.

'THANK GOD,' the doctor bellows back. 'I'M SOAKED . . . IS RIA WITH YOU?'

'OVER HERE,' a female voice calls out. 'CAN I GO IN?'

'Yes,' Miri says.

'YES,' Harry bellows.

'THANKS,' Ria shouts.

'She said thanks,' Harry says.

'I heard,' Miri says, offering him a quick smile, which for Miri is a microscopic twitch of her lips. Safa pulls a face at Harry. Emily lifts her eyebrows as Ben grins at the big man. Miri doesn't smile at anyone other than Harry.

'Bloody rain,' Ben remarks as they start walking back.

'When you've been in a war with rain,' Emily quips with a grin at Harry.

'Worse than jungle rain this,' Harry says, taking no offence at all.

'It's very wet rain,' Safa says as Emily, Ben and Harry all nod and make sounds of agreement.

Miri stares at them from under the hood of the poncho. Only the British could say rain is wet and understand what it means. They can spend hours discussing and dissecting it. They have so many words for it too. Strange people, for sure.

They trudge back across the clearing on the wide plateau on top of the hill above the bunker. The Blue comes back into view slowly. Glimpsed through the rain before shining clearly. Ria stands next to it. Waiting for them in an army-green poncho with an M4 assault rifle gripped in her hands.

'Hey,' Ben calls ahead. 'Chopper landed on me.'

'Oh, well.'

'Lots of sympathy then.' Ben grins at her.

'No,' she says. 'Why did we finish before you got back?'

'I just said – the chopper landed on me.'

'It's not real,' Ria says, tilting her head back to peer out from the hood.

'He was being a dick,' Safa says. 'Did Bertie do the sound effects?'

'Nope,' Ria says. 'I did.'

'You did?' Ben asks. 'They were brilliant.'

She shrugs and stares round at them. Pain in her eyes masked and hidden. Her voice dull and lifeless.

'We going through or chatting like twats in the rain?' Safa asks.

'Twats in the rain, I think,' Ben says, smiling at Ria.

They pass through the light to a room only a few hundred metres away. *Live connection*, Bertie calls it. He did explain something about the manipulation of time so that it simply connects one place to another.

'It's all just binary,' Ben mumbles, sighing as he moves from the rain to a dry room. Big towels stacked and waiting to dry hair, faces, hands and arms.

'Is it getting less weird yet?' Emily asks, looking at Ria.

She shrugs again. 'Done it so many times now,' she replies.

'Say that again,' Ben says. 'We going to see Bertie later?'

'Aye,' Harry says. 'Do with a bit of sunshine.'

'I'm done,' Emily says, hanging her poncho on a hook on the wall. 'We going back out?'

'Yep,' Safa says to a chorus of groans.

'Practice makes perfect,' Miri says.

Rifles are dried off and stacked on metal shelves fitted to the wall. Harry detaches the box of blank firing ammunition in the belt feed from the heavy machine gun and works to clean the excess moisture off the weapon.

'I'll get the drinks ready,' Ria says, walking from the room.

'We can do it,' Ben calls out. The sound of the inner door to the main room opening and closing comes clearly as he winces and tuts.

'She's fine,' Emily says. 'Let her do it.'

'She's not a slave,' Ben says.

'No,' Emily says quietly, 'but she just lost her mother and she's now outside a hologram of her own home throwing flash-bangs and firing blanks at us while we practise shooting in to the place where her mother died . . . While knowing we can't go inside and rescue her mother. I think the girl has the right to be weirded out.'

Ben widens his eyes, the corners of his mouth turned down. 'That messes my head up, let alone hers.'

'And you've had over six months to adapt,' Emily says. 'She's had about a month.'

'Work helps grief,' Miri says, as flat and blunt as ever.

'Blah, blah,' Safa announces. 'I'm going to get a drink.'

'Safa, you talk to her,' Ben says.

'Not a chance,' Safa says, stopping in the doorway.

'She likes you,' Ben says.

'She likes me because I don't keep asking her if she's okay and if she wants a beanbag to sit on so she can cry and hug a fucking teddy.'

'You're brutal,' Ben says, walking towards her.

'You're a bellend,' she says, walking backwards. 'Watch out, the prisoner is behind you.'

'Still funny,' Emily says, behind Ben.

Safa comes to a sudden stop as she pushes the door open to the main room to peer suspiciously. 'Don't tell me.'

'I won't,' Ria says from the main table.

'Got it,' Ben says, smiling smugly at the others.

'Hate you,' Safa grumbles. 'Sofa,' she says, pointing at a huge dark-red leather sofa against the wall to her right.

'That was here yesterday,' Emily says. 'We sat on it last night.'

'Oh, yeah,' Safa says.

'Table,' Emily says, nodding at the small table next to the sofa against the wall.

'No,' Ria says.

'Got it,' Harry says, walking on towards the table.

'Have you?' Safa asks. 'What is it then?'

'Look,' Harry says simply.

'So annoying,' Safa says, looking round. 'That chair.'

'No,' Ben says.

'That other sofa,' Safa says.

'No,' Ben says.

'New rug!' Emily says, pointing at a red rug on the floor under the chair Safa pointed at.

'No,' Ben says.

'Lampshades,' Emily says, looking up at the tiffany-style shades fitted over the lights.

'Two days ago,' Ria says.

'Fuck's sake,' Safa grumbles.

Miri walks in, pauses, looks round and walks on. 'Got it.'

'Oh my god,' Safa snaps.

Sofas. Armchairs. Pictures on the walls. Rugs on the floor. Standing lamps. Table lamps. New tables. New chairs to sit on when they eat at the new tables. Throws. Side tables. Coffee tables. Vases of flowers. An eclectic blend of shades and colours that all work in perfect harmony to make the big room look somewhere between a luxury hunting lodge and a Swiss chalet. Sumptuous, warm, homely and very inviting.

'Can we give up? I really want a drink,' Emily whispers to Safa.

'Shall we pretend we know?' Safa whispers back.

'Got it!' Emily announces.

'Ha!' Safa grins.

'Twats,' Ben says.

'Fuck's sake,' Safa mumbles.

'Give up,' Emily says.

'New table,' Ben says.

'Where?' Safa asks.

'Oh, yes,' Emily says, cocking her head over to look. 'That's really nice, Ria.'

Safa tracks the line of sight from Emily to Ria. She frowns, scowls, gets ready to call everyone a twat, then grins, sudden and wide. 'Got it,' she announces proudly.

'Do you like it?' Ria asks her, pausing mid-drink and making to look at Safa.

'It's alright,' Safa says with a shrug, then clocks the glares coming from Ben and Emily. 'Yes! I love it. It's awesome.'

Ben groans. Harry rolls his eyes. Emily shakes her head.

'It's very table-like,' Safa says, admiring the new table now holding their food, drinks, plates and eating stuff. 'Wooden and . . . and . . . it looks flat.'

'Oh god,' Ben mumbles, turning away.

'And sturdy,' Safa adds. 'Which is good for a table.'

'It's great,' Harry rumbles, placing a huge hand on Ria's shoulder. 'Bunker looks lovely now, Ria.'

Ria smiles up at him. Seeing his genial face so broad and big and full of beard.

'You'll have to do my room,' he says in the way of Harry – easy, steady, deep and so reassuring.

'I'd love to,' Ria says.

'And mine,' Safa says, coming to a stop on Ria's other side. 'Is that mine?' She plucks a mug of coffee from the table. 'But nothing weird though,' she adds to Ria. 'I like black,' she says. 'And white.'

'Black and white?' Ria asks.

'Or some other colours,' Safa says. 'Not shit ones though. Actually, do Emily's first cos she's got good taste, then . . . Actually, no, you got good taste too, so do what you want, go nuts. Pass an apple over, cheers . . . Is it weird being outside your hologram house?'

'Yes.'

'Bet it is,' Safa says, holding the apple in one hand and the mug of coffee in the other. 'We're in a bunker in dinosaur times and the prisoner that tried to kill us is now my bezzer mate. Everything's weird. How's your brother anyway? Still batshit crazy?'

Twenty-Six

She was here before. Many years ago. She knew it would still be here. Only time and the evolution of the world will ever take this place away.

She arrives on the ninth floor below ground level to the same repugnant stench of damp, rotten air. She has varied the arrival location each time. Yesterday was the eighth floor below ground level. The day before was the tenth. She has the coordinates for different places on each floor.

She came here when it was still the old Soviet Union. That was back in the day. Now she is here again but this is different. For a start, the objective is a whole bunch more serious, and her resources are a whole bunch less.

A small torch lights the way as she moves out of the cell and into the main walkway. Each room was designed to hold people in the event of a nuclear or chemical attack. Four to a room the size of an average American prison cell. The Russians didn't buy into the concept of personal space. They would have crammed tens of thousands in here over the ten floors buried deep beneath the ground, each floor a vast network of rooms and corridors. They said it was to save people, but never answered why each room had a door lockable from the outside.

It felt weird coming back here, but she knew it was one of the only places in the world safe enough for the task in mind. No one comes here now. The razor-wire topped fences surrounding the vast grounds outside stop most. The external doors are welded shut too, so only someone with serious intent and serious equipment would break through.

She finds the stairs and treads down with the faint echo of her boots on each step. It would be pitch black without the torch. A complete absence of light. A total darkness that would freak out the hardest of people.

She sees the light spill as soon as she turns the corner. A glow ahead that seems to be fighting the darkness for the right to live and exist.

'MIRI?'

Desperation in the voice. Fear too.

'MIRI? I CAN'T TAKE THIS . . .'

She walks on towards the light. Purposefully treading harder to create sound that will signify her approach.

'MIRI!'

He's freaking out. She knows he recognises her footfall, but the fear inside his mind will be driving him crazy. His imagination running wild.

'MIRI! THIS IS INHUMANE . . .'

She stops and waits with her torch pointing down so the light doesn't reach the area he can see.

Roland stares through the bars. His face covered in days of growth. His once-lacquered hair now in clumps. Bags under his eyes. Cheeks sunken. His hands tremble as he grips the bars and tries to see down the corridor.

He screams out in fright when she steps from the blackness into the pool of light outside the cell. His heart thunders. His nerves frayed. He is almost at breaking point. Almost.

'Roland,' Miri says, lifting her hand to show him the pistol gripped steady and unwavering. 'Move back.'

'Miri, please . . . I can't stay here.' He sobs the words out, tears spilling down his dirt-encrusted cheeks.

She stares at him. Devoid of expression. He has cleaning materials. He has a safety razor. Water, food, supplies, reading materials and enough comfort to keep him occupied and safe. The fact he isn't washing or taking care of himself is down to him and him alone.

'Okay,' she says flatly, and moves to drag a wooden chair into the pool of light.

'No, sorry, sorry,' he whimpers, moving back from the bars.

'I will stay here.' She sits on the chair and rests the notepad on her knees.

'No, please, please, come in . . . I can . . . I can make it cleaner . . .' He rushes off to move bits of litter and empty tins across the floor. His movements frantic and rushed. His whole manner now showing complete servitude.

'From the beginning,' she says, opening the notepad and clicking her pen.

'Miri, please . . . I can't take it here anymore . . .'

'From the beginning.'

'I CAN'T DO THIS,' he screams out, animalistic and full of rage. He lunges at the bars. His face twisted in fury. 'You can't do this to me . . .'

She waits with her pen hovering over the notepad, then checks her nails and flicks a tiny piece of dust away from the tip of one finger.

'Miri . . . I'm begging you . . .' An instant switch to pleading. The tears come again. Sobbing as his chest heaves. 'Please . . .' His voice becomes a hoarse whisper. He even starts sliding down the bars, as though ready to collapse, but his eyes dart to take in her lack of reaction. 'CUNT,' he screams out.

A month to the day since they extracted him and his children. Leaving him in the bunker with the others was not an option for Miri. She needed him sterile and away from everyone else. She needed him starting to break. She needed him made weak and reduced to base human traits.

The cell was stocked with supplies and enough batteries to ensure the lights never went out. Enough food to grow fat and enough drink to never grow thirsty. That was all part of the mind game. A show of care with soft touches that contrasted so starkly with the horrific location and the ongoing captivity.

Miri lets the emotions play out. He did the same yesterday. He flits between denial, rage, impotent threats, then to begging, pleading and offering money, wealth and anything she could ever want. She's heard it all before, and not just from him. This alone shows his staggering ineptitude. He invited her into this game. Roland came to her and asked for her help. What did he think would happen?

Miri doesn't say a word, but waits with the pen hovering over the notepad. Her posture is perfect. Her back ramrod straight. It hurts her to sit for any length of time like this, but she chooses to be read in a certain way right now, and that way is unforgiving.

'Fine,' he gasps while sitting on the floor to slump like a child. 'I killed myself. My son invented a time machine to go back and stop me killing myself. Someone broke the world. I extracted Ben, Safa and Harry, and now here we are. All done? Happy now, you evil fucking vile, treacherous, nasty . . .'

'Properly. From the beginning.'

'Miri, please.' He sobs. His whole world crumbling around him. To stay another night in this place is too much. The noises he hears. The demons in the shadows. The monsters watching him. His mind warping from the loss of knowing where he is in time and space.

'Approximately ten billion human beings die in an event which is attributed to your son . . .'

'I know this. I told you this. I came and got you for this very reason.' He spits the words out bitterly, with the anger surging back up.

Miri has known people survive years of this treatment and never lose a shred of pride. She has served with people who have done it. She has worked on others held captive too, but Roland is a record. She hasn't known anyone break this quickly. He's not even been tortured or deprived of food or sleep.

He has no choice. He knows that, and so he starts from the beginning properly. Recounting the same story she has now heard so many times she could repeat it in her sleep.

The first few debriefs saw a Roland entirely focussed on the risk to humanity and how everything had to be done to save the world. How important it was to extract Safa, Ben and Harry. How hard it was to get the bunker built and ready.

He was honest too, and said he'd bitten off more than he could deal with, and in the end he was spending less and less time in the bunker. It was frustrating for him that Ben got sick, and he felt very intimidated by Safa.

At first, he tried making out it was so he could be with his family, but then admitted he was getting hooked on stock markets again. The same way he did when he lost everything before he tried killing himself. This time, however, he was dealing in stocks and shares with the benefit of a time machine. But instead of making vast sums, he became addicted to trying to make money without influencing the timeline.

What becomes clear is that Roland loves his family, but he also loves money, wealth, power and himself either equally, or in some cases, more. He is a greedy coward, but not evil. He tried to do the right thing, and given the circumstances he actually did very well. He lies easily, but not convincingly.

What also becomes clear is that the man is actually very resourceful when he puts his mind to something. He was a government minister once, and admits he was tempted to pass the device to the British government.

In short, Roland is a typical aristocratic man of wealth.

Through her own investigations, Miri ruled out that Roland leaked the device or played any overt part in the British Secret Service finding them in Berlin. It was simple ineptitude.

'We're done,' Miri says. She checks her watch and makes a note of the time, then stands up swiftly. Roland blinks in surprise. Trapped in a loop of monologue about his life and feelings, but his eyes come alive with the glint of hope.

'Please,' he whispers, rising unsteadily to his feet with a show of complete submissiveness. 'Please . . .'

'Is there anything you have not told me?' she asks.

His heart thrills at the new question. Something is different. He edges closer to the bars of the door held secure by the thick chain and padlock. 'Nothing . . . I swear it, Miri. I swear on my children's lives.'

She pauses, listening, waiting with her head cocked over. She can feel she is being watched. She knows she is being watched.

'What is it?' Roland asks, panic in his eyes at seeing her reaction.

'Okay?' she calls out. Roland blinks. Confused. The sound of a shoe scraping on the rough floor floats over clear and distinct. Miri nods and looks back at Roland. 'We're done here.'

'Really?' he asks, his voice quavering with emotion, which drops off as she comes forward while lifting the pistol. 'No . . . No, please . . . MIRI . . .'

Shots fired from a small pistol held one-handed that send the rounds through the gaps in the bars that embed in his body. A double-tap to his centre of mass that drives him back. A step forward, an adjustment of aim to place the last shot through his head. Killing him outright.

Roland is not evil, but this is Miri's show now. This is her game and the last thing she wants is someone connected, wealthy and influential looking over her shoulder.

Besides, a question is now answered. A mystery solved. She allows a second of reflection while thinking about fate and destinies. Histories and lives linked in an ever-revolving chain of existences.

She was here before. In this same place. She stood in this same spot in the mid-1990s as part of a UN investigation team ensuring treaty compliance of the Soviet cessation in production of chemical agents.

They were all confused back then, and she's thought about it ever since. The Russians suppressed it. It was never leaked or mentioned.

Miri takes the bag left in the next cell along then returns to unlock the door to Roland's room. She checks the body first. Ensuring he is dead. She opens the bag and takes out the incendiary charge that she places next to the corpse. Every movement seems prophetic and loaded with meaning. There is enough charge to destroy everything in this cell, but not enough to damage the structure of a building constructed to withstand a direct missile strike.

With the timer set, she walks off. The damage will be enough to destroy any evidence. She knows that for a fact.

Miri reaches the portal on the ninth floor and pauses for a few seconds until she hears the dull whump of the explosion and stands to think for a second.

They all wondered, back when they visited this site, how a man died in a fireball in a cell ten floors below ground level in a bunker welded shut from the outside that had not been accessed for over a decade.

Now she knows.

She killed him and made it happen.

Twenty-Seven

Ben waits in the portal room. Pensive and quiet. A large black holdall at his feet. He knows what she is doing. They all do. Emily told them what she saw when she came back with Miri that night. He never liked Roland, but still, the thought of the man being executed in such a way is abhorrent. Only Miri and Emily have seen the underground complex Roland is held in, but Emily's description was enough for them to know that Miri's treatment of him is uncomfortably close to torture.

He questioned it, of course. Quietly, when he and Miri were alone. She just looked at him and told him to let her work. He declined to accept that answer. She declined to explain. They argued. In the end, she gave enough of an explanation to satisfy him. Again, he knew he was being manipulated, but at least it was overt and obvious, and although the end is justified by the means, it still leaves a bitter aftertaste.

She comes through, nods once, then focusses on the tablet to change the setting.

'You killed him?'

'Yes.'

Roland is too great a risk. His ego is too vast. His vanity and addiction to wealth and power would constantly place them in danger. That's what Miri had said. Roland's own actions almost cost the life of his son and daughter and the loss of the device. *This is the level we are working at, Mr Ryder, and not all our decisions will be easy ones.*

She looks up from the tablet to Ben, thoughtful for a second. 'We know where he is, Mr Ryder. If we need him, we can go back and get him. Bag?'

'Here,' Ben says, handing it over with a heavy sigh. 'Want me to come?'

She takes it, wincing at the weight. 'No.'

The blue light blinks off, then back on. She picks the sunglasses up from the side and nods at Ben while pushing them on.

'I don't mind coming . . .'

Miri hears Ben's words cut off as she steps through to a dazzling sun reflecting off a gorgeous blue sea.

'Miri!'

A transition of character. From cold to warm. From austere to friendly. She smiles warmly at Bertie rushing towards her and drops the heavy bag on to the rocks not far from the water's edge.

'Look what I found . . .' he gabbles, holding up a seashell. 'These were extinct for, like . . . like, tens of thousands of years in our time . . . Look! It's what? Two or three years old? So amazing.' His gaze flicks from her to the seashell the size of a house brick clutched in his hand.

The island is tiny. Just a rocky outcrop with thick vegetation some-where in the Aegean Sea between the coasts of what will eventually become Greece and Turkey. It's not the Cretaceous period, but old enough to be safe.

'How are you?' she asks, softening her tone.

'Oh, fine, totally fine . . . Like, yeah, fine and . . . Oh, I saw a meteor shower last night! So beautiful. Like, just amazing. Never see anything like that in our time. Light pollution. Yeah, so, um . . . it's all just binary really . . .' He stops talking and stands with the now-forgotten seashell in his hand.

'Ria?' Miri asks.

Bertie looks round. 'Somewhere . . . I think she's at the shack. I woke her up for the meteor shower last night and she cried again.'

'Grief, Bertie.'

'Yeah,' Bertie says with a slightly vacant look on his face.

'Can we talk?'

'Talk?' He looks stunned at the question.

'In the shade?'

'Oh, totally,' he says, nodding seriously. 'Miri. Would you like a drink? I've rigged up a rudimentary cooling system using those solar panels you got me. Could you get some more? And some wiring . . . And I need a few capacitors and transistors, diodes and, like, don't get new stuff. Get old stuff, like old computers and I'll, like, totally strip them down.'

'You said that yesterday.'

'What's in there?' he asks, looking down at the bag with genuine interest.

'The things you asked me to get yesterday.'

'Oh,' he says slowly, 'what was that?'

'I need some shade.' The sun hurts the scars in her scalp hidden beneath her tangle of hair.

'So,' he says, waving the seashell at her while leading the way. 'I had a thought while I was watching the meteor shower last night. I mean, it's just binary, isn't it? Like, everything so . . . um . . . we're over-thinking the whole space-flight problem.'

'Are we?' she asks, glancing across at him as he drops back to walk by her side. He doesn't offer to take the heavy bag, but she knows it is only because he hasn't thought to ask. Bertie is not thoughtless. He is the opposite of thoughtless.

'Oh my god, Miri. Is that bag heavy? Let me take it . . . um . . . So you hold the seashell and . . . No, actually I can put the seashell down here and . . .' He gently places the seashell on the flat rocks. His movements are childlike, overly precise, and the way he squats and stands suggests someone with learning difficulties instead of possibly the greatest genius that may have ever lived. When he stands, he beams at her, as if he has already forgotten why he put the seashell down in the first place.

'Bag,' she says. 'It's heavy.'

'You should let me take that . . . What's in it? Wow, that is super heavy.'

'Can we go to the shack now, please, Bertie?'

'Of course,' he says with a huge grin as he shoulders the bag. 'So I rigged up this cooling system using the solar panels . . . I mean, the sunshine here is just epic. Like, so pure. Anyway, so, like, I've got the average temperature down to two degrees above zero . . . Celsius, of course . . .'

'Of course.'

'And, yeah, so, haha! The space-flight problem. Like meteors don't ever run out of steam do they? Haha! Can you imagine if meteors used steam-engines? So . . . I mean . . . it's the propulsion, isn't it? They get going and they go . . . and, I mean, like, they have gravitational pull forever pulling them towards a larger body, but . . .'

Miri listens, and everything he says makes sense. Meteors will simply keep going *like, forever and ever, like, epic.* So what keeps them going? What made them go in the first place?

Miri has lived a life of many places and many peoples. She has killed for many reasons, some true and righteous, others blurred and indistinct, but in all those years and in all those places, she has never met anyone like Bertie.

He catches her looking at him and smiles before switching subjects in the blink of an eye and starting to describe the mating habits of the local crab population.

Miri didn't factor for Ria and Emily coming through the portal, but she's lived a life of adaptation and changing expectations, and moved swiftly to assess, evaluate and take action to ensure everything is still done correctly.

Everything had to be done right.

Bertie had to be kept away from his father and everyone else. Roland had to be kept away from his son and everyone else.

Harry, Safa and Ben had to be debriefed. Roland and Bertie had to be debriefed. Emily had to be debriefed.

Every day for the last month, Miri has gone to each in turn to debrief and go over everything they know and exactly what happened before she arrived. Their isolation was key. Retaining sterility of the subjects during the debriefing stage was crucial. Bertie and Ria were brought here, and whereas Roland was tricked into going, she simply asked Bertie and Ria and said she wanted them kept apart until she had spoken to everyone. A month is a long time to debrief, and by asking the same questions each and every session she knew she was irritating them, but therein lies the subtlety of the manipulation.

Now Roland is dead and Emily is a member of the team. This is the game, and Miri is back in it. The thrill is there. The lust to be in the lead and winning.

'Hi,' Ria calls out, rising from the patch of sun she was lying in. She looks better, but the same sadness is in her eyes. The same drawn, introspective look that comes from deep personal grief. The bruises on her face now almost gone.

'Ria, how are you?' Miri asks, her tone still soft and warm.

Ria offers a smile and shields her eyes as she looks at Miri.

'You're taking the sun,' Miri says, observing the glow on Ria's skin. 'Be careful you don't burn.'

'I shall, thank you,' Ria says politely. 'How is everyone?'

'Fine,' Miri says.

'Bertie would love to see them again . . . He adores Harry and Ben . . .'

'Soon,' Miri says.

Ria offers the smile again, weaker this time. 'Bertie, can you get Miri a drink, please.'

'Totally,' Bertie says, nodding eagerly as he strides off, still with the heavy bag over one shoulder.

'How is he?' Miri asks once Bertie is out of earshot.

'He's Bertie. Nothing bothers him for long. He's over it already . . .' She trails off again, staring after her brother. 'I told you about the dog. He wept like a baby for a few hours, then it was like it never happened. Same with our grandmother . . . He . . . he processes things differently . . .'

'Yes.'

'I hate him for that.'

Miri doesn't reply, but waits as Bertie goes into the shack, getting caught in the doorframe by the bag on his shoulder, then spending a full minute trying to figure out how to fit both himself and the bag through at the same time.

'It's not a bad hate,' Ria adds into the quiet, glancing at Miri. 'Not a bitter hate. I just wish I could . . .' The last words choke off with the memory of her mother trying to run through the house amidst the carnage.

Miri rests a hand on her shoulder. Grief is powerful, and it must be given time to vent and play out. 'I'll give you a few minutes,' she says quietly before walking off.

The shack isn't a shack at all, but a timber-built summerhouse. It was a flat-pack self-build Miri bought from a huge home construction depot in California. Before that, Ria and Bertie had a large canvas army tent, but Miri knew that having a solid structure would help them settle and give Ria something to think about.

Miri had collected the summerhouse with Doctor Watson. Two older people making a purchase together drew no attention. They used a hire truck to get it to the waiting Blue, hidden in the countryside; then they brought Harry, Ben and Safa through to help carry it on to the island. The whole exercise served many purposes. It introduced them all again and enforced the knowledge that Ria and Bertie were safe and being cared for.

Bertie was thrilled to see them and talked non-stop of the things he had seen during the days on the island. He was clearly drawn to Ben and Harry, and told them about how he spent the nights *like, totally mapping constellations with Ria*. Bertie even followed them back through the portal to the bunker to help carry the lumber, without a flicker of a glance at anything. He was so enraptured in telling them what he had seen that it just did not occur to him to look round or question where they were. He made the time machine and had used it many times, so it was nothing new to him. He just followed them in and out until the lumber was stacked. Two minutes later, he had forgotten they were even there as he started sorting the wood and tools.

The shack was built within two days. It was built perfectly too.

Over the course of the two weeks, Ria and her brother had asked for very little in terms of supplies. Ria because of shock and grief, Bertie because he just didn't think of anything. Miri leaves them plenty of food, drink, reading materials and essentials. They are both washing. Bertie is shaving, and they are eating.

Bertie has the same height and build as Roland, and the same dark hair, but whereas Roland normally kept his lacquered and neat, Bertie pays no heed and lets it stand up wild and unruly. It suits him though. Even now, walking barefoot round an island with his top off and wearing baggy shorts, he looks entirely at ease.

For her part, Ria has the same dark hair but the facial features of her mother. A large girl, bookish and geeky-looking. Awkward, and seemingly always bordering on embarrassment.

'Is that a chair?' Miri asks, looking at the item in Bertie's hands, then round at the stripped electrical products she'd previously brought him. Spools of wire wrapped around thick twigs in order of size and usability. Piles of component parts, and the cases stacked neatly to one side.

'I made it for you,' he says, rushing to carry the wooden chair over. Tree branches for legs and left-over planks from the summerhouse used for the seat and backrest. 'For your bad back,' he adds, nodding earnestly.

'Thanks.'

Bertie carefully adjusts the angle of the chair and checks the position of the sun, before he spots the bag he dropped and runs off to rifle through the contents. The chair is surprisingly comfortable. 'Very good,' she says. He doesn't reply, but acts like a child on Christmas Day. Giddy with pleasure and happiness at the bundle of presents.

'That'll keep him happy,' Ria says, walking up to them. She sits on the ground and leans her back against the side of the summerhouse. 'Debriefing again?'

'Do you mind?' Miri asks.

'Carry on,' Ria says quietly. 'How many times do we have to do it?'

'As many as necessary. Bertie, I'll start with you.'

'Okay,' Bertie mumbles, examining an old transistor radio as if it holds the secret to immortality, which it may well do to him.

So it begins and again the contrast with Roland could not be starker. Bertie speaks as though this is the first time they have discussed the subject, while also picking up tools and starting to work on the old radio.

His father died and he decided to build a time machine, so that families can go back and ask their loved ones not to kill themselves. That's it. That was his sole motivation for building a thing that so many others had only dreamt of. *It's all just binary.* Everything is binary. He has access to a secret language made of zeros and ones. A language that holds the mystery of the universe, but in order to have that access, his brain has to be wired differently. Miri considers autism and a range of spectrum disorders, but it's impossible to label Bertie.

She thought of asking Ria if he had ever been diagnosed or tested, but held back. Ria hadn't volunteered the information, and it made no difference anyway.

Bertie built the device in his basement workshop, and once built, he applied the laws of scientific research by conducting tests to ensure it was working properly. During that time, he popped in and out of several different eras. All of which fascinated him at the time, but it is now just something he once did. He recounts how he walked through ancient Rome for half an hour smiling at people who *like, were so totally friendly, but, like, all really short, but like not midgets or anything.*

What staggers Miri is that he went into the future. He had access to advanced technology and scientific awareness, but paid no attention to it because that would be *like, cheating,* and anyway, it wasn't what he was there for. It was on the second test jump to the year 2111 that he discovered the *world was, like, broke. Like, totally ruined.* He panicked, and assumed he had caused it. She asked him what he saw. He said he went through the portal, saw it was bad, then went back into his workshop to find his drone and used that to film it all. She wanted to ask if he checked radiation levels or saw any signs of what caused it, but avoided doing so to prevent planting ideas or false memories, being unsure of his level of grasp until she knew him better.

It was after Bertie saw the full devastation that he went back to stop his father from *like, doing the suicide thing.*

'Harry is, like, really big,' Bertie says, giving voice to the thoughts in his head. 'Like, totally make a bigger chair for him. Dad said Safa's beautiful, but, like, totally tough, and you aren't allowed to tell her you think she is beautiful. But if someone is beautiful, why would they be angry? I mean, like . . . everyone is, like, beautiful, and you should say that so they feel good . . . You're beautiful, Miri.'

She blinks with an exceptionally rare flicker of surprise as Ria chuckles softly.

'What about me?' Ria asks him.

'You're, like, my sister,' Bertie says, pulling a face.

'I am your sister – I'm not *like* anything.'

'Hang on,' he blurts with a grin. 'Like . . . if I put this in here now . . . and . . . ' He detaches an old MP3 player from the solar panel charge he has also made and attaches a wire leading from the circuit board to the inside of the radio. A hiss, and then the music comes. Played from the MP3 player, but routed through the speakers of the radio, which give a wonderful crackle to the Spanish guitar music. 'Haha! Got music now,' he says, nodding at the old radio with obvious glee.

'Well done,' Miri says, seeing the look of absolute pleasure on his face. 'Ria, do I need to go through everything with you again?'

'No,' she says while watching her brother. 'I can't think of anything.'

'Is there anything you have not told me?'

'No,' Ria says thoughtfully, 'I really don't think there is.'

Ria is three years younger than her brother, and although intelligent, she is nowhere near the level of genius of Bertie. *No one is near Bertie. My brother is an anomaly.* Ria led what she believes is a normal life. It was hard when her dad committed suicide, but they got through it. Her mother had a series of relationships, but nothing really lasted. Malcolm and Konrad stayed working for the family estate until they died in a car accident in 2052. Ria explained that Bertie was more upset about that than at any other time they had ever seen. Malc and Kon. They were always down in the basement, drinking tea and listening to Bertie's ideas and seeing the things he had made. Ria suspected that hidden away in the layers of Bertie's unique mind was the thought that he could also save them. *Who knows? Only Bertie knows what he thinks, and even if he told us, we wouldn't understand it.*

Ria was completely overwhelmed when Roland came back. It had been fifteen years since his death, and of course Ria and her mother had to deal with the fact that he looked the same as the day he had left. They had aged, grown, matured and developed, but he had not. Roland had walked out of the family home, and walked back into it fifteen years later, but for him it was the same day.

Roland did not discuss his plans. He did not go out, and once the shock of his family seeing him again wore off, he set about trying to do what he could to *save the world*. What exactly he did, he kept to himself. Neither Ria nor her mother had any idea that he had brought back Malc and Kon.

Gradually, over the months that passed, her father became the man she remembered. Busy, and absorbed entirely in himself. Ria saw her mother at first become rejuvenated at being reunited with her husband, but then Susan began to worry that she was suddenly too old for him. She had cosmetic surgery and started wearing younger clothes. Ria watched her mother slowly breaking down from being reunited with her dead husband only to see him growing as cold as he always was.

'And you?' Miri had asked, examining the woman's non-verbal communications closely. 'Tell me about you.'

'Nothing to say. My family are wealthy, so I was bred to be a shallow creature of greed . . .'

That was the first answer. Short, and filled with a grief-ridden show of self-loathing, but gradually Miri drew the woman out and thanked the gods of fortuitous fate for letting Ria get through the portal.

'That was the last debrief,' Miri announces, closing her notepad.

'What now?' Ria asks after a few seconds of silent thought. 'Do we just stay here?'

'I have tasks for you both,' Miri says, her tone gradually firming from the soft, caring manner to that of a person in charge of the mission.

'Tasks?' Ria asks, showing surprise as she looks at Miri. 'What tasks?'

'You designed sets and costumes for a holographic film production company. I need . . .'

'Oh no,' Ria says, cutting in quickly. 'I said I helped out . . . I only did it as a hobby because mother knew the wife of the . . .'

'Do not interrupt me, Miss Cavendish.'

Ria closes her mouth. Miri's tone wasn't loud or harsh, but the sudden authority in the woman renders Ria silent.

'The bunker is sterile. It needs soft-furnishings, furniture, colours . . . I have neither the time nor the inclination to do it. My team will not have the time to do it. You will do it.'

'But . . .'

'Ben's mental health decline was brought on by a combination of shock and the medications he was given when he arrived. Doctor Watson firmly believes the severe, austere environment played a significant part in that. You will work to prevent that happening again. We also need clothes for different time periods . . .'

'Oh my god, Miri . . . are you being serious?' Ria asks, rising to her feet with a look of panic.

'I am always serious.'

'Miri, listen . . .'

'I have listened. It is my job to listen. It is also my job to make decisions and delegate. You have a role in this. You are here, and your presence will mean we do not have to extract someone else to do that role.'

'I am in grief right now,' Ria says, hardening her voice.

'Work helps grief. It occupies the mind. You can choose to remain here with your brother or come back to the bunker and reside there. You can move between the two by asking me to open the portal to enable it to happen. The other members of the team can also come here if they so wish. This is a pleasant environment and it was chosen specifically for that reason.'

'No. I am not going anywhere near that bunker if my father is there. He ran off and left us. My mother is dead because of him . . .'

'Your father is not returning to the bunker. He is no longer a part of this. I am not asking. You *will* work. Do you understand?'

Ria stares open-mouthed and shocked.

'Expediency matters,' Miri continues. All trace of softness gone. Her words are flat, dull and hard. 'It will be done as quickly as possible . . .'

'Maria's, like, totally awesome at decorating and stuff. Like, she helped Mum do the house and bought my clothes and helped Mum get new stuff when Dad came back and . . .'

'Bertie! You are not helping,' Ria snaps.

'Bertie, can you make another device?' Miri asks, turning from Ria to the man now working the back off a large tablet.

'It's just binary,' Bertie mumbles, 'but, like, I made one and Dad said I totally couldn't make another one and, but, no, totally . . .' He stops talking to nod eagerly as Miri processes the last sentence back to herself.

'You had plans in your workshop for the same thing but with a red portal. Is it the same?'

'Haha!' Bertie says, getting the back off the tablet and staring at the inner workings.

'Bertie, is it the same?' Miri asks.

'He doesn't work like that,' Ria says.

'Totally. S'just binary.'

'What colour do you need?' Ria asks, long-practised at fielding comments and questions for her brother.

'No colour. Invisible.'

That does it. His head snaps up as his entire features show instant, laser-like focus.

'And smaller. Something a person can carry and use easily.'

He drops the tablet and stands quickly. 'How would you see it?' he asks, staring intently at Miri.

'Not the apparatus, just the field. That needs to be invisible, see-through.'

'An invisible time machine?'

'Yes. Smaller.'

'A portable, invisible time machine?'

'Yes.'

'That,' Bertie says, his eyes narrowing, 'is, like, totally the best idea ever.'

Twenty-Eight

Steaks sizzle on the big, gas-fed barbeque grill bought from Walmart. Onions fry in a skillet. The air fills with smells of cooking. Old Greek café tunes play through speakers in the background.

Ria takes the bowl of salad over to place down on the table as everyone else chats and relaxes after a hard day's training in the pouring rain outside the bunker. Bertie sits between Ben and Harry opposite Safa and Emily, beaming from ear to ear. Miri and the doctor at one end talking quietly.

A beautiful Aegean evening. The water surrounding the island is blue and calm. The sky deep and clear.

Ria goes back to the grill. Busying herself cooking the evening meal of steaks, jacket potatoes and salad.

It's been two months since Miri finished debriefs, and while Ria has developed a routine, she still feels weird. Her days are spent outside her hologram home throwing flash-bangs at the others and firing blanks in the rain. Her evenings are spent cooking and doing laundry and chores.

Thinking of Cavendish Manor makes her think of her mum, a fresh surge of emotion welling up inside. Why can't they go back and get her? Bloody Miri. Bloody bunker. Bloody everything, all because of bloody, sodding Bertie. He's a genius and a pain in the arse. He had to go and invent a time machine, the bloody idiot.

There isn't time to rescue her mother. She knows that. The portal has to be set back far enough to be away from any ground troops and protected from satellite view by the dense foliage of the big trees bordering her house. Safa and the other three have to run close enough for Harry to use the heavy machine gun. She knows they then have to run to higher ground for Ben to use the sniper rifle before they sprint to the back of the house for someone to fire the missile launcher at the helicopters.

She pokes the steaks and turns the potatoes. Having a time machine is confusing. She asked why they couldn't just keep coming back to do the different things at different times. Miri said they had to do it in one go, and that having multiple sets of *them* helping *them* would get messy, confusing and dangerous – and what if the wrong Harry, Ben, Safa or Emily went through the wrong portal at the wrong time?

She also knows two heavily armed gunships crash through the roof and probably kill everyone inside. Including her mum, if she's not already dead by then.

'Can I do it?'

She blinks from her train of thought to see Safa standing next to her looking at the meat cooking on the grill. 'Can I turn them,' Safa says in her way of asking while telling.

'Sure,' Ria says. She hands the tongs over and moves along to start unwrapping the potatoes from their silver-foil jackets.

'Train with us,' Safa says, poking a steak.

'What?' Ria asks.

'Do some phys – good for you, releases endorphins. I don't want you getting moody like Ben did.'

'I'm fine.'

'Up to you,' Safa says. 'No more red meat this week. Bad for the arteries. Get some chicken or fish, or something.'

'Okay, Safa.'

'Going without meat won't hurt them either.'

'Okay.'

'You depressed?'

'What?'

'Are you depressed?'

'My mum just died.'

Safa pokes a steak. 'Get over it. World moves on.'

'It was a few weeks ago.'

'Three months, and so? Go mad. Cry. Scream. Take a training stick and batter Harry. He'd love it. Get drunk. Run about. Do what it takes. Get it out. That shit's no good inside.'

'I'm not like you,' Ria says quietly.

'Like what?'

Ria shrugs and winces at the hot potato burning the tips of her fingers. Safa watches her, puts down the tongs and picks a wrapped potato up in her bare hands. Ria stares as Safa starts unwrapping it, heedless of the agony she must be feeling.

'Know what pain is?' Safa asks. 'Pain tells you when something is wrong, but not all pain has to be listened to. The pain receptor in my hand is telling my brain to let it go. My brain is telling my hand to fuck off and get over it cos my brain knows the heat isn't bad enough to cause damage. So I can hold it for a bit without it doing anything bad. If it gets that bad I can swap hands, but that's giving in to it, so you hold it and man up and ignore it – that tells the pain to do one.'

She unwraps the potato and holds it naked in her hand while looking at Ria. 'It hurts, but I control what I do.' She places the potato down in the bowl with the others and goes back to poking the steaks on the grill. 'These need turning?'

'Please,' Ria says. She looks at the potato, as though wanting to pick it up and hold it and tell the pain to fuck off and do one. She wants to control what she does. She wants a six-pack and muscles in her legs, and for her cellulite to fuck off. She wants to go back and get her mum.

'Come here,' Safa says, moving back to pick up the potato. 'Hold your hand out.' Safa takes her wrist and places the hot potato in her palm. Immediate heat. Immediate pain. A signal to pull back her hand. A signal to drop it, to throw it, to do anything except hold it. Safa doesn't say anything, but watches her closely. Her own hand still on the top of the potato. 'Man up, it's just pain.'

Ria nods. It hurts like mad. It hurts like crazy. Tears threaten to prick her eyes. She swallows. Safa lifts the potato away and looks at it. 'I'll have this one.'

'I want to get her.'

'Your mum? Not happening. No time.'

'I'll train and get fit . . . I'll do it.'

'No. Some things can't be done. We can't open the portal into the mess inside the house. We can't go into the house with the choppers coming through the roof . . . And anyway, Ben said if we had done it, we would have done it. Confuses the hell out of me, but he's an egghead.'

Ria just stares, feeling stupid for asking. Feeling weak and soft next to Safa.

'These done?' Safa asks, poking the steaks.

They eat at the big table. Communal dining al fresco, with big, meaty steaks served with hot potatoes and salad. Ria's hand hurts. She glances to see Safa's hand is red, and knows hers will be the same. She wants to be like Safa, but becoming anything like these people is a path too difficult to take.

In truth, she is equal parts intimidated by, in awe and resentful of them all. Safa and Emily are both so fit and healthy. Ria's belly wobbles when she runs and her thighs rub together. She's not fat, but then she's not fit either. Not fit at all. Okay, maybe she is a bit fat. Not obese though. Curvy. Safa and Emily have six-packs. Actual six-packs. You can see the muscles and everything. Ria has never seen a woman with a six-pack in real life who hasn't had cosmetic surgery. Even the actors she saw on set were digitally edited to make them look better.

Ben Ryder is an actual urban legend. Something from folklore, and even though he is always polite and friendly, she still feels weirded out when he talks to her.

Harry is lovely, but so quiet, and Ria finds it hard to find anything to say to him that doesn't sound like trite, immature gibberish.

The doctor is nice, but spends most of his time with Bertie.

Miri is just scary.

Ria thinks ahead to the night and tries to decide where she will sleep. The island is like paradise, but spiders keep getting in the shack and Bertie refuses to remove them *cos, like, they're totally so cool.* Bloody Bertie. She'll sleep in the bunker tonight. Her rooms are nice now.

She pushes her steak round the plate and munches on a green leaf while listening to Miri and Ben bickering over the Barrett.

'Thing kicks like a mule. Listen, Emily is a better shot than me . . .'

'No,' Miri says bluntly.

Ria knows Ben is struggling to handle the Barrett fifty-calibre sniper rifle. She's not surprised. The thing is enormous. She picked one of them up once and could hardly carry it, let alone imagine firing the thing.

'You said time isn't fixed,' Ben says. 'So we change. We'll use something Emily can handle, and let her do the . . .'

'No.'

'Why not? Time isn't fixed, Miri . . .'

'No, Mr Ryder.'

'I cannot fire the fucking thing when I've been moving. Emily is a trained sniper.'

'Miss Rose undertook a sniping course, which is a big difference to being an active sniper.'

'Here they go,' Emily murmurs.

'Yep,' Safa says.

'We are using the Barrett, Mr Ryder.'

'Emily can't handle the Barrett.'

'Which is why you are using it.'

Ria pushes her steak and chews on a green leaf. Safa and Harry are no good at sniping. Ben is a brilliant shot, but he's struggling to hit moving targets after running. Ben and Miri bicker. Harry and the doc talk quietly. Emily and Safa the same. Bertie stares round in absolute glee and awe. Ria prods her steak. She misses her mum. She needs her mum. She wonders where her dad is, then immediately feels the bite of anger at him. He deserted them. He ran off. It was Ria and her mum throwing themselves at the people in their house.

'Finished?'

'Huh?' She looks up to see everyone staring at her.

'You've hardly touched your food, Ria,' Doctor Watson says. 'Feeling okay?'

'Fine. Not hungry . . . I, er . . . snacked . . .'

Ria rises to gather the dishes to hide the blush spreading across her cheeks. Everyone else starts trying to help. Ria wishes they wouldn't. It's easier to do it on her own. Quicker too. She packs the dirty dishes in a basket ready for washing. Waste food is thrown into the sea to feed the fish with food from the future that will change their genealogy and alter the course of the world; or maybe they'll just eat it and make it into fish poo. Ria doesn't care. Harry moves off to smoke. Miri goes after him. The two of them silent in their company of dirty smokers. Ria sniffs the air, scenting the toxic aroma of cigarettes. She has smoked before. She tried it at parties when everyone was doing it. It made her feel sick, but there was also something nice about it.

'Hey.'

Ria looks up in surprise to see Emily walking towards her.

'You okay?' Emily asks.

'Yep,' Ria says.

'That was a lovely meal.'

'Okay.'

'Oh, did you get the thing for Harry?' Emily asks quietly.

'Yep. Got some popcorn too. Don't know if Harry's had popcorn before.'

'Harry will love it. You joining us? We'll need someone to set it all up.'

'You can do it.'

Emily is from her time. She knows how to use a tablet. Besides, Emily was an uber secret agent and speaks every language ever invented ever. Ria can speak a bit of French, and that's only the swear words.

'Join us. We'll crash out, eat popcorn . . . It'll be great.'

'No, thanks. Got some stuff to do. Like . . . supplies and . . .'

'Okay,' Emily says easily. 'Oh, listen, I was thinking . . . Did you want some personal training or anything? You don't need to. I don't mean that. You look great. I meant, you know, if you did? We could do it quietly.'

Ria would love that. 'No, thanks,' she says, wishing she could take the words back as they come out. Why does Emily say everything like it's a sudden thought? *Oh, listen, I just had this idea.*

'Oh, okay. Well, listen, just you know, keep it in mind. I can come here or . . . you know, in case you were worried about the others seeing. I get that. I totally get that.'

Ria doesn't think Emily does get it. Emily is almost perfect. Safa *is* perfect. 'Thanks.'

'They're still bloody going,' Safa says, walking over to join them as Ben continues his debate with Miri. 'Ria, you don't have to do all the chores. They'll get lazy if you do everything for them. Just tell Miri to fuck off. Want me to tell her?'

'It's fine.'

'Up to you.'

'I like doing it,' Ria says.

'Weirdo.'

Ria chuckles. She likes Safa's directness. No sympathy, no empathy, no asking if she's okay or wants to talk.

Ben marches over, shaking his head. 'That woman is stubborn as anything.'

'Most women are,' Emily says.

'Aw, the Ryder charm not working?' Safa asks him.

'Ben! Can I show you now,' Bertie calls out, rushing from the table with the doctor behind him rolling his eyes.

'Sure,' Ben says.

'Are we invited?' Emily asks.

'Yeah, like, totally,' Bertie blurts, grinning widely. 'It's so cool, but, like, I can't get signals through it, but, like, the energy from the displacement field is acting as a barrier to certain . . . like, space. Like, no energy to carry the . . . In space no one can hear you scream and the explosions in the movies when they have fire and noise are, like, so wrong cos space is, like, a total vacuum and the displacement field has the same properties which, like, totally kill sound waves and . . .'

'Okay, okay,' Emily says, cutting into his rapid speech. She loops an arm through his. 'Come on, show us.'

'Is Ben coming? Ben, are you coming?' Bertie asks.

'Right behind you, mate,' Ben says, reaching out to grab Safa's hand before she can dart off. 'Safa's coming too. She wants to see it.'

Ria follows behind them to the shack. She's seen it already, but feels the same ever-present sense of protectiveness over her brother.

Bertie leads Emily over, gabbling furiously while constantly turning to check Ben is still coming. They cram into the shack. Ben and Emily going in with Bertie while Safa, Ria and the doctor gather by the door.

One side of the main room given over to tables. Hologram computer programs shining from tablets; images hovering in the air with reams of binary code and what looks like hieroglyphics. Scraps of paper everywhere. Chewed pencils. Notepads. Sheets pinned to the walls with sketches and diagrams or full of block text written in hand.

'Jesus, Bertie,' Ben says in genuine surprise on seeing the small, red square of light at the end of the table. The pattern is the same. The way it shimmers and seems alive with a solid wall of colour, but red instead of blue, and the size of an old computer monitor.

'Epic.'

'Bertie. Is that a time machine?' Ben asks. 'Has Miri seen it?'

'She has – she comes over all the time,' Ria says from the door.

'Er, no,' Bertie says.

'Pardon?' Ben asks.

'Eh? What? What is? What that? No,' Bertie says, gabbling in his excitement of showing Ben.

'Can I touch it?' Ben asks.

'Like, totally.'

Ben stretches his hand out to the red light. No heat, no sensation at all. He leans over and sees his hand coming out the back.

'Er, so is it working then?' Ben asks.

'Displacement field's off,' Bertie says, nodding eagerly. 'It's, like, totally the same as the other one, but, you know, testing it . . . Electromagnetic pulses don't go through, so . . .'

Ria clears her throat and leans in through the door. 'Bertie is testing it to push radio signals and cellular waves through . . . I mean, they don't go through the time machine now, do they?'

'Oh, mate,' Ben says, 'that's brilliant.'

'S'binary,' Bertie mutters, still grinning at Ben.

'Well done, mate,' Ben says.

'It's, like, red,' Bertie says. 'Cos, like, the other one is blue.'

'It's, er, yeah,' Ben says.

'Finished your woodbine?' Emily asks as Harry looms behind Ria and Safa.

'Aye,' the big man says, slightly confused at the question.

'Got a surprise for you,' Emily says.

'For me? Harry asks.

'Aye,' Emily says deeply.

'What?' Ben asks.

'You'll see,' Emily says. 'We heading back in?'

They stroll down the path with everyone asking what the surprise is and Emily grinning, but refusing to say.

In the portal room, Ria slips out ahead of the others to fetch the tablet and bags of popcorn. She walks back into the main room to see Emily telling Harry to sit down and make himself comfortable on the huge red leather sofa. The big man complies easily, stretching his legs out with a wry smile as Emily winks at Ria. Ben, Safa and the doctor take seats. Miri stays by the door, curious, but not part of it.

'Popcorn?' Emily asks.

'Here,' Ria says, holding the bags out. 'Sweet, salted . . . Some toffee too.'

'Popcorn?' Ben asks. 'We watching a movie then?'

'Movie?' Harry asks, looking round the room. 'No screen.'

Emily takes the popcorn to distribute, then tucks herself on the sofa next to Harry. 'You'll love this,' she tells him.

Ria switches the tablet on and sets it down. She looks up at everyone sitting and watching expectantly, and realises her brother has come through and is already eating popcorn while staring in awe at Harry and Ben.

'Ready?' Ria asks Emily.

'Ready,' Emily says, clearly pleased.

'Lights, please, Miri,' Ria says. Miri flicks the lights off. The room drops to a darkness broken only by the glowing light of the tablet. Ria presses the screen and moves away swiftly before the hologram image of the old Warner Bros logo blooms out in the air above the screen. Music plays. Harry grins. Ben and Safa say something. Bertie laughs with delight. The Warner Bros logo fades to be replaced with a perfect 3D image of a night sky with a moon shining far in the distance and a large bird of prey perched on a road sign for Privet Drive.

'Bloody hell,' Ben gasps. 'No way.'

'Oh, yes,' Emily says. 'They converted it to 3D a few years ago. Cost them a fortune.'

An old, bearded man comes into view. Harry sputters, leaning forward to glare. 'Dumbledore!' he roars. 'That's Dumbledore . . .'

Emily settles back with a huge grin as Harry continues to watch in fascination at *Harry Potter and the Philosopher's Stone* playing out in the main room of the bunker.

'Ria?' Emily calls, on seeing the girl heading towards the door. 'Come and sit down, have some popcorn.'

'I've seen it, like, a hundred times,' Ria says, feeling a jarring rush of emotions, being genuinely happy at Harry's reaction, but not wanting to sit and join them. Like she doesn't belong. An outsider, not a team member. They all have important roles. The only thing Ria can do is cook food, wash their clothes and buy supplies.

'Ah, come on,' Ben says.

'Got some stuff to do. Enjoy,' Ria says. She walks out of the room to see Miri in her office. She clears her throat, feeling that instant sense of discomfort at being in Miri's presence. The older woman looks up to fix those cold eyes on her.

'I'll do the laundry.'

Miri doesn't say anything.

'Er . . . so . . . is it okay if I hang out for a bit and come back later?'

Miri looks at her, weighing up the question. 'Hang out?'

Ria shrugs. She's in her twenties. She doesn't need to ask permission. Miri makes her feel like a child. 'Get a coffee while the washing's on. You know, just, er . . . walk around, maybe get some things for the bunker . . .' She trails off. Awkward and uncomfortable.

'You are an adult, Miss Cavendish. You are free to *hang out*, but I have to impose a time restriction for the security of the device and the bunker. Three hours enough?'

'Sure,' Ria says.

'Money,' Miri says, walking across her office to a big chest in the corner. She lifts the lid, takes a wad of notes and carries them back to Ria. 'Enough?'

'There's, like, five grand there, Miri,' Ria says, looking at the wad.

'Want more?'

'No, no, that's fine,' Ria says, taking the money. 'Thank you.'

'You know the rules, Miss Cavendish.'

'I do,' Ria says.

'What are the rules, Miss Cavendish?'

'No single large purchases without a backstory. Don't draw attention. Make sure I am not followed, but if I am, then come straight back here or go to the local police station and wait for you.'

'Good,' Miri says, moving to the desk.

Ria walks down to her rooms to change into jeans and a top. She checks herself in the full-length mirror in the corner of her bedroom, seeing the curves of her own hips and ample chest. She wonders what it would be like to be as lean as Safa and Emily. In the bathroom, she applies make-up. Simple foundation, mascara and eyeliner. She brushes her long black hair, checks her teeth, sprays perfume and goes to the portal room. She changes the setting from *island* to *Milwaukee* and watches as the blue light blinks off, then back on again. She checks her small bag for the money, picks up the waiting washbag and steps through. She steps back and crosses to Miri's office to see her holding a set of keys in her hand.

'Thanks,' Ria says, stretching out to take them. 'Forgot.'

Twenty-Nine

Ria was briefed, of course. She knows that in 2010, the year she is currently using, the population of Milwaukee stands at around half a million. She learnt other stuff too. She knows the city is on the shore of Lake Michigan, which once had a problem with algae. She did consider, while listening to Miri, if maybe they had brought something from the Cretaceous period into this time that caused the algae. That would be quite funny, she thought, or at least ironic, what with Miri lecturing her about changing the timeline.

Ria knows the demographics, as of 2010, are approximately forty per cent white, forty per cent black and then everyone else. Miri did tell her the breakdown for Hispanic and other cultures, but Ria was still focussed on the whole algae-in-the-lake thing. In short. Lots of people live here, but Milwaukee is known for being shit towards African Americans because Miri said there is a disproportionate gap in sentences for crimes committed by white people and black people, and also in education standards. Ria had no idea why she was being told all that until Miri explained that by understanding local social issues, she can better judge incidents and situations.

Miri also came with her the first few times.

Ria waits in the van. Miri said they have to wait and make sure no one is looking, paying attention, staring, that sort of thing. The car park is enormous. Miri called it a parking lot and said a big old van parked at the end wouldn't cause a problem for a while. At least a few weeks, and by then they'll switch to another city and time period. The van is legally owned. Miri paid cash for it and added an extra few notes to make sure the previous owner didn't update the records too quickly. It's large enough for the portal in the back too.

She goes through the heavy blackout curtains fixed to the van's ceiling and makes sure the curtain behind is put back before going through the next set. At the front, she stares through the windscreen at modern life in the car park of an enormous American shopping centre, or *mall*, as Miri said. Cars everywhere. Hundreds of them. Rows and rows of cars, vans and pick-up trucks. People everywhere too. Loading vehicles. Getting out of vehicles. Parking vehicles. She waits for a bit to make sure no one is *actively monitoring* and unlocks the driver's door before dropping down and inhaling the dirty air with a satisfied groan.

She walks at the pace Miri taught her. Casual, but not lazy. Busy, but not rushed. *Walk like you know where you are going and look like you know what you will do when you get there.*

She falls in behind a man and woman discussing whether they should eat out tonight or cook at home. The man wants to have home food and save money. The woman wants to eat out, as she is sick of cooking. Ria wonders what their lives are like. Are they happy, fulfilled, content, or just as miserable as everyone else? They have no clue that a woman from the future is walking behind them. A woman from the future who lives in the very distant past in a bunker with weird people who play outside a hologram house with pterodactyls flying about.

The couple look round as Ria chuckles. She smiles and turns away.

She wanted to fake an American accent, but Miri said no. *Be natural. Be dull. Be boring. If anyone speaks to you, just be dull. They'll soon get bored.*

The washbag is heavy. She adjusts it on her shoulder and heads for the launderette. A vast room filled with washing machines and dryers. She gets change and sets about filling the washing machines with the black training clothes they all wear. The towels go in another machine. Underwear and casual clothes in yet another. She idly thinks about bacteria and things from the Cretaceous period being on the clothes and getting into the water supply, and thinks again about the algae in the lake. She puts powder in and sets the cycles to start.

If someone told her seven months ago that her dead father would come back, she wouldn't have believed them. If someone then said he would bring back Malc and Kon from the dead and then fuck everything up by building a bunker and using a staging area in Berlin that was discovered by the British government, who killed Malc and Kon and . . . She blinks, losing the confusing train of thought. Whatever. It's all just weird. She misses her mum so much. The pain inside is immense. Like, crushing. It's not getting better either or going away. *Just give it time*, the doctor said. Time? How much time? It hurts so much. She can't stop thinking of the look on her mum's bleeding face as they tried to protect Bertie. The fear and confusion. The utter terror.

'You coming back, honey?' An American drawl, a friendly tone. Ria starts, and turns to see the withered old lady attendant staring at her.

'Just going to the mall,' Ria says.

'Take your time,' the old lady says. 'You want them dried?'

'I can do it.'

'Nah,' the old woman says, waving a wrinkly hand. 'Be young, go do young things. Damn British, so polite. Wish my granddaughter was polite. Damn kids.'

'Thank you.'

'You're welcome, have a nice day,' the old woman says, back on auto-pilot.

Ria walks out and down the pavement, *sidewalk*, to the main entrance to the mall and joins the throng of people moving like zombies, and suddenly three hours of freedom seem too much. She doesn't know anyone. She doesn't belong here. She has no home.

She spots the golden arches and heads that way. The smell of grease hangs in the air. She hates eating in front of Safa and Emily. Her own perception of being judged for eating when she isn't in perfect physical shape. Whatever. She's hungry. She's fat already. Fat and ugly and lonely. She spots the good-looking man behind the counter. She's seen him before, but he's never served her. She watches him while she queues. He's got lovely arms.

'Help you?' says the man behind the counter.

She orders a large Big Mac meal and six nuggets.

'You Australian?'

'British.'

'British, huh? What y'all doing here?'

'Holiday.'

'What?'

'Vacation.'

'Vacation? To Milwaukee? That's shit.'

She smiles and takes the food to a plastic table, where she sits on a plastic chair in a plastic restaurant to eat and people-watch.

She has been told about the American obesity crisis. She can see it. She looks round and feels thin. It gets worse too, in the future. Much worse. Britain and Europe aren't far behind, but at least they pass laws to reduce sugar and fat content.

Tastes nice though. She eats slowly, but only so she can people-watch and hear snatches of conversations. These people are probably all dead by the time she is born. Hang on, this is 2010. Ria was born in 2039, so that's twenty-nine years from now. Okay, maybe they're not all dead. Some. The rest are just old.

Nihilism settles. A profound sense of *what's the fucking point? Why bother?* She misses home and hanging out on sets. She was quite good at costumes and set design too. Not the actual sets, but the little things in the foreground or background that added realism. She thinks back to the day she stepped in when the set designer walked out in a huff. She designed a whole scene. Furniture. Background props. Everything. It was the main scene too. The part where the bad guy gets his come-uppance. That was the best day ever. She got a kiss on the cheek from the director, and even had her name in the credits. She was so thrilled. She posted it straight away and had the biggest reaction she ever had on social media. She misses drinking and sex. She misses being promiscu-ous and not giving a shit because she was wealthy and didn't care; now she has access to millions of dollars and a time machine and couldn't feel more empty inside. She finishes eating, but wants more. Food is comfort.

'Help you?'

'Six nuggets, please.'

'Hey, British girl. Still hungry, huh? You wanna apple pie? Free. Call it a vacation gift.'

'Won't you get in trouble?'

'Nah, I'm leaving in a week. Enlisted. Marine Corps.'

'What, like a soldier?'

'Yeah, but better – a US Marine, hooyah.'

'Cool. Well, good luck.'

'What's your name, British girl?'

'Maria.'

'Hispanic?'

'No, I said I'm British. Everyone calls me Ria.'

'Ria. Nice. I like that.'

'Thanks.'

She goes back to the plastic table to watch people, although now she is glancing over at the boy behind the counter. Not a boy. A man. Young. Black. Very handsome. Big arms. She likes big arms. His teeth are very clean too. She likes clean teeth. She dips a nugget in some ketchup and bites into it as he looks over and smiles. She smiles back, then covers her mouth because it's rude to smile or speak when you are eating. He seems to find that funny and laughs.

She's full, but she wants to get more nuggets so she can talk to the nice boy. She thinks about getting another drink, but this is America and she can refill from the soda machine on her own.

'Hey, Ria, British girl, more nuggets?'

'Um, no, thanks. Do you have a napkin or a serviette, please? I spilled some Coca-Cola on my leg.'

'Hey, sure thing. Let me get you a wet wipe.'

'Thanks.'

'So how's the vacation in Milwaukee?'

'Boring.'

'How old are you?'

'Twenty-two. You?'

'Twenty-one. Last week.'

'Happy birthday for last week.'

'Thanks. Say, y'all gotta get back somewhere?'

'Pardon?'

'I said, y'all gotta get back? Go home. You know, you on a curfew?'

'Curfew? I'm twenty-two.'

'Hey, just checking,' he says, holding his hands up and smiling broadly. 'Wanna go to a party?'

'Me?'

'No, the girl behind you.'

'Oh, sorry,' Ria says, looking round.

'Yes, you,' he laughs. 'Wanna go? Few beers, nothing serious, you know.'

'Where is it?'

'Bar near here.'

She knows she shouldn't. Miri told her the rules. Fuck Miri. Fuck everyone. 'Okay, what time?'

'I finish in an hour. Wanna eat more nuggets and wait, or, like, come back?'

'I can't eat anymore nuggets. I only got those because you're cute.'

He laughs. 'I thought British girls were, like, totally shy.'

'I am,' she says. 'I'll come back. One hour?'

'Sure thing. One hour.'

'What's your name?' Ria asks, hoping that's it's something totally cool and American, like Brad or Chuck.

'Derek.'

Never mind. He's got nice arms and clean teeth.

She walks slowly round the mall feeling like a fat bloater for eating a Big Mac, twelve nuggets, an apple pie and the largest cup of Coca-Cola she has ever seen. She burps softly, checking to make sure no one heard her. She shouldn't be going to a party or drinking with anyone. Miri said to keep interactions to an absolute minimum. Ria can't understand why though. Everything bad that happens takes place in 2061, which is the future from here, and even if someone else has a time machine, which she knows is a possibility Miri has not ruled out, it still means these other time travellers would have to know where they are. Whatever.

She stops at a window display and immediately gets an idea for Emily's room. Emily seems more mature and refined, so her room should reflect that. It should be serious and elegant. Ria stops herself from falling into a trap of decorating rooms to reflect perceptions of character, otherwise Harry's would be a military cot with camouflage netting on the walls. What about the corridor at the end? That needs something. Painting definitely. That will really help get rid of that austere look. The gaps in the main room too. They need sorting.

What happens after all this? What then? They'll train to get ready and go back for the thing at her house – but then what? The end-of-the-world thing, she supposes. And after that? Will she just live in the bunker forever? She strolls through the store half seeing the displays while half lost in her own thoughts, then spots the white, shabby-chic

low chest and instantly knows it's perfect for Emily's room. She lifts the
lid to make sure a pair of assault boots can fit inside.

◆　◆　◆

'Hey, you came back,' Derek says an hour later.

'I did.'

'What's that?'

'A shabby-chic chest.'

'Damn,' Derek says, staring at it on the low trolley.

'Help me take it to my van?'

'Sure thing. You buy furniture on vacation?'

Shit. 'For my aunt. She's American.'

'From Milwaukee?'

'California.'

'We're in Milwaukee.'

'She's from California. She lives here now.'

'Where she live?'

'In Milwaukee. I like your arms. You work out?'

'Every damn day, hooyah. I ran track in school. I was a quarterback
too and had trials, but I wanna serve my country. I enlisted.'

'Yes, you said.'

'Marine Corps. Hooyah. Yes, ma'am.'

'Wow,' Ria says, nodding at him as he pulls the trolley out the doors
of the mall and into the car park.

'Where's the truck?'

'Van. Over there, other side.'

'Your aunt like furniture then?'

'She likes guns. Where's the bar?'

'Over there.'

'Do you live with your family?'

'Nope, co-sharing. My buddies and me got a place. I'm moving out in a week though. Enlisted. Yes, ma'am.'

'Hooyah,' Ria says, offering a smile that Derek returns slowly. 'I mean, that's great! Wow, I'm, like, so impressed and, like . . . totally impressed. So you ran track?'

'Yes, ma'am. Hundred metres, relay . . . I can bench, like, two hundred and twenty pounds too.'

'Wow,' Ria says again. 'Er, this is my van. We can just pop it in the side bit . . .' She unlocks the sliding door and pulls it back along the runners.

'Damn,' Derek says, 'you got curtains?'

'Just to keep the light from the back when my aunt is sleeping. So wow, two hundred and twenty pounds is so much. You must be so strong.'

'Yes, ma'am,' Derek says, hefting the white, shabby-chic low chest into the van.

'Wish I was fit and healthy,' Ria says, watching his arms bulge as he pushes it in.

'Y'all look fine to me,' Derek says, going slow to give her the gun show.

'Ah,' Ria says, looking down at her chest. 'If you like big boobs.'

'Yes, ma'am,' Derek says, now looking at Ria's boobs instead of the black curtain that pulled back a bit to reveal a glowing blue light. Ria leans in, brushing her breasts over his arm and plucks the curtain back.

'So,' she says as he swallows. 'Where's this bar?'

Thirty

'Brilliant,' Harry booms as the movie ends. His white teeth flashing through his black beard in the darkened room. 'Aye,' he adds. 'Brilliant.'

'You liked it then?' Emily asks.

'Ach, brilliant,' he says.

'Was great,' Ben says. 'Even Safa sat still for more than an hour.'

'Blah, blah,' Safa says, groaning as she stretches out on the big sofa. 'Keep rubbing my feet.'

'I've been rubbing them.'

'Well, keep going then,' Safa laughs, trying to sound aggressive and nice at the same time.

'You ticklish?'

'Try it and die, Ryder.'

'You don't scare me, Patel.'

'Try it then.'

'Er . . . nah,' he says as she chuckles.

Emily looks over at them and thinks they should just get a room and get over it. The amount they touch each other is ridiculous. Her feet on his lap. His hands rubbing her feet. Shoulder-brushing, hip-bumping, pushing and shoving each other all the time, and Safa liter-ally walking past him in her underwear every chance she gets. He puts his hands on her hips now to move her out the way too, and she either grins like an idiot or play-fights him. It's increasing too. Safa was pretty much pissing around Ben when Emily first arrived, and that reaction seems to have opened a door for her. Like a teenager starting to accept there are emotions other than anger and happiness. It's almost like Safa is testing him and constantly pushing the boundaries, while he remains entirely passive and casual about it.

'Where's Bertie?' Harry asks, looking round the room.

'Went back to the island,' Emily says. 'He told you he was going. He said Dumbledore gave him an idea and rushed off.'

'Did he?' Harry asks. 'Brew?'

'Aye,' Emily says deeply. 'Want me to make it, old man?'

'Old,' Harry tuts, rising to his feet.

'You are an old man,' Emily says, watching him walk over to the big table. 'You're almost a hundred and thirty years older than me.'

'Three years,' Harry says.

'Where you going, beardy?' Safa asks as Harry changes direction and walks towards the door.

'Ask ma'am if she wants a brew.'

'Arse-licker.'

'Aye,' Harry says, pushing the door open and flicking the light on at the same time to a chorus of groans at the others getting blinded. He chuckles and calls through, 'Brew, ma'am?'

'Yes. Movie finished?'

'Aye, has,' Harry calls back.

Miri checks her watch. The movie is just over two and a half hours long, and given the comfort break taken for Harry to have a smoke it means Ria is due back now. She folds the newspaper she was reading and moves from her desk to place it on top of the end stack. She's working year by year. Reading paper editions from English-speaking countries to gain an insight into the world as it moved on after her period. Emily said she can download and access them all on a single tablet, but she likes the act of reading newspapers and she knows the others keep taking them out to read too. Apart from Safa, who just moans when everyone is reading.

She walks from her office into the corridor and stares into the portal room, then checks her watch again. She'll wait another ten minutes. She moves up to the door and into the main room to see Safa stretched out on a sofa with her feet being rubbed by Ben, and thinks the two should just get a room and get over it.

'Movie good?' she asks Harry.

'Aye.'

'Good.'

'Seen it?'

'No.'

'Should.'

'Will.'

'You two have the shortest conversations ever.'

'Thank you for your observations, Miss Patel.'

'You got Miss Pateled,' Ben says.

'Thank you, Mr Ryder.'

'Haha! Rub, you bellend, don't fucking tickle.'

'Rub your bellend? Something you want to tell me, Safa?'

'Twat.'

'Sorry, that was childish,' Ben says to the room at large.

'S'fine,' Emily chuckles, taking advantage of Harry being off the sofa to stretch out. 'Was funny.'

'Miri? You okay?' Ben asks. 'You've checked your watch twice since you've come in.'

'Ria is late.'

'By how long?' Emily asks.

'Two minutes.'

'I'm sure she is fine,' Emily says.

'You worried?' Ben asks.

'Not worried. Concerned.'

'Same thing,' Safa says.

'It is not the same thing, Miss Patel.'

'She'll be fine – she's twenty-two,' Ben says.

'Young twenty-two though,' Safa says.

'Only by your standards,' Ben says.

'Meaning?' Emily asks, lifting her head to look at Ben.

'Both of you were doing serious stuff at that age. Ria hasn't, but that doesn't mean she is less than . . .'

'Safa never said that,' Emily says.

'Yeah, I know, but . . . What I mean is, Ria is young by your standards of not being professionally trained and disciplined, but by normal standards she's probably fine. You two are the rare ones. Ria is normal for that age . . . or at least what people that age were like in my time.'

'Makes sense actually,' Emily says thoughtfully.

'The egghead has spoken,' Safa says. 'Where were you at that age, Emily?'

'Israel.'

'What about you?' Ben asks, looking to Safa.

'Dunno, rub my feet.'

'I am.'

'Awesome. I joined the police because of you, then joined the Diplomatic Protection Team because of you, and now I'm on a sofa having my feet rubbed by you. Fucked up, but it is what it is. Rub my feet.'

The brutal, raw honesty brings a sudden silence to the room that even Safa detects. She lifts her head, looking round at them.

'Would you rub my feet?' Ben asks.

'Will I fuck! That's disgusting. I'd literally puke on you.'

'Other people in the room,' Emily says, holding her hand up.

'Twats,' Safa laughs. 'Cheers, beardy,' she adds, sitting up swiftly to take the mug held out by Harry.

'My Ben,' Harry says, offering the other.

'Never going to live it down,' Ben says. 'Cheers, mate.'

Miri checks her watch and feels the irritation. This is why civilians are no good in missions.

'Come on,' Ben says, heaving himself up to his feet at seeing the look on her face. 'We'll get ready.'

Changed. Dressed. Shirts on to cover pistols holstered on belts. Weapons made ready. Radios into pockets. Earpieces in. Comms checked, and all while they finish the drinks Harry made.

'Milwaukee, 2010,' Miri says, holding them in the portal room next to the shimmering blue light. 'Time is synced to here, currently twenty-one fifty hours. It will be dark with urban lighting. Opposition is not expected. Blue is in a van at the edge of a parking lot across from the mall. You have all seen it. Questions? Good. Safa on point. Locate and extract. We are not drawing attention. Go.'

Safa walks through to the van and pushes aside the curtain. She looks back, seeing Emily coming and not seeing the white, shabby-chic low chest that her shinbone rams into. Instant pain. She swears under her breath.

'What's up?' Emily whispers.

'This fucking thing,' Safa says, kicking the chest.

'Oh, that's nice,' Emily says. 'Is it a chest? I like that.'

'What's up?' Ben asks, coming through the portal.

'Oops,' Harry says, behind Ben. 'Hold up?'

'Fucking chest,' Safa says, still rubbing her shin.

'It's nice though,' Emily says. 'Shabby chic, I think.'

'Shabby pile of shit,' Safa says.

'Hold up?' Miri asks, coming through behind Ben and Harry.

'Chest,' Harry says.

'Shabby chic,' Ben says.

'It's nice,' Emily says.

'Ria there?' Miri asks.

'Is Ria there?' Ben asks.

'No, just a chest,' Emily says.

'No, just the chest,' Ben relays. 'Shabby chic, apparently.'

'Go over it,' Emily says to Safa.

'I am . . .'

'Don't stand on it,' Emily says.

'How the fuck do I get over it then?'

'Just step over it.'

'It's too big . . .'

'Why are we still here?'

'Miri wants to know why we're still here?' Ben asks.

'Step over it,' Emily says.

'I'll kick it out the fucking door in a minute.'

'Stand it on one end,' Harry rumbles.

Silence.

'Should do that,' Emily says.

'Yep,' Safa says.

The chest is moved to stand on one end. They go past it to view the front and a mostly deserted car park. Streetlights glow here and there. Lights on in the mall and the late businesses still open.

'Clear,' Safa says. She goes to open the passenger door and drops out to land deftly. Emily follows. Ben comes out. Harry drops down and holds position to offer a hand to Miri, who glares at it for a second before accepting the assistance without a word said.

'I said we should use the back doors,' Safa grumbles.

'Welded shut,' Miri says.

'Unweld them then . . . This air stinks,' Safa says, pulling a face.

'Does,' Emily says.

'If one of you stays with the van, I'll check the launderette,' Ben says.

'I'll stay,' Harry says.

'Two stay – looks more natural,' Miri says.

'I'll stay,' Emily says.

'Lead on,' Miri says, looking at Ben.

'Mind if I smoke?' Harry asks Emily as the others head off over the parking lot.

◆   ◆   ◆

They reach the launderette. Lights on. People inside. A sign proclaiming the facility is self-service after 10 p.m.

'Wait outside,' Miri says to Safa. She goes in behind Ben, who walks through looking over the tops of the machines. Miri goes along the front to view down the aisles formed by the rows of washers and dryers. People folding clothes into baskets, loading and unloading machines. Low music from hidden speakers. No Ria anywhere.

'Hi, do you work here?'

The old lady stands, grimacing at the pain in her lower back. She looks at Ben, then behind to Miri. 'The British girl, right?' the old lady asks.

'Er, yes, that's right,' Ben says, charming, easy and super-concerned all at the same time. 'Black hair, er . . . sort of medium build.'

'Curvy,' the old lady says. 'She didn't come back. Went into the mall. Clothes all folded in the bags over there.'

'That's very kind of you. Did she seem okay?'

'Seemed fine to me,' the old lady says, walking off. 'Saw her with a black kid. He works in the mall.' She stops to turn back. 'Nice kid, not a gangbanger.'

'Thanks,' Ben says. 'These bags?'

'Yep,' the old lady calls back. 'What are ya? Soldiers?'

'Soldiers?' Ben asks.

'Clothes,' the old lady says, making a few heads turn to listen. 'All black, like soldiers.'

'Er,' Ben says.

'Laser-quest,' Miri says with a laugh that animates and brings sudden warmth. 'Damn kids running about playing. Vacation from the UK – they don't have it over there. Whole family doing it now.'

'Damn kids,' the old woman laughs. Ben looks round to see a few of the other women tutting and shaking heads as they go back to folding clothes.

'Owe you for the wash?' Miri asks, pulling a small clutch of notes from her pocket.

'She paid,' the old lady says.

'Thanks,' Miri says.

'Hope you find her,' one of the other women calls out. 'Ain't safe here late. Too many damn kids with guns.'

'Thanks,' Miri says. 'We'll find her.'

'Wow,' Ben says softly once outside. 'That was very good.'

'Mall,' Miri says. 'Safa, take the washing back to the van.'

'On it.'

Ben and Miri walk in through the main doors of the mall to see a uniformed security guard marching towards them. 'Closes at ten-thirty,' he says quickly, his accent thick. Miri takes him in. Nigerian, maybe Ghanaian.

'Looking for a girl,' Ben says.

'Cops?'

'No, family. Black hair, this tall, curvy . . . Speaks with a British accent.'

'No, not see. I not see her. Close at ten-thirty. Two minutes, I lock doors.'

'We'll have a quick look,' Ben says, walking off.

'Two minutes.'

'Yes, you said,' Ben says. 'We'll be quick.'

'I get trouble if late. Ten-thirty.'

'What's his problem?' Ben asks, walking up the main aisle with Miri.

'Jobs are scarce,' Miri says. 'He's worried.'

Ben looks back to see the concern on the security guard's face as he glances at his watch.

'*Emily, you still at the van?*' Ben says into the discreet transmitter fitted under the collar of his shirt.

'*Confirmed. With Harry. Safa walking towards us.*'

'*Check that chest in the van. See if it's got a receipt or something.*'

'*Doing it now, over.*'

'Good idea,' Miri says.

'Place is deserted,' Ben says. 'They'll have cameras though. Worth checking?'

'Won't let us look. We're not cops.'

'We've got a time machine – we don't need to ask.'

Shutters going down. Staff making final adjustments and preparations to close for the night. They pass McDonald's to see a group of kids eating burgers at a table while an Indian woman mops the floor round their feet.

'*Ben, receipt says Terry's Treasures.*'

'*Seriously?*'

'*Afraid so.*'

'*Cheers.*'

'Over there,' Miri says, pointing to a glass-fronted store. Throws and furniture arranged artfully in the window. He spots another white, shabby-chic chest in the corner.

They go inside to see a man at the counter working the cash register with a big notepad open next to it.

'Closed,' he says, glancing up. 'Open in the morning.'

'Sorry to disturb you,' Ben says politely. The man stares at him. 'We're looking for a girl. She might have bought a chest here, the same kind you have in the window.'

'British girl. Dark hair. Sure.'

'Yes, that's her. Er, how long ago did she buy it?'

'Why? She not get home?'

'Not yet,' Ben says, showing a worried look.

'Saw her down at McDonald's talking to a kid who works there. Black kid. Derek, I think. Nice kid. Joining the Marines.'

'McDonald's?' Ben asks.

'Sure,' the man says. 'Hope you find her.'

'Thanks.'

Back out and down to see the kids laughing and throwing fries at each other, while the Indian woman tries not to notice as she mops. She looks exhausted. Bags under her eyes. Sadness in her features.

'Hi,' Ben says, drawing her attention. 'Does Derek work here?'

The woman looks at him, then at Miri. She doesn't smile or show any expression. Fries land next to Miri's feet. The Indian woman looks down at them.

'We're looking for a girl, my sister,' Ben says. 'British girl, black hair, curvy . . .'

More fries land. Cackles of laughter. Slurps of beverages that spill from cups on to the floor the woman just mopped.

'Help you?' a man asks, walking out from behind the counter.

'Yes, hi,' Ben says. 'We're looking for Derek.'

'Who are you?' the man asks, his face flushed from cleaning down the surfaces. His tie tucked in between the buttons on his McDonald's shirt. 'Cops?'

'Family,' Ben says. 'Looking for my sister. British girl, dark hair, curvy.'

The man shrugs. 'Can't help you.'

More fries land. More drinks spilled. The Indian woman mops the floor.

'Sorry, mate,' Ben says, smiling at the manager. 'My sister isn't from here. Someone saw her talking to Derek. Is he here?'

'Don't give out company information,' the man says, scowling at the Indian woman, then over at the kids.

'I'm not asking for company information. I'm asking if you saw her, and if Derek is here so I can ask him.'

'Derek left three hours ago,' the man says quietly. 'Gunjeep, clear that fucking mess up,' he barks at the woman, pointing at the mess.

'Maybe you should tell those kids to stop throwing it on the floor,' Ben says.

'Maybe you should leave before I call the cops,' the man retorts. 'Gunjeep! Clear that fucking mess up. Bitch is deaf . . .'

'Ben!'

'Listen to me, you fucking twat,' Ben says, bending the manager backwards over the counter. 'That was rude, very rude . . . I fucking hate rude people . . .'

'She *is* deaf! Gunjeep is deaf, man! She can't hear anything.'

'What?'

'She's deaf! She's deaf. She can't hear. She got the job through a programme. Learning difficulties, man . . .'

'Oh,' Ben says, still holding the man over the counter. 'Right, well . . . still shouldn't call her a bitch,' he adds stiffly, slowly releasing the manager.

'Long day, man,' the manager says weakly, clearly terrified. 'Other manager sick . . . I been here since seven this morning.'

'I see,' Ben says, nodding. 'Er, so . . . Derek finished work, did he?'

The manager nods. 'About three hours ago. He's a good kid. Joining the Marines. Probably in the bar having a beer.'

'Bar,' Ben says politely. 'Right, and where is that?'

'By the parking lot, man. You didn't need to grab me up, dude.'

'Yeah, sorry. Thank you, and sorry for, er . . . you know . . .'

'Whatever, man,' the manager says.

Ben smiles at him, then smiles at Gunjeep staring dully. 'Thanks.'

'She's deaf, man. I just said that.'

'She might lip-read.'

'She doesn't lip-read, man. She's Indian.'

'Right, well, we're going now. And you kids, just stop throwing chips about. Messy shits. Mall closes at ten-thirty.'

'Smooth, Mr Ryder.'

'Sorry.'

'You go now. Close now. You go.'

'Yes, alright!' Ben says to the worried security guard. 'What about those kids? You kicking them out?'

'Ben,' Miri says quietly.

The security guard stares back.

'In McDonald's, throwing chips about.'

'Fries,' Miri says.

'Throwing fries about,' Ben says.

'Owner's kids,' the security guard says. 'You go. Close now.'

'Right,' Ben says. 'Thanks,' he adds brightly.

'Smooth, Mr Ryder.'

'Sorry.'

'Think before you speak. Look before you speak. Process the world around you. Your communication skills are exceptional, so try engaging your brain at the same time.'

'Sorry.'

'Don't let Safa rub off on you. You are not Safa.'

'Okay, sorry, Miri.'

'Safa would have made him answer, but that's because she is Safa. You are not her. You have other skills.'

'Sorry.'

'Don't be sorry. Learn. Be better.'

'Yes, Miri.'

'Aggression is a tactic to be used when necessary.'

'Yes, Miri.'

'Intelligence is the tool we use all the time.'

'Okay, sorry, Miri.'

'When you and Safa have sex, do not let it impact on the dynamics. Safa will be fine, but make sure it does not affect *your* abilities.'

Ben stops and stares at her as they head to the car park. 'Sex?'

'Yes, sex.'

'We're just friends.'

'Sure. In the meantime, try masturbation. Release the tension.'

'Miri!'

'You get anything?' Safa calls out as they near the van.

'Kid works in McDonald's,' Miri says. 'Derek. Might be in a bar here.'

'Bar there,' Emily says, pointing across the car park to bright lights over a door marked *Bar*.

The five set off towards it. Ben mutters and shoots glances at Miri. Miri ignores him.

'Everything okay?' Emily asks.

'Fine,' Ben says.

'I suggested Mr Ryder try ma . . .'

'Yes, thank you,' Ben cuts in.

'Try what?' Safa asks.

'Nothing,' Ben says.

'No, what?' Safa asks.

'Tell you later,' Ben says, buying time.

'No, now,' Safa says, not wishing to sell time right now.

'Looks like a nice place,' Ben says, looking ahead to the bar.

'What should Ben try?' Safa asks, looking at Miri.

'Can we just drop it?'

'Masturbation.'

'Miri!' Ben says.

'What, wanking?' Safa asks.

'Oh my god,' Ben groans.

'Yes,' Miri says.

'Oh,' Safa says. 'Why does Ben need a wank?'

'Can we please fucking drop it?'

'Tension,' Miri says.

'You tense then?' Safa asks him.

'I fucking am now,' Ben mutters.

'Have a wank then,' Safa says.

'Jesus,' Ben says.

'You should,' Emily says, nodding at him seriously.

'What!? No!'

'Helps,' Emily says.

'I'm not tense,' Ben says.

'You sound tense,' Emily says.

'Have a wank,' Safa says.

'Ask Safa to walk past you a bit more in underwear.'

'Emily!' Ben says in horror.

'Fucking funny,' Safa says, laughing at the comment that a month or so ago would have resulted in outright violence.

They stop outside the bar. Five of them gathered by the door, trying to peer through the glass to the darkened, gloomy interior.

'See anything?' Emily asks.

'Nope,' Ben says. 'Too dark, and apparently I'm too tense to see anything.'

'Get over it,' Safa says. 'I'll go in and have a look.'

'Is that wise?' Emily asks.

'Why?'

'She might be talking to the boy from McDonald's. You'll just get angry and hit him.'

'I wouldn't,' Safa says with a scowl.

'I'll go,' Ben says.

'You can't go – you'll embarrass the hell out of her,' Emily says.

'Miri then?' Ben asks.

'God no!' Emily says.

'Well, we can't all go in and look,' Ben says.

Thirty-One

Ria sips the beer and stares into his dark eyes. His right arm propped on the bar reaching out so his fingertips can gently stroke the soft skin on her left arm. She giggles and listens, leaning in to pay attention and glancing at the shape of his bicep. She doesn't mention there is no party and no buddies to meet. It doesn't matter.

'I bet you'll look hot in the uniform,' she says.

'Yes, ma'am,' he says, smiling coyly.

'I'd love to see that. Have you got it yet?'

'No, ma'am,' he says, still smiling coyly. He likes Ria. She's so different to anyone he has met. Her accent is so nice and soft, yet she told him the merits of the M4 assault rifle in adverse weather conditions, what oil is the best to use and how the magazines sometimes get a bit sticky. He asked how she knew, and she just laughed in a rather beguiling way and made a joke about being from the future, but from the past. He laughed too and drank his beer.

'Oh, shame,' she says, dropping her hand to rest on his thigh. 'Well, you have a McDonald's uniform – that's something.'

She knows about proteins and carbs too, and about good fats and bad fats. Girls don't know that kind of stuff in Derek's world. Not in the detail Ria does. She seems sad though. Derek glimpses the pain in her eyes between laughing. It makes him want to know why, but Derek is a good kid, so he doesn't pry. He likes her boobs and curves too. He likes the warmth of the soft skin on her arm and the way she laughs at his crap jokes.

'Wanna 'nother beer?'

'Love one. Let me get them.' Ria pulls out a wad of banknotes from her clutch purse.

'Hey, y'all put that back,' Derek says quickly, looking around in alarm.

'What? Why? It's fine.'

'Not round here it ain't,' Derek says, his tone serious. 'Don't show that here, Ria. These folks will rob you easy.'

'Sorry,' she says, peeling off a single note while offering him an apologetic smile.

'Where you get that from anyway?' he asks, glancing round again to make sure no one saw the money.

'Smurfs.'

'What?'

'Nothing. My family is wealthy.'

'Hey, two beers,' Derek calls out.

'Sure thing,' the bartender says. He brings over two uncapped bottles, takes the note and brings back the change.

'Cheers,' Ria says, holding her bottle out to Derek and not giving a shit about the bunker or Miri or the portal in the van or the launderette or anything at all other than this nice boy smiling at her.

'Cheers,' Derek says. He learnt that from Ria too.

'Stout.'

Ria freezes, the bottle pressed to her lips.

'What?' the bartender asks.

'Stout.'

'What's stout?' the bartender asks.

Ria closes her eyes.

'Ale. Stout. Maybe bitter?'

'Bitter?' the bartender says.

'Aye, bitter, beer.'

'Beer? You wanna beer?'

'Aye.'

'I'll have one too, please, mate.'

'Ladies?' the bartender asks.

'Orange juice.'

Ria winces at each voice. Her eyes closed.

'Sure thing.'

'Er, I'll have a beer too, thanks. In a glass though. Not a bottle.'

'You drink beer?'

'What? I like beer.'

'Okay, fuck that then. Scrap the orange juice. I'll have a beer too.'

'So four beers?'

'Five,' Miri says from behind Ria, who slowly opens her eyes, purses her lips and stares at Derek.

'Hey,' Derek says, 'I think they're British too . . .'

Ria turns slowly on the bar stool.

Harry glances down and smiles. Ben nods. Emily waves. Safa glares past her to Derek. Miri looks round the bar.

'What the fuck?' Ria asks.

'Oh, hi,' Emily says, as though surprised.

'Seriously?' Ria hisses. 'What the fuck?'

'Problem?' Safa asks, still glaring at Derek and not liking the way he is looking at Ria.

'Safa, stop it,' Ria blurts.

'Hi, I'm Ben,' Ben says, leaning across Ria to offer Derek his hand.

'Oh my god, Ben,' Ria seethes, having to lean back as they shake.

'Harry,' Harry says, taking Ben's place to tower over Ria in the offering of an enormous hand to Derek.

'Sir,' Derek says, staring up at the huge bearded man.

'They got stout here?' Harry asks him.

'What?' Derek asks.

'No, Harry, they won't have stout,' Ria says. Wishing the ground would open up.

'I'm Emily.' She squeezes in next to Harry to offer her hand. 'You must be Derek.'

'Oh my god,' Ria mutters, hardly believing this is happening.

'Er, hi,' Derek says, clearly bewildered. 'Nice to meet you. May I get you a drink? Are you Ria's family?'

'Ach, nice manners, that lad,' Harry booms as Ria winces again.

'That was polite, wasn't it?' Emily says, smiling at Derek then back to Harry.

'Ria, you okay?'

'I am fine, Ben.'

'Cool. We, er, we just wanted to, er . . . get a beer and . . . check you were alright.'

'I am fine, Ben.'

'Good,' Ben says slowly, rocking on his heels.

'Five beers,' the bartender says, placing the bottles down as Ria plucks a note from the purse and holds it out without looking round.

'Hey,' Derek says, alarmed again at the show of money. 'Don't show that here.'

'We're more than safe,' Ria says flatly. 'Trust me.'

'Oh, sorry,' Emily says, 'could I have a glass?'

'Sure thing.'

'Make sure it's clean,' Safa says.

'Er, yeah, clean glass, sure thing,' the bartender says, rushing off to find one.

'Harry, don't eat the nuts – they're covered in piss,' Safa says as Harry mouths a huge handful from the bowl on the bar.

'So,' Emily says, grinning at Derek. 'You work in McDonald's?'

'How do you know that, ma'am?'

'Saw you there,' Miri says from the back.

'We saw you there,' Emily says.

Derek nods and peers round to see an older woman staring round the bar slowly. 'I leave in a week. Enlisting.'

'Oh no,' Ria groans, sinking on the stool.

'Enlisting?' Harry asks, mouthing more nuts.

'In the military?' Emily asks.

'Really?' Safa asks, staring at Derek a bit harder.

'Yes, ma'am. Marines, ma'am.'

'Marines?' Miri asks.

'Yes, ma'am. US Marines.'

'Good lad!' Harry booms, clapping him on the shoulder.

'Well done,' Emily says.

'Good lads, the Marines,' Harry says. 'Worked with them in Italy in . . .'

'Beer, Harry,' Ben says, passing the bottle over.

'Can you join then? Being a negro . . .'

'Oh my god, Harry!' Ria blurts.

'Harry!' Emily says, moving in swiftly from behind Derek. 'We're from a different place,' she says to the lad. 'Different terms for things. Oh, did you drop this?' She holds a folded brown leather wallet. 'It was on the floor.'

'He's not racist,' Ben says, as Derek takes the wallet, glancing from Harry to Emily to Ben.

'Fought with some in Africa,' Harry tells Derek, pulling his attention back. 'Good lads too.'

Derek nods and swallows. He was brought up well. To be polite and respectful, but to challenge when things are wrong. 'Sir, that word isn't used now,' he says to Harry.

'What?' Harry asks.

'Negros, sir.'

'Oh,' Harry says. 'What is it then?'

'I'm black,' Derek says. 'Or African American.'

'Seriously, what are you doing here?' Ria asks.

'Came for a beer,' Emily says.

'You so did not come for a beer.'

'I gave a time, Miss Cavendish.'

'I know, but I'm staying out.'

'We had to come find you, Miss Cavendish.'

'Ria! My name is Ria. I am twenty-two years old, Miri.'

'You could have told me you wanted more time.'

'I don't have to tell you anything.'

'I have security concerns, Miss Ca—'

'Ria! My name is Ria.'

'Take it easy,' Ben says.

'If you want more time, you ask for more time,' Miri says.

'What? Am I a fucking prisoner then?'

'You are not a prisoner, but I . . .'

'You are not my mother. She's dead. I'm an adult, and I'm going to get drunk and have sex with this boy.'

'What?' Derek asks.

'I'm not leaving. I'm not running away. I just want to get fucking drunk and have sex!'

'What?' Derek says.

'I'm coming back. I just . . . I just . . . He's cute and he's got nice arms, and he said I look nice and he likes curves . . .'

'What?' Derek asks.

'Problem?' Harry asks, looking round at the suddenly quiet bar. 'Be on about your business now.'

'The shabby-chic chest is lovely,' Emily says, breaking the heavy, charged silence. 'And you look really nice, Ria.'

'Sorry,' Ben says, resting a hand on Ria's shoulder as she fights back the tears.

'It's fine,' Ria says, holding a hand to her mouth. 'I'm sorry. What you're doing is important . . . I'll come back now and . . .'

'No, no, no,' Emily says. 'Stay, it's cool.'

'No, I should . . .'

'Stay,' Ben says. 'Have some drinks.'

'You're an adult,' Emily says. 'We were just worried . . . No phones, remember?'

'I know,' Ria whispers, looking round at them with tears in her eyes. 'Bertie's working on it.'

'It's fine,' Emily says. 'You look lovely, so lovely, and I love your curves. I wish I had curves.'

'You've got a six-pack,' Ria snorts, half-smiling, half trying not to cry. 'I bet men love it.'

'Men?' Emily asks, smiling at her. 'You don't know?'

'Know what?'

'I'm gay.'

'What?'

'I'm gay,' Emily says. 'So trust me when I say you look gorgeous and your curves are lovely. Stay. Have fun.' She leans in to kiss Emily's cheek. 'He does have nice arms,' she whispers. 'And a lovely smile.'

'He does,' Ria says, smiling as Emily pulls back.

'You okay?' Ben asks from behind her, his hand still on her shoulder. 'Need anything? Money? Gun? M4 assault rifle? Bazooka?'

Ria laughs, wanting to cry again but with different emotions coursing through her. 'I'm fine, honestly.'

'Okay,' Ben says, leaning down to kiss the top of her head. 'You know where we are if you need us.'

'I'll be fine . . .'

'Miss,' Harry says, leaning over to kiss her forehead, the bristles of his beard tickling her skin. He smells of woodbines and popcorn. 'Nice to meet you,' Harry says again, holding his hand to Derek. 'Sorry I called you a negro.'

'Sir,' Derek says, shaking his hand again.

'Nice arms,' Safa tells Derek. 'Do more cardio – you'll define better. And wear a condom, or I'll snap it off and shove it up your arse.'

'Whoa, time to go,' Ben says, guiding Safa away. 'Nice to meet you, Derek.'

'Sir,' Derek says, staring in alarm at Safa.

'I'm watching you,' Safa calls out as she walks across the bar.

'Ma'am,' Derek says. He watches as they file out through the door and the bar slowly comes back to normality. The door opens. Safa leans in, pointing two fingers at her own eyes then at Derek before Ben pulls her out.

'Families, eh?' Ria says, smiling tentatively at Derek.

He looks back at her, then over to the door again. 'Sure, families. Hooyah . . .'

Thirty-Two

'Are you gay?' Ben asks, his hand still clamped on Safa's wrist as they walk across the car park.

'No,' Emily says. 'I just said it to make her feel better.'

'Really?'

'Maybe?' Emily says with a smile.

'Name?' Miri asks, pulling a small tablet from her pocket.

'Derek Collins, middle initial T. Date of birth, 20 June 1988,' Emily says from the glimpse of his driving licence she gained while Harry created a distraction.

'Did you know Emily is gay?' Ben asks Safa.

'Yep,' Safa says. 'We should go back and get her. I don't like him.'

'Did you know?' Ben asks Miri.

'Yes.'

'I didn't know,' Ben tells Emily.

'Should you then?' Emily asks.

'Eh? No! I mean . . . No, I never, you know . . . I didn't . . .'

'It's fine, I'm playing. Yes, I am gay, but I also like men.'

'Bi-sexual?'

'Ah,' Emily says, 'they labelled it all back then, didn't they?'

'Er, so they don't in your time?'

'We should go back. He had beady eyes. I don't like beady eyes.'

'He was fine, Safa,' Ben says.

'No, they don't,' Emily says to Ben. 'Not like they did in your time.'

'And he looked shifty,' Safa says.

'He did not,' Emily says. 'Good-looking boy. And he was polite.'

'Yeah, until he wants something, then he won't be polite,' Safa says.

'Not all men are like that,' Emily says.

'Fucking are.'

'Is Ben?' Emily asks.

'. . . all men other than Ben are fuckers.'

'Ahem.'

'And Harry.'

'Got him,' Miri says. 'DMV has Mr Collins registered at one zero four nine Tenth Avenue, Milwaukee.'

'I still don't think we should be doing this,' Ben says.

'World ends, Mr Ryder. We'll do what it takes.'

'How does the world ending have anything to do with Ria?'

'How do we know it doesn't?' Miri counters.

'How can you justify placing her under observation on the basis of an incident that takes place a hundred years in the future from this time?'

'How can you justify not taking all necessary steps to ensure the safety of our team?'

Ben narrows his eyes. 'Low blow.'

'Effective response.'

'Cheap shot.'

'Cheap shots are still shots, Mr Ryder.'

Safa, Emily and Harry look at Ben.

'Fine, you win,' he says.

'I always do,' Miri says.

'He still looked like a creep,' Safa says.

'He did not look like a creep,' Emily says. 'He looked like a very nice young man.'

'That's what they said about Jack the Ripper,' Safa says. 'Very nice young man. Then look what happened. Hey, we should go back and find him.'

'Who?' Ben asks.

'Jack the Ripper.'

'Yeah, we can't do that.'

'Why not? Who says we haven't already done it? Maybe we already do it and it's done, so therefore we can do it . . .'

'But . . .' Ben says.

'And they never found out who he was,' Safa cuts in.

'Yeah, but . . .' Ben says.

'So there,' Safa says. 'We're gonna get Jack the Ripper.'

'We're not.'

'We already did.'

'We didn't.'

'Social networks,' Miri says, handing the tablet to Emily.

'Pardon?' Emily says.

'Mr Collins. Social networks. Check him.'

'Oh, right,' Emily says. 'Er . . . so . . . we're in 2010, so . . . Facebook? Christ, this is ancient . . . There's no 3D or . . . What operating system is this? It's so slow . . . and this screen is just awful. It's not intuitive or . . . Where's the catch-all program?'

'There isn't one,' Miri says.

'How do I do it then?' Emily asks.

'Still a Two,' Safa coughs into her hand.

'No,' Emily protests. 'This is, like, years behind my time.'

'Want me to do it?' Ben asks.

'I was still a Two because all the Ones were taken.'

'I'll do it,' Ben says, taking the tablet from her.

'It takes years to be a One.'

'I'll log in with my old account,' Ben says with a sudden jolt. 'Oh shit, I remember this . . . I had to reset my password. They said someone in America logged in.' He laughs at the thought, shaking his head. 'This is fucked up.' He double-taps the Facebook icon, then taps into the username field and starts to write his old email address. He tabs over to the password. *StephMyers2015.* It feels wrong to write her name. The application opens to his Facebook page as of 2010.

'Is that Stephanie?' Emily asks, glimpsing the profile picture of a smiling woman.

'Er, yeah. Yeah, it is,' Ben says. 'I couldn't have pictures of me . . . You know . . . the whole Calshott Ryder thing. I, er . . . I only put hers there to . . .' He glances at Safa's frozen face staring at the screen in his hands. 'I only put it there so I had a picture . . . People ask questions otherwise . . .'

'Ooh,' Emily says, glancing at Safa's face. 'Not awkward at all.'

'Whore,' Safa mutters.

'What?' Emily asks.

'Her, not you,' Safa says, turning away from the screen with a look of utter distaste. 'Can we just get the fuck on now?'

'Er, Derek Collins,' Ben says, typing the name in. 'Common name . . . Loads of . . .'

'That's him,' Emily says, leaning over and pointing.

'Got him,' Ben says, opening the profile to see the smiling young man from the bar. 'Pictures . . . Parties, sports . . . family . . . He's anti-drugs,' Ben adds, seeing the shared posts. 'Pro-police, pro-military . . . Tons of stuff on the Marines . . . Seems okay,' he says with nod. 'Nothing that bad here.'

Miri takes the tablet back, ends the current screen and opens a new program. She thumbs the screen, pursing her lips with focus. 'Where did you put it?'

'Collar, back of the neck,' Emily says.

Miri presses the screen and waits while the connection is made. The speakers hiss, background noise, the sound of glasses or bottles clinking.

'. . . rry? Er, yes, he is a soldier, but in England.'

'Who was the other guy?'

'Ben, but I don't want to talk about them. Tell me about the Marines again . . . Do you want another beer?'

'Y'all like beer a lot.' Derek's voice, laughing.

'Do you have beer at your house?'

'My house?'

'The place you live. Your flat.'

'Apartment. Sure, I got beer there.'

'We should go. I'd love to see it.'

'Ma'am, you said you wanted to have sex . . . I want you to know my momma raised me good and . . .'

'Stop gabbling. I hate gabbling.'

They all look at Safa, who shrugs.

'. . . go to your flat, apartment . . . Whatever, let's go there.'

'She's throwing herself at him,' Ben mutters.

'. . . come on, do you want to? I want to.'

'But, ma'am, Ria . . . listen . . . I . . .'

'We'll just go back for a beer, then I'll go home.'

'Christ,' Ben tuts.

'. . . sure, we can do that,' Derek says, his voice showing a level of uncertainty.

'Don't worry,' Emily says, seeing the look of worry on Ben's and Harry's faces. 'This is quite normal for my time.'

'You want another beer here?' Derek asks.

'Nope, we'll have it at yours. Come on. How far is it?'

'Not far.'

◆ ◆ ◆

Ria and Derek walk from the bar to a deserted parking lot. Ria looks over to the van at the far edge and round with the sensation of being watched that she shrugs off as she reaches for his hand.

Derek leads the way. Hand in hand and feeling confused, flattered, horny, concerned and full of testosterone all at the same time.

'You sure you wanna come back?' he asks, his voice muted now they're out of the bar. 'We could meet up tomorrow, catch a movie . . . pizza . . .'

'I want to come back,' she says, squeezing his hand. She needs this. She needs this contact, this comfort, this warmth of another human being. She flits between needing to cry and needing to laugh. Between feeling warm inside from the beer and feeling homesick for the bunker and for her old house. She wants to take Derek to the island and sit on the rocks to stare out over the moonlit sea. She wants sex. She wants to be held, to be loved, to be at home and to see her mother. She wants everything and nothing and to be away from the perfection of Safa and Emily, and the worried looks Ben and Harry always have. 'So,' she says, snapping out of her sudden introspection. 'Are you looking forward to it?'

'Sex?' Derek blurts.

'No! The Marines,' Ria chuckles. A sound behind them. Like a snort of laughter snapping off. She turns to look, but sees nothing, only empty sidewalks.

'Drunks,' Derek says, not seeing anything either.

'I'M TWENTY-TWO . . .' she shouts back at them.

'Shush,' Derek says quickly. 'This ain't the place to draw attention.'

Ria walks on. They wouldn't follow her, would they? She glances behind again, but still sees nothing. No. No, they wouldn't. That would be too much. What do they care anyway? They came to look for her, satisfied themselves and now they've gone back to eat popcorn and watch holos. They're fit and clean and healthy and perfect, and they have each other. She doesn't have anyone. They didn't come for her anyway. They came for Bertie. Bloody Bertie. It's always about Bertie. *My son is a genius. My son got three Master's degrees when he was bloody fourteen . . . thirteen . . . whatever.* Bloody Bertie.

'What?' she asks, blinking at Derek.

'I won't miss here,' Derek says wistfully. 'Can't wait to go.'

'Don't wish it away,' she says, the sadness creeping back into her voice and eyes.

'Hey, so maybe I should walk you home.'

'No,' she says, forcing a beaming grin and moving closer into his side. 'I want to see your flat.'

'Apartment.'

'Flat,' she giggles, pressing her boobs into his arm. 'I'm fine, honestly.'

'You said your momma died.'

'Don't want to talk about that. Tell me about the Marines. Tell me about nice things and, and . . .'

'They got grief counsellors in England?'

'What the fuck? I'm fine. Are you excited about the Marines? Where do you go to train? What are those other guys called? Seals or something?'

'Navy Seals. Special Forces.'

'You should do that,' she gushes, clinging to his arm. 'You'd be so good.'

'Hooyah,' he says, smiling, worried, confused, turned on.

'Hooyah,' she laughs.

'My place,' he says, nodding at the door over the road. 'Listen, Ria . . .' He stops walking to stand on the sidewalk. 'Maybe I'll walk you home, huh?'

'Do you want to?' she asks, dropping her voice to a low murmur, closing the gap between them. 'I mean . . . if you don't want me to come back . . .' She trails off, seeing his eyes flick down to her chest, now inches from him. She reaches out for his hands, taking them in hers,

smiling at him, fluttering eyes, demure and sexy. He swallows, blinks
and tries to steel himself to say no, to say he will walk her home. She
senses the rejection coming and moves in to press her mouth on his.
He stiffens. Unsure. The worry increasing, but she's warm and soft and
she smells so good. He thinks to pull back, but her hand comes up to
snake round the back of his head, pulling him in. She doesn't push it,
but kisses softly, easing her lips against his, feeling his heart thumping,
feeling his hard body. 'I'm leaving soon,' she whispers, pulling her lips
back from his. 'One night.'

'I . . .'

'Don't you want me?'

'Sure, you're . . .'

'Do you think I'm pretty?'

'Yes, ma'am, very damn pretty.'

'Let's go inside. I want to go inside.'

'Okay.'

They cross the road, pushing into each other, arms round waists,
shoulders, kissing, touching, and through the door to climb the stairs
to his apartment.

◆ ◆ ◆

'She needs to come home,' Safa says.

'She's an adult,' Ben whispers back.

'She's drunk. She's going to do something she'll regret. I'm bringing
her back . . .'

'No,' Emily says. 'She's fine. You heard him – he's being really nice.'

'She's upset. She shouldn't be doing anything,' Safa says.

'Her choice,' Miri says. 'We're here to ensure protection. Not to
guide her life.'

'Exactly,' Emily says.

'Young lady should come home,' Harry says, upset at seeing the girl needing affection so badly she's throwing herself at the lad.

'She is fine,' Emily whispers firmly. 'If this is how she copes, then let her. It's her life. Her mistakes.'

'*Oh god, I am so horny . . .*' Ria's voice continues.

'Fuck's sake, turn it off,' Safa snaps.

'*You sure, Ria? You sure you wanna . . .*'

'*Stop asking me! Yes. Yes, I am sure . . . Where's your room? Oh my god, you are so fit.*'

'Turn it off now,' Safa says, her voice rising.

Miri shakes her head. 'No. If it is uncomfortable for you, Miss Patel, then go stand over there.'

'We are not fucking listening to her having sex.'

'We are listening to ensure she does not say anything about the Blue.'

'I won't listen to this shit,' Safa says, striding off.

'Aye,' Harry says, following her.

'Tango Two? Want to leave?'

'My name is Emily,' Emily says quietly. 'And I'm fine, thank you, *Mrs Sanderson.*'

Miri glares with cold grey eyes.

'Apologies,' Emily says.

'*Fucking hell . . . your willy is huge . . .*'

'Yeah, okay, I don't want to listen,' Emily says, walking off.

Noises. Thumps. Bangs. Grunts. A hiss of static. Background voices. A television or stereo. Music playing softly. A commercial advert. Heavy petting. Clothes being taken off. Zippers.

'*STOP . . . STOP, PLEASE . . . NO!*'

Safa, Harry and Emily burst to life. Sprinting down the alley as Ben waves his hands at them.

'It's a movie . . . Just a movie,' he says urgently as a tinny American voice pleading for someone to put the gun down comes from the tablet.

Miri changes the tablet to the lowest volume setting, but listens intently. Loose lips sink ships, and a word uttered in passion has overthrown governments before. She knows. She's done it.

Ben reaches out to touch Safa. She pulls away from him with pure fury pouring off her. She hates it. She hates that Ria is doing this. She should have more pride in herself, but Safa also feels something else. A weird jealousy. A sense of someone having the emotional freedom and sexual maturity to simply know what they want and to have it. She walks further into the shadows. She wants to go and not listen, but what if Ria gets in trouble? Ben stares at the ground. Miri is right. The potential risks are too great and they don't know Ria. They don't know Emily either, but it's different.

'Can't listen,' Harry says, walking off further down the alley. Safa goes with him. The two side by side until they get enough distance not to hear anything.

A sound of a sob. Emily goes to move again, aiming towards the mouth of the alley towards the direction of Derek's apartment. Ben stops her. Shaking his head.

Ria cries. The heavy breathing and rhythmic sounds of the bed ending suddenly.

'*Keep going . . . please . . .*' Ria says.

'I can't listen,' Emily says. 'Sorry, I'm not an agent anymore.'

'*I'll stop . . . You're crying . . .*'

'*No! Please, I'm fine.*'

'*Ria, listen . . .*'

'*Just fuck me, please.*'

Miri locks eyes on Ben, as though daring him to turn and go with the others. This is what it takes. To work at this level means doing this. To listen to everything. To hear everything. To know all the pieces of the game. Ben refuses to be cowed. That he is sickened at what he hears shows on his face, and he gives thanks that Miri finally portrays the essence of a human being and closes her eyes in distaste, but then he immediately suspects that very reaction was just a show too.

It's over quickly. A build-up. A grunt. Silence.

'You okay, Ria?'

A sniffle, a quiet sob. *'I want to go home.'*

Ben stares across the road at the building.

'Sure, can I call someone? You wanna drink? Coffee?'

'I miss my mum.'

'What happened? You want to talk?'

'Christ, he's a nice lad,' Ben whispers, looking away.

'She died . . . I . . .'

'It's okay, you can cry . . .'

'I just . . . I . . . I can't see her again . . . never . . . She's gone and . . .'

The words come between sobs. Derek's soft tones giving comfort. The bed creaks. Ben visualises the lad moving closer to her.

'It's hard, sure it is,' Derek says. *'Your momma loved you though. What about your daddy?'*

'He was a cunt,' Ria sobs with a half-choked laugh. *'I didn't mean that . . . Oh god, I didn't mean that . . .'*

'Hey, it's fine, sure it is. Those people? In the bar? They good?'

'Yeah . . . busy . . . Everyone's so busy . . .'

'They talk to you?'

'Try, but . . . I don't know them . . . My brother is, like . . . He's this genius and . . . Oh fuck, it hurts, Derek. It hurts so much . . .'

'Hey, it gets better. My daddy died. It gets better . . .'

Silence for a second. Ben can visualise Ria looking up at him. *'Your dad?'*

'Yes, ma'am. Iraq. Ten years ago.'

'He was a soldier?'

'US Marine.'

'Oh. Oh, I see . . . Oh, that's so sad.'

'He died serving his country. It hurts. Sure it does, but it gets better.'

Miri stiffens. Her face hardening. Ben sees the flash of pain in her eyes, fleeting and quick, but real. Then it's gone and the mask is once more set in place.

'*My mum died protecting me and Bertie . . . my brother . . .*'

'*That's brave.*'

'*She was so scared. The look on her face . . . She was cold . . . She tried stopping them . . .*'

'*Them?*'

'Be ready to move,' Miri murmurs.

'*Some men . . . They came into our house . . .*'

'*Like a home invasion?*'

'*Er, yes. Yes, like that. Me and Bertie got out, but . . .*'

'*Your daddy?*'

'*He ran away,*' Ria says softly, weakly, '*left us . . . He's a coward. Those people you saw in the bar?*'

'Careful, Ria,' Ben mutters.

'*They were there, they helped . . . They were so brave . . . They didn't run . . . They . . .*' She breaks off to sob quietly. '*They . . . they would have died for Bertie . . .*'

'*And you,*' Derek says.

'*No,*' Ria says with kind sorrow in her voice. '*My brother is special . . .*'

'Can't we get her mum out?' Ben asks.

'You know we can't.'

'Can't we go in after? Take, like, a second to pull her out.'

A blink of an eye. Every situation offers opportunities to plant seeds. If she wins Ben, she wins the team, and she needs all of them to win the game.

'I admire your morals and honour, Mr Ryder, but it cannot be done.' She pauses for effect. 'The British government will torture the mother if she survives, and all of Bertie's friends, and all of Ria's friends and everyone that ever knew them. If they don't, the Russians will, or the Chinese, or the Americans . . .'

'If the mother survives, we can take her,' Ben says.

'This is the level we are at, Ben. We must do whatever it takes. We cannot use the device to go forward past the attack on the house to see the world or how it lies because time is not fixed and it does not matter what happens, but only what we make happen. Do you see? I need you to see. The only thing of importance now is what *we* do.'

Ben listens to Miri. He listens to Ria crying and Derek giving what words of comfort he can find which right now is better than possibly anyone else in the world. The view of it all opens, and for a brief second the isolated life they have in the bunker vanishes.

'How do you make a government stop?' Miri asks, staring at him.

Ben goes to answer, then stops with the surreal notion of such a strange rhetorical question.

'*Listen, you're a lovely boy, but I want to go home now.*'

'*Sure, yeah, sure, Ria. I'll walk you home.*'

'*No, it's fine. Honestly.*'

'*It's not safe here. I'll walk you back . . . Hey, you got money. I'll call a cab.*'

'*Honestly, it's fine. I think my, er . . . well, the people at the bar, they'll be nearby . . . Miri will be anyway.*'

'*Miri?*'

'*The older lady. She's amazing. Like, so cold and brutal, but . . . She'll be near here waiting.*'

'She's smarter than we thought,' Ben whispers.

'*Will I see you again? When do you go?*'

'*I'm not sure.*'

'*I'd like to see you again. Can we email? You on Facebook? Hey, gimme your number and . . .*'

'*I don't have a phone. We lost it in the . . . the thing . . . and I haven't replaced it yet.*'

'*Oh, damn, I got an old phone. You want it?*'

'*What's your name? I'll find you on Facebook.*'

'Derek Collins. Milwaukee. I finish work tomorrow at six if . . . you know . . .'

'I'll try. I'll ask Miri if . . . maybe . . . We've got a lot to do, but I will try.'

'You'd better say yes,' Ben whispers, looking at Miri. 'If you bloody don't, I'll tell her she can go.'

'What's your name?'

'Ria.'

'No, your last name . . .'

'Oh, er, gosh, sorry, had a bit to drink . . . Calshott. Ria Calshott.'

Ben snorts a laugh. Miri deigns to twitch the corners of her lips.

They listen to the kisses goodbye, which grow into heavy breathing and even heavier petting. Ben leans against the wall. Miri stares at the wall opposite.

'You are so beautiful,' Derek whispers.

'You're lovely too,' Ria whispers back.

Finally, they hear the door open, but then more kissing comes. The stairs creak. More kissing. They get to the ground floor inside the building and stop to kiss. They reach the street door and kiss. Ben hums to himself. Miri thinks forward to tomorrow and what she has to do.

'Come see me tomorrow,' Derek says as the street door finally opens.

'I'll try, promise . . .'

Ria walks out and looks left, looks right, then goes back to kiss him again before pushing him back in the door and telling him to go to bed. She finally walks out across the road, peering round before spotting the mouth of the alley. She hesitates, as though unsure, then heads for it.

'Miri?'

'Here,' Miri says, shutting the phone down and stepping out from the shadows.

'Hey,' Ben says, moving out.

Ria looks at them, her face showing fleeting emotions one after the other.

'We just wanted to make sure you were okay,' Ben says. 'Everything alright?'

'Yep,' Ria says simply. 'He's a nice man.'

Ben nods. He wants to tell her Derek is a very nice man and that men like that don't grow on trees, and that in actual fact he wants to walk over and shake his bloody hand for being such a decent human being. But he doesn't. He smiles instead and walks out to offer his arm. 'Walk you home, m'lady?'

'Thanks,' she says, smiling shyly, hesitant at looping her arm through his. He is Ben Ryder after all. 'He asked my name,' she says, taking his arm. 'I said Ria Calshott. Was that okay? I said I lost my phone too . . .'

'It's fine,' Ben says, leading her back behind Miri. 'Absolutely fine. You want to see him again?'

'Um, he, er . . . Well, he said he finishes work at six tomorrow, but I'll ask Miri. I said we're busy . . . but I didn't say anything about the . . . the thing or . . . anything. I promise.'

'Oh,' Ben says, as though taking it all in and thinking. 'Well, he seemed a good lad, you know, just from meeting him briefly in the bar. So, yeah, sure, why not? Maybe watch a movie or something with him. Do you good to get out of the bunker a bit.'

'He is nice, and he has a huge . . .'

Ben coughs, sudden and hard. Something caught in his throat.

'Are you okay?' Ria asks.

'Yep,' Ben gasps.

'I was saying he has a huge old television . . .'

Thirty-Three

'Ben . . . you asleep?'

He snaps awake at her voice pushing through the layers of sleep. Her tone is different; she sounds worried. He looks up to see her standing in the doorway to his room, bathed in a silvery glow of moonlight streaming through the windows. A screech outside. A thunderous roar from far off. An instant reminder of where he is in time and place.

'Ben?'

'Yeah,' he whispers, gruff and deep from sleep. 'What? What's up?'

She hesitates, not speaking. He can sense her nerves.

'Safa? What's up?'

She goes to turn away, but stops and moves forward, then stands with her hands at her side, suddenly afraid and not knowing what to do. He rejected her before, but that was the old Ben. Not this Ben. Hearing Ria and Derek has played on her mind. Seeing Ria coming back so much calmer tonight, laughing and smiling softly. Still sad, still with tears in her eyes, but like the bad energy is gone. She thought what Ria did was wrong but right. Things are black and white to Safa. Anything in between is too difficult and weird, so she shies away and puts the wall up and tells everyone to fuck off.

Ben sits up, instantly worried. 'Safa? You okay?'

She moves fast, as though worried something will happen to stop her. She closes the door and crosses through the moonlight to his bed. 'Budge over.'

'Eh?'

She doesn't wait, but sinks down on to his mattress as he slides over to make room. She lies on her right side facing away from him. He stares. Too stunned to do or say anything.

He swallows, blinks and starts easing himself down with the instant worry of what to do. She's right there and only wearing a vest top and knickers.

She turns to look up at him, the whites of her eyes so clear, the shape of them, the contours of her face. She saw a picture of Steph tonight and hated it. She hated it with a passion. She hates that Ben had that connection. Like jealousy, but not jealousy. She doesn't know what it is, only that she didn't like it.

'Lie down,' she whispers, her voice strange in both their ears.

He lowers slowly, taking care that his groin does not touch her backside. His right arm goes under the pillow. His heart thunders.

'Safa . . . are you okay?'

'Fuck's sake, hold me.' She tries to sound like Safa, bossy and hard, but it comes out soft and asking instead of telling. She turns again, blinking at him. 'If you want to . . .'

He moves to cocoon, sensing it is right, feeling it is right. His right arm moves under the pillow as she lifts her head so he can slide it under her. His left arm goes over. She moves back into him. Her heart whumping through her back so hard he can feel it. Her whole body trembling. The thought of Safa being scared makes him move closer, holding tighter. She curls up and moves back. He moves forward and lowers his head so his mouth is but a millimetre from the top of her head hardly believing this is happening.

'We're not having sex.'

He smiles into the darkness at the blunt voice of the woman he adores so much. 'Okay.'

She winces at herself. *Why did she say it like that?* This is bliss, lying here. It's so nice. He's so warm and cuddly. Safa doesn't do cuddling, but right now she loves cuddling.

'I want to have sex . . . but . . . not now.'

'Okay.'

That's even worse. Now she sounds like a cock-tease.

'I'm not a cock-tease.'

'I know.'

Stop talking.

'I did want sex that night I came in . . .'

'Yeah?'

'Like loads . . .'

Oh god, now she sounds too eager.

'I'm glad we didn't,' he says.

Why did he say that?

'Me too.' No, she's not. She wishes they did have sex. 'I did want to have sex, and I wish we did.'

Oh, you twat.

'Me too,' he says.

'But we can't have sex now.'

Stop fucking talking.

'Okay.'

'I want to have sex now.'

'Er . . .'

Now she's confused him. *Stop confusing him.*

'Am I confusing you?'

'No. You're Safa.'

What does that mean?

322

'I'm shit at this stuff, Ben.'

'It's fine.'

'I never had friends before.'

Oh my god. Why did she say that? Why isn't he saying anything back?

'Why aren't you saying anything back?'

'I'm listening.'

'Not like a girlfriend. Like a girl who is a friend . . . Not a lesbian friend.'

Shut up.

'Okay.'

'I'm not homophobic. I meant I never had a mate, like a girl mate. Like Emily.'

Seriously. Shut up.

'Okay.'

'Or a boyfriend.'

'Okay.'

'I fancy you.'

Don't tell him that.

'I fancy you too.'

Yes! He fancies her.

He moves position, re-adjusting to get closer, more comfortable. She pulls his hand in to her chest and realises the back of his hand is pushing against her left boob. Can he feel the nipple? What if he feels the nipple?

'Can you feel my nipple?'

Shut the fuck up. Please. For the love of god.

'Er, no . . . No, I can't.'

What if the nipple gets hard? What if he gets an erection? What then?

'Safa?'

'What?'

'Stop worrying.'

'Okay . . . but what if you get a hard-on or my nipple gets erect?'

'It's fine.'

It's fine. Ben said it's fine.

'Ben?'

'Yep?'

'Some cunting, fucking bastard sexually abused me . . . so . . . And, like, men always say how pretty my eyes are and try and fuck me, but I did want sex with you that night. And I want sex now and I fancy you and I'm horny, but I got worried and . . . And Ria did that tonight and it made me think and I saw that cunt Steph and . . . And I'll never lie to you or anyone and I'll never let anyone ever hurt you like that Steph did and I know I'm a fucking nightmare, but . . . Well, say something then, for fuck's sake.'

'Okay.'

'Okay? What does that mean? Just okay? What's okay?'

'I'm not the man who did that. You have friends now. You have Mad Harry Madden and me and Miri, and Emily likes you, and I will never lie to you. I won't try and fuck you ever. Men don't do that, Safa. Real men don't do that. I won't do that, and if you tell me who that man is, I will kill him, and if I don't, then Harry will. You are gorgeous and I am willing myself not to get an erection and offend you, but if it happens, then it is because I adore you more than you could ever know, but on every level of you being you and not just because you have tits and nice eyes, so, yes, this is more than okay. You make everything okay.'

'Oh.'

Wow. He said all that.

'Okay?' he asks.

'Okay.'

Okay. It's more than okay.

'It's more than okay. Sleep now.'

'Okay, Safa.'

'If you get an erection, it's fine now.'

'Okay.'

'And if my nipple goes hard, then that's also fine.'

'Okay.'

'Night, Ben.'

'Night. Safa.'

'You can kiss my neck if you want.'

Thirty-Four

'Morning,' Emily says, walking into the main room.

'Morning,' Safa replies, already eating at the table. 'Coffee's here.'

'Thanks,' Emily says cheerfully. Too cheerfully. She takes fruit from the bowl, grabs a plate and heads over to the table. 'Another one?' Emily asks, lifting the flask of coffee.

'Cheers.'

'You're probably tired.' Emily lowers the flask and peers at Safa, as though examining her. 'I'm looking for a warm afterglow.'

'Fuck's sake,' Safa says, shaking her head.

'Got up for a wee in the night.'

'Did you?'

'Your door was open.'

'Was it?'

'And your bed was empty, you hussy . . .'

'Morning,' Ben calls out, walking in with a brief wave. 'Coffee on?'

'Damn it,' Emily mutters.

'Flask here,' Safa says.

'Morning, Ben,' Emily says.

'Morning, Emily. You okay?'

'Aye,' Emily says deeply at seeing Harry walking in.

'Aye,' Harry says with a smile at her.

'Coffee's here,' Safa says. 'We'll practise the house assault for the morning, then do marksman drills for you, Ben.'

'Awesome,' Ben says, taking two mugs from the big table over to Emily and Safa. 'I spoke to Miri last night, while we were waiting for Ria.'

'Listening to her having sex, you mean,' Safa says.

'And that,' Ben says, ignoring the edge to her voice.

Safa pauses with the knife peeling the skin from the orange. Emily sits down. Harry comes over to lift the flask and start pouring.

'Ria here yet?' Ben asks.

'Not yet,' Emily says, glancing round to the door leading to the smaller corridor.

'Miri said they'll torture her mother if she's taken alive, same with all their friends . . . everyone that ever knew them.'

'They will,' Emily says.

Safa looks up, frowning slightly. 'Can't she just go forward and see.'

'No point,' Ben says. 'Time isn't fixed.'

'Don't get it,' Safa says, peeling the fruit.

Harry sits down and leans back, listening as he always does, intently and quietly.

'If we go forward now and see what they're doing after the house assault, we'll see one thing,' Ben says, 'but what they do will change pending what we do. Miri's got it into my head and it makes sense: *we* create the time now and make it bend to what *we* want.'

'Bend? Bend what?' Safa asks.

'Not bend – bad word to explain,' Ben says sitting down. 'Miri said we have to stop a government, but . . . well, it's not just one, is it? We're dealing with more than one government. UK, US, Russia, China . . . Fuck knows who else . . .'

'All of them,' Emily says.

'How?' Safa asks. 'There's five of us, including Miri, and she's not combat-ready.'

'I'll sit down with Miri tonight and go through it,' he says thoughtfully.

'Makes sense,' Harry says.

'What does?' Ben asks him.

'We have a time machine,' Harry says simply. 'They can't have it. Controlled aggression. Best way. Bad things happen in war. You said the Yanks dropped a big bomb in Japan.'

'Nuclear bomb,' Ben says with a nod.

'Ended the war?'

'Certainly helped,' Emily says while Ben thinks on the question.

'Yanks dropped a big bomb and killed many, but saved more,' Harry says. 'That's what war is.'

'Guess so,' Ben says with a smile. 'At least we're not planning that.'

'Planning what?' Harry asks.

'Dropping a nuclear bomb on Roland's house.'

'Why not?'

'Fuck, Harry,' Ben says.

'Ach, listen to Miri,' Harry says, leaning over to steal an orange from Safa's bowl. She offers the knife, which he takes to start peeling. 'We're not going to stop a government with a few rifles now, are we?'

'Morning, morning.' Doctor Watson bustles in, heading for the table while rubbing his hands together. 'Coffee on, is it? Slept on the island last night, I did. Went for an after-dinner snooze in the hammock and woke up to see Bertie mapping the constellations. Portal was closed, so I stayed there. Where's the coffee? Ah, over there, is it? Morning, Emily! So I went back to sleep, and this morning he wakes me up going on about something. Of course, I had just woken up, so didn't have a clue what he was on about.' He empties the last of the flask into a mug. 'Turns out he has calculated the time period we are in on the island . . .'

He lifts the mug to sip, and gives a satisfied groan. 'To the year, I might add. The clever sod has worked it out. No telescope. Nothing. Just the stars and geology, and what not. I came through just now and checked the date on the tablet. Blighter's bloody right too.'

'Seriously?' Ben asks.

'Oh, yes,' the doctor says, sitting down.

'Maybe he saw the date on the tablet,' Emily says. 'He's been through enough times.'

'Bertie wouldn't think to look,' the doctor says. 'He'd say *that's, like, totally cheating.* So that's our genius at work, and that was all done while he works on the second time machine *and* tries to work out how to get radio signals through the displacement field.'

'We could have one permanently open to the island then,' Emily says. 'And one we use for whatever.'

'Did I miss anything last night?' Doctor Watson asks, stealing an orange from Emily's bowl as Harry hands the knife over.

Ben smiles into his coffee mug. Emily suddenly looks up and away. Harry whistles softly.

'Twats,' Safa says. 'Ria had sex with a boy from McDonald's.'

'Oh,' Doctor Watson says, peeling the orange.

'Didn't something else happen?' Emily asks innocently, widening her eyes, as though trying to think. 'I'm sure there was something else . . .'

'This bunker is too small,' Ben mutters as Ria walks in looking somewhat sheepish. 'Hey, morning. Hangover?'

'Nope, feel fine,' she says.

'To be young,' the doctor says with a tut.

'Sit down,' Ben says. 'I'll make a fresh flask.'

'I'll do it,' Ria says.

Life in the bunker rolls on. The morning after the night before in an enclosed environment, where small things stand out. Safa went to Ben's room last night. Ria had sex with a boy from McDonald's. Miri

said they have to stop a government. Bertie worked out the year by
looking at the stars as something to do in between building a second
time machine.

Miri walks in, brisk and business-like in her manner. She takes a
mug and sits down as Ria strolls over to take a seat with a defensive look
etched on her face. 'This where you tell me off?'

'No,' Miri says simply.

'What the fuck?' Safa asks, looking round the table. 'Are we having
a breakfast meeting or something?'

'Yes,' Miri says.

'What for?'

'To talk.'

'Talk about what?'

'Last night and . . .'

'What about last night?' Safa asks, the glare hardening instantly.
'It's my business if I want to get in bed with Ben. Got fuck all to do
with . . . What? Why are you groaning?' she asks Ben as he covers his
face in his hands. 'It's got nothing to do with anyone. We didn't have
sex, so . . .'

'Oh my god,' Ben groans.

'What!'

'I didn't mean that, Miss Patel, but thank you for sharing.'

Safa glowers, seethes, frowns, scowls, then shrugs and goes back to
eating her orange. 'Fair one.'

'So moving on,' Emily says, looking at Miri.

'I wasn't there all night anyway,' Safa adds.

'Great,' Emily says, looking to Safa, then back to Miri. 'So . . .'

'Like, a few hours,' Safa says.

'Do you want to talk about it?' Emily asks.

'Do I fuck.'

'Then stop talking about it.'

'I am.'

'Great. So what were you saying, Miri?'

'Need to get bigger beds,' Safa says to Ria as Ben bursts out laughing and Harry chuckles into his mug. 'What?'

'Safa!' Emily says.

'I'm just saying. No point pushing two beds together, cos I'll fall down the gap in the middle.'

'Oh my god,' Emily says. 'Done sharing?'

'Piss off. Who stole my other orange? Oh, and a lamp for my side of the bed. On a little table or something. It was pitch black when I got up, couldn't see a thing . . . I tripped over one of Ben's boots. Maybe get him a chest like you got Emily. Stop laughing! I never had a boyfriend, so I don't know how this stuff works. Twats.'

Miri listens and watches. Showing patience where patience is needed. This is it. Her team has been built. It's time for the endgame.

'I need to talk about Cavendish Manor.' Her tone eases the humour from the room. The smiles fade. The joviality abates. As she speaks, her voice becomes increasingly blunt, without any trace or inflection of emotion.

They listen in rapt attention. Faces become focussed and hard. Surprise and shock show. Miri watches each closely. Reading reactions.

She speaks for several minutes without interruption. From the start to the end. When she finishes, there is but silence. Heavy and charged.

'No,' Safa says, the first to speak out. Her voice strangely quiet, almost timid. 'No way.'

'It is the only way,' Miri says. A master at work, with a deft touch of tone and inflection. She waits, expecting the next response from Safa.

'Ben? Is she right?'

Miri waits, expecting the next response from Ben.

'I don't know.'

'We're not doing it unless you say it's right,' Safa tells him.

331

'How do you stop a government?' Ben says to himself, but his voice carries round the room to everyone else watching him. He looks at Miri. 'I need to know what you know.'

'Of course. But we'll train and make ready nonetheless.'

A buzz inside Miri. A tingling. This is the endgame. Win Ben. Win the team. Win the game.

Thirty-Five

They work to train and be ready to do a thing they will only do if Ben says it is right, because what Miri said made even Harry's eyes go wide.

'*As of our time, nine countries had nuclear weapons. As of Ria and Bertie's time, fifteen countries have nuclear weapons. NATO failed. The sanctions to prevent more countries enriching uranium failed. Where do the warheads point, Mr Ryder?*'

Days and weeks blur. There is only work. Sleep, eat, train. Repeat.

'*We are not here to stop the Brits gaining the device. We are not here to stop one country gaining it. We are here to stop them all.*'

'*Can't we just talk to them? We'll open dialogue and say we've got it.*'

They work in monsoons with driving rain so thick they can't see more than a metre in front of them. They work through howling winds that blot noise. Through energy-sapping humidity that dehydrates and causes headaches. Safa drives them on, heedless of the warnings given by the doctor, heedless of everything.

'*This is not about oil or money, but about power beyond anything any nation has ever possessed. This changes everything.*'

In the darkness. In the rain. In all elements at all times. Room clearance. Scenario training. Attacking the bunker. Attacking the shack on the island. Defending both. Hand-to-hand training. Weapons training.

Sniper training. Ben grows sick of the Barrett. The power of it. The noise of it. The weight of it.

'The US is allied to the UK. The French are allied to the US. Israel and Iran hate each other. India and Pakistan the same. North Korea is right there. Russia is allied to China. China is allied to North Korea, but all bets are off if the Brits have the device. Will China ally with the UK? If they do, does the US attack China? What happens then? What if Russia launches against the UK? Who retaliates for the British? The French? Does Israel take advantage of the chaos and unleash on Iran? Does China attack the US to prevent them gaining more power? Think, Mr Ryder. What we do now defines everything for the whole of the world.'

Miri's office slowly fills with stacks of newspapers and magazines, piles of encyclopaedias and tablet devices. A huge map of the world on one wall. Coloured pins denote the nuclear powers. Coloured string fastened between each to show the threats, political situations and warring factions.

The pace is relentless. Miri works with them on attacking the house. Miri and Ben work in the evenings or when they can snatch time to study and learn. Miri trains with them when she can. Joining room-clearance drills to hone her skills and to learn how they each move.

While Miri and Ben study, so Safa, Harry and Emily set the scenarios up, clean weapons, make adjustments to kit and run through tactical options. Harry's training is brought up to modern standards, but likewise, his ability to draw on countless real combat missions helps the others.

The sense of excitement in Miri becomes almost tangible. She's never felt more alive. This is the biggest game of all. This is power beyond anything, and it's just her against everyone. To pit her five against everyone else.

The portal room gains another shimmering light. Red and blue next to each other. One with a handwritten sign above it saying *LIVE* and one above the red saying *ISLAND*.

John Watson, an intelligent and highly experienced medical doctor, becomes an assistant to a young man with a shock of unruly black hair. The two go back and forth, testing radio and satellite signals, digital and analogue signatures and sound waves to try and push them through. *It's all just binary.*

Ria works too. Keeping clothes clean. Providing food. Hiding when she feels sick. Running the bunker. *The Quartermaster,* as Harry calls her. She takes coffee into Miri's office and listens to Ben and Miri talking as they stand in front of the huge map. She spots the markers and tracks the ever-changing lengths of coloured string that propose the strike patterns of nuclear weapons.

A few days later, she presents a hologram program of planet earth big enough to replicate the two-dimensional paper map on the wall, with different coloured lasers instead of the strands of material, and an ability to tap and bloom out information panels.

She presents it coyly, thinking they will take it as a gimmick or a toy. The map on the wall was forgotten after that evening and the new holo used instead.

After the night with Derek, Ria is given freedom of movement and access to the tablets that control both devices. There is an assumption she is now *fixed*. That she got the bad energy out of her system.

She doesn't tell anyone when her period fails to come. Nor does she say anything when she pisses on a plastic stick bought from the pharmacy in Walmart that turns blue, and she doesn't notice that everything she does is seen by Miri.

Ben has to reach the conclusion on his own. He has to know for himself because to know is to counter, and to counter is to win. *If we do not win, everyone will die.* The manipulation is steady and careful. Ben is smart. Miri respects that.

Win Ben. Win the others. Win the game.

'*Bertie Cavendish was in the mainstream media for gaining triple Master's degrees at a young age. He was quoted as saying he wants to invent time travel. The Brits launched a significant attack in Berlin, which we know was the centre of the search and full of agents from every country. Within an hour or two, the same agency launched an attack on Cavendish Manor. The rest of the world will follow the breadcrumb trail and that information alone is enough for every other agency to think the Brits have secured the device. It does not matter that the British will deny having it, because who in their right mind would admit such a thing?*

What does the world look like the day after Cavendish Manor? This situation now could cause the world to be destroyed by 2111, but we cannot go forward to look as it makes no difference. We fix this situation and then go forward, because the day after Cavendish Manor could be the day those warheads are unleashed. We know who will attack who. We've studied it. We have that information. We know where the warheads are pointing. We do not have a choice, Mr Ryder. Do you see now? I need you to see this.'

She saw on the day she arrived the way Safa and Harry deferred to Ben's intelligence. The way they both held back and waited while Ben asked the questions. They respect Ben. They trust his judgement. Emily is now the same.

Manipulation to reach a conclusion Miri knew when the game first began. Everyone else just needed time to grow the bond and believe that what they are doing is righteous and proper.

Win Ben. Win them. Win the game.

'Miri's right,' Ben tells the rest that evening.

The confirmation is received quietly with grim determination. To the last they accept it must be done and the thrill of the game grows only stronger.

Thirty-Six

'END EX, END EX.'

That was the best one yet. Ria can sense it. The last few days have seen a marked change. Almost like the confirmation Ben gave cemented the belief in the need to achieve the goal.

They had more hologram soldiers today too. Ria re-configured the program and moved the tablets about so they would pop up in different places.

She makes her weapon safe and slings it to the rear, grimacing at the weight and the stench of the flash-bangs hanging in the air. One of the chemicals within them turns her stomach. She should say something. She should tell them. She doesn't know why she is not saying anything, only that each time she tries, the words don't come out. She feels stupid and immature. What they are doing is important and big. Bigger than anything. *Hey, sorry, I know you're all trying to save the world and everything, but I think I'm pregnant.* No way. She can't say it. Not now. The pressure in the bunker is immense. Crushing, heavy and growing worse every day. An energy building up ready to be vented and unleashed.

She keeps telling herself she will tell them after, but what if she wants an abortion? Does she want an abortion? She could speak to the doctor and arrange a termination now, but again the mental block is there. John is working with Bertie every day anyway, in between nursing sore ankles and tutting over the bruises on Ben's shoulder caused by the immense recoil of the Barrett.

She pulls the hood down on the poncho, suddenly too hot, and feeling swamped and trapped by the waterproof cover. Rain lashes her face, wetting her hair against her scalp. It feels nice. Refreshing. She cannot bring a baby into this world. What is she thinking? Say something. Do something. She could attend a walk-in clinic. The UK has them. She wouldn't even need to give her name. Just walk in, get it done and leave.

'*Ria? We're heading back in.*' Safa's hard voice coming through the radio under her poncho.

'*Okay,*' she shouts, jabbing at the button through the material.

She heads back across the clearing that is now so familiar. She looks up to the tree line that is now so familiar. She walks closer to the bank and sees the top of the bunker that is now so familiar. This is home, but it doesn't feel like it.

Ria is not stupid. Not stupid at all. She just refuses to give voice to the idea that having a baby will give her something of her own. Bertie is a genius. He is the reason all of this is here. The others are all gifted in what they can do. Ria isn't gifted in anything. She can't do anything. She feels stupid around them. Fat and unfit, too slow, too dense. She wants the baby, but she doesn't want the baby. She wants her mum.

Their paths converge as she reaches the Blue at the same time as the others. Faces flushed. Brows sweaty despite the rain.

'Went well?' Ria says.

'Did,' Ben says, grim-faced. He looks exhausted. 'Look okay from your point of view?'

She nods. 'Really good, best yet.'

'Soldiers were brilliant,' Emily says to her. 'Popping up all over the place.'

'Too many?' Ria asks.

'Oh god, no, really good,' Emily says.

They go through into the portal room. Shedding kits, boots, weapons, ponchos and bags. Miri comes through after them with the doctor.

Ben puts the Barrett down. He was hoping it would become an extension of his body or something that he would gain an intrinsic connection to, but it's just a gun. A big, noisy, heavy gun, and he hopes never to touch the thing ever again. Harry works to strip the Browning. Emily checks her assault rifle. Safa drops to start pulling her boots off. Tension in the air. Tension that grows every day.

'Grilled chicken tonight,' Ria says, hanging her poncho.

'And fish,' the doctor adds, as though trying to lift the mood.

'I didn't get any fish,' Ria says.

'I got them,' the doctor says.

'Where from?' Ria asks.

'From the sea.'

'We can't do that,' Ria replies instantly. 'I mean, we said, didn't we? No food from these times. No berries. No fruits. Nothing . . .'

'Oh,' the doctor says benignly.

'That could be dangerous,' Ben says. 'The whole food-chain thing is way out, isn't it?'

'Ah, it's probably fine,' Doctor Watson says, waving a heavy hand about.

'We're not getting fucking food poisoning,' Safa snaps.

'Don't eat the fish then,' he replies.

'Or you,' Safa says. 'You're the medic. We need the medic to not be dead. They tend to work better.'

'Ah, it's probably fine,' the doctor says again, heading for the door.

Ben drops to a knee to start unlacing a boot. 'How long?' he asks after the doctor.

'Oh, about a month now,' John calls back. 'Bertie and I do a spot of night fishing.'

'Fuck's sake,' Safa snaps.

'It's fine,' Ben mutters.

'He fed Bertie million-year-old fishes.'

'It's not a million years – more like tens of thousands, and they're not old if they're caught fresh and they're both still alive.'

'Whatever.'

The pressure grows. Palpable and real. They filter out into the bunker to walk down the now-painted corridor.

Emily goes into the main room first. Early evening. The light coming through the window is fading. She walks round flicking switches on lamps to bathe the room in soft, warm light.

Harry brushes past her to set the water to heat. Ben walks behind him, moving round his solid bulk to grab an apple from the bowl. Miri takes an apple and turns to lean against the table while eating. Safa sits on the armrest of the big sofa that Emily flops on with an audible groan. Nobody speaks. The atmosphere feels thick and charged. The day has been long and gruelling. The days before that were longer and more gruelling. Weeks of it. Unrelenting. They all feel it. Like a thing building. Like a force growing stronger.

Emily stretches out. She loves this sofa. This is her sofa. This is bliss. She wouldn't change being here for all the money in the world, but it's still hard. Very hard. She idly watches Harry making drinks. Of all of them, he is the calmest. This is not new to Harry. The rest mask the restless energy with usual behaviours, but Harry is the same as always. Calm and controlled.

The doctor comes through. Ria gets the mugs ready. Harry pours. The air fills with the sound of the water going into the mugs and the chink of the spoon as Ria stirs. She hands one to Ben, then moves out to pass Safa's and Emily's over. Harry passes Miri's before taking crackers from a tub and loading a plate with sliced cheese. He crosses to the sofa. The one that Emily thinks is hers, but is really his. She pulls her legs up. He sits down. She watches him load a cracker with cheese. He lifts it to eat. She leans forward. He holds it out. She takes a bite. He eats the rest. No need for words. No need to speak. She leans against him.

Ria watches them discreetly. Trying to detect if they are flirting, but it doesn't feel like it. Mind you, Ben couldn't sit down and rest against Harry, so maybe there is a degree of flirting, but mild, like passive and non-sexual, which makes it just friendship.

Emily likes being near Harry. Alpha was an enigma. A demi-god. The best of all of them. Frighteningly capable and brutally efficient, but Harry lifted Alpha off his feet with one arm and ragged him like a doll. She rubs her forehead on his shoulder. He loads a cracker and offers it. She takes a bite. He eats the rest. Friendship.

Safa sips her coffee. Ben drinks his. Miri eats her apple. The doctor sits down heavily in an armchair in the thick, charged air. Tension grows. Pressure builds.

Ria feels the urge to speak out and say something. Just say it. Announce it and be done. She forms the words to say. Running through it in her mind as her heart beats faster and nerves fill her stomach that tightens with a sense of dread. She wants her mum. She really wants her mum right now.

'We're ready,' Safa says suddenly, breaking the silence.

Ben freezes with his mug to his lips. Harry pauses, loading a cracker. Emily looks over. Miri holds the apple close to her mouth. The doctor purses his lips and nods slowly.

Ria's heart thunders. *Say something. Say it now before it's too late.*

'Beardy,' Safa says, looking at Harry, who is now back to loading his cracker. 'You've done the most missions. When's the best time to go? Now while we're in the zone, or . . .'

'No,' he says, working on the cracker. 'Rest tonight. Go in the morning.'

Safa sips her coffee. Ben drinks his. Harry holds the cracker for Emily to bite.

Ria stares at the floor. It feels like her vision is closing in, that the room has become too small, too confined.

'Tomorrow then,' Safa says, glancing at Miri.

'Agreed,' Miri says before biting into the apple.

It's done. They're going to do it tomorrow. Ria wants to scream and shout and beg them not to do it. She stares at the floor and doesn't say anything.

Emily groans, long and audible. Ben looks over at her, seeing the smile slowly spreading across her face. 'Thank god,' she mutters.

'Aye.'

'Definitely,' Ben says as the tension in the room slides away. A lifting of worry. An easing of pressure. Finally, they are ready. Finally.

Each feels the finality of the decision and the relief it brings. Apart from Ria. She forces a smile and makes her legs move to carry her across the room towards the door.

'You okay?' Ben asks her.

'Fine,' she says lightly, nodding quickly. 'I'll get the chicken on.'

'That,' Safa states, 'is a bloody good idea. I am starving.'

Thirty-Seven

The night passes. They eat grilled chicken and fish on the island with Bertie and Doctor Watson. They drink water and juice. They talk lightly, but the energy is there. The feeling of something coming. The build-up. Pre-mission tension. Ria sits with them. Her right hand holding the fork. Her left unknowingly on her belly. Doctor Watson notices it. Miri too. Nothing is said. This is not the time. A look between them. A nod. Ben sees that look and casually glances down to see Ria talking to Emily with her left hand on her stomach. He pauses, thinking, connecting and looks back at Miri. His eyebrows lift. She purses her lips and goes back to eating. The secret is out.

'What time is kick-off?' the doctor asks.

'Early,' Safa says. 'We'll warm up and go for it.'

'I see,' he says. 'I shall make ready to receive casualties.'

'Stay out of the portal room,' Safa adds. 'Risk of rounds going through.'

'Understood,' the doctor says gravely, waggling his fork in the air.

'Progress on the sound waves?' Miri asks Bertie.

'S'just binary, but yes, but haha! I don't know.'

A murmur of chuckles at Bertie's reply. Getting a straight answer out of him is impossible.

'Like, totally no reason they won't go through. Matter is, like, totally matter. The whole world is full of sound. Like, epic and awesome and . . . The sun makes noise and everything makes noise, but, yeah, no, so . . .'

'You'll get there,' Emily says.

'We were shouting through it today,' the doctor says with a smile at Bertie. 'We spent the best part of two hours walking back and forth singing songs and trying to determine the exact second the noise ends . . . or begins . . . depending which side you are on.'

'S'just binary.'

'And making the displacement field see-through?'

'Not started that yet,' the doctor answers.

'Would be good to see what's on the other side before we go through,' Miri says, forking a chunk of grilled chicken.

'Oh my god!' Bertie blurts, then bursts out laughing.

'What?' Ben asks.

'See-through, like to see through? Like, to totally see the other side? Like . . . like . . . window! You want a window? Haha! I thought you meant just see through, not see-through . . .'

'A window, Bertie,' Ria says. 'So they can see what's on the other side.'

'Haha! I mean, totally just rewrite the laws of physics and . . . um . . . epic. Okay, Miri. A window. Why are you rubbing your belly? Have you got bellyache?'

'What?!' Ria blurts. 'I'm not,' she adds, bringing her left hand up while her face flushes crimson. 'Period pains,' she mumbles.

'Urgh,' Bertie says, grimacing.

Emily tuts and reaches out to rub her arm. 'Nasty. Maybe John can give you something?'

'S'fine,' Ria mumbles.

'John? Anything you can give Ria?' Emily asks down the table.

'I'm fine,' Ria states, hating the patronising, condescending show of kindness from someone so fit and strong.

'Perhaps we can have a chat after dinner,' the doctor says, holding his gaze on Ria.

She squirms on her seat. Hating all of them. Hating the sudden attention. She can feel her face burning. Everyone is staring at her. She can feel it. She glances up to see none of them are looking at her.

'How's the shoulder?' the doctor asks.

'Fine,' Ben says. 'Bit sore, but nothing really.'

Conversations roll on. Idle chat. Ria stabs the chicken on her plate. Her appetite gone. She worries about tomorrow as her whole body fills with that sense of dread. She can't stop thinking about it. Why are they going tomorrow? That means she has no more time to think and decide what to do. Her mum is in the house.

'Be a long day tomorrow,' Emily says casually, reaching out for the salad bowl.

'I still don't know why you're doing it all in one go,' the doctor says. 'Stagger it out. Why rush it?'

'Not rushing,' Miri says. 'Execution of the mission in one fluid motion.'

'But you have the option,' the doctor says. 'If something happens, I mean. Someone trips or twists an ankle, say, or . . .'

'We have the option,' Miri says, nodding at him.

'We discussed it,' Ben says. 'A lot. We discussed it a lot. Best to go straight through. One hit. Start to finish.'

'Well, you chaps know what you're doing,' the doctor says. 'Just watch out for the old . . .'

'Oh, fuck off,' Safa laughs.

'What?' the doctor asks with a grin.

'Let him say it,' Ben says, chuckling as he nods at Emily to pass the salad bowl.

'Fuck's sake,' Safa mutters.

'My advice,' the doctor announces.

'Go on then,' Safa says.

'Watch out for the old crossfire.'

Low laughs, chuckles and grins round the table.

'Got to watch the crossfire in a firefight, you know.'

'When you've been in a war with the old crossfire,' Emily says deeply.

'Aye,' Harry says, smiling over the table at her.

'Aye,' Emily says.

'Aye,' Ben adds.

'Twats,' Safa says.

They eat, but not too much. They sip a cold beer each. Only one though. Miri and Harry drift off to smoke and sit in comfortable silence. Safa, Ben and Emily rest on the warm rocks with bare feet in the cool water and watch the doctor casting a line from a rod while wearing his ridiculous sleeveless fishing jacket. Ria frets.

She worries. The sense of dread builds. The threat of a panic attack drives her to clear and wash the dishes, tidy, clean and move about. The others offered to help. She said no curtly. Safa, Emily and Harry guess the tension of tomorrow is making her snappy. Miri, Ben and the doctor suspect something else, but now is not the time.

The night comes. The darkness falls. Stars shine. They relax on the island before retiring back to the bunker. Emily and Harry race to grab their sofa. Safa and Ben take one of the others. Safa toes her flip-flops off and lands her feet in Ben's lap with a grin. Emily does the same to Harry, who shoves them off. She puts them back. He grabs her ankles with one hand and tickles. She screams out and pulls back while hitting him on the shoulder. They pass time, and each counts the seconds that now seem to be crawling by. Each wants it to happen now. Get it done. They've trained for it. They're ready for it.

Ria watches the seconds going by too fast. The countdown is on. The panic inside knots her stomach. She paces her rooms. Worried sick.

Miri takes her lists into the main room for a final verbal briefing of the order of play. The others nod, listen, make comments and mentally prepare.

Then it's time. Time to say goodnight. They drift to their rooms. Safa and Emily sit on Emily's bed chatting for a while. Harry reads Mark Twain. Ben lies on his bed deep in thought.

Emily lies awake thinking of tomorrow. How will it feel going back? She knows Miri will be watching her closely. She also knows that if she even attempted anything stupid, the Blue would pop open next to her and Miri would come through with a pistol aimed at her head. Not that she would do anything stupid. Emily is with them to the end. They are the good guys. This is the front. She likes eating crackers and cheese with Harry too much to be anywhere else.

Harry sleeps. A mission is a mission. Nothing new. Nothing to get flappy about.

Safa strides barefoot up the corridor in knickers and a vest. She opens the door, goes in, closes the door and crosses to his bed. He pulls the cover back. She sinks down and rolls on her right side. He rolls to curl up behind her. Cocooning. She smiles and shuffles into him. He smiles and kisses her head.

'Do what I say tomorrow,' she says quietly.

'I will,' he says.

'If it goes wrong, I'll come back for you.'

'Same.'

'You did that once before,' she says, rolling over to look at him.

'I did,' he says, kissing her cheek.

'You worried?' she asks.

'Not worried – apprehensive, I think. You?'

'No. You said it's the right thing.'

'It is.'

'Okay,' she says, she turns a bit more, tilting her head up. He pauses, unsure of the movement. She smiles, looks at his mouth and swallows as the smile fades. It happens quickly. She moves without thought. Without thinking. Without worrying about what it means. She twists and rises to push her lips at his. Clumsy, awkward, too sudden, too fast. Hungry and needing to do it now. Just a kiss. They kissed in the ocean. Didn't they? Did she? Neither of them know. Neither could tell what happened after. She thinks about it constantly. She has wanted to kiss him so many times. Every time she comes into his room, she wants to do it. Every hour of every day, she wants to do it. The wall she built was big and thick and it has taken months to lower it enough for this second to be right.

He freezes, completely surprised. Then he melts into it. Softening as her warm, soft lips push into his. His eyes close. His hand moves up her back to push through her hair. She pushes harder. Kissing firmer. Mouths open, tentative and slow, gently, testing, teasing, seeking confirmation that this is okay. Is it okay? It is okay. It's more than okay.

He can feel her heart whumping through her chest. He can feel the tremble in her body. Lips part. Tongues meet. She groans at the touch of it. At the sensation. She murmurs and kisses harder, needing more. She sinks down, pulling him with her. Her hands slide over his shoulders, down his back, pulling him closer. She opens her legs to wrap round as he moves between them. Still kissing. Kissing harder. Mouths pressed. Breathing each other. He grows and stiffens. She feels it. Heat blooms. A need. An urge. A hunger inside. He does nothing without consent. He doesn't touch or grope, but he waits and holds back. She takes the lead, needing to take the lead, needing to control the motion and what happens.

She takes his hand and guides it to her breast, then gasps at his touch. She tilts her head so he can kiss her neck, and gasps at his touch. She lifts her top and pulls it off, then gasps more as he kisses down her neck to her breasts and stomach. Everything slow. Everything safe. Everything with love and care. He comes back up, pausing to kiss as she stiffens in his mouth. The feeling is incredible. Like nothing she has ever felt before. Slow and gentle. His mouth finds hers. He doesn't grind or push, but waits. She can feel the rigidity of him and senses the willpower exerted to resist the urge to move.

She moves. She tells him it's okay. A tiny motion at first, and still he waits. Still he holds. He will wait forever. He will hold forever. She is brave, courageous, fearless, tough, hardened, combat-experienced, but this is new, this is different.

She moves. She tells him it's okay. The tiny motion grows more. They kiss and touch. They hold and stay close. The heat builds. The urge grows with it. Her hand goes down to find him. Touching. Gasping at the hardness. He swallows and blinks at her touch, but still waits. That he can do that tells her the depth of his inner strength. She pushes his boxers down, freeing him. She uses her feet to slide them down his legs. She takes his hand to move it between her legs. The breath catching in her throat. Her eyes closing. Gentle. Slow. So slow.

Everything is okay. It is more than okay. She pulls her knickers down and smiles when he lowers to slide them from her legs, then smiles again when he comes back to kiss her. Naked they lie. Him between her legs. Still waiting. Still holding. Still showing he will wait forever. They kiss and breathe. Her hands run over his body. His stroke her cheeks. She moves more. Needing to move. Telling him this is okay. No need for words. No need to speak. She cannot speak. The feeling is too much. The growing desire becoming a tangible thing to be held and nourished. She moves more, gasping again when she feels the hardness touching her. She moves again, slowly back and forth. He moves with her. Gradual, easy, gently. Nature is as life intended, and without help he finds her. She feels him holding, not going in, waiting, exerting that control. She moves to take him inside. The groan escapes her mouth, slow and long and filled with something far greater than pleasure. He is inside her. That thought captivates her for a second. That thought whirls through her mind. He is inside her. Still he holds, still he shows the greatest of respect, still he kisses gently, lovingly.

'You okay?' he whispers. Needing to know. Needing her to tell him this is okay.

She nods, she nods quickly, firmly, holding him. 'Yes.' It is okay. It's more than okay. 'You move,' she breathes into his mouth, still kissing. She wants him to do it. She wants him to take control now. He has proven himself, and more. He has shown such tender care that the wall crumbles to fall away and it's okay to be vulnerable now. It's okay to show weakness. 'I love you . . .' She whispers the words, feeling the liberation of being able to show emotion, of being able to express something that otherwise causes confusion and angst. He moves, and what she felt before magnifies tenfold. Emotions surge inside. 'I've always loved you . . .'

He moves. They kiss. He lowers his head to her ear; she can hear him breathing. She always wants to hear him breathing. He moves. She closes her eyes, never wanting this to end. This feeling. Never realising it could be like this. Never daring to dream this could happen.

He hasn't said it back. Sudden worry. Sudden fear. Did she go too far? Did she say it too soon? The vulnerability shows. The fear grips.

'I love you.'

Instant relief. She needed to hear it. He had to say it. He didn't want to say it straight back for fear of sounding trite or cheapening the power of her words and what they meant to him, but the same emotions that she feels are inside him. She realises that, and it's okay. It is more than okay.

He moves as he takes the control given. Understanding and knowing this is right. His body on hers. Her hands on him. He moves with a power that grows. With an intensity that builds. She moves too. She has to. Her body tells her what to do. Instinct now. Organic. Everything organic. He moves faster. She groans harder. She breathes faster. She runs her hands down to his backside that she grips and holds and guides him to move more. Still with love. Still with care.

It can never end. It should never end. It has to end. It's been a long time. He comes, sudden and powerful. She gasps at the sensation and the heat, at his body driving into her. His mouth finds hers. She takes him in. Kissing passionate and long. Kissing as the waves of orgasm sweep through his body and mind. Kissing as the driving urge abates to ease and slow. She can feel his heart thundering. His muscles locked. The intensity of him, and all for her. Only for her. Still the kiss goes on. As he sinks to lower. As he softens. As his heart rate slows, still the kiss goes on.

At some point, they stop and lie with each other. At some point, they drift to sleep. Neither could say when. Everything organic. Everything natural. It is okay. It's more than okay.

At the other end of the bunker, it is not okay. Not okay at all. Ria sobs in the darkness. She has never felt so alone.

Thirty-Eight

Pistols checked and made ready. Spare magazines pushed into the slots on their tactical vests. Bootlaces tied and double-knotted. Muscles thrumming from the warm-up of running light circuits outside. Sweat shines on brows. Faces grim and ready.

They gather in the main room. Coffee brewed. Coffee drunk. They are not hungry, but the day will be long, so they eat. Harry prepares the Browning. Loading the first links of the live ammunition belt. Emily checks her assault rifle and the contents of her pouches. She fastens the strap of the pistol round her leg.

Miri wears the same as them. Sinister in black. Her greying blonde hair scraped back into a ponytail. The lines on her face that could be scars show livid and deep. Her cold grey eyes are hard. She pushes the pistol into the holster and hefts the assault rifle to check and make ready.

The doctor bustles back and forth. Caught up in the energy. One of the rooms in his section is ready with an operating table and side units full of equipment. He cleaned it last night. He cleaned it this morning. He'll clean it again when they deploy. He wears a white lab coat. A stethoscope hangs round his neck. Surgical scrubs worn underneath.

Bertie is on the island with strict instructions not to bloody move. *Do not bloody move. Do not come to the bunker. Stay there. Do you understand? What did I just tell you? Say it back to me.* The doctor made sure he understood. They did consider holding him in the bunker but didn't trust him to not stroll out and wave at the nice soldiers.

Ria hides the fear inside and watches them getting ready with that dread growing inside. She has hardly slept. She looks like shit. Bags under her eyes, her face drawn and tired.

'Fucking thing,' Ben mutters, hefting the Barrett to make it ready. Harry pulls two missile launchers on to his back. Emily takes one. Ben straps an assault rifle to his. Everyone loaded with kit, but this is how they have trained and drilled. What they do now is nothing different to what they have done many times.

'Harry,' Safa groans, glaring at his boots. 'You had the new ones,' she adds, shaking her head.

Ben looks round to see him in his 1943 boots. Miri hates them. She told him not to wear them. He is Harry. He will wear what he bloody wants. Emily grins at him. Loving him for it.

'I'm ready,' Safa says, pushing the magazine in her assault rifle and yanking the bolt back. 'Shithead?'

'I take it that's me,' Emily says. 'I'm ready.'

'Beardy?'

'When you've been in a war,' he rumbles, earning a round of grins.

'Ben?'

'Yep.'

'Good,' she says, the woman in charge, the team leader. Ben thinks about last night and can't help but smile. She smiles too. Sensing the thoughts before looking round. 'We've drilled for this. We've gone at it from every side. No matter what happens, we have planned for it. They won't have anywhere near the opposition Ria threw at us. If anything, the whole fucking thing might be an anti-climax. Harry, remember to shout if that thing jams up. Ben, be ready to cover Harry if it jams.'

'Got it,' Ben says.

'That's it then,' Safa says. 'Miri? Anything from you?'

'Negative. Stick to the plan, but stay fluid.'

'Fuck it then,' Safa says. 'We're ready for this. We're better than they are. We're the good guys. We're going in hot, but we're going in ready. On me.'

She takes the lead. She is Safa. She always takes the lead.

'Good luck,' the doctor booms.

'Good luck,' Ria calls out, her voice sounding flat and strained.

Through the doors to the portal room. Miri takes the tablet as final kit checks are done.

'Can we eat cheese and crackers tonight?' Emily asks, trained and experienced, but still feeling that last-minute burst of tension.

'Aye,' Harry says softly, reassuringly as deep and calm as ever. 'Watch a holo.'

She nods. 'Sounds good.'

He holds the Browning one-handed and rests an enormous hand on her shoulder, bringing an instant calm to her mind. No words needed.

'Ready?' Miri asks, her thumb hovering over the pre-set destination on the screen.

Ben stiffens. Gripping the heavy sniper rifle. Safa looks at Emily, at Harry, at Ben, then moves to stand in front of the gap between the two poles. She flicks the safety off and brings her rifle up ready and aimed. 'On three,' she says to Miri. 'One . . . two . . .' Miri presses the screen. The Blue comes on instant and live. 'Three.'

Safa goes first. Walking through to an instant change in air, in temperature, in light, in environment. Her assault rifle up and aimed. The grass and trees are so different to the clearing they drilled in, but the sound effects created by Ria match the noise of the rotor blades from choppers thudding overhead and the gunshots in the distance. She takes it all in with a sweep round before sticking her hand back through the Blue with a thumbs-up.

Emily goes through. A look round. A scan of all sides. The choppers overhead. The heli she came in on with Alpha and the others. The two gunships. The time in the bunker melts away. It's as if she was here yesterday.

'Clear,' Emily snaps. 'Move out.'

Safa paces a few strides. Trees blot the view ahead. The foliage is dense. She takes a knee, holding position.

Harry comes through. The Browning gripped and ready.

'Harry clear,' Emily reports.

Emily's hand goes in. Ben comes out. His eyes showing the split second of adjustment to the new environment. A scan round to a terrain so different to the clearing they drilled in. A glimpse of the house in the distance. Trees all round them. A canopy overhead covering the Blue from the satellite they know is monitoring the area.

'PEOPLE IN THE HOUSE . . . LIE DOWN WITH YOUR ARMS OUT . . . PEOPLE IN THE HOUSE . . . LIE DOWN WITH YOUR ARMS OUT . . .'

The voice is huge and one they all remember. A surreal second. Emily was on the other side when they first heard it. The pilot in the helicopter repeats the commands. Safa visualises the soldiers running for the house. Emily visualises the agents and operatives inside and herself with the others on the landing.

Miri steps out and takes it all in without a flicker showing on her face.

'PEOPLE IN THE HOUSE . . . LIE DOWN WITH YOUR ARMS OUT . . .'

'On me,' Safa calls out, waving a hand forward. She takes point with Emily. Rifles up and aimed. Safa checks her watch. Through the undergrowth they go. Feet lifting to avoid snagging on tree roots and fallen branches. Miri waits by the Blue. Her face a mask as she watches her small team deploy towards Cavendish Manor.

Remember. Mother deploys the soldiers as Bravo goes into the room. That's the marker. You have to wait for the soldiers to go in.

Inside the house, bodies lie dead and injured. The battle is underway. Alpha glares over the bannister. Tango Two and the others with him. Pistols firing from the drawing room. Agents killed. A flash-bang goes in. Gunshots. Screams. Red laser sights shining. The noise is immense. The booming voice of the amplified helicopter pilot. The rotor blades of the gunships. Chaos unfolding.

'Agent down . . .'

'Fall back, fall back . . .'

'DO NOT FALL BACK . . . Bravo, get down and lead them through . . .' Alpha orders.

'Be happy to oblige,' Bravo mutters. 'Anyone with a flash-bang can throw it in that room now.'

Emily worked them through it. Guiding them to what was happening on her side while they were taking cover on the servants' stairs. They push on through the trees, working towards the house. Knowing they deployed further back from the soldiers forming the ring of steel.

'They're scared to return fire,' Charlie says inside the house.

With the trees and foliage masking their arrival, Safa and Emily run aiming and ready. Harry carrying the Browning. Ben with the Barrett. Heart rates building. Tension growing. This is it. This is the start of the show of force.

'THIS IS ALPHA . . . SHOOT TO KILL . . . MAXIMUM AGGRESSION . . . MOTHER, IF YOU CAN HEAR ME, DEPLOY THE SOLDIERS TO THE GROUND FLOOR . . .'

'Flash-bangs,' Emily mutters. They hear the explosions. Tens of them thrown on the order of Bravo into the drawing room. The booms sound and roll. Percussive and full of bass. Glass smashing. The windows blowing out. 'Bravo goes in,' she says.

'IN IN IN,' Bravo roars in the house. His strong, cultured private-school tones so loud and deep. Seconds later, the sound of sustained gunfire comes through to the four still working their way towards the house. One submachine gun at first. Then more. More and more. Harry remembers the man reaching his hand in to fire into the stairwell.

'Faster,' Safa orders, increasing the speed. They see figures in camouflage pouring across the grounds towards the front door.

They will not send every soldier in the house. The British Army is one of the finest fighting forces in the world. They are excellent at what they do. You have to work harder to be better, to be faster.

'LEFT SIDE,' Emily snaps, the figure seen. Her finger squeezes the trigger, the first shots from their side are taken. The first kill gained as the soldier spins in surprise, blown back off his feet. The sound of the M4 assault rifle masked by the cacophony of noise searing the air.

'FASTER.' Safa runs now. Leading her team. A camouflaged figure glimpsed ahead. She aims, waits for him to come into view behind the tree and fires, shooting the soldier dead. She snatches a glance at her watch. Four minutes.

'AHEAD, AHEAD,' Safa screams. 'DOWN DOWN DOWN . . .'

Figures running at them, drawn by the shots. She aims and fires. Rounds whip through the foliage. Fire is returned. Emily holds, aiming, waiting. She fires a burst, a figure drops. Safa kills another. Emily takes the third, pauses and tracks the fourth running away. She guns him down, shooting him in the back.

Four minutes twenty.

'FASTER,' Safa orders.

In the house, Harry runs with his arm covering his face to protect it from the debris flying past. Noise everywhere. He drops. Unable to move on. His arms and face bleeding.

They sprint through the undergrowth. Safa checks her watch. Four minutes fifty. She sees the spot. The foliage between them and the house now much thinner. Soldiers still running in. Soldiers all around them.

They take advantage of the chaos to run through and hope to hell they reach the mark.

'*WE'VE GOT THEM PINNED*,' Bravo shouts into his radio.

Safa looks at her watch. Four minutes fifty-five. She fires while running at a soldier. Rounds slam into his chest. Emily fires to the side. Ben and Harry stay behind. Knowing the drill. Seeing the spot they have to reach.

On the servants' stairs, Miri glares at her stopwatch. 'Five minutes six seconds, five minutes six seconds.'

'GO NOW, GO NOW,' Harry roars a few feet from her. He changes the magazine in his pistol as he prepares to go down and engage to buy time.

'HOLD,' Miri shouts.

Bravo grins. He's got them pinned in place.

Outside the house, Harry reaches the spot. Emily and Safa go left and right. Harry goes in between them, dropping to brace the heavy machine gun on the bipod. Ben stops behind them. Lifting the sniper rifle to sweep round.

In the drawing room, Bravo turns towards the door with his hand lifting to the radio mic to transmit the situation and suggest they look for the exit point from that corridor.

Outside, Harry sees the soldiers and black-clad figures pouring fire into the wall. The room full of them. So many. More still running into the house. A growl. A lip curls. His finger pulls back and all other sound around them is blotted out by the enormous thud of the Browning roaring to life.

He pours rounds through the window. Bravo's heightened instincts and speed of reaction save his life while all around him men die screaming.

Ben said this has to be done, so Harry fires to slaughter them from the rear. This is war. Bad things happen in war. His whole body judders from the recoil as he feeds the belt into the gun.

The noise of the heavy machine gun draws the soldiers who are still outside the house. Emily and Safa fire hard and fast. Killing them as they run.

The soldiers take cover and fire back. Ben breathes. Focussed and controlled. He sweeps round, staring down the sights. Waiting, doing what he practised. He fires without thinking. He fires suddenly and takes the recoil in his already sore shoulder with a glimpse of the pink mist left where the soldier's head was before the fifty-calibre round took it away.

'TIME TO GO . . . MOVE NOW . . .' Safa shouts.

Harry surges up, lifting the Browning as he rises. Emily and Safa covering his flanks. They run on, aiming for the patch of higher ground.

Echo staggers from the door ramming into his back on the landing. The five agents turn to see the famous face of Safa Patel with that split second of hesitancy buying her the time to press the attack. Safa Patel against five of the best agents the British Secret Service has. She holds them off. She doesn't win, but neither do they. A blur of arms. A blur of bodies moving, twisting, blocking and countering. *Safa held five of you off on her own. You ever see anyone else do that?*

Ben sights the door of the house. That's his marker. Behind him, Harry strafes the undergrowth, suppressing the forces. Safa and Emily flank Ben. Covering his sides. Calm now. Easy now. Ben breathes, steadying his nerve as he lifts the aim from the door and up to see through the windows. There she is. Safa fighting five people on her own. The sight is stunning. Mesmerising. An incredible display of her prowess. She moves like water. So graceful. So brutal. So fucking fast. He spots Emily, Tango Two. She looks so different there. Attacking Safa. Being beaten back by Safa. All of them being held off by Safa. Ben grins. He can't help it.

'I fucking love you, Safa.'

'Focus, bellend.'

Ben sees Harry run from the door on the landing to slam a vicious kidney punch into Charlie's side. The whole thing is a blur. Figures seemingly dancing and weaving. He sees Alpha kick at Harry. He sees himself run from the door into the fray. He drops the sight to the stairs. Seeing the soldiers and agents starting to climb. A twitch of the sights back to the fight on the landing. Miri leading Bertie, Ria, Roland and Susan.

'Fuck me,' Ben mutters at seeing Harry rise with Alpha gripped by the throat. The strength in the man is staggering. The look on his face is crazed. Mad Harry Madden unleashed.

He twitches back to see Miri on the landing staring at her watch, her lips muttering silently. She surges up, grabs Bertie and pins him to the wall as Ben gains the sight on Charlie running at them. He fires, removing Charlie's head with an instant kill.

'Got him,' he mutters. The sound lost in the chaos around him. He spots Delta, and although he knows he misses, he takes the shot. Time is not fixed. Not fixed at all. He still misses, but takes pleasure in the look of surprise on Delta's face that buys time for Safa to kick him in the bollocks.

He tracks Harry running to the stairs. Covering the big man in the house while the big man covers him now.

Calm inside. Icy cold. His heart rate slow. His breathing easy. A soldier rises to stab at Harry on the stairs. Ben fires, and the high-powered round lifts the man from his feet and slams him back into the wall. He sights another and fires.

'Seen me yet, bitch?' Emily mutters, glancing up at the sky. She risks a pause to flick a middle finger, hoping the satellite feed sees it.

Mother glares at the screen. 'WHAT THE FUCK IS GOING ON?' she rages. Aides flinch at the pure fury in her voice. All eyes on the screen watching the four black-clad figures slaughtering soldiers in the grounds. She spots the face looking up and a middle finger. No. It can't be. No way. '*TANGO TWO, WHERE ARE YOU?*'

'*Landing, middle floor.*' Alpha's voice booms with a background noise of carnage.

Ben fires the Barrett. Sensing the power of the weapon and understanding why Miri insisted on using it. The noise is something else. The power of it. The message it sends. Miri said there are accounts of enemy soldiers running from US troops just from hearing a single shot from a Barrett.

Miri waits at the Blue. Casually smoking a cigarette while holding the rifle one-handed, braced in her shoulder.

Ben sees the sudden battle for the doorway on the landing as everyone runs for it. He fires again, but the single shots he can take are a pittance against the numbers they have in the house. It doesn't matter. They are almost done. Weeks and weeks of solid drills and Safa was right, it's almost an anti-climax. All they have to do is run to the back of the house, fire the missile launcher at the gunship, then this part of the mission is done.

Thirty-Nine

'The US President, Prime Minister,' the aide says, holding the secure phone out. The PM takes the handset as the aide flaps his hands to tell the many people in the emergency planning room to be quiet. A tense silence falls. The PM clears her throat and presses the button to make the connection live. 'Hello, Sarah,' the PM says calmly.

'Veronica,' the US President says. 'I do hope you are in your bunker because your little country is about to be wiped off the face of the earth. Moscow and Beijing are both repositioning their missile systems.'

'Is this a threat, Sarah? The British government does not give in to threats . . .'

'Can it, Veronica. Do you have it or not? We'll protect you if you have it, but I need to know.'

'I cannot confirm . . .'

'PM,' an aide whispers from nearby, holding an identical handset. 'Moscow on line two . . .'

'I'm watching the damn feed, Veronica! We all are. Moscow is watching it. Beijing is watching it. This is too big for the UK to contain. You should have come to me first. Now do you have it or not because our *special* relationship will go out the damn window if you do not cooperate.'

The room bursts into frantic activity as aides and ministers rush to establish if the satellite uplink has been compromised.

The PM stares at the big screen on the wall. Cavendish Manor in the centre. Two gunships hovering overhead. Bodies scattered across the grounds to the front of the big house. She watches the four people at the edge of the undergrowth unleashing hell on the soldiers surrounding the house.

'Sarah,' the PM says. How her tone stays so calm is beyond everyone. 'If you are watching the feed, then you will see this operation is unfolding as we speak. I cannot, at this stage, confirm or deny anything, but please be reassured that the UK seeks to work closely with the US in any and all matters of security.'

'We come first,' the US President states. 'We are watching.'

Sarah Conway, second term US President, cuts the line off and glowers round at the five-star generals, admirals and special advisors all flicking their eyes from her to the huge screen showing the satellite feed of Cavendish Manor. Sarah was honest enough to say they hacked the satellite feed, but she held back on saying they also hacked the radio network. The room listens to Mother screeching in ever-increasing panic that signifies a loss of control.

'Be ready to launch.' She utters the words. There is no choice. The rest of the world has to see the United States is prepared and ready. A time machine changes everything. No country other than the US can have such a thing.

In the same bunker under Downing Street that Safa Patel secured the then Prime Minister in nearly forty years ago, Veronica Smedley holds the handset out to one aide and takes the other while mouthing *Who is it?* The aide mouths back *Moscow*. 'Veronica Smedley. To whom am I speaking?'

'It's Alexander. Do you have it?'

'Alexander. May I first say that . . .'

'We are watching it, Veronica,' the Russian President cuts in, his accent holding only a trace of Russian – but then he was only a year ahead of Veronica at Oxford. 'You must tell me. We can protect you. The UK is too small for this, Veronica. You cannot defend yourselves. Let us deal with Beijing and Washington. Work with us.'

'Alexander, the operation is unfolding as we speak, but please be assured the UK seeks to work with Russia in any and all matters of security.'

'Call me as soon as you know,' Alexander asserts. 'Russia will stand with you.'

'PM, His Highness the King is still on line three. He's demanding an explanation.'

'I'm sure he is,' Veronica says, having severed the line to Russia. 'He can wait. Get me Mother now . . .'

◆ ◆ ◆

In a control room in a building in central London on the banks of the River Thames, Mother watches the satellite feed with wide eyes as the vein in her forehead bulges with pulsing fury.

'WHERE IS TANGO TWO?' she screams into the radio network, unaware of and indifferent to the fact that the US and now Russia are listening to every transmission. She looks again at the four figures outside. Her eyes narrow. Her mouth twitches. Frantic activity everywhere in the room. Phones ringing. Messages incoming. Hologram computer networks glowing. Voices speaking to process information. Two of the four were recognised instantly. Safa Patel and Ben Ryder. Mother allowed a second of shock at that recognition before screaming at everyone to *get back to fucking work*.

The big man is familiar. Harry? Harry? 'WHO THE FUCK IS THAT ONE?' she screeches, jabbing at the screen.

Aides flinch and mutter. One lifts a hand tentatively. 'Harry Madden?'

'WHAT? FUCKING WHAT?'

'Looks like him,' the aide says weakly.

'FUCK FUCK FUCK.' Mother stands straight, pushing her hands into her hair with utter despair. 'WHO'S NEXT? BIGGLES?'

'Mother, got the PM on line one . . .'

'Tell her to fuck off . . .'

'Um . . .'

'Give me that phone . . . Veronica? I am really quite busy right now.'

'What is happening?' The voice is calm, controlled.

'I don't fucking know . . .'

'Mother,' another aide shouts. 'We're detecting more changes to missile positioning . . .'

'Who?' Mother demands. 'Who the fuck is pointing missiles at us?'

'Er, everyone is?' the aide says, blinking rapidly at the information flowing into his system.

'That is why I am calling you,' the PM states, drawing Mother's attention back to her. 'I have received direct warnings.'

'From who? Tell them to fuck off . . . WHERE IS TANGO TWO? Someone get Alpha on the line . . . What the fuck is happening? WHERE IS TANGO TWO? Is that Tango Two outside? What the fuck is she doing outside? Is she still inside? PM? Who threatened us?'

'They all did. They all are . . . I need an update. Do we have it?'

'Fuck,' Mother mutters.

'The US President is watching this feed,' the PM says. 'Moscow and Beijing too.'

'WHAT? HOW? Hang on . . .' She pulls the phone away for a second. 'Is that Tango Two outside? WELL, FUCKING FIND OUT . . .'

'They will launch at us if they even think we have it,' the PM says into the phone. 'We need to confirm or deny. We have no choice . . .'

'It's a live operation,' Mother says, glaring round the chaos of her office. 'If the US President is watching, she will see that.'

'Now is not the time for semantics. We have US military aircraft in UK sovereign airspace. We have Russian military aircraft heading our way. Every missile facility in the world is currently pointing at us. I need answers. Confirm or deny.'

'It's her,' someone shouts, pulling up the stock images of Tango Two to compare to Emily seen on the live feed. 'Confirmed. That is Tango Two . . . real name Emily Rose.'

'*WHERE IS TANGO TWO?*' Mother screams into the radio as the PM holds the phone away from her ear with a wince, while her aides look on in varying states of fear.

A muffled voice amidst the chaos within the house. '*WITH ME, TOP FLOOR . . .*'

'*GUNSHIPS . . . TOP FLOOR . . . FIRE NOW, FIRE NOW . . .*' Mother screams.

'Mother, be careful . . . If we are seen using heavy military equipment, it will send a signal that we are losing control,' the PM says, trying her best to stay calm.

'Fuck off,' Mother snaps, throwing the phone across the room. She flips a switch to transmit on every channel deployed to the attack in Hampshire. '*KILL TANGO TWO . . . KILL HER NOW! . . . GUNSHIPS . . . TOP FLOOR, FIRE NOW, FIRE NOW . . .*'

Forty

Ria stares at the shimmering light with tears streaming down her cheeks. Her hands trembling. Her stomach in knots of fear, dread and abject pity. Her legs threaten to give way. They'll kill her mum. She needs her mum. Her mum is in the house. She can get her out. She can do it. She needs seconds, that's all.

She sobs as she takes the second tablet for the Red. She has to get her mum. She is pregnant. She doesn't know what to do. It's always about Bertie. Always about what he's done. Her father didn't care. He didn't care before he committed suicide and he doesn't care now. He ran off when they were being attacked in the house. He ran off and saved himself. He's not even here now, but off hiding somewhere.

She has an assault rifle. She knows how to fire it. She's watched the others enough times. She's even put a magazine of live bullets in it.

Tears fall on the screen of the tablet. Panic surges up. Her breathing comes faster. She hyperventilates and smothers her own mouth with a hand to stop the noise carrying down the corridor to the doctor in his rooms.

All she can see is the look on her mum's face when she tried to defend Bertie. The utter terror and confusion in her eyes. Her mum is a good person. Loving and caring. She doesn't deserve this. Ria needs her. Her mum needs to be here in the bunker or on the island with Bertie. Mum will love the island. Mum loves the heat and sunshine.

Rational thought vanishes. The need to have her mum back outweighs anything else. She convinces herself she can do this. She can go through and grab her mum to bring her back. She's even timed it for when everyone else is on the top floor trying to rescue her bloody brother.

She fights to recover her breathing and stem the tears falling down her cheeks that mist her vision. She fights to gain composure and push the crippling fear away.

Miri smokes outside the Blue. Her mind running fast. The thrill inside is strong and beautiful. The same thrill she used to get when she executed missions, but this is better than all of them put together.

She looks at the cigarette. Dammit, she hates smoking. She loves smoking. It stinks so bad, but feels so good. A lingering glance to the blue light behind her. A twitch at the corners of her mouth, then she looks forward to the direction of the house.

◆　◆　◆

Through the scope on the Barrett, Ben watches Echo lead the charge up the main stairs. He knows Echo will throw the flash-bang up. Miri and Bertie will be stunned. John will get them into the bedroom and the last bit will happen. Several operatives and soldiers remain on the middle-floor landing, but what they do is of no relevance now.

Ben lowers the weapon. Blinking as his eyes adjust from the sights to real vision.

Safa leads them on, running towards the corner of the house to complete a mission that has gone like clockwork. Better than clockwork. It's been almost easy.

◆ ◆ ◆

Miri smokes. Her eyes cold and fixed. A few feet behind her and a hundred million years in the past, Ria inhales deep and slow next to the inert Red. Her hand holding the tablet trembles as she keys the coordinates.

◆ ◆ ◆

Ben, Safa, Harry and Emily run. Miri smokes. Ria summons courage and on the middle landing of Cavendish Manor, while everyone else fights on the top landing, Alpha drags a terrified woman by her hair across the ruined carpet. His face twisted in fury. Bravo with him.

Soldiers and operatives watch as Alpha slaps Susan Cavendish across the face several times. Each one a solid whack that snaps her head over. Blood spills from her nose. Her eyes already swelling. She cries out and spits blood from her mouth. Bravo draws his pistol to press the barrel into Susan's forehead.

In the grip of terror, Susan looks up into the almost friendly face of Bravo smiling down at her. She has no idea what is happening or who these people are. She didn't even know Bertie had built a time machine until her dead husband walked back into their house not a day older than when he left. She fainted when she saw him, and believed it to be a dream until she woke and saw him again.

Her family were reunited. It was glorious and wonderful and beyond anything she ever dreamt of. She was suddenly years older than her husband, but worked hard to recapture a youthful appearance. Ria took her shopping. She had cosmetic surgery, breast augmentation, nips and tucks.

All she knew was that Bertie had *glimpsed something nasty in the future. Best I get that sorted for him.* That's all Roland said. She never questioned Roland about his business activities before he died, and was so caught up in having him back she never asked him again. Then he slowly reverted to how he was before. Self-involved. Focussed and cold. He kept saying it would only take a while to sort out, then they could go away somewhere. Somewhere special and amazing.

Now she is kneeling on the carpet on the middle floor of her home, battered and bleeding, with a warm, friendly face smiling at her while a gun is held to her head.

Bravo knows he has a friendly face and he plays it to the maximum now. Jarring her senses to increase the sense of confusion. Alpha hits her again, but Bravo tuts and shows disdain at her being hit, then shakes his head at Alpha, who takes a step back. They've done this same routine many times.

Bravo drops to a crouch, the pistol still held at her head. 'Who are they, my dear?'

She whimpers, shaking her head slowly, unable to speak or form coherent thoughts.

'Come now, do tell me, who are those people?'

'I . . . I . . .' Susan mouths, but she cannot think to answer. She doesn't know. She doesn't know anything. Only confusion and fear.

'*KILL TANGO TWO . . . KILL HER NOW! . . . GUNSHIPS . . . TOP FLOOR, FIRE NOW, FIRE NOW . . .*' Mother's voice screeching through every radio. Noise overhead upstairs on the top floor. Alpha moves in closer and slides a knife from his belt.

Bravo tuts sadly as he pulls the earpiece from his ear. 'That is a shame, my dear. We'll have to cut you open and feed your insides to your children.'

Susan's head snaps up. Sharp focus in her eyes. Bravo smiles, wolfish and full of charm. 'Who are they? Tell me or I will kill everyone you ever knew . . .'

Miri lights the second cigarette. The first one crushed under her boot. Footsteps coming. She lifts the rifle, aiming with two hands with the cigarette wedged between her lips. He's young. Eighteen? Nineteen at the most. Fresh out of basic. He looks terrified. Consumed with panic and not watching ahead, only the sides. Running from the heavy machine gun and the sound of the Barrett.

'Stop,' she says dully. He crashes to a standstill. Eyes wide. His assault rifle held lowered. 'Don't do it,' Miri says calmly. 'Just drop it . . . Go on now . . . Drop it and live, or raise it and die.'

He drops it instantly. Gasping for air. His chest rising and falling. His face blotchy with red spots.

'How old are you, kid?'

'Ei . . . eight . . .' He swallows. 'Eighteen,' he finally blurts.

'Lie down, hands on your head. I won't shoot you. Go on now. You stay still and quiet, and you'll be fine.'

He nods. Believing. Hoping. He drops to his knees, then lies flat on the ground with his hands interlocked on the back of his head.

She adjusts position to cover him with the rifle held one-handed while she carries on smoking. 'You ever smoke?'

'No,' he whimpers. 'Once . . . couple of times . . .'

'Stinks, don't do it.' She glances back to the Blue, then once again across towards the house.

It's too much. Susan's mind starts shutting down to protect her from the horror of the situation. She can feel the knife going in and she can feel the man with the friendly face gripping her chin, but it's not her body anymore. She becomes detached from reality. Bravo spots the glaze stealing across her face and slaps her hard. She comes surging back to the now and the pain searing in her stomach. She tries to scream, but his hand smothers her mouth and suddenly his face is not so friendly. The knife sinks deeper. The pistol presses harder into her head. Bravo shouts louder. Demanding to know who they are. Telling her he will kill everyone. A red light. Shimmering and beautiful. She looks past Bravo to see every colour in the spectrum seemingly gliding over the gateway to hell.

Safa spots it. A flash of red light coming on inside the house as they run past the front. A shade of red unlike any other. Shining, shimmering and iridescent as it glows from the landing on the second floor.

'BEN!'

'What?' Ben snaps round to see Safa staring inside the house. Emily and Harry cover, aiming and firing back towards the grounds. Ben spots it instantly. Knowing instantly what it is. Knowing instantly what is happening.

Ria stares at the Red. Her whole body trembling. Her knuckles white from gripping the assault rifle. She has to go now. Right now. Her mum is out there. Tears stream down her face. Her eyes puffy and red. Silence, save for her own gasps. Determination rises. Wild determination. Courage summoned from delusion and panic brought on by the shock of everything. She has to save her mum.

The chain guns of the attack helicopters come to life. Over six thousand large-calibre rounds per minute. A deafening searing noise of bullets slamming into brick and plaster, and through windows and wood. The walls vibrate, sending shockwaves through the floorboards to make the whole house seemingly quake from the onslaught. Missiles launch and hit. Detonations. Guns firing. Explosions.

As the world around them gives way to noise and sensation, so the middle landing of Cavendish Manor bathes in red light. Twenty armed men snap heads over to the shimmering iridescence glowing and pulsing with ripples of every colour on the surface.

Miri smokes with a strange smile etched on her face as she stands close to the young soldier lying on the ground.

Mother watches the gunships lay waste to the house. The PM stares at the screen with an almost resigned air. The US President grim-faced. The Russian President the same. In China. In Israel. In India. In Pakistan. In France. In North Korea. Every government of every country that could hack the satellite feed watches and prepares to strike, counter-strike, defend and attack as Ria plucks the final shred of maddened courage to go through, while Miri's eyes twinkle as she reaches down to take the radio from the soldier.

The centre of the world is here. This is the game.

Ria screams as she runs through. Her rifle held poorly, but her finger on the trigger and the safety already clicked off. The noise hits her first. The sheer cacophony of her house being fired at by chain guns and missiles. The whole building shaking and trembling. Chunks of plaster falling from the ceiling. Bodies on the floor. Blood smeared on the walls. In a split second of utter realisation she knows she has made a terrible mistake. As that realisation hits, she sees her mum kneeling on the floor and being held by two black-clad men. She sees one of them pushing a knife into her mum's stomach. She sees that look of pure terror on her mum's face and squeezes the trigger of her assault rifle.

Time slows like it did when he was seventeen and walking home down a country lane. Like it did when he was on the platform at Holborn Tube station and when he fought in the bunker against the guards with Safa and Harry. Like it did in the ocean and in this same house. Everything in perfect clarity. Every move laid out in front of him. There is no panic, only calm. *Ben is smart. He doesn't panic. I need that.*

Ria kills her mother. Firing blanks was easy. She never needed to aim but just fire. She sprays the landing with rounds. The soldiers and operatives are trained for such a thing and drop to roll or burst away. Her mother doesn't. Susan stares fixed at the gateway to hell from which her daughter runs as the rounds slam through her chest and neck.

Time slows. Everything in perfect clarity. The Barrett already handed to Safa. The rocket launcher already pulled round. Ben sees Ria firing the assault rifle, wild and unfocussed. He sees the plaster falling from the ceiling and the dust particles hanging in the air. He sees the soldiers recover quickly to bring aim at Ria as the air on the landing glows with red lasers seemingly drawn of the same hue shining behind the girl screaming out as she sees her mother drop dead and bleeding.

Time slows. Everything in perfect clarity. He squeezes and fires. The missile launches with a bright burning trail from the front door into the space between the men and Ria. The explosion is instant and huge. A booming detonation of fire and noise that only adds to the carnage in Cavendish Manor. Ria is taken off her feet, sprawling out on the floor.

Time slows. Everything in perfect clarity. Ben drops the missile launcher and reaches back to take the Barrett from Safa, swinging the weapon over as he brings it up to brace in his already sore shoulder.

'Leave the bazookas . . . Go now . . .'

He braces and readies to stare down the scope through the dust and smoke billowing in the house. He spots a camouflaged figure moving and fires. He spots a black-clad figure and fires. He fires quickly into bodies and into the middle of them. He fires the enormous weapon as Safa, Harry and Emily run for the stairs.

Ria has to be protected, but more than that, more than anything, the Red has to be protected. *This is the level of what we must do, Mr Ryder. The safety of the device will always be the priority.*

Ben pulls the trigger. The recoil slamming into his shoulder. The noise is immense. The solid whump of the sniper rifle marking their presence. Marking their arrival.

'GET THROUGH IT.' Alpha screams the order while hunkering down behind several bodies. Using their forms as a shield. Others scream in panic, but he is Alpha. He does not panic. Through the smoke and debris, he spots Ria sprawled on the floor. His right hand brings the pistol up. The Barrett fires again, killing a man rising up near Alpha. Hot, wet blood spatters on Alpha's face, but he pays no heed as he aims and fires. Men rise to charge at the red glowing light, only to be shot down by Ben twitching to aim and fire while he waits.

Safa takes the top of the stairs and runs down the landing with her own pistol out, firing into the mass of soldiers and agents. Harry and Emily do the same. They run past the Red to go deep into the attackers. Everything on instinct. Everything on reaction. *Safa held five on her own. You ever see anyone do that? I need Safa.*

'*MINE, BEN,*' Safa screams into the mic. Ben drops the Barrett.

Safa slams her knee into a head and twists to flip with a high kick, striking the side of a skull. Harry smashes two through the ruined bannister that land with a sickening crunch of bone next to Ben, who draws his pistol and shoots both before hefting the two remaining missile launchers up. Emily grabs a head from behind and snaps hard, severing the spinal column.

◆ ◆ ◆

Miri smokes and holds the radio taken from the soldier. She listens to the sounds coming from the house. She looks up to the sky, as though towards the satellite, then checks her watch.

◆ ◆ ◆

The three on the landing twist and spin to block, to snap arms, sweep legs and stamp on throats as Ben strides from the lobby to a back room. He lowers one missile launcher, lifts the other, makes ready and fires at the back wall, removing it from existence.

◆ ◆ ◆

Miri smiles and presses the button on the side of radio. '*Hello, Mother . . . My name is Maggie Sanderson . . .*'

Ben walks to the gap in the ruined wall and stares up in awe at the sight of two military gunships firing both sets of chain guns. Spent casings spew in long trails from the side. Glinting as they fall to scatter unheard on the ruined lawn.

In a control room in a building in central London, on the banks of the River Thames, Mother freezes as the room becomes instantly quiet.

In a bunker under Downing Street, every aide and minister ceases what they are doing at the new voice coming through the radio network and a name they all know from a person that was meant to have died many years ago.

Washington and Moscow grow silent. They all know that name. Anyone who ever worked in intelligence and security knows that name.

Miri holds the radio and the attention of the world in her hand. '*I need you to understand who is in control here . . .*'

Harry's heavy 1943 boot drives into a soldier. He swings a fist into the face of another. Someone hits him. He doesn't blink. He doesn't flinch. He slams his head forward, dropping the attacker instantly. A kick, and the body sails over the edge to land on the lobby floor. Alpha and Bravo see Tango Two. She is upstairs. But she is also here. Time travel. Doesn't matter. They go for her. The two best agents in the country aiming for the woman as she fights on.

In the glade next to the Blue, Miri draws breath and checks her watch. '*Look at your gunships . . . Watch what happens . . .*'

Ben lifts and aims. He flicks the sight up and adjusts. No rush. No panic. He blinks slowly and presses the trigger. The missile swooshes. A glowing trail of bright light marking the trajectory as inside the top room Tango Two sees the arc while fighting for her life without a clue as to why.

'*That is what happens . . .*'

'Oh, fuck,' Mother mutters at the sight of Ben Ryder aiming from the hole in the back of the house. The missile launches and soars up into the gunship on the right. Rotor blades strike with a flash of sparks that send screaming metal ramming into the house as both aircraft spin out of control down to crash into the roof of Cavendish Manor.

'*Ben Ryder. Safa Patel. Harry Madden. Emily Rose and me, Maggie Sanderson. My five against all of you . . .*'

Emily ducks, spins and comes up behind a soldier to grab his head. She tenses and snarls to bunch the explosive force needed to break the neck. Only a few metres away, Ria lies in shock on her side, clutching the gunshot in her stomach. Silent. Pale and staring only at the face of her dead mother lying amongst the bodies and debris. The pain is immense. She sees the two men that held her mother now running at Emily and thinks to scream, but stays silent in the chaos and noise.

The speed of them. The vicious power as Alpha wrenches Emily back and spins her round for Bravo to rain withering, brutal punches into her face. Emily tries to block, to counter, but the two best agents go at her. Neither relents. Neither stops. Her nose breaks. Blood sprays out. She blocks a few hits and lashes out, but the psychological effect of just knowing she is fighting Alpha and Bravo give them the edge. She tries, but they are too fast. She screams out as the hard kick takes her down with a dull thud.

Alpha's foot lifts to stamp. His own bloodied face twisted in malice. The foot comes down, but she smiles up almost in pity at the two men who have no idea what's coming.

I need Harry. Mad Harry Madden takes the two men from the side. *The man is fearless.* The sheer power of him lifting both up and along as he drives them into the wall. Mad Harry Madden won't stop. Mad Harry Madden will eat crackers and cheese tonight with his friend, and he'll kill every living thing here to do that. He drops to punch. Landing huge hits one after the other into eye sockets, bursting ear drums, breaking noses.

'Harry . . .'

He snatches round to see Emily on her feet behind him and moves aside. Emily draws and stares down at the battered men. *Pick a side, Tango Two.* She aims, fires once then twice and goes back into the fray.

'*Your best are dead. Your best will die. Dammit, I hate smoking. You okay, son? You stay there. It'll be over soon.*'

Mother closes her eyes. Maggie Sanderson. Christ, they don't stand a chance. The PM listens to the flat American voice that comes through speakers to emergency bunkers all over the world as aides, generals and advisors shake heads in confusion.

Ben sprints up the stairs to see Ria down and bleeding. He grabs her wrists to drag her, screaming, through the Red to the instant silence of the bunker.

'DOC . . . IN HERE . . . !'

'Coming . . . !' he hears Doctor Watson shouting, and goes back to the noise, heat and smoke of Cavendish Manor. No panic. Calm inside. He draws, aims and fires his pistol into one going for Safa. He twitches to fire into another one.

'FALL BACK . . . FALL BACK . . . *Miri, Ria activated the Red. It's live in the house. We're going back through it now . . .*'

Safa, Harry and Emily retreat in a disciplined line. Pistols drawn and firing at anything moving, as all around them the whole house trembles and shakes from the gunships crashing down through the roof.

'RUN,' Ben screams as the aviation fuel in the gunships ignites. They run across the landing towards Ben to fall through the Red into the bunker as Cavendish Manor is lost in a fireball that plumes up to be seen in perfect detail by the satellite feed.

They land hard, as they did the first time they came running from Cavendish Manor. They land hard and sprawling in the portal room as Doctor Watson works on Ria. Flames come through the Red. Heat and debris smashing into the walls around them. The doctor drops to protect Ria with his body as Ben scrabbles to get the tablet and swipe the screen to cut it off.

◆ ◆ ◆

The young soldier on the ground flinches as the house explodes. His eyes locked on Miri as she speaks into his radio. Her voice so calm, so controlled, so powerful. She reaches down to pat his shoulder and winks, telling him it'll be okay.

'Miri . . .' Ben comes through the Blue. 'Ria's been shot in the stomach . . . Doc's working on her now with the others . . . Who the hell is that?' he asks on seeing the soldier.

'Just a kid,' Miri says. 'Tell John the bullet passed straight through Ria. No serious internal injuries . . .'

'How do you . . . ?' He trails off, too in the heat of the moment to care for the answer. He watches Miri lift the radio to her mouth and press the button. She speaks slowly. Deliberately and with care.

'*Are you all listening safe in your bunkers? My name is Maggie Sanderson. I will complete my mission, then destroy any and all devices. If you interfere with my team again, I will release the bubonic plague in your cities and poison your water. I will either find you as children and kill you, or be there when you wake in the night old and frail to see me watching you. I will find your families. There is no place I cannot go and there is no thing I will not do to achieve my objective. What you are, I am, but worse, because I did it first and I did it longer . . . If you have any doubt as to my words, let me show you what I can do . . . Let me show you how a plan is executed . . .*'

'*Maggie! This is Mother . . . Don't you fucking dare . . . For the love of god, don't do it . . .*'

'*I already am . . .*'

Forty-One

How do you stop a government?

They ate because they knew the day would be long and it was decided to punch through while the energy was high.

A few minutes for Safa to check Emily's injuries to her face. It should have been the doc checking, but he stays with Ria. Refusing to believe Miri that the bullet passed through and caused no serious internal damage. Having a time machine is one thing, but he is a doctor and he will check for himself, thank you very much.

They drink water. Rinse faces and reload weapons before gathering in the portal room in front of the two inert devices.

How do you stop a government?

'Ready?' Miri asks, holding the tablet.

Safa waits to take the lead. She is Safa. She always takes the lead. 'Ben? You sure about this?' she asks quietly, her pistol held in a double-handed grip in front.

How do you stop a government?

'I am,' Ben says, holding his own pistol in the same way. They all do. All holding pistols double-handed and ready. Hearts hammering. Eyes fixed and staring.

'Ready,' Safa says.

How do you stop a government?

The Blue comes on. Safa charges forward with pure aggression on her face to a voice booming through a radio network.

'*Maggie! This is Mother . . . Don't you fucking dare . . . For the love of god, don't do it . . .*'

'*I already am . . .*'

In the same bunker she secured the then Prime Minister in nearly forty years ago, Safa Patel appears from a shining blue light. The current Prime Minister, Veronica Smedley, flinches at the sight. Aides scream out. A uniformed guard goes for his sidearm and is shot dead with a double-tap to his centre of mass.

Emily, Harry and Ben surge in behind Safa. Pistols up and aimed. Eyes tracking for threats. They trained for this. They drilled for hours and hours in every room in their bunker, and even Bertie's shack, to make this go right. Soldiers and police officers are killed. Veronica stays frozen at the head of the table. Frozen in fear and resignation. Harry shoots into the doorway of the emergency planning meeting, killing the armed man running in.

They gain control of the room in mere seconds. Bodies lie dead and bleeding. Ears ringing from the shots inside the confined place.

Miri strides through the Blue and heads straight towards the Prime Minister. A uniformed man rises to block her. Older, military. His hair greying. His eyes hard. She draws and aims at his head. He lowers back to his seat with his hands up. She moves to the PM and glances at the screen on the wall showing the satellite feed of Cavendish Manor.

'*MAGGIE? MAGGIE?*'

Mother's voice screeching through the speakers in the room. Miri stops at the side of the PM and stares down at the woman with those cold grey eyes so unreadable.

'My name is Maggie Sanderson. I will complete my mission, then destroy any and all devices. If you interfere with my team again, I will find you and I will kill you. Do not take any action against any other country. What we are doing does not concern you. Do you understand? I need you to understand.'

The PM nods, once and firm.

◆ ◆ ◆

How do you stop a government?

The Blue comes on. Safa goes forward.

'*Maggie! This is Mother . . . Don't you fucking dare . . . For the love of god, don't do it . . .*'

'*I already am . . .*'

Sarah Conway, the US President balks at the sight and dives from her chair to the floor. The reactions from the Secret Service are fast. Safa fires, killing one instantly, as Harry, Emily and Ben come through to shoot down the others still trying to draw pistols from holsters.

Aides run screaming. More armed men and women run into the room. More shots are fired. More death is given. An aide rushes at Harry and drops unconscious with his nose broken from the punch given by Emily.

Miri strides from the Blue with her pistol already out and gripped. She told the others the Secret Service are good. She spots the same feed on the screen showing the same view of Cavendish Manor engulfed in flames.

'*MAGGIE? MAGGIE?*'

Mother's voice on the hacked radio system. Miri crosses to the cowering Sarah Conway and drops to kneel at the woman's side.

'My name is Maggie Sanderson. I will complete my mission, then destroy any and all devices. If you interfere with my team again, I will find you and I will kill you. Do not take any action against any other country. What we are doing does not concern you. Do you understand? I need you to understand.' Miri drops lower to speak softly. 'If I need help, I will come to you, but stay the hell out of my way until I ask you.'

◆ ◆ ◆

The Blue comes on. Safa goes forward.

'*Maggie! This is Mother . . . Don't you fucking dare . . . For the love of god, don't do it . . .*'

'*I already am . . .*'

Moscow is worse. More guards. More men and women with guns. More death. Safa kills two before Harry, Emily and Ben can get through. The emergency room is bigger too, with more people screaming and running in panic. More angles to cover.

Cavendish Manor on a screen. Mother screeching into the radio. Men and women diving on top of the Russian President trying to cover him with their bodies. Control is still gained. Albeit short-lived while the alarm sounds to summon more guards and soldiers.

Miri speaks in Russian this time. Fluent and perfect.

'My name is Maggie Sanderson. I will complete my mission, then destroy any and all devices . . .'

As she speaks, so her team commence firing at the doorways to hold back the arriving reinforcements.

◆　◆　◆

The Blue comes on. Safa goes forward. She leads them each time. The first through and the last back. Her instincts and reactions save them time and again.

'*Maggie! This is Mother . . . Don't you fucking dare . . . For the love of god, don't do it . . .*'

'*I already am . . .*'

Cavendish Manor on a screen. Mother screeching into the radio.

'My name is Maggie Sanderson . . .'

◆　◆　◆

Again and again they deploy to arrive at the exact same time in bunkers and emergency rooms the world over.

North Korea is the hardest. That's where Harry is shot, and it's the only time they need to throw a grenade to gain space to get back through the Blue, with Emily clamping her bare hands on Harry's bleeding arm.

Emily stayed on Harry, screaming for a medic, as they landed in the portal room. Straddling him, with blood pushing between her fingers, coating her hands. It was only a flesh wound in the end, but there was a lot of blood. Harry didn't flinch. The dressing was applied and he carried on as if nothing happened.

◆   ◆   ◆

'Maggie! This is Mother . . . Don't you fucking dare . . . For the love of god, don't do it . . .'

'I already am . . .'

Cavendish Manor on a screen. Mother screeching into the radio.

The same words spoken by Miri. Emily speaks twice. Once in German and once in French. Languages learnt via an intracranial device she wore as a child that she told Miri about in Berlin when a plan was forming.

◆   ◆   ◆

How do you stop a government, Mr Ryder? You show it a power beyond its own. You show an ability to come back and kill it whenever you wish.

They ate because they knew the day would be long, ferocious, savage and unforgiving. Between each deployment, they gulp fluids and take pain relief.

There is no time to rest. They have a time machine. It could be staggered and done over days, but they go while the energy is high, while the ferocity of the fight is still in them. To take that energy with them into each place to do what must be done.

When the final one is finished, they go back to Berlin to a time before the staging area was ever established. They go back to hide explosive charges to blow the street and make the first statement when Alpha leads his team away.

A plan formed. A plan executed.

◆ ◆ ◆

A hundred million years in the future, in a glade just in front of a shimmering blue light, Miri kneels next to a young soldier, while in the distance Cavendish Manor burns from the aviation fuel of the gunships.

Two minutes for all of them. Months of planning and a whole day to achieve perfection of execution.

She knows that right now in each bunker and emergency room there is chaos and disorder caused by her, but there are also speakers still connected to the hacked radio network from this place.

'*Time travel is possible. I have the device. I have the inventor. I do not want anything from you. My name is Maggie Sanderson. I will bend time to win . . . and I will win . . .*'

She stubs the cigarette out and places it in the plastic bag with the others. The soldier watches her. Confused. Mesmerised. She places the bag down next to him. 'Make sure Mother gets that.'

'My mum?' the young soldier asks, bewildered.

'Not your mum, Mother. You'll know soon enough, and tell her from me if she harms you, I will find her. What's your name?'

'Private Armstrong . . . Colin . . . Colin Armstrong.'

'Goodbye, Private Armstrong. Been nice meeting you.'

'Wait! Who . . . What . . .'

Miri and Ben go through the Blue. The young soldier sees it. They walk through a solid wall of light, then it's gone. Just gone.

'Did she say anything else?' Mother asks him, days later in the concrete underground cell.

Colin shakes his head, then stops to look round at the scary men standing round the Prime Minister. 'She said . . . She said, if you harm me, she'll find you. She knows my name . . . I told her my name . . .'

The PM nods. Mother smiles. 'You've been touched by an angel, Colin. Maybe a devil. I don't know. Either way, you are free to go . . .'

About the Author

RR Haywood is an Amazon All Star author. He is the creator of the bestselling series *The Undead,* a self-published British zombie-horror series that has become a cult hit with a readership that defies generations and gender.

Living in an underground cave, away from the spy satellites and invisible drones sent to watch over us by the BBC, he works a full-time job, has four dogs and lots of tattoos. He is also a certified, badged and registered hypochondriac, for which he blames the invisible BBC drones.

Should you not have a drone to hand, you can find him at www.rrhaywood.com.

Made in the USA
Monee, IL
09 November 2023

46052405R00236